PR...

"Mullen's new series starts with an absolute bang. Following his award-winning YA work, Mullen's transition to the contemporary crime genre is effortless, and his command of muscular prose is evident. Cass Callahan is a can't-miss character."

— JAMES WADE, TWO-TIME SPUR AWARD-WINNING AUTHOR OF *BEASTS OF THE EARTH*

"The harsh, powerful descriptions of the dangerous border country of south Texas make Dead Land as vivid as a punch in the gut. Once you open this book, you're not going to close your eyes until you know former Houston detective Cass Callahan has found justice for the dead. A great start to a new western thriller series!"

— W. MICHAEL GEAR AND KATHLEEN O'NEAL GEAR, *NEW YORK TIMES* BESTSELLING AUTHORS

"Chris Mullen's writing is sharp and action packed. His talent and enthusiasm are enviable."

— CHRIS ENSS, *NEW YORK TIMES* BESTSELLING AUTHOR

"Chris is a new, exciting Western author."

— HOWARD KAZANJIAN, AUTHOR AND AMERICAN FILM PRODUCER

DEAD LAND

To Margaret ~
Welcome to the
🅰️!

— signature

ALSO BY CHRIS MULLEN

Rowdy Series
Rowdy: Wild and Mean, Sharp and Keen
Rowdy: Redemption
Rowdy: Dead or Alive
Rowdy: Rescue
Rowdy: To Catch a Killer
Rowdy: Return

DEAD LAND

CASS CALLAHAN

BOOK ONE

CHRIS MULLEN

Dead Land
Paperback Edition
Copyright © 2024 Chris Mullen

Wolfpack Publishing
9850 S. Maryland Parkway, Suite A-5 #323
Las Vegas, Nevada 89183

wolfpackpublishing.com

This book is a work of fiction. Any references to historical events, real people or real places are used fictitiously. Other names, characters, places and events are products of the author's imagination, and any resemblance to actual events, places or persons, living or dead, is entirely coincidental.

All rights reserved. No part of this book may be reproduced by any means without the prior written consent of the publisher, other than brief quotes for reviews.

Paperback ISBN 978-1-63977-381-7
eBook ISBN 978-1-63977-380-0
LCCN 2023948622

For those that serve, those that dream, and those that give all of themselves because it is right.
And for my buddy Chance.

DEAD LAND

DEAD LAND

PROLOGUE

Under the cover of darkness, three men moved with stealth, a mere blur among the shadows beneath an open sky where their trail remained hidden as the moon had yet to rise. The terrain, far beyond that which any man could pass without the help of four-wheel drive and far from civilization where authority did not come from men in uniform but was imposed by those who ruled through power and fear, cut a path that flowed like a pipeline from south of the border without objection onto sovereign soil. Ruthlessness played its dirty game, and blood ran warm for the loser.

Time was the only adversary threatening the small band causing sweat to drip even as the night air cooled their faces. In rhythm, they pushed onward toward the distant bluffs overlooking first, the river, and then a land where freedom and opportunity become reality. Like a mule, they packed cargo to be delivered.

Gambling with gravity, they clung to a concealed ladder tucked behind brush and rock, their every movement deliberate and calculated, their hearts pounding as their descent brought them ever closer to the payment of a promise.

The ripple of water grew louder as they approached

the river. Without hesitation, each stepped into the flow, sloshing through the shallows, then waded deeper until swimming was the only option. Coming ashore, one by one, they mucked their way to dry land. Soaked through, they headed further inland, leaving the melodic trickle of the Rio Grande to fade into the night behind them. With muddy shoes, they trudged along until they reached a small grove of cottonwood, the spot described to them as the drop point. Now, all they needed to do was protect their packs and wait.

A night owl swooped overhead, startling the travelers causing one of the men to question if the risk of his part was worth its cost. Thoughts of his little girl in Camargo, Mexico, and the life he sought in Texas pressed upon him like an unrelenting force, yet he had no choice but to carry his load. There was much more at stake than his life alone. Shivering from cold and uncertainty, looking one way then the other, he wished for a quick end to the job.

Dressed in black and watching from within the shadow of a dying cottonwood, a lone figure appeared before the mules. All that was discernible were the whites behind the stranger's eyes as they captured the crescent moon rising over the towering cliffs.

The travelers stood, their nerves palpable, eager to unload their burdens and to fill their pockets with promises made. They nodded their heads, acknowledging their contact, then blinded by quick flashes of light flaring once, twice, three times from the shadows, each man fell, bathed in warmth as blood spilled from the holes in each of their bodies.

With unsettling satisfaction, the figure stepped forward and looked over the dead.

"Bienvenidos a los Estados Unidos."

PART ONE
ALMOST HEAVEN

CHAPTER ONE

The smooth idle of my jet-black 2021 Ford Explorer had one job, keep the air conditioner running high enough to fend off the thick waves of sweltering morning heat that pulsed from the hood and the rising humidity that covered the windows with a thin sheen of vehicular sweat. August in Houston is hot as balls, and that was a fact no one could ever dispute.

The radio chirped a series of coded chimes, followed by a monotone voice announcing a 10-19 at the corner of Richmond and Jeanetta, a busy spot in west Houston littered with bars, hookah lounges, and an Asian massage parlor busted more times than I choose to count for *services* not on the menu. I reached for the transmitter.

"Leave it, Cass. It's too damn early, and we're at least ten minutes from scene. Let a blue-and-white respond."

My partner and royal pain in the ass, Detective Ray Tucker, reached forward and tweaked the volume on the receiver.

"Ain't why we're out here anyway," he added.

Ray was five years my elder, wore a pot belly like a beer-chugging badge of honor, and tended to speak his mind regardless of the audience. A lack of respect for superiority was a strength in which he excelled. In the field, it was a weapon, but once we were back at the house, it caused an inordinate amount of friction between him and the higher ranks. He had been busted down to patrolman a time or two, but always clawed his way back into the good graces of the right people at the right time, and *well-ah*, here he sits with me waiting for *number six* on Houston's most wanted list to show himself from the ramshackle apartments across the street from where we sat. No man could intimidate Detective Ray Tucker. That was his wife's job, and she was damn good.

I looked at Ray and shook my head, knowing fair well I was not going to win this round but was compelled to reach for the transmitter anyway.

"What the hell are you thinking?" he said, eyes bulging in surprise that I would even entertain responding to the call. "That ain't our job."

Ray always made his point with as few words as possible.

Before I could reach the handle, the radio squelched, and a voice more suited for the Upper East Coast sounded out.

"10-William-56, enroute..."

"See? Now we can return to our job of sitting and waiting on this fucker to show himself."

Ray flicked the face of DaVon Robinson's most recent mugshot, then tossed it onto the dashboard and rolled down his window. He hocked and snorted a large spitball and let it sail onto the pavement. He wiped his mouth with his sleeve, then glanced over at me and smiled.

"I hate this shit."

A wall of warm, sticky air surged in through the window, immediately clinging to my exposed skin. It felt heavy to breathe and caused my fingers to feel as if they had been doused with tree sap, sticking together while I cupped them in front of the A/C vent to keep cool. Sweat formed on my neck and began to drip below my collar.

"Roll it up already," I said.

I switched the controls on the a/c to blow full blast, then leaned back, inviting the cool air to fight off the invading Texas heat. My eyes felt heavy from a long night of sitting, waiting, and listening to the ramblings of Ray telling one inappropriate story after another. I had known him since the Gulf War and swear that I had never heard the same story twice. He was a black hole of political correctness and every hardened liberal's nightmare, but I would not trade him for anyone else. When the shit hit the fan, Ray would be there, and God help anyone in his way.

With my head against the headrest, I closed my eyes, feeling the draw of sleep taunt me. The cold air found its way around my body replacing what had escaped through Ray's open window. In the few moments of blackness, thoughts of my wife and son played their way into view, making everything, for the moment, better.

Raven, my high school sweetheart and love of my life, was a teacher but had stepped away from the classroom just after school let out for the summer. An incident at home had thrown her into a tailspin of emotional frailty, and though I was her rock, I could tell that even I was falling short of being able to rectify an occurrence well out of my control.

Spencer was away at school enjoying his sophomore year at Texas A&M University. It had been his lifelong dream to become an Aggie. Try as I might, I never quite got it. Every time I thought I had it figured out, Spencer would laugh and say, "It's not something you can see from the outside Dad. You have to live it to understand." In the end, I did not care one way or the other. As long as Spencer was happy, that was good enough for me.

I drifted deeper down the rabbit hole, surfacing under a black sky riddled with foreign stars. The momentary quiet of the desert and the vast wasteland of Saddam Hussein's crumbling country filled my vision. Chatter crackled in my earpiece as I drove the HMMWV Army tactical vehicle through the dead of night. All was quiet, but even in dreams, terrible things happen when least expected.

A flash of light followed by an enormous explosion rocked the Humvee, turning night into day with its plume of yellow and orange flame. With a harsh jolt and hairpin turn to the left, the Humvee stopped.

"GO! GO! GO! Get clear of the flames. Get clear of the fire..."

Fire...Fire...

"CASS!"

I felt my shoulders rock back and forth.

"CASS! Wake up!"

I opened my eyes, feeling the cool blast from the a/c once again, but the intense pounding on my shoulder continued.

"What?!?" I yelled out.

"Got a call, Cass." Ray spoke with an air of concern.

"What call?"

"Dispatch radioed a ten-twenty-five. We gotta roll!"

"Ten-twenty-five? Since when do we answer for a fire?"

"Cass," Ray lowered his tone and spoke in a calm, serious voice. "It's your house."

CHAPTER TWO

Raven!

The engine seemed to howl her name, growling louder as the engine revved. I slammed my foot on the accelerator, and we surged forward, wheels spinning before catching hold of the pavement. In a tear of screeching rubber and white smoke, the Explorer shot ahead, leaving a trail of tire marks from the parking lot to the street. A woman walking her dog raised her hand and yelled while waving her middle finger as we fishtailed onto Main Street and tore off.

Ray did not say a word. Instead, as he braced himself, he reached forward and pressed a switch that lit our dash lights. The radio crackled again with that same monotoned dispatcher announcing...10-59...*pause*...1983 Chevy Chase drive...*pause*...fire department and EMS are on scene.

I reached for my phone and fumbled with the numbers to unlock it. I had to hear her voice. I had to know she was out of the house.

"Give me the phone, Cass," Ray said as if he were talking a jumper off a ledge. "I'll call. You get us there in one piece."

I glanced at him out of the corner of my eye, then released my phone and grabbed the wheel with both hands.

There were no such thing as red lights, speed limits, or detours this morning. All that mattered was that I got home as fast as possible. No reprimand for disregard for public safety could ever match the regret I would live with should I not reach Raven in time.

We sped toward Highway 59, screeching through a tough left turn beneath the overpass, then whipped onto the entrance ramp and took off like the lead car in the Daytona 500.

"Anything?" I asked. "She pick up?"

"No, Cass. It went straight to voicemail."

All I heard was *NO*. The rest sounded like the teacher's voice in a Charlie Brown episode. Just once I wished one of the kids would look at the camera and say, "What the hell is she saying?"

We sped south on 59, hurling past the few commuters that littered the highway before us. We drove against the grain of Houston traffic, but once we reached Loop 610, all bets were off, and everyone, and I mean everyone, better respect the lights and make way.

"Try again," I said, my voice shouting, filling with nerves and anxiety.

Ray could have argued that he had. He could have told me to keep my speed in double digits. He could have tried to console me, but I would not have listened, and that was not Ray. He pushed the contact on my phone that read *Little Bird* and placed the phone to his ear.

"Voicemail," he said.

My heart sank, then felt as if it would explode as we approached a wave of red taillights that filled every lane ahead of us. Construction at 610 and 59 was the worst, won by the lowest bidder, and built with no regard for time or speed. Whatever councilman or woman signed off on this project should be made to stand next to the merge lane in a yellow vest and hard hat while holding a sign that says, *SLOW—THIS IS ALL MY FAULT*.

The Explorer teetered forward as I braked behind the sea of red. I yanked the wheel, steering us half onto the shoulder, and chirped the horn. Most drivers respected the lights and made room, but there was always that one driver, oblivious to the world who had no intention of moving for anyone or any reason. Ray rolled down his window, stuck his head and arm outside to wave it over, yelling, "Get the fuck out of the way!"

As if they were not doing anyone any favors, the driver turned on their blinker and eased into the adjacent lane. I pressed the accelerator. The engine roared, and we sped past. Another hundred yards and we would be past the loop and clear of the mosh pit of vehicles.

The a/c blasted, but I was covered in sweat. The radio crackled again, but I ignored the call.

"Westpark or Beltway?" Ray asked.

I answered with a tug of the wheel, flying over three lanes to the right, then hauled up the entrance ramp and onto the Westpark toll road. The westbound lanes were clear, but the eastbound was stacked bumper to bumper with no place to go.

I glanced at our two o'clock, toward home, and saw something that almost made my stomach empty itself. A building trail of black smoke rose in the air. Its thinning plume looked like a finger taunting and pointing, exclaiming *You will never get here in time*.

I had never felt fear on the job, or even in the war for that matter. We had orders to follow and missions to complete, but my mindset had always been one of focus. Anxiousness was always present, but more like the nerves an athlete experiences before a big game. They are not afraid. They are ready to play. To win. That was how I always saw things, which kept my mind at ease and my focus on what I was responsible for doing.

I had my "old ladies" with me, protecting me as I

would them, but I never once felt fear like I was feeling right now. A helpless, hapless mix of emotions stirred at my core. Guilt snuck its way in, poking at my gut, squeezing my throat.

"I should not have left her alone," I said to myself. "She wasn't ready."

"Horse shit," Ray said, overhearing me. "Raven is as tough as nails. She did what she had to do. If you ask me, she's a hero."

I did not answer. I tightened my grip on the wheel and let focus regain control. Traffic on the northbound lanes of the Beltway was bad but not insurmountable. I pressed forward like a wolf on the hunt, watching the sheep startle, then scatter away hoping I was not after them. Two exits whirred by in a blur of multicolored cars and rubberneckers until at last I caught a break. A green light at Westheimer and the feeder road was like finding a ten-dollar bill in an old pair of jeans.

I slowed just enough to keep us from rolling over in the intersection when my phone rang. I fumbled to reach it, then realized Ray had already answered and was listening.

"Raven?" I asked, my eyes pleading for good news.

Ray shook his head. "It's Spence."

He continued to listen but would not hand me the phone. He nodded, looked at me, then nodded again.

"You hang tight, Spencer. As soon as we know something, your father will call you back."

He hung up, then slid the phone into the chest pocket of his jacket. He sat back again as if we were out for a weekend road trip and did not say a word.

I could sense the unease and curiosity of traffic as the smell of something burning began to filter in through the A/C. We passed car after car, and within each vehicle, the driver or passenger wore a peculiar look as if puzzled by the smell, wondering where it was coming from or what was causing it.

Like thin fog, a haze began to form over the streets, tangling in tree branches and upsetting birds that flew away from the stench to cluster and perch on power lines much higher where fresh air was to be found. Their chirping judgment added to the growing scene in my mind as I imagined how bad it could be.

I could hear sirens in the distance. I pulled a hard right onto Walnut Bend Lane and blew through every stop sign until I saw the flashing lights of an HPD patrol car blocking the entrance to Chevy Chase Dr. *My street*. A patrolman stepped into the street as we approached and circled his hands instructing us to go around.

Does he not see my lights? I screamed inside my head.

I ignored the patrolman and mounted the curb just short of where his blockade began, taking out a row of rose bushes, and cut a path of tire tracks through the yard to the frenzied street one block from my house. I would pay for that later in more ways than one.

Black smoke billowed from the roof of my house. Firefighters worked to fight the flames, standing dangerously close to the blaze.

Where was Raven?

Neighbors grouped together and watched, concerned looks on their faces while their children stood in their own flock, mesmerized, enjoying the excitement, waving their arms around like they were watching a parade on the Fourth of July. To the little ones, this was fun.

Lights pulsed atop the fire trucks like strobes in a dance club, illuminating the faces and reflecting off the yellow neon gear the firefighters wore to protect themselves.

I screeched to a stop two houses down from mine, threw open the Explorer's door, and raced toward the scene. Ray followed close behind.

I could feel the pulsing heat against my face. The crackle of wood and the roar of the fire sounded like I was racing toward the sidelines of a monster truck rally.

Where was Raven?

I reached the rear of the fire marshal's Chevy Tahoe before running face first into Captain Janet Gilcrest. Janet was an old friend, captain of station 69, and as hard a woman as one could ever meet.

"Whoa!" she yelled. "Hold up there!"

I tried to push by, but she stepped in my way. When I attempted to move around her, she sidestepped and bear-hugged me, pushing me back.

"Ray!" she yelled. "Keep him back!"

Ray's firm hands settled on my shoulders, their grip a gentle yet unyielding reminder of the raw strength he possessed, capable of overpowering me and driving me to the ground with a mere twist of his wrists. Captain Gilcrest, Janet, remained in my way until the message sank in, and I stopped trying to run toward my burning house.

"Raven! Where is she?" I yelled.

Janet backed up one step but remained on guard should I try anything stupid.

"I've got firefighters searching for her now. Stay back and out of the way. The more time spent with you, the less time I have to find your wife and save the house."

I relinquished what remaining tension I had in my muscles and succumbed to my fear. We had made it to the house, but for what? There was nothing I could do except wait and pray that Raven was not inside.

I heard someone yell behind us but was too engrossed in the scene before me. My eyes searched every window, trailed every movement, and studied every detail, and yet I saw nothing but burning embers, rising smoke, and water shooting from all directions. Even the pressure of Ray releasing his hold on me went unnoticed.

Captain Gilcrest stepped away to further direct operations. I fought the urge to ignore her warnings and run inside. I turned my head and saw that Ray was heading up the block, arguing with the patrolman we had bypassed. Arms flew and fingers pointed. I turned away, feeling nothing except angst for my wife.

I watched as two firefighters used a Halligan bar to break the glass of the picture window Raven had so loved and which had only been installed six months prior. Smoke poured through the broken window. Flames surged to inhale the fresh air only to be met with a wide spray from a powerful hose as a team of firefighters pushed forward to fight the inferno.

Like a moth staring at certain death, I watched them battle. I felt a tug on my arm and looked to find Captain Gilcrest urging me to follow her.

"They got her," she said.

"Is she...alive?" I asked, but Janet had already moved away.

I ran to catch up. We weaved our way through the battlefield just out of reach of the unbearable heat, until we came to the rear of an ambulance. Janet approached one of her firefighters who was dripping with water and dressed in protective gear. I could not hear what they were saying. I was too concerned with what was happening in front of me.

Raven lay on a gurney, exposed skin reddened and sore, black stains on her feet and under her fingernails. An EMT placed a breathing mask over her mouth, then disappeared into the front of the ambulance. I felt my heart lurch in my chest. I lost my breath and for a moment felt as if I had been left alone to tend to her without knowing what I should do or where I should start.

Was she alive?

I tried to speak, but all I could do was step closer and lean on the rear of the ambulance. Sweat dripped down my neck while salty tears burned my eyes. I forced myself to hold them back, but I was not strong enough. Free-flowing, they carved their way down my face.

"I can't lose you," I whispered. "Please, don't go."

Time seemed to stretch, each second an eternity, as I stood there yearning for any news that my wife would be all right. I felt a large palm press on my shoulder. Ray had returned. He stood by me and said nothing, which was vintage Ray. A man of few words.

CHAPTER THREE

The rolling blacktop hummed beneath the Explorer's Michelin Pilot Sport All-Season tires as we cruised at seventy miles an hour along Highway 90, heading west just past Hondo, Texas. The terrain was flat, the horizon seemed unreachable, and the relentless sun showed no mercy.

"Everything is brown," Raven said as she leaned back in her seat and stared out the window.

Three words, then silence. Since leaving Houston early this morning, she had kept to herself. Quiet. She slept some, but when she was awake, Raven stared out the passenger window as if she had drifted to a far-off place, leaving me to drive alone and wonder what she was thinking. I glanced at her. Her toes dangled off the front of her seat, and her knees were pulled snug against her chest covered with an old, knitted throw her grandmother had made years ago. It had seen better days. Then again, we all had.

I did not mind her silence. She could go all day without saying a word if that was what she wanted. She was alive and sitting next to me. That was all that mattered.

I reached for the knob on the radio, hoping to find

some music to fill the void. Maybe that would soothe her. With one hand on the wheel and cruise control handling the speed while keeping me centered in my lane, a handy yet unbelievable step forward in technology that drove the car by itself, I scrolled through the dial.

I scanned each frequency, tuning past static and distortion until the radio chirped to life and an enthusiastic voice called out over the speakers, "*Estás escuchando la mezcla en la radio española.*"

My hopes for Billy Joel, Journey, or even Axel Rose adiosed as the broadcast turned out to be music better suited for our favorite Mexican food restaurant back home. I pushed the knob, turned the radio off, then returned to watching the solid yellow line lead us west while the hum and vibration from the road kept me company and reminded me it might be time for new tires.

By noon, we drove through Uvalde. I could not help but look around and wonder how they were able to pick up the pieces after such a terrible, dark day. It had been well over a year since tragedy laid its black claws upon Robb Elementary School, and yet, signs of healing brought color and life to an otherwise ordinary West Texas town. We passed by murals painted on buildings that memorialized child after child, each who had been so violently robbed of life. Flowers lined the downtown plaza. My heart ached for the families while my mind tried once again to understand how and why operations went so wrong.

Raven had been an elementary school teacher, and I had been a volunteer "Pilot" at her school when my schedule allowed me the opportunity. She was passionate about teaching, and I was able to catch a glimpse of that from time to time as I walked the halls and grounds as an additional protective presence on campus. When the opportunity arose, many dads and teachers' husbands answered the call.

Time heals, and life moves on to the next news story of

the day, yet driving through Uvalde reopened a Pandora's box filled with questions. Questions that, to this day, remain unanswered.

We slowed to a stop for a red light at the corner of Main and County Road 353. A sign that read Old Uvalde Cemetery with an arrow pointing toward the entrance another fifty or so feet ahead caused a chill to fan out from my temples and creep down my spine. I did not know anyone buried there, nor anyone in Uvalde for that matter, but I felt the loss weigh down on me one more time.

I glanced at Raven, at the scarring on her neck and the puckered remnants of blisters on her arms from the fire, and felt guilty. Of all things, why did I feel *guilty*? The past few weeks had been rough, but we had made it through and were headed for a fresh start. I suppose the memorials we saw and the cemetery staring me in the face reminded me that on my blackest day, my loved one survived.

I squeezed the steering wheel and closed my eyes. My lips moved as I whispered a prayer to myself. Then, in my moment of reflection, I felt the warmth of a palm on the back of my hand. I opened my eyes and looked at Raven. She smiled, eyes red and watery.

"Light's green."

I let my right hand go of the steering wheel and intertwined my fingers in hers. She squeezed my hand three times, our secret code to say *I love you*. I felt what she felt and knew where her thoughts were taking her.

A friendly honk sounded out behind us, asking with shrill politeness that I move along. I pressed the gas and continued west on Highway 90 with Raven's hand wrapped in mine. For miles, neither of us let go.

We passed through Del Rio, which looked more like a DMZ made up of Texas Highway Patrol and Border Patrol vehicles. Black-and-whites seemed to be stationed at every curve while the green-and-whites patrolled the streets like wolves on the prowl, always in packs and always hungry. In Houston, I saw a smattering of this, but nothing compared to what I observed today.

We crossed over the Pecos River and sped on toward Marathon. When I was a kid, my uncle Stewart would bring me out west to hunt and to visit his ranch during summer break. I went every year from fifth grade to high school and have vivid memories of stopping to throw quarters into the Pecos River. He said it would bring us good luck. I saw it as money I could have used to play Pac-Man or Defender at the arcade in Sugar Land. I smiled at the memories, absorbing the rhythmic *thump, thump, thump* that reverberated through the car as we passed over the expansion joints of the bridge. We did not stop and continue the tradition, though as we drove on, I hoped that had not been a mistake.

In Marathon, Texas, we turned south on Highway 385 and headed toward Big Bend National Park. This route weaved its way through vast deserts with distant rising mountainous peaks, a treasure that some say may be the most beautiful National Park in the country. Raven saw things different.

"You're sure we're heading in the right direction?" she asked.

"I'm sure," I answered. "We'll cut through the park, then head on to Terlingua for the night. I have the perfect spot picked out for dinner and a cold margarita waiting with your name on it."

"Hope they have a *grande*."

Raven looked out the window again and sighed. I could tell she was tired. Tired of being in the car, tired of people asking if she was *okay*, but most of all, tired of being afraid.

We had lost just about everything in the blaze. Fire investigators determined that our living room curtains ignited when a candle on the windowsill burned out of control due to an elongated wick aggravated by a draft from a ceiling fan, but that did not lower my suspicions that Raven may have had a hand in starting it.

She was a modern-day Al Herpin, though she did not suffer from the same sleepless condition as he. A combination of ritualistic late nights preparing for her next day's classes and her natural night owl tendencies led her to run on very little rest. When she did come to bed, she would sleep for three or four hours, then pick up where she left off the day before. It was like when we were in college, and the nights never died. Every day was the same, full of energy, never once taking a nap, but after her incident, she began to change.

When firefighters found her, she was lying down on the bed in our room. Even as smoke filled the house, 911 was never dialed from our home number. It was neighbors from across the street that first reported the fire, thinking no one was home. Turns out they were wrong.

Uncle Stewart did not have children of his own, so when he passed last year, a family attorney informed us that he had left his ranch, the CR, to me. As it turned out, my summertime home in West Texas became our refuge when our world turned black. I did not know if relocating to the ranch would be permanent, but it did get us away from the city, away from the burned-out skeleton of our dead house and the daily reminders of how bad things got when my job led danger to our front door. At least, out here, all of that was behind us.

I looked at Raven as she leaned her forehead against the passenger window. She had sunk back into staring out the window, distant in her thoughts, but one.

"Brown," she said. "It's all I see."

CHAPTER FOUR

The view from the porch of the Starlight Theatre restaurant and bar in Terlingua captured Raven's attention as we sat in wait of a table and watched colors explode across the horizon. Her dreary brown landscape became blanketed in shadow as the palette of early evening spilled amber and crimson across what light blue canvas remained. Drifting lower and becoming more brilliant, the diving sun cast a pink hue across the distant rocky slopes and crags, illuminating each before stretching to the valleys below. It was the most beautiful way to end such a long, taxing day. I could tell by the deep stare in Raven's eyes that she too became encapsulated within the twilight atmosphere of West Texas.

When our table was ready, she did not want to move.

"Can't we eat out here?"

"We can eat wherever you like," I said.

I gave the hostess a "can you hook a fella up" look and slipped her a five-dollar bill. Like a pro, she palmed the cash and led us to a table where we could witness all of God's glory until the hard arms of night pulled themselves over us. Even then, we were not disappointed.

A stream of stars flooded the sky overhead, spreading

out in all directions. Back home in Houston, we were lucky to find the Big Dipper on a clear night, but out here, there were more constellations and clusters of blinking white than our eyes could keep up with.

"Is it always like this? So bright and beautiful?" Raven asked.

I leaned forward, placing my elbows on the table, and folded my hands. I stared at Raven, remembering how things were before, hoping that we would soon return to the good ole days once again.

"As far as I remember," I said.

The hostess returned to tell us our waitress would be right over, then slid me a fresh mug of draft beer and a glass of red wine for Raven.

"It's on me, sugar," she said, then walked away.

Raven raised an eyebrow at me and smirked. "Sugar, huh?"

I shrugged my shoulders and lifted my glass toward her. She raised hers, and we toasted to being off the road after such a long drive.

"I'm glad to see you smile," I said, wondering if I had gone too far even with that simple compliment.

Raven dipped her head, then looked into my eyes and took a long, slow, sensual sip of her wine. I felt her foot brush against my calf under the table. It was the first time since the fire that she had been...interested. I gave her an eyebrow raise of my own and enjoyed the subtle caressing of my leg.

Unlocking her gaze, she looked past me and took another sip of wine. In a blink, the color drained from Raven's face as if she had seen a ghost. She flinched in her seat, drawing her legs underneath her, poised to bolt from her chair. Her eyes widened, her pupils shifting left and right like they were attempting to decipher some unknown code, then with a sharp gasp, brought both hands to her face and covered her mouth.

"It's him," she said, quivering.

I reached across the table for her hand, but that only caused her to flinch and scoot her chair back. I stopped, then turned my head to look around.

The porch was filled with people waiting for tables to open. An older couple, from the looks of which spoke professional RV-ers, stood chatting close together. The man wore a hat better suited for Crocodile Dundee, a Mexican *Guayabera* that did a poor job covering his man-gut, and oversized shorts that reached to the top of his balding kneecaps. His wife was short and plump, with dolled-up red hair and a perpetual smile. Her teeth glistened. She wore a T-shirt that said 'Big Bend or Bust' written in bright red letters that arched over a cartoon sketch of an eighties-style camper speeding toward a cliff.

A pack of she-wolves laughed and drank and danced their way in and out of the crowd, disregarding everyone, then as if on cue, raised their hands to the sky and screamed like they had each just been asked to be the other's maid of honor.

I glanced back at Raven. Her eyes were glued in one direction. This time, I followed her stare and saw a group of men sitting around a table just beyond the socially dysfunctional girl pack. One of the men locked eyes with me, his glare unwelcoming and intense.

Instantly, I understood. I turned back to face Raven and leaned across the table. "It's not who you think."

"You're wrong. It's him. I know it's him!"

"Sweetheart, we've been over this. There is no way it..."

"But it is," she interrupted, flinching again and knocking over her wineglass, spilling what was left onto the table.

I grabbed some napkins to sop up the spill. A handful did the trick, but the results looked like a pile of bloody bandages.

Raven had episodes, most of the time stemming from a drawn-out day of depression, but sometimes they hit like a motorcycle running into a brick wall. Our evening had been going well, so when she crashed, I had to work fast to pick up the pieces.

I pulled a twenty from my pocket and flipped it onto the table, then stood and walked around behind Raven. She still stared at the man, who now was growing irritated by her attention. I kneeled close and whispered into her ear.

"Let's go."

She did not move. I stepped to her side and gently laid my hands on hers. She trembled as if caught in a freezing wind that only she could feel.

"Come on," I said with a whisper.

Raven allowed me to guide her to her feet. I wrapped my arms around her and held her close as we headed for the exit. We passed by the hostess on our way out. She looked at us with a mix of judgment and confusion. I met her gaze and smiled.

"We're all right," I said. "Left some cash on the table."

"But you didn't order anything," she said.

"It's fine."

The Explorer was parked about one hundred feet from the front of the restaurant in a gravel lot filled with vehicles from all over. Texas, New Mexico, Arkansas, Maine. Who the hell drives here from Maine? A single light pole cast a dim yellow circle on cars parked beneath but failed to reach ours, causing its jet-black color to blend in with the shadows. Live music blared from inside as a cover band demolished Bon Jovi's hit song, *Livin' on a Prayer*, surging louder then becoming muffled each time the front door opened and closed.

I cradled Raven as we walked, but her head twisted as we left, eyes locked on the man who frightened her so. He remained engaged with her, not understanding, but finding offense with her inseparable stare. An angry dog will bare its teeth, growl, and stand its ground, but calm, deliberate movements can help prevent a potential attack.

I did not mind angry dogs, but this mutt did not play by the same rules.

A few more steps and we would be off the porch and heading down the gravel slope that descended into the parking lot.

"What's her problem?"

The man bit. Once was tolerable, but his teeth had sunk in, and he was hungry.

"I said, what's her problem?"

I glanced back. The man stood up and followed us at a slow pace. I had hoped he would stop at the porch. I felt the weight of my concealed Sig Sauer 229. It called to me, *ready when you are*, but unless things turned dangerous, it would be disappointed. We were leaving, and there was no need to take this any further, but some people do not know when to let go.

Gravel crackled under our feet as we walked into the dark toward the car. A pause in the music between sets gave way to the sound of more than one set of boots on our tail.

"You need to tell that bitch to mind her business."

Dogs are pretty smart, but the one thing they fail to realize is that no matter their bite, there is always a bigger dog.

I stopped.

"The car is just ahead. Go get in," I whispered.

I pulled my arm from her shoulder and gave her a gentle nudge. She turned to me, eyes hollow and afraid.

"Go," I said and handed her the keys.

Hesitant, she backed away, then turned and shuffled her feet toward the car. One look at her frailty coupled with the single moment from when we parted was all it took to stuff the fearful thoughts of her reliving her worst day and turn them into a controlled rage. I turned to face the man who felt the need to verbally attack a woman, took a slow, deep breath, and clenched my knuckles.

The man continued his approach. It was dark, but my

eyes had become accustomed to the lack of light, allowing me to get a good read of him. He stood about five feet eleven inches, about 185 pounds, was bald, had a tangled nest of hair dripping from his chin, and wore a leather vest with patches sewn on the front. One grabbed my attention as it came into view. A white stripe with black lettering arched over a gray skull with a cigarette in its mouth read *Life Don't Matter*.

He stopped two paces in front of me, chest puffed out like a fighting cock, arms twitching at his sides. An angry grin slit his face. His eyes widened to show the whites pooling around their dark, beady centers. Two of his buddies dressed in similar garb watched their alpha from behind.

I will admit he had the look of intimidating asshole. What he did not know but would learn soon enough, was that men like him were easy. It was the quiet, manipulating ones that worried me.

We stood facing each other for a moment. I heard a car door open, then close behind me. Raven was safe. Another moment passed and the music picked up again inside the Starlight. It was bad, but not as bad as things were about to get out here. Music is thought to soothe the savage beast, but it did nothing but encourage the man in front of me.

The familiar chords of "Eye of the Tiger" reverberated from the theater, but something seemed amiss. The beat was out of rhythm, and the vocals were delivered in a scratchy death growl that marred the essence of this cherished anthem from my youth.

"Kick his ass, Cletus," one of the men yelled from behind him.

I could not help myself. A smirk edged out of the corner of my mouth.

"Cletus?" I said with a hint of sarcasm. "Why don't you and your boys head back inside and have a drink."

Throughout my life, I was raised to walk away or talk

myself out of a fight. When I was younger, that worked a time or two, but most often, I found myself wrestling on the ground with whatever bully tried having their way with me. Advanced Taekwondo training in high school paved the way to a national championship in 1997. I loved sparring but was faced with an even greater responsibility to avoid physical altercations outside of the ring. My military and law enforcement training kept me in top shape and added critical techniques meant to keep me safe while inflicting the most pain possible on my opponent.

My main objective was always safety first—for me, my partner, and then the perp. When all else failed, which they sometimes did with the crackheads and escapees I have faced, or if my partner, no-filter Ray, escalated things, it was comforting to know that all I needed to do was dip into my bag of tricks and choose from a variety of offensive maneuvers. I looked at each situation like a game of chess, thinking two and three moves ahead. Multiple strategies led to an exponential number of outcomes, but I had my favorites. I would much rather be playing chess right now.

"Something funny?" Cletus said, his temper rising.

I glanced at his buddies. Both were smaller than Cletus and looked harmless enough. They wore matching vests that I was sure made them feel like they were some sort of gang or club, but all I could think of at the time was the Black Widow's comical role in Clint Eastwood's *Every Which Way But Loose*. Those fellas were glorified cheerleaders at best.

"I said..."

I interrupted.

"You said, 'is something funny?' Well, here's your answer."

My words deflected my shifting stance. I stepped my right foot forward, keeping eye contact the entire time.

"If you feel that being misidentified by a woman with whose history you do not know, then becoming offended because she looked your way, then I would have to say I might find that a bit amusing. You, on the other hand, may feel that warrants aggression and the use of foul language in an attempt to frighten, of all people, a woman. That, I don't find funny at all."

Cletus's nostrils flared. "You son of a bitch."

"You see? There's that word again. Let me suggest this to you one final time. Turn around, take your buddies, and cool down with a drink. You'll feel much better."

Cletus turned his head to look at his cronies. "Ready for some fun?"

They whooped and hollered, spouting obscenities themselves though the mix of chatter on the porch and the band brutalizing a classic muffled their voices.

Cletus turned back to face me but was unprepared for what happened next. I would have him doubled over, face first on the ground in three moves, tops. He lunged ahead, swinging at me with an unrefined left hook. I slid forward just enough to disrupt the distance between us, blocked the punch with my right forearm, then threw an elbow strike with my left. Hardened bone connected with the side of his Adam's apple, pressed deep into his throat, bruising and tearing muscle as I turned his evening of heckling into an instant nightmare, but I did not stop there.

Once my elbow was clear of his throat, I straightened my arm, clutched his left shoulder while gripping his assaulting wrist in the process, and stepped farther into him. In one motion, I pulled up and twisted his wrist and pushed down on his shoulder blade with my opposing hands, toppling him over into a very painful and submissive bent-over position. Wrestling free was useless. I increased the pressure on his arm to the point where I had complete control over him.

His two buddies rushed in but slid to a stop when I twisted Cletus around to block their path. My sudden movement caused him to squeal. The pain was real. One could say more real than he had ever experienced. The two men slid to a stop, seeing I had complete dominance over their friend.

"Let him go," one of them said.

"Aren't you the one that said...how did you put it...oh, yes! Kick his ass?" I said.

He looked at his friend, then back to me. The other had the wherewithal to stay quiet. Cletus whimpered something beneath his breath.

"Can't hear you, tough guy, but I'm guessing you've had enough?"

He nodded his head in short, violent bobs. I could feel his muscles begin to relax and his breathing slowed, though his pulse pounded to the rhythmic beat of Survivor's only hit song still blaring through the Starlight doors.

I glared at his friends. A single bead of sweat dribbled down my cheek.

"If you or any of your girlfriends come at me or my wife again, I won't stop."

The fire in my eyes was enough to send them packing.

"Nah, man. It's cool," one of them said.

The two men raised their hands in surrender and backed away. I kept Cletus in a tight, painful kowtow until I was sure my point was made. When I was satisfied with their retreat, I squeezed just a bit tighter, causing Cletus to whimper once more, then leaned over and whispered into his ear.

"Who's the bitch now?"

With a harsh shove, I pushed him forward, face first into the gravel lot, his nose crunching on impact. Cletus groaned as he eased onto his back. In excruciating pain, he clutched his left arm with his right hand and lay in a heap of defeat. Blood carved trails through gray gravel dust that powdered his face from the fall.

I backed away, watching them as I went. Cletus remained on the ground. One of the men went over to check on him. The other returned to the porch and took a long swig of the beer he had left behind.

"Welcome to West Texas," I whispered to myself.

I turned around and took the last few steps to the Explorer and gently tapped on the passenger window. Raven sat with her feet on the edge of the seat, legs pulled to her chest as they were earlier today. She turned and looked at me. Her face was pale. Tears drenched her cheeks. I mouthed the words, *everything's okay*, then walked around to the driver's side door.

Though blanketed by darkness, I could see Cletus being helped to his feet. *We left the city to get away from crap like this*, I thought. I opened the door and sat down behind the wheel.

We stayed put for a moment until the dome light timed out and we sank into blackness again. Light. Dark. Black. White. East. West. They each needed the other. Balance was what kept them in symbiosis. If Raven and I were to find a way to move forward with our lives, we too would need to find that same balance.

A simple push of the ignition button brought the car surging to life. The Explorer's xenon lights cut through the black. As we drove down the gravel road, I reached over and rested my palm on Raven's knee. Lost in silence yet again, she sat and stared out the window.

The salted sky above was a sight to see, though our evening had become clouded by unnecessary setbacks. The Explorer's orange blinker flashed as I turned left onto Ranch Road 170 and headed for the motel I had arranged earlier in the day. I squeezed the wheel, frustrated and worrisome. And to cap off a long, strenuous day, my empty stomach growled.

CHAPTER FIVE

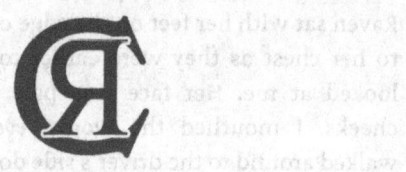

Except for the soft breaths Raven took as she slept, a direct effect of the 150 mg Trazodone she swallowed once we settled in for the night, and the on-again-off-again buzz of the window unit air conditioner, everything was still inside our modest motel room just south of RR170.

I drifted in and out of sleep but had been up since the red numbers on the alarm clock read 3:33, an odd time to awake and notice numbers as such. In an attempt to fall asleep again, I counted ceiling tiles of all things, more times than I would like to admit. Thirty-seven seemed to be the number that kept coming up. Enough light escaped through the open space between the unleveled bathroom door and the worn-torn carpeted floor to illuminate the far wall and cast a dull yellow hue that stretched out across the ceiling. I had tried everything I could think of to turn it off last night, but a faulty switch was to blame and any further investigation on my part may have led to the entire motel burning down. Other than flipping a switch, I knew nothing about being an electrician.

Little Orphan Annie would have hidden under the covers as the illuminated streaks overhead looked more like the arms and claws of a goblin reaching out over the bed. I squeezed my eyes shut, then reopened them. Childhood tales and nightmares, it seemed, never truly vanish. Instead, they linger, evolving and growing more potent, ready to pounce when least expected.

I rolled onto my side and read the clock again...6:20.

The blackness behind the drooping venetian blinds had begun to show signs of faltering. I pulled the covers off me and swung my legs over the edge of the mattress. When my bare feet touched the floor, the carpet felt moist. I had to remind myself this was not a Hampton Inn or Best Western.

I tip-toed to the bathroom, relieved myself, then slipped on my shoes without socks and walked past the bed to the motel door. Sliding the security chain off and leaving it to dangle against the wall, I unlocked the door and crept outside.

A rush of warm air met my face while the coolness of our room fought to hold it back. To the west, the sky sparkled in the inky cloak that held onto night. But to the east, the beginnings of dawn cracked the horizon, turning the sky and everything in its path to colors better suited on canvas for artisans to marvel over than this big-city detective to witness alone.

I thought about waking Raven but held back. There would be many mornings like this once we made it to the ranch. She could enjoy those on her own time when she was not struggling to find her own light. Looking back at the motel door, I hoped more than anything that our move would help all things between us and within us to heal.

I stood and watched the birth of my first day as an adult in West Texas. The morning glowed like a fire raging in the distance, reaching out in colorful wisps extinguishing the starlight, causing day to erupt with a flaming brilliance. Stretching outward, over the plains, then up the slopes of the distant Christmas Mountains, swirls of red and yellow and orange wound their way and then fell through the foothills like the coming of a great flood.

The sky itself reminded me of the old saying, "Red sky in the morning, sailor take warning," but I was determined to have a positive outlook for the day.

A loud buzzing from inside our room broke the peaceful sunrise. I rushed to open the door and lunged for the alarm clock on the nightstand. Bright red numbers flashed 6:40, and buzzing screeched out as I tried to find the right buttons to push to turn off the alarm. Nothing was working.

"Damn it," I gruffed as I pushed at the buttons like a maddened teen losing a Call of Duty battle on a PS5, but that did not help, nor make me feel any better.

Ending my madness, I yanked on the cord and pulled the plug from the socket. It snapped from the wall like a bullwhip and smacked me in the cheek just below my right eye.

"Son of a..."

"Everything all right, Cass?"

Raven cut me off before I could finish, though I screamed the words inside my head as I tossed the dead alarm clock onto the carpet. The red 6:40 stopped flashing and faded like the eyes of a Terminator succumbing to a heavily armed and battled-hardened Sarah Conner.

"Yeah," I said. "Some yahoo forgot to disable the alarm before they left, I guess."

I sat on the bed next to her. She rolled over and looked up at me. A glaze of light filtered its way into the room between the slats of the blinds as I gazed upon her face.

"You look beautiful this morning," I said.

Raven reached out her hand, fingers twiddling in midair. I clasped her fingers, then brought them to my mouth and kissed them. She smiled, then sighed. I could tell that most of last night's emotions were tucked away, but the sigh suggested a slight residue may still be lingering about.

"You hungry?" I asked.

"Starving."

"Well, I doubt there is room service here." I chuckled.

"What? You mean this isn't the Four Seasons?"

Her mood brightened my day more than any sunrise could ever chance to replicate.

"Wanna pack up and leave this joint?" I said in a terrible attempt at a New Jersey accent, but it made Raven smile.

She nodded her head, then rolled onto her back, pulling me with her. We lay close together, and though I wanted more than ever to take this to another level, I knew she was not ready. Her lips moved as she whispered something to herself. I could feel the warmth of her breath as she repeated the pattern of words spoken too soft for me to understand. She had her daily routines that got her moving, which I never questioned but was always curious about.

When she was ready, she exhaled in a long, calming manner, then looked me in the eyes.

"Pancakes?"

Thirty minutes later, we cruised along the narrow road following the rise and fall of the pavement while eating breakfast tacos purchased from a roadside taco truck, the only thing open at o'dark thirty.

The glow from earlier now spread to full light rising, yet still capped the cliffs just across the Rio Grande in Mexico in a fiery reflection of brown and red earth and rock. Below each crest lay a subdued shadow, like remnants of night hiding in the valleys and along the shoreline of tangled trees and muddy banks. This stretch of RR170 through Big Bend Ranch State Park was by far my favorite, more so even than that which leads into and around Big Bend National Park. It brought back memories from my childhood days of enduring the longest car ride in the world from East Texas to the windy, rolling terrain that followed the US/Mexico border. In those days, it served as a reminder that we were getting close to my uncle's ranch.

When Uncle Stewart passed, we received a letter from The Clark Law Firm, PC, informing us that we had been named in his will and that we should contact them regarding the matter. As it turned out, Uncle Stewart left me his ranch in its entirety. Five thousand acres that stretched from RR170 to the Rio Grande was home to some of the most beautiful scenery one could ever hope to see.

The Callahan Ranch, or CR, as it was called, had been known for cattle and horses, though in its later years, most of both stocks had been sold off. Now, a portion of the CR's acreage was leased to neighboring ranchers, Floyd Huckaby and Roy Sinclair, so their cattle could graze the land beyond their own fence lines. Following Uncle Stewart's death, word spread that he had left the ranch to a distant relative. I was unclear about how the news tracked back to me, and how so quickly following the discovery letters began showing up from both Huckaby and Sinclair, as well as numerous others offering to purchase the CR outright. I dismissed each bid to buy, but found one from as far south as Monterrey, Mexico, rather intriguing. The offers were generous, but the directness of the many follow-up letters of inquiry I received started to rub me the wrong way. While each wanted the land for themselves, it felt as if they were more threatened by the possibility of city folk gaining control. Did I know anything about west Texas ranching? Not one bit. Was I going to let that bother me? Hell, no. I figured I would learn along the way as a tenderfoot might have during the days of trail drives and range living. When all else failed, I would lean on Uncle Stewart's foreman, Levi Flint.

Flint remained after Uncle Stewart passed. He was paid through a trust that had been set up during Uncle

Stewart's failing years to ensure that the ranch remained in good standing even after he was gone. Flint started working the ranch about the time I started college. I made excuses for why I did not have time over the summers to visit or work as I had in the past, most of which revolved around my interest in a certain College of Education student. Uncle Stewart knew the game better than I gave him credit for but loved me the same, nonetheless.

I reached out to Flint after we learned about my inheriting the ranch and again when Raven and I made plans to relocate to the CR, each time missing him for one reason or another. I could not decide if he was always busy or resentful that after all his years of faithful service to my uncle, the ranch was left to some tenderfoot in the big city. Whatever the reasons, we were less than an hour away from learning the truth.

"What do you think?" I asked Raven, pointing to the dips along the road and the winding Rio Grande.

She leaned forward and followed my finger with her eyes.

"Well, I see some color. And the way the cliffs tower over the river gives this area a little more mystery than the flat land from yesterday," she said, then grabbed my finger in her hand and held on. "I like it. Just wish it didn't take all day and then some to get here."

"Believe me, I feel you," I said. "When I was a kid, I thought the drive would never end. Then, just when I couldn't take it anymore, the road turned into a roller coaster, and I knew we were close to Uncle Stewart's. He would tell me to hold on and we'd speed down the slopes and soar around the bends in the road. It felt just like riding the Texas Cyclone at Astroworld before they closed it down."

"I never went. Guess I missed out," Raven said.

I pulled away and gripped the steering wheel with both hands. A smile crept across my face as I squinted my eyes and focused on the road ahead.

"Stay seated and keep your arms and legs inside the vehicle."

I revved the engine, and the Explorer shot ahead.

"Enjoy your ride on the West Texas Cyclone!" I yelled.

Up and down and around the bends, we raced ahead, taking each curve like we were on our own set of wooden rails. As we soared over each crest, our stomachs lurched into our throats, only to be pushed into our seats again as we scuffed the base before the next impending rise in the pavement. Raven squealed. I let out a yee-haw like I was one of the Duke boys leaving Sheriff Rosco P. Coltrane to eat our dust behind the General Lee.

We surged to the top of the next rise and came into full view of a vast, leveling terrain ahead. I glanced at the dashboard and saw the speedometer read 78. I let up on the gas as we started our descent.

POP!

The smell of burning rubber filled our noses as the car wobbled on the blacktop. I eased the brake and dove into my EVOC, Emergency Vehicle Operations Course, training, slowing the Explorer while trying not to overreact and flip the vehicle. The rumble of dead rubber and the metallic scrape of the wheel grinding along the roadway made my teeth ache.

As our speed decreased and I gained more control over the car, I let out the breath I had been holding and glanced over at Raven. Her right hand held the *Oh Shit!* handle in a death grip and her left palm was pressed against the dash. I faced the front, steered the car onto the shoulder, and eased us to a complete stop.

"You okay?" I asked.

"Aside from almost peeing myself? Yeah."

We shared a smile. Raven crinkled her nose at the smell of hot rubber and waved a hand in front of her face. I unbuckled my seat belt, but before I opened the door to inspect the damage, I asked Raven one more question.

"Wanna go again?"

Raven tilted her head and raised her right eyebrow at me.

"Um, No. I think I'm starting to understand why they closed Astroworld down."

I laughed and gave her a wink, then stepped out of the Explorer and looked back along the road. A long streak of black stained the pavement. Chunks of tire littered the road, and the smell of hot rubber still lingered. I walked to the rear of the Explorer and inspected what remained of the driver's side tire and noted the fresh road-rash scars on the rim. I knelt to get a closer look as if I had some secret method to make what was left of this tire still work when I felt an instinctive pull at my gut. I stood and looked both ways along RR170.

I heard the passenger door open, then close, and the crunch of Raven's All-stars on the gravel as she walked back to join me.

"Is it bad?"

I did not answer at first.

"Everything all right?" she asked.

I turned my gaze away from the road ahead to look at her.

"Yeah. Just need to put on the spare."

I began to kneel again when Raven spoke up.

"Someone's coming."

The roar of an engine grew louder as I stood and listened. About a quarter of a mile away, a vehicle approached, then slowed as it drew near. I felt the weight of my Sig on my belt and hoped we would not be subject to a similar offering of the West Texas hospitality we were shown last night.

Raven stayed close by me as a white, older model Dodge Charger approached. Then, with a pulse of red and blue, strobe lights on the dashboard of the car began to flash.

CHAPTER SIX

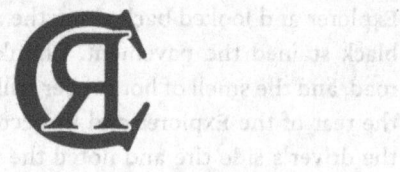

My tension subsided, and the weight of my Sig settled, but I still felt some anticipation as the Charger rolled to a stop on the opposite side of RR170. Painted in reflective ivory yet hidden beneath a thin film of dirt that covered the driver's side of the car, were the camouflaged words, *South Brewster County Sheriff*. The car sat idling for a solid minute before the driver's side window opened. I could see the silhouette of a man in a cowboy hat sitting behind the wheel, and I could hear static from the radio. A garbled voice rang out from the speaker, to which I heard the officer respond, *10-46*.

"Why is he just sitting there?" Raven whispered.

"He's just checking in with the house," I said. "Standard procedure."

"You can understand what they're saying?"

"Yeah. Once you get an ear for radio talk, it becomes second nature."

The radio squelched once more, then silenced as the driver's door opened. A man about 5'11" and around 200 pounds stepped out of the vehicle. He looked at us and nodded. From head to toe, he looked the part of West Texas law enforcement, from the silver-belly-colored

Stetson resting on his head down to his black cowboy boots. A silver badge pinned on the left breast of his beige uniform glistened in the morning light. His eyes remained hidden behind dark Ray-Ban sunglasses, but the smile that brimmed beneath a black Spanish mustache set my mind at ease.

"Morning," I said.

"Mornin'," he replied, walking over. "I'm Sheriff Chance Gilbert. Looks like ya have a bit of trouble."

He stopped in front of us. We both looked back at the trail of tire marks and nubs of rubber scattered along the pavement.

"With all the dips and curves, yer lucky ya didn't end up in the culvert across the way. It's all too common 'round here for tourists ta get caught up in the drive and not look where they're goin'. Come across too many far worse than y'all."

He looked at me, his smile still brimming. He was friendly enough, but I knew the game.

"Yeah," I said. "It's beautiful country out here."

"Hope ya got a spare. Could call a wrecker, but findin' Hector Chavez this early in the mornin' may cost extra. He's an ornery cuss, especially this time a day."

"No need. We've got a spare. Thanks for the offer, though."

Sheriff Gilbert nodded and placed his hands on his hips before twisting side to side for another look at the damage to the Explorer. He whistled through his teeth, then spoke under his breath.

"Lucky, indeed."

I stepped to the rear of the Explorer and activated the lift gate. A robotic beep sounded out as the rear hatch raised open. Sheriff Gilbert joined me at the rear of the vehicle.

"Ya got a lot of bags an' things. Where ya headed?"

I smirked. His gamesmanship was good. Friendly. Unintrusive, yet such an innocent question was loaded with underlying interrogative properties. I reached for the brown plastic Randall's bag filled with snacks Raven had bought for the drive and pulled it out of the way first.

"You mind putting this up front?" I asked her.

"Sure," she said, taking the bag.

"Actually," I said, turning to face the sheriff, "we're almost there."

"That so?" he responded.

"I used to come out here over the summer, years back, to stay with my uncle. He's since passed and left some property to me."

"Callahan?" he said, raising an eyebrow. "Yer Stewart Callahan's nephew?"

"That I am. You knew Uncle Stewart?"

"Mighty fine gentleman, he was. Stirred up quite the interest in his property when he passed."

Tell me about it, I thought.

Raven returned from the front of the car and stood by my side. I offered a hand to Sheriff Gilbert, and we shook.

"The name's Cass. This is my wife, Raven. Spent last night over in Terlingua. Hoped to get an early start today, but you can see things aren't really going our way."

"Terlingua, huh," Sheriff Gilbert said. "Guessin' ya didn't stay at a Four Seasons?"

That made Raven smile, as it had been her exact observation. Sheriff Gilbert smiled back.

"Least I can do is help ya get back on the road. Yer not that far from the CR. Maybe fifteen minutes er so."

"Thank you, Sheriff Gilbert," Raven said.

"Please. Call me Chance. Most folks around here do."

Raven looked at me with a curious, interested grin, then aimed her smile back at her new friend.

"Well, all right...Chance."

"Good," he said. "Now, let's change this tire and git ya on yer way."

It took twenty minutes to unload the rear of the Explorer, locate the scissor jack and spare, and change the tire. Sheriff Gilbert supervised while I did the heavy lifting. He talked about local to-dos and recommended a few restaurants we should try, then cautioned us about one in particular.

"Margaritas at *El Hefe* restaurant are some of the best around, but stay away from the guacamole."

Only one car passed by while I changed the tire. As I tightened the lug nuts, Sheriff Gilbert stepped onto RR170 and motioned for the driver to slow, then waved him past.

With the spare set to take us the rest of the way, I went to work reloading the rear of the Explorer. Raven started to pitch in, but I suggested she put her feet up instead.

"Don't have to tell me twice," she said.

She reached in front of me and offered her hand to Sheriff Gilbert.

"It was nice meeting you, Chance. Thank you for stopping."

"My pleasure Ms. Callahan."

"Hey," she said. "It goes both ways. Call me Raven."

Sheriff Chance Gilbert's black mustache curled as he smiled at my wife. He released her hand and then ceremoniously bowed before her.

"It's my pleasure, Ms. Raven."

Raven glanced at me, and I could tell that she liked Sheriff Gilbert. It had been weeks since she had opened up to people with such ease, but I could tell that there was something Raven had sensed about Sheriff Gilbert that made her feel comfortable. Safe. She turned and walked to the passenger door, opened it, and sat down inside.

As I was loading the final bag, a garbled call came over the radio from the sheriff's car. We exchanged glances.

"Time to get back to work?" I asked.

"It would seem so," he replied. "Welcome ta South Brewster County. I'm sure we'll be seein' each other around from time to time."

He offered his hand. We shook, and I nodded.

"Be safe out there, Sheriff Gilbert."

"It's Chance. Always Chance for my neighbors."

We parted hands and exchanged friendly smiles. He looked both ways before stepping across RR170, then paused and tilted his head in the direction from where we had come. A low rumble rose in the distance, surging louder and louder.

I looked through the rear window and saw Raven was reading one of her magazines, unaware of the approaching sound. I stepped next to Sheriff Gilbert and watched as three motorcycles crested the hill and sped their way down the slope. With the sound of roaring mufflers, the riders downshifted as the flashing lights from the sheriff's car came into view, slowing their approach.

As they rolled closer, I felt a surge of adrenaline prick at the back of my neck and my gut spoke to me. After all my years of police work, I had learned to trust that feeling over most everything else.

As they passed by, they rode in a V formation, moving across the center stripe of the road. The bikers slowed further, allowing me to get a good look at each of their faces. The rumble blared, but for me, all was silent as I stared into the eyes of Cletus, the very man who had confronted us last night. His face was still red from the altercation. He scowled at me as they passed.

Sheriff Gilbert picked up on the negative vibe and gave a stare of his own, no doubt committing as many details as possible of each rider to memory.

When they had passed, they revved their engines and sped away. I followed Sheriff Gilbert onto the road and watched as they turned into tiny specs before us.

"Friends of yours?" he asked, still watching them ride off.

"You might say that."

"Do I need to know more of the story?"

"No. It's a dead issue."

Sheriff Gilbert turned and squinted an inquisitive eye at me.

"Poor choice of words," I said. "Anyway, I don't expect any trouble from them going forward."

"Let's hope not, but just in case," Sheriff Gilbert said as he reached into his shirt pocket and retrieved a business card. "Call me if things turn south."

A gold badge emblazoned the left half of the card. To the right, text read, Sheriff Chance Gilbert...South Brewster County Sheriff's Department...432-837-3488...*Serving the Public Good*.

I looked it over, then slipped it into my pocket.

"Thanks, Chance."

He nodded, then walked to his car and sat behind the wheel. He reached for the radio, called in code *10-106*, and turned back to me, tipping his hat. With a slip of the wheels over gravel, he made a hard U-turn and sped off in the same direction as the bikers, lights still flashing on his dash.

I walked to the Explorer and opened the driver's side door. Raven leaned over as I sat down and buckled up.

"He sped off in a hurry. Everything all right?"

Sure, I thought. *Just another run-in with our pals from last night hoping to send you into another emotional flurry and ruin what is turning out to be a very promising day, flat tire notwithstanding.*

I smiled, then leaned over and kissed her forehead.

"Everything is just fine. Sheriff Gilbert seems..."

"Chance," Raven interrupted, smiling once again.

"Right. I forgot you two were on a first-named basis."

She punched my shoulder and playfully bit down on her bottom lip.

"Anyway...Sheriff Gilbert, Chance," I said with a jolt of sarcasm. "He had another call to see to. Nothing to worry about."

"Good," Raven replied.

Good, I thought.

Raven leaned over the center console and rested her head on my shoulder.

"Chance said we were only fifteen minutes away from the CR."

"Yep. You ready to see our new home?"

"I'm ready to be off the road and out of the car for a while."

"Me too."

I pressed the ignition button, shifted the Explorer to drive, and headed out for the final minutes of our cross-Texas journey to my uncle's ranch. I still had a hard time calling it ours. Once we settled in at the CR and found some peace and quiet, that may start to grow on me.

Once back on RR170, I found a clear broadcast from a radio station in Alpine. I caught the tail end of the morning forecast on Big Bend Radio, station KALP 92.7FM, then began to hum along as they played John Denver's, *Take Me Home, Country Roads*.

Almost heaven indeed.

PART TWO
THE CR

CHAPTER SEVEN

CR

Just as Sheriff Chance Gilbert had said, we reached the turnoff that led to the CR within minutes after pulling the hobbled Explorer back onto RR170. I eased us across the empty oncoming lanes and turned onto a gravel road that stretched so far in front of us it looked as if we might drive straight into Mexico from here. We rumbled over the metal bars of a cattle guard, then followed the spiny twists of barbed-wire fencing, our tires spitting a trail of white dust in our wake. The crackle of crushed limestone under our wheels vibrated throughout the car, sending a funny sensation across our bodies.

"Almost there," I said.

"It's going to take a while to get used to this," Raven said, looking out her window. "All of this."

"It's not so bad. Just a little bumpy."

The morning sun bathed the sky in azure hues, and as it rose, the bluffs to the south and west shifted from their earlier brilliant orange to a subdued, dull brown. We passed scattered clusters of cows fenced in on either side of us. A handful raised their heads to watch us go by, but most remained disinterested as we were not a part of the daily routine. In the distance, I could see buildings come into view.

"Look," I said, pointing ahead. "There it is."

Raven leaned forward and followed my finger. "I just hope there is a tub and some hot water. All this dust in the air is making me feel dirty."

"Now we're talking," I said with a hint of excited sarcasm.

"Cass!" Raven replied, then playfully punched me on the shoulder.

It made my day watching her smile. There was nothing in the world comparable to the way she beamed when happiness was in charge. It was when *the other* found a way to disrupt and take over that worried me.

The buildings I had pointed out grew into the form of a ranch-style house, a barn, and two other smaller structures that looked like miniature houses from HGTV's *Tiny House Nation*. I did not remember those from my childhood, but I did remember everything else as if I had been here yesterday.

An opening in the fencing gave way to another cattle guard and a tall ranch gateway with a wide metal arch stretching from one side entrance to the other. Hanging from the pinnacle of the arch was a piece of ironwork that looked like an oversized cattle brand formed with the capital letter *C* and a smaller capital letter *R* set within the arc of the *C* but reversed.

We passed under the arch, rumbling over another cattle guard, and pulled in front of the house. I looked at Raven and smiled, reenergized and ready to explore as I had done many times in the past. I knew she still held on to her one wish, to disappear into a warm tub and soak the miles away. We paused a minute to let the dust settle. From across the yard, masked behind our cloud of dust, the figure of a person appeared.

"Who is that?" Raven asked.

"Dunno. Maybe it's Uncle Stewart's foreman," I said.

"Don't you mean *your* foreman?"

"I guess that's the new way to look at it. Let's go introduce ourselves."

As the dust thinned, it was clear the figure was indeed a man. He watched from afar without so much as a welcome wave.

"Friendly guy," Raven said. "You go say hi. I'll stay in the car, just in case."

"In case of what?"

"In case he's a crazy West Texas murdering squatter intent on keeping what he thinks is his and wants to kill us for trespassing," she said with a smile, yet underneath I could tell that she meant it.

"Don't forget who yer married to, little lady," I said in my worst cowboy accent.

"Oh my god," she replied with a laugh.

I grunted, winked at her, then opened the door and stepped out.

"Go get 'em, Quick Draw McGraw," she said with a smirk.

I closed the door and caught the stare of the man from across the way. He wore boots, dark work jeans held up by a large golden belt buckle, a plain long-sleeve button-up shirt, dark sunglasses, and a weather-beaten cowboy hat that had stories to tell.

The man watched as I stepped closer. He waited, sizing me up as I approached. I wondered what my faded blue jeans and baseball cap told him about me. "The proof was always in the pudding," my uncle Stewart used to say. A cliché, but correct, nonetheless.

"You Levi Flint?" I asked.

The man took his time to respond. He removed his sunglasses, spat a wad of phlegm into the dirt, then took a step closer to me before speaking up.

"You must be the city folks Mr. Callahan left the CR to," he said.

"Yeah," I answered. "I'm Cass. My wife Raven is over in the car."

He glanced at the car, then squinted back at me. We stood through what I felt was an awkward moment of silence, then he offered a bit more of himself.

"I run this place. Have since before Stewart died."

"So, you are Levi Flint?"

"Flint. That's all."

"All right, Flint. Raven and I are happy to meet you. We'll get settled and then we..."

Flint cut me off.

"Got work. Find me if ya can, but I have a shit-ton ta do."

Without so much as a handshake, Flint turned and walked around the side of the barn. When he appeared again, he was riding a horse toward a small herd of cattle grouped beyond the barn. They looked up as if they were expecting him. As if they knew him. A small trail of dust rose behind the clomping hooves of the horse.

Behind me, I heard Raven close the passenger door of the Explorer. I looked back to see her holding one hand over her eyes to shade them from the morning glare. It was not even midmorning, but the West Texas heat had already begun to announce its arrival.

At least it was a dry heat, I thought.

I reached into my pocket and pressed a button on the remote key fob to open the rear hatch of the Explorer as I walked over to Raven.

"Everything all right?" she asked.

"Yep."

She looked at me with curiosity.

"Was that the foreman?"

I turned and looked at the shrinking figure of man and horse riding away from us.

"That's Levi Flint. Says just to call him Flint, though. Salty guy if you ask me. I guess we'll see how it goes."

"See how it goes?" she said. "You worried about something?"

"No. Not really. It's going to take some time to adjust to each other, that's all. Let's go inside and have a look around," I suggested. "Find you that bathtub you were hoping for."

"That sounds good to me. Maybe you could brew some coffee while I'm in there?"

"Sure," I said.

I grabbed a handful of bags from the rear of the Explorer and headed up the three steps to the porch. Raven followed, then reached around me to pull open the screen door as I fumbled with the bags and the keys to our new "for now" home.

"Here. Let me," she said, taking the keys.

She placed one hand on the doorknob and was about to slide the key into the lock when the knob twisted, and the door opened. We shared a glance.

"Guess it was already unlocked," she said. "Kinda spooky."

"After you," I said.

"No, I'm good. Uncle Stewart left this place to you. You should go in first."

Raven stepped aside and placed her hands on my hips, pushing me toward the door.

"Okay. Okay."

I nudged the door open with my foot. Smells from what seemed like a hundred years ago wafted into my nose. Old memories played on an ancient reel-to-reel projector in my head with silent actors portraying a time when the ranch was filled with people and animals and where hard work and happier times were a part of daily life on the CR.

I looked at the front room. Aside from a thin layer of dust, it looked as it always had. A worn leather couch took up the middle of the sitting area. Lamps sat on pinewood tables on either end, the base of each was made of a porcelain cowboy fighting to stay in the saddle of a bucking bronco. The shades were stained from years of use and dirt. A painting of a rancher atop his horse surveying a herd of cattle being rounded up for branding hung on the far wall. Red shag carpet covered the floor from the entryway to the opposite side of the room and down the far hall that led to the bedrooms. To my immediate right was a gun cabinet. The glass door hung ajar. A glance inside confirmed my thoughts. *Empty*.

I walked to the couch and placed the bags I carried on the floor. Raven followed and looked around. I hoped she was imagining how she could put her own touch on the place rather than filling with concern over the work we had ahead of us.

"Why don't you see about your bath? I'll finish unloading. When that's all done, and you're ready, we can figure out what we want to do next."

"Okay," she said.

It took three trips to unload everything and one return trip to place the blown tire and wheel inside the rear of the Explorer. I would need to find a replacement as soon as possible. Seeing that my hands were blackened from lifting the tire, I headed to the kitchen sink to wash up.

"Woo-hoo!"

Raven's cheer echoed from the opposite side of the house.

"Hot water!"

I smiled as I scrubbed the tire stains away in the sink, then walked to the picture window by the kitchen table. Looking out to the range of land between the house and the distant cliffs of Mexico just across the Rio Grande, I thought what an adventure it would be to ride out there on horseback. I was a rancher now. Truth be told, I was not sure what that meant, but I was one, like it or not.

I considered walking the property while Raven took

her bath but decided against it, thinking it may cause her undue stress to be left alone in a new place right off the bat. Instead, I sat on the leather couch and flipped through an old *True West* magazine. The cover read, "BORDER RIDERS, A Dangerous Job, Then and Now" – January/February 2009.

"Some things never change," I said to myself as I read along.

Forty-five minutes later, Raven emerged from the bathroom with a towel wrapped around her hair, looking refreshed. She was glowing, as if all her cares and troubles had washed away with the trip-grime and hotel funk she had carried since yesterday.

"I'm hungry," she said.

It was nearing lunch. We had only car snacks to eat, and I was not yet brave enough to peek inside a refrigerator that had not been opened in weeks.

"Let's head to town and get some lunch. We'll grab some groceries and find that Hector guy, Sheriff Gilbert..."

"Chance," she interrupted.

"Not gonna let that go, huh?"

She smiled as a six-year-old might when knowing a secret, then plopped down on the couch next to me.

"Anyway, if we can get the tire replaced today, that would be a big help. The sooner we get the donut off, the better."

"What is it with cops and donuts?" she joked.

"Really?" I said, reaching out and grabbing her waist. "Really?"

I tickled her, to which she giggled and kicked her legs this way and that. The towel around her head unwound, plopping in a moist heap on the floor.

"Stop it." She laughed. "Stop it."

"Make me," I said.

Without hesitation, Raven surged forward, wrapped her arms around my neck, and pressed her lips to mine.

She held me in an embrace and kiss that rivaled any other jaunts at love I had tried to initiate over the past three months. I lightened my grip and fell back into the deflating cushions of the old couch. Raven held tight, pressing her lips to mine, exploring my mouth with her tongue, then in brief release, came up for air before repositioning herself to straddle my body with her legs. My heart raced and my breath felt heavier to draw, but I was not about to let this moment with the love of my life pass without exploring how far she was willing to go.

With an arousing gentleness, her hands moved from the back of my neck, finding their way to my chest. Her hips rotated forward and back over my jeans. My damn jeans! She leaned over, brushing her wet hair against my face, and bit the lobe of my left ear.

"I love you," she whispered.

I slid my hands from her waist, gliding them up and down her back, then under the border of the *Life is Good* T-shirt she had just put on, letting my fingers trickle on her bare skin like warm water running over her. Why my mind wandered at that moment to agree that life was, in fact, *good*, I'll never understand. In an instant, my focus sharpened, and I lost myself in the pleasure of our bodies intertwining, becoming further entangled in each other's embrace.

BLAM!

Like teenagers caught doing *things* by disapproving parents, we sat straight up and looked around.

"What was that?" she asked.

"Sounded like a gunshot," I said, standing up. "Stay here. Stay inside."

Raven sat back on the couch and pulled her legs to her chest, wrapping her arms around them. Her eyes widened as I headed for the door. My gun screamed at me to be pulled and begin the hunt, but I was not about to go that far in front of Raven. When I reached the door and no further gunshots sounded out, I felt there had to be a reasonable explanation. Raven trembled on the couch.

"It'll be okay," I said, trying to sound reassuring though she had fallen behind a curtain of safety and did not acknowledge my words.

It better be okay, I thought as I opened the front door and stepped outside.

CHAPTER EIGHT

I squinted as the midmorning sun glared down like a spotlight in an interrogation room from one of those midfifties black-and-white movies. I pulled my Sig, holding it low at my side, and surveyed the property. Stepping off the porch, I walked behind the Explorer and looked at the miniature houses, then the barn.

BLAM!

Another blast echoed from beyond the barn. I looked and spotted Flint on foot, walking away from the cattle he had ridden toward. He held a rifle to his shoulder and was sweeping his aim across the open terrain before him.

BLAM!

A third blast sent a thin trail of smoke to fan away from the muzzle of his rifle and disappear in the breeze.

"What the hell is he shooting at?"

I pulled the keys to the Explorer from my pocket and hopped behind the wheel. It would be a rough drive, but if I was going to find out why he was shooting and at what, or *who* a voice whispered from deep within, I needed to get out to him fast. I pressed the ignition button and fired up the engine.

It was a tight fit, but I squeezed the car between the barn and a small corral and rumbled over the uneven earth straight for Flint and the cows. As I neared the small herd, most looked up at the strange black thing coming at them, then proceeded to move away at a walk. The closer I got, the faster the herd moved, spreading out like spilled milk on the kitchen floor. There was no pattern or control, just an innate need to flee.

I saw Levi Flint lower his weapon and look my way. He glanced back in the direction he had been shooting, then headed toward me at a brisk pace.

I stopped the Explorer and opened the door.

"Get back in that piece of shit and turn it around!" Flint sounded pissed. "What the fuck do you think you're doing?"

He noticed the gun in my right hand and pointed at me with a very strong, agitated finger.

"You gonna grease some gang bangers or somethin' with that?"

I had stepped into something I knew nothing about, but I was beginning to dislike his attitude.

"Heard shooting. Figured there was trouble."

"Oh, you *figured*? You the new sheriff in town, huh. Well, you *figured* wrong, asshole. We got coyotes runnin' around out here lookin' to take down a couple of these late season calves. Had the herd grouped together, SAFE, while I shoot the furry bastards! But you come runnin' out here ta save the day just served 'em up on a platter."

Realizing I had made a huge mistake, I looked around. In the distance, I saw a flash of gray scurry across the ground, followed by another.

"What can I do to help?"

Flint bit his bottom lip and looked at the ground before speaking. When he looked at me again, his eyes cursed me just as his words had.

"You ain't a cowboy and you sure as shit ain't a rancher. Ain't nothing you can 'cept stay the hell outta my way."

"Mr. Flint..."

"I got work ta do. More now than ever, thanks to you."

Without another word, Flint turned around and headed for his horse. I stood and watched him mount up, slide his rifle into a saddle scabbard, and ride off to round up the scattered cows.

A warm wind kicked up some dirt near my feet, twirling it around like a tiny dust devil. It spun in wild disarray, then dissipated without a trace.

"Well, shit."

I turned around and headed back for the Explorer. Before getting in, I looked at Flint as he whooped and hollered, working to drive the startled cows back together by himself. There was nothing I could do, or knew how to do, to help. I opened the door and sat down behind the wheel.

"You're not in Houston anymore, Cass," I said as I made a hard U-turn and drove back to the house.

I bounced along at a slow pace, replaying the harsh words Flint had said. As much as I disliked being on the ass end of a chewing, he was right. One of the first things I learned in training was never to blindly rush into something. If I had done that back in Houston on the job or in Iraq during the war, I could have gotten myself killed and put the rest of my team in a dangerous situation at best. Now, it seems I may have put some of the cows at risk, and it was safe to say that I was not one of Flint's most favorite people.

I parked the Explorer and headed inside to check on Raven. She was still sitting on the couch in the same position when I left her.

"Everything's fine, sweetheart. It was just Flint trying to scare off some coyotes that were roaming too close to the cattle."

I sat down next to her. The glow I had seen in her before was gone. She looked pale.

"Let's run into town and grab some lunch. You'll feel better with a full stomach."

I wrapped my arm around her and tried to coax her off the couch. Instead, she leaned into my chest and cried.

Even out here, in one of the most remote places I know, the demons that tormented Raven were just as merciless. I hated what had happened. I hated that I was not there to protect her. I hated that I was not the one to pull the trigger. Like the coyotes in the pasture, her memories prowled inside of her, waiting to attack when least expected.

CHAPTER NINE

Adjusting takes time, and for now, we had plenty of that to spare. Moving out west allowed us an opportunity to heal and to start again.

In the two weeks since our arrival, we had met a few families in town, discovered a local diner that served the best Denver omelet I have ever eaten, crossed paths with Roy Sinclair and Floyd Huckabee on more than one occasion, and shared a drink with Sheriff Chance Gilbert at *El Gran Chihuahua*.

We found a taste of home at the Dairy Queen off RR170 on the way into Brewster, the county seat for South Brewster County and the nearest glimpse of civilization before driving further north to Presidio or south to Lajitas. We ordered dipped cones and sweet tea to help combat the heat and found a small table near the window to enjoy our treats. Raven became chatty with the young lady who served us.

"Charlotte? What a beautiful name," Raven said.

"Thank you, ma'am," Charlotte answered with a smile.

Raven looked at me, then back at the girl.

"You know, we have a son about your age off at

college. We'll have to bring him by when he comes out for a visit."

Charlotte was polite but the redness in her cheeks told me she was growing embarrassed.

"Don't mind her," I said, swooping in for the save. "Thanks for the ice cream."

Raven kicked my shin under the table causing Charlotte to crack a smile before returning to work behind the counter.

"She's a cutie," Raven whispered.

"And you're acting the part of creepy stranger."

I gave Raven a playful squint, winning this round.

We sat and enjoyed the ice cream and the fact that life was coming together for us in West Texas after all.

Raven recovered from her initial episode when we first arrived. At her doctor's request, she had found a therapist to talk with and had weekly running appointments in town. She also frequented La Mariposa Mística, The Mystical Butterfly, most times coming home with scented candles or oils. Upon learning her name, Cruzita Vásquez, the quirky owner of Raven's new favorite shop, convinced her to buy a Milagro charm carved in the shape of a bird. A raven. According to Señora Vasquez, the necklace would keep evil spirits away from her, and the Mexican patron saint of protection, *Nuestra Señora de la Santa Muerte* would guide her. I thought it was ridiculous, but Raven felt otherwise. If it made her happy, who was I to disagree?

Levi Flint had not quite warmed up to the idea that we were the new owners of the CR, but a six-pack of beer following my Lone Ranger incident had been a good start to douse the flames between us. He became tolerant of me and was courteous to Raven whenever their paths crossed. At my request, he took the time to show me around the property on horseback—a ride I enjoyed, though my backside vehemently objected.

My tour of the CR took the better part of the day. Covering five thousand acres was no walk in the park. Flint knew that going in, which I am sure was cause for some pure enjoyment on his part as I struggled to muscle through the day. Clear skies led to climbing temperatures. The pastures closest to the ranch house ran flat, similar to that which bordered either side of the property. In my view, it was why both Roy Sinclair and Floyd Huckabee, opposing neighbors, were so aggressive in trying to acquire the CR. As we rode farther, the terrain became less hospitable. Jagged bluffs and rocky crags rose and fell the closer we came to the river. Our only respite was under the cover of a small cottonwood grove about four hundred yards from the water.

Flint was not much for conversation and kept his answers short without offering much detail when I asked him questions. I walked beneath the shade of the tall trees, enjoying the warm breeze on my face and the absence of a saddle between my legs. How cowboys rode all day and were still able to father children was beyond me.

I looked at the rising bluffs towering to the southwest of us.

"Those cliffs in Mexico?" I asked.

"Yep."

No what they were called or historical fact that happened around here. Just, "Yep."

"Ever try to climb them?"

"Nope."

"How about the river? Any fish in there?"

"Probably."

Remind me to ask for my money back, I thought.

We did not stay long in the grove. Flint led us up and around a series of rocky outcroppings and cut ravines, most of which were perfect spots for rattlesnakes or for Indians of long ago to hide in before ambushing us.

I stopped my horse and slid out of the saddle to get a closer look. Flint noticed after the fact and reined his horse around, cutting me off before I got too close to the edge.

"Wouldn't want ya ta fall in. May not be able ta pull yer ass out again."

Flint's face looked as if it were made from the same material forcing its way out of the ground. Stone.

"They that deep?" I asked.

"Yep."

He blocked my path forward, which made me wonder if he was concerned about me falling in or if there was something out here that he did not want me to see.

"Okay. Okay. I know when to take a hint."

Flint sneered. I returned to my horse and mounted up. The burn between my legs grew fiercer, but I was set on making it through the day without complaint. I pulled my phone from my pocket to drop a pin on our location, but we were so far out that I had no cell reception. Looking around for landmarks, I took a mental note of the location in case I got the urge to make my way back and poke around a bit. It was my land after all.

Along the banks of the Rio Grande, a flat stretch of shoreline allowed us access to the water. Two formidable boulders rose from the river, their distance spanning twenty yards apart. Jutting out of the water, swirling currents danced at the bases of each rock, adding a lively touch to the tranquil setting. The flow was steady, but the water looked more like coffee running toward the Gulf of Mexico.

"Know why it's so brown?" Flint asked.

At last! Something with meat on it. I thought for a moment, then said something about how the sediment mixed with the mud and that the recent drought played a part in the current conditions of the water.

Flint laughed.

"Nope. It's 'cause all them Mexicans swimmin' across. Turned it spicy brown."

My shoulders slumped. He laughed again.

With the afternoon threatening to close down with us so far from the house, I suggested we forgo the rest of the tour and head back. Like a pad of butter melting atop a ribeye steak, the sun began to disappear into the heart of Mexico just over the bluffs across the river. It was clear that Flint was more than happy to acquiesce. The pace at which we rode home was double that from our early walk. If I were to make a return trip out here, it would have to be on an ATV. The fire that was cooking in my jeans was not something I wanted to experience again any time soon.

I followed Flint the entire way back. No talking. No kidding around. Just Flint in the lead and me gritting my teeth tighter with every bounce along the trail.

Seeing Raven standing on the porch of the ranch house as we rode up to the corral was a sight for sore eyes and sore butts. What made it even better was when she waved, then hopped off the porch and walked over to meet us. A fresh smile preceded her, which was something she had been doing more of these days.

Flint dismounted first and wrapped the reins around the middle rail of the corral fence to secure his horse. I watched and tried my best to copy the method.

"Getting the hang of things?" Raven asked.

I heard a grunt escape Flint, but that was all, and Raven did not hear.

"Well," I said. "I survived."

She turned her attention to Flint.

"Do you have plans for supper, Mr. Flint?"

I could feel my eyes bulge at Raven's offer, but then again, she usually had a pocket full of olive branches. There is no squashing the compassion of a teacher.

I wiped the surprise from my face and turned to look at Flint. He glanced at me, then straightened his posture before answering.

"I still have things to see to, Ms. Callahan, and it looks as if you already have company."

Flint pointed at the entrance of the ranch. A brand-new King Ranch Ford pickup turned under the gateway and rumbled over the cattle guard before kicking up a trail of dust as it drove toward the house.

"Who could that be?" Raven asked.

"From the look of it, Floyd Huckabee," Flint said.

"Wonder what he wants," I said.

"Same as most everyone around here these days," Flint replied.

Raven and I turned like synchronized swimmers to look at Flint.

"And that would be...?" she asked, her words drawing out in curiosity.

Flint turned back to his work but said one thing loud and clear, more as a warning than an answer to Raven's question.

"The CR."

CHAPTER TEN

"Howdy, neighbor!"

Floyd Huckabee stepped around the front of his massive truck, complete with roof rack running lights, a grille guard that had the words KING RANCH welded into the design across the front, a tow winch with a large and very shiny hook affixed and ready for duty, and at least a four-inch lift with tires that looked like they could chew through anything.

Huckabee was short and overweight, with a face that looked more tired than a splintered lane at the nine-pin bowling alley, but he wore a smile that cut through the hardened features of a man pushing seventy years. He wore alligator boots and a brown, felt Tecovas hat with a large feather flaring back from the left side of his hat band. His jeans were typical cowboy cut with a silver buckle in the shape of Texas, and he wore a large turquoise stone bolo with silver tips. Raven and I walked toward him, both wondering why he had come out uninvited.

"Good evening, Mr. Huckabee," I said, offering a hand. "To what do we owe the pleasure?"

We shook, then he acknowledged Raven with a tip of his hat.

"Well," he said, taking a glance around the property. "See you have Levi Flint with ya still."

"You could say that. He had an agreement in place with my uncle Stewart long before he passed. Figure I might learn a thing or two from him along the way."

The three of us stood looking back and forth, smiling. Feeling more awkward by the second, Raven spoke first.

"Do you want to come in for a glass of iced tea, Mr. Huckabee?"

"That's mighty kind of ya, ma'am, but I'll only be a minute."

"Kind of a hike for only a minute's worth of time," I said. "What's on your mind?"

"That's just it. It's what's on everyone's mind."

I waited for him to elaborate. He looked at me, then at Raven, smiled again, and looped his thumbs in his pockets.

"It's just, you folk don't seem the ranchin' type. I knew your uncle for many years. Heck, watched him sell off most of his land across 170. Roy Sinclair bought a stretch. Phil Buckthorn and Manny Ramirez, too. You may not know, but the CR was the premier ranch back in the day."

I know, I thought.

"Anyhow..." Huckabee paused and looked around again.

Flint appeared from the barn and stood watching from a distance for a moment, then turned and walked toward the miniature houses, one of which was his living quarters.

"As I'm talkin'," he continued. "It sounds more like I'm tryin' ta run ya off. Couldn't be further from the truth. I simply wanted to remind you that should you decide to hang it up, my offer to buy the CR stands. Could be next week or in five years, if I'm alive."

Huckabee laughed off the last few words.

"Thank you for the offer, Mr. Huckabee."

"Call me Floyd. No sense keepin' with formalities.

We're neighbors. Business partners, too, sort of. I do appreciate yer honoring the contract Stewart and I formed over grazing rights to the southwest portion of the CR."

"No problem, Floyd."

He nodded his head, then reached into his pocket.

"Almost forgot."

Removing his hand, he produced a roll of twenty-dollar bills and handed it to me. I took it, looked it over, then tried to give it back.

"What's this?" I asked.

"Oh, it's part of the money I owed Stewart for the lease. Comes due every quarter. There's a little extra added on as a late fee."

Floyd looped his thumbs in his pockets again and jostled his jaw as if trying to reposition a false set of teeth.

"Mr. Huckabee…Floyd, I'll check Uncle Stewart's records, but I think you're all squared away for last quarter."

A thin smile curled up his cheeks, revealing a perfect set of teeth.

"You let me worry about that," he said.

He tipped his hat to Raven, then whirled around and walked back to his truck. Before climbing in, he paused for a wave.

"Cash in hand when yer ready."

If I did not know any better, I was watching Little Enos Burdette from Smokey and the Bandit load up right in front of me. Always wanting to make a deal or place a bet. Money was next to nothing to men like him, fictional or otherwise.

The truck roared to life, then like a bear walking over a deadfall, its meaty tires crushed their way to the gravel road that led to RR170. A plume of black exhaust polluted the entrance to the CR as he pounded the accelerator and drove away.

I stood a moment longer with Raven and watched the dust settle over the road and barbed-wire fence that bordered the property. She put her palm out asking to hold the roll of bills. I placed it in her hand, then noticed Flint had been sitting on the front stoop of his tiny house, cooler at his feet and a can of some kind of beer in his hand. He sat angled away from where we were standing, but I was sure he had staked out the whole scene.

"Come on," I said to Raven. "Let's go inside. I could use some iced tea."

I walked only a few steps when I heard giggling. Looking over my shoulder, Raven covered her mouth with her hand, then fell victim to uncontrollable laughter.

"What is it?"

"It's...It's..." She doubled over holding her stomach. "I'm gonna pee."

I wondered what she found so amusing, then, feeling the sting between my legs, realized the cause.

"The way you're walking, Cass. You sure you're cut out to be a cowboy?"

"You should see the horse," I said.

I joined her in the fun, then overacted a few more steps before my jeans caught just right and sent a flaming burn along the inside of my legs to my crotch. I stopped, placed my palms on my knees, and took a long, slow breath. Raven walked over and patted me on the butt.

"Ouch!" I groaned.

Raven continued to snicker, then reached for my hand and led me to the house.

"Come on, Hop-a-long. Let's get you cleaned up."

After suffering through a warm shower, I stood and air-dried myself beneath the bedroom ceiling fan before sliding into a pair of boxers and an old T-shirt. Raven brought me a jar of cream she had bought at none other than La Mariposa Mística and instructed me to rub it over the affected areas.

"You mean you're not going to help?"

"Eww," she said. "No way."

"What about all that 'in sickness and in health stuff?' We both said it."

"Yeah. You do the sickness, I'll do the health. Love ya, Cass."

She gave me a wink and almost seemed to float out of the room. I read the jar, "*Balsamo de mariposa azul.*"

"What the...?" I said to myself as I walked with bowed legs to the door and leaned through. "You gave me gelatinous butterflies?"

"Trust me," she called out.

I turned and walked like the saddle-sore tenderfoot I was and sat on the edge of the bed. Opening the jar, I lifted it to my nose and took a whiff.

"Not bad."

I dipped a finger into the cream and spread it over a small area of irritated skin. In an instant, I felt a cooling sensation.

"Damn stuff works."

That bit of relief told my fingers to dive in and not look back. With a glob ready to go, I toasted the jar in honor of my tender skin.

"Here's looking at you, *mariposa*."

When Raven returned with some iced tea, she nearly dropped the tray at the sight of me lying spread eagle on the bed still holding that jar of magical goodness in one hand and rubbing the inside of my left thigh with the other. I tilted my head up and smiled.

"I see it's working," she said as she placed the tray on the nightstand and sat down next to me on the bed.

"Yep. Not only is it cooling, it kind of..."

Raven raised an eyebrow in wait of what I was going to say.

"Well," she said.

I shot her a sarcastic grin, and exhaled with an erotic groan.

"It tingles."

CHAPTER ELEVEN

CR

Three days later, having made one trip to La Mariposa Mística to replace Raven's jar of heavenly butterfly cream that soothed and healed my saddle sores, and one drive up to visit Bo Jangles Motorsports in Presidio, I found myself back at the CR with last year's model Polaris Ranger 1000 Premium 4x4 side-by-side. It was a beast. Equipped with rugged-looking PXT2 tires, 1000 lb capacity rear cargo bed, 61 HP ProStar Engine, 4-inch LCD instrument panel, LED headlights, and a tow rated to 2500 lbs, I was in love. The icing on the cake was that the cockpit was more comfortable than the driver's seat of the Explorer, which meant my rear was in good hands, so to speak.

"Looks pretty mean," Raven said.

"It's great! Wanna go for a spin?" I said, sitting atop my new favorite toy, pretending to rev the engine.

"I think I'll pass. You go have your fun."

Raven tilted her head and smirked.

"You know, Spence is gonna be jealous," she said.

"Maybe that'll get him to come out for a visit," I replied.

Entering his sophomore year at Texas A&M University back east in College Station, Spencer was less than thrilled about our decision, my decision, to move out to Uncle Stewart's ranch. His disappointment about losing what memories he had made during his teenage years to the fire that took our home in Houston was understandable, but was more outspoken than I would have liked when we told him of our plans to start over at the CR.

"West Texas? Come on. That's like BFE!" he had said.

My partner Ray had to explain the terminology, BFE, to me.

"You know, Cass. *Butt-Fucking Egypt*? Means so far out there that who the hell would want to go?"

All in all, Spencer was not wrong. It was a long way from what we were used to. Raven and I were both hopeful that he would make time for a visit. The problem was that the fall semester had just started and he was drinking the maroon Kool-Aid like it was free-flowing from every water fountain on campus. I was happy for him, and a little jealous. To be young and carefree again. Who would not want that?

One thing Spencer had an eye for, besides the girls in short skirts and boots on game day, was extreme sports. He excelled in Taekwondo as I had, but he gravitated more to high-risk activities, including rock climbing, cliff diving, snow skiing, mountain biking, and four-wheeling. He seized every chance to engage in these daring adventures when the opportunity arose.

Raven turned to head inside. I started the Ranger and revved the engine, causing her to jump. She whirled around and glared at me. I smiled back and blew her a kiss.

"I'll remember that," she said.

"The kiss or that I got ya?"

"Wouldn't you like to know?"

Her glare caved, and she tossed me a loving wink, then headed the rest of the way into the house. I revved the engine again, released the brake, and sent a flurry of small stones sailing up behind me as I darted off toward the wide-open ranges of the CR. I figured it was only right to break her in.

My family had lived and worked on ranches back in a time when the West was as wild as the streets of Chicago are today. I had heard stories of how my ancestors had ranched somewhere out west, New Mexico, Arizona, then picked up and moved to West Texas, which is how the CR came to be almost over a hundred years ago. It was much larger then, spanning over 100,000 acres. Over time, pieces of it were either sold away or split among family. Uncle Stewart kept the best section, the *Gateway to Paradise*.

I made sure to avoid Flint and the work he was doing, though my curiosity was piqued when I saw him head beyond the fences that separated the cows from the rocky outcroppings that led to the Rio Grande.

I throttled up, sending a roadrunner scurrying away, and sped off in a different direction toward the northern border of the property. Roy Sinclair leased a thousand acres that stretched from the river along the north edge of the CR to RR170, another deal Uncle Stewart had entered prior to his death and one I would continue to honor. If I was going to lease to Floyd Huckabee, Roy Sinclair should get the same consideration. Their contributions helped pay the yearly land taxes, so I would be hard-pressed to risk losing that supportive income.

As I approached the draw between open CR range and leased CR property, I saw three men on horseback walking toward the south gate and decided to investigate.

Wonder if that's ol' Roy with them, I thought.

I had yet to meet the man, but I had heard my fair share of stories. Never took a day off, always had a hand in what was going on, grew calluses like they were fingernails, and would rather spit blood than shed a tear. On top of that, he had been rather aggressive in his pursuit of purchasing the CR, just as Floyd Huckabee and a slew of others had been. Our paths were bound to cross, so I might as well get it over with. What was the worst that could happen?

I raised a hand as I slowed the Ranger in front of the riders. None returned the gesture.

Okay, so they're not so friendly.

I turned off the engine and waited as they took their time riding over. They stopped obtrusively close, one on each side and one, whom I presumed to be Sinclair, dead center. I was surrounded.

I looked up at the three men, seeing each had a rifle resting in a scabbard at arm's reach. They also wore pistols on their hips, though not in the style of a traditional cowboy. The older man who hovered in front of me packed a .45 caliber Beretta PX4 Storm. Its stainless slide gleamed in the sunlight and the three arrows molded into the grip were a dead giveaway.

Dare in Brocca. Hit the target.

This was not the type of pistol I expected an aging rancher to be carrying. Maybe an old Colt single action or Smith and Wesson, not a weapon with tactical implications. I glanced at the other men and saw one of them wearing a similar sidearm.

"Gentlemen," I said looking back at the older man.

He glared down at me as one would an ant when considering whether or not to stomp the life out of it. While I was uncomfortable, I did not feel as if I were in danger, yet.

"You fellas from the *Double S*?"

The older man spit before addressing me.

"A-yuh. I'm Sinclair."

I stepped out from behind the wheel and offered him a hand. He did not reciprocate. Instead, he offered his thoughts on my taking over the CR.

"Son, I know'd who ya are. Most do round here by now. Ya stick out like a dead cactus with yer ball cap and city jeans. Problem with a dead cactus is they still pack mighty prick. Ya can dig 'em up but burnin' 'em out is the safest bet."

My planned welcome disintegrated to a defensive position.

"Mr. Sinclair, I believe we may have gotten off on the wrong foot."

"Only thing wrong is ol' Stewart leaving this place to a soft city slicker like you. Maybe ya ought ta consider packin' it in. Head on back ta Austin er San Antone."

"Houston, actually," I said.

I was beginning to get angry. Who was he to tout his arrogance over me? The more he disparaged me, the more I was beginning to reconsider his agreement with Uncle Stewart. It was my land now, after all. Any deals made before were subject to my approval. I could see the contract burning up right alongside the cactus this prick had been describing.

"Mr. Sinclair, I wanted to introduce myself, but seeing as how you seem to know more about me than I expected, I suggest we part ways as friends before this becomes uncomfortable for the both of us."

He squinted his eyes so only the black of his pupils showed through. Wrinkles curled away under his eyebrows, stretching like jagged trenches to the edge of his hairline. He wore a weather-beaten Stetson atop his head that hid the gray frills of what aged hair he had left. Bristled skin sagged under his chin, wavering as he sat stewing in the saddle. I could see his boney knuckles flex as he tightened his grip on the horse's reins.

"Mister, watch your tone," the man to my right warned.

He looked at me with contempt and a sheer desire to jump from the saddle and teach me a lesson. Sinclair spoke up, interrupting his man's unspoken provocation.

"Let 'im be, Earl. He may not understand how things work out here, but like it or not, we are on his land. He kin talk how he likes, long as he remembers his place when he ain't on his land."

Nice, I thought. *More threats. Indirect, but deliberate.*

I glanced at the third man on my left. He had not said a word, and the look on his face had not changed one bit since our conversation started. Silent. It was guys like him that gave me the most concern. Loud mouths were just that, self-glorified bullies. The fighters were predictable, relying on force and power, but the silent types, no matter their size or condition, were the ones who saw three moves ahead in their mind games and had multiple reactions already staged when they chose to act. Like me. I would burn his face to memory.

Spanish or Castilian background, darkened caramelized skin, brown eyes, black hair, block chin, 175-190 pounds, scar below his left ear, trailing ends of a black tattoo clawing its way up his neck. Were those fingertips? If they were and this was a Black Hand tattoo, his ties ran across the border with possible cartel or mafia influences, but I'm sure Sinclair already knew that.

I mounted my iron horse and gripped the wheel, eyes locked once again with Sinclair. He had some bad dudes on the payroll, but held enough control over them to keep this failed attempt of being a good neighbor from escalating to an all-out feud. Still, I had had enough of all of them.

I flipped the ignition to ON and revved the engine, my farewell *fuck you* moment to the lot of them. Their horses startled, whinnied, and backed away from the sound. Sinclair glared and Earl fumed, but Mister Spanish heritage regained control of his horse and studied me.

"Y'all have a nice day," I said before reversing.

I was not about to take my eyes off them.

At a distance of about twenty yards, the three men reined their horses away and walked on toward the Double S. I sat and watched them go, wondering how bad things could get. I decided that this little incident would remain between us. No need to give Raven a reason to be nervous.

The Ranger's smooth idle beneath me purred like a large cat. It was time I woke her up and headed for home. I could use a drink. Unfortunately, the only brew I had at home was light beer, and that would not cut it.

"El Hefe it is," I said to myself.

A plume of dust shot from behind the offroad tires as I tested the limits of my new toy on the way back to the house. I caught sight of Flint returning from the far reaches of the CR. It made me realize that I did not know the exact makeup of his job description. I made a mental note to speak with him about it, but first I needed a fair helping of tequila. No sense in starting another fire before the first one was out.

CHAPTER TWELVE

R

It was too early for dinner, so I asked Raven if she wanted to head into Brewster for a drink and maybe bring some take-out home. She declined but put the onus on me to bring her something to eat when I returned.

"Fine," I said. "Extra guac?"

"Ewww! No. You remember what Chance said about the guacamole, and he was right. More like crapamole. Just bring me some flautas and a little of that spicy salsa they have in the little plastic containers."

"Red, or green?"

"Red, of course."

"You got it, Little Bird. I'll be back in a bit."

I walked to her and kissed her forehead. She smelled of coconut and fresh carnations. Her scent alone made me want to scrub my plans and inhale the rest of her. I moved my palms to her hips.

"What are you doing?" she asked.

I answered with the one look that said it all and took a long whiff of her hair.

"Yeah, about that. I may smell like roses, but the petals are falling if you catch my drift."

I stepped back and removed my hands from her body.

"Alrighty then," I said. "Definite raincheck on that one."

"Yeah," she said, smiling. "Don't forget my flautas!"

I twisted around and walked to the front door, eyeing the bathroom along the way.

"Flautas and a cold shower."

"What was that?" she called out.

"Nothing, dear, Nothing. Lots of flautas coming up."

I grabbed a few things that were sitting on the end table near the couch, checked my KWP, keys-wallet-phone, and headed out for a much-needed drink.

The Explorer roared to life, and I was off for El Hefe on the far side of Brewster. I tuned the radio to KALP 92.7FM and listened to a mix of eighties music brought to me by Vesey's Lawn and Garden Supply. *"For greener pastures made easy, stop by and shop at Vesey's."* It was a ridiculous slogan, but it stuck with me.

Journey, Air Supply, and the Red Rocker himself, Sammy Hagar, serenaded my drive into town.

"I can't drive...*fifty-five!*"

I sang along enjoying the music when a familiar-looking vehicle pulled up behind me and flashed its lights. I slowed, pulled over to the shoulder, and stopped the car. I left it running and with the push of a button, opened the passenger side window.

"Mind telling me where you're headed?" a friendly voice bellowed from the shoulder.

"Hopefully same place you are, Chance," I answered. "You're looking off duty in the civies?"

Sheriff Chance Gilbert leaned on the window looking worn out. He wore a Resistol straw hat, a front-snap brown Wrangler shirt with decorative off-color yoke, and a bicentennial Texas belt buckle with a tooled leather belt wrapped around his waist. Per county regulations, he wore his gun on one hip and carried cuffs that were tucked into a leather sleeve and looped through his belt on the other.

"*Gracias a Dios*, yes. Been one of those days, *amigo. Largo y loco.*"

"I'm headed over to El Hefe, wanna come along?" I offered.

"Come along? How 'bout an escort?"

"Let's do it."

Five minutes later, we pulled into El Hefe and parked alongside the most recognizable truck in all of South Brewster County.

"Looks like we may run into Floyd Huckabee inside," Chance said.

"Yeah, was kinda hoping so," I replied.

Chance gave me a look, then dismissed whatever question he had in mind.

"Come," Chance said. "First round's on you."

"Me? How do you figure?"

"Well, I could write you a ticket."

"For what?"

I stopped and turned to Chance. His face widened with a grin that would make anyone smile.

"Noise pollution. It's why I pulled you over. I saw you singing in your car. Thought I'd do the world a favor and stop you before it was too late."

My jaw dropped. Chance laughed, then slapped me on the shoulder.

"Come on. I'll let you off with a warning," Chance said, then pulled the door to El Hefe open.

All the smells of Mexican home cooking filled my nose as we walked inside. The low light and traditional mariachi music gave this small restaurant an ambiance that transported its patrons to old Mexico.

We headed for the glow of neon lighting that hung over a bounty of tequila bottles on the bar and took a seat on stools at the counter. Chance helped himself to a basket of peanuts, popping one after the other, brushing the shucked shells away after each mouthful. I looked around and exhaled, relieved to put the run-in with Roy Sinclair behind me.

The bartender walked over, smiled at us, and batted her long, fake eyelashes at us.

"Oh, Rosa. Where were you twenty years ago when I needed you?" Chance joked.

"More like forty years, big poppie," Rosa said, laughing. "What'll ya have?"

"*Dos margaritas, por favor*," Chance said, pointing to the two of us.

He raised his hand to his mouth and whispered something to Rosa. She stepped back, nodded, then smiled at me.

"Nice of you to pick up the tab, Mr....?"

"Cass," I said. "My friends all call me Cass."

"Now yer gettin' the hang of it," Chance said and slapped me on the shoulder again.

Rosa went about fixing our drinks. Chance continued to empty the basket of peanuts. Looking around, I spotted one final task I wanted to handle as soon as the opportunity arose.

"Excuse me a sec, Chance."

I stood up and walked across the restaurant to a group of four men sitting together. Their table was filled with chips and salsa, queso flameado, and half-finished glasses of beer, and they kept the company of Floyd Huckabee. I did not know the other men, but they looked the sort who had lived in this town of Brewster for years on years. Huckabee smiled when he noticed me walking over.

"Well, ain't that Slim Pickens if I ever saw 'im," he said.

The other men turned to look at me, amused by Huckabee's remark.

"Hey there, Mr. Huckabee."

He pointed at me and raised an eyebrow as if I had made some kind of mistake.

"Floyd," I said, correcting myself.

The table laughed again, then each offered a hand as I was introduced by Huckabee. I shook hands, nodding cordially, ending with Floyd's small, but very powerful, grip.

"I appreciate you swinging by the other day."

"Ain't nuthin' about it, Cass. What can I do fer ya today? Decide ta sell already?"

Floyd licked his gums and rubbed his hands together, then laughed at me, the rest of the table joining in with him. By the look, and smell of them, I sensed their tab was long overdue to be closed.

"No, sir. It's just I'd hate to be thought of as one who would take advantage of a neighbor, such as yourself."

I reached into my pocket and pulled out the roll of twenty-dollar bills. Knowing he would not take the money from me, I balanced it on the table in front of him.

"I run a pretty tight ledger, Floyd. I had a feeling you had overpaid, and I was right. I wouldn't want us to get confused down the line. Thank you for stopping by, though. Guess I'll hear from you in a couple of months?"

Floyd looked at the money, rolled and wrapped and just as he had delivered it three days ago. I saw his smile retreat. The other men were curious but indifferent. I nodded to each, ending with Huckabee, then turned and headed back to the bar without saying another word.

As any good policeman would, Chance observed my conversation from afar, followed me with his eyes as I returned to my stool, then looked me over for any sign of psychological distress.

"Care to share, *amigo*?"

"It's nothing. Just tidying up a little business between Floyd Huckabee and Uncle Stewart. No more, no less."

Rosa delivered our drinks, a fresh basket of peanuts for Chance, and another basket filled with warm tortilla chips for us to share.

"Good," he said, pointing to himself. "I'm off duty."

I smiled at Chance.

"Guys like us are never off duty, Sheriff Gilbert," I said.

He took a sip of his drink, then stuffed a handful of chips into his mouth.

"Yeah," he crunched. "Yer right about that."

The blend of tequila, Cointreau, and lime juice seemed to be weighted in favor of the tequila, which was fine by me. I had hoped a small buzz would roll in to cloud at least the less desirable memories from the day. I nursed my drink, snacking on chips between sips, but still fell victim to the inevitable brain freeze. Stabbing cold pierced the rear of my left eye. I took deep breaths, stuck my tongue to the roof of my mouth, and shoveled a handful of warm tortilla chips into my mouth, only to endure the frozen maragrtia's torturous cycle.

"If ya drink it on the rocks, ya won't have that problem," Chance told me.

Feeling relief set in, I nodded and smacked my lips.

"True, but that might be a little too dangerous. They're easier to drink for sure, but if the potency is even slightly similar, you may have to haul me in so I can sleep it off."

"Nope, it's like I said. I'm off duty."

We shared a laugh and took another drink.

"You ever get the help you requested from Marathon?" I asked.

South Brewster County's population was sparse but had an equal if not greater need for a substantial law enforcement presence than Alpine or Marfa, which were a hundred miles to the north in North Brewster County.

Like many border towns, Brewster was on the front lines of the rising human trafficking, drug smuggling, and mass illegal immigration issues that had inundated the evening news as of late. Border Patrol and the Texas Department of Public Safety were no strangers to the area, but the brunt of keeping the peace fell upon the sheriff's office, and Sheriff Chance Gilbert was overworked and understaffed.

When Chance first learned I was a detective, he approached me about joining the sheriff's department, but declined. While I empathized with his disappointment, I did not move to the CR to return to law enforcement's front lines. My priorities were elsewhere, beginning with ensuring Raven's well-being.

We sat at the bar nursing the bottom half of our drinks when I turned to Chance.

"You've been a good friend to us. Me and Raven. I appreciate that. She's been through a lot."

Chance put both elbows on the counter. He looked at our reflections in the mirror that hung behind a row of bottles lining the bar in wait of their final pour before being tossed to the local landfill.

"She seems happy whenever our paths cross," he said. "So that's good."

"It is," I replied. "It's the days you don't see her that worry me the most, but I'm grateful to say she's making significant strides for the better."

"You ever want to talk about it, you know." Chance looked at me, pursed his lips, and nodded. It was an open invitation to lay my frustrations and concerns out there in a safe space between the two of us. It was a genuine offer between professionals, friends, and while we were still getting to know one another, I felt comfortable sharing the story of how we came to move to the CR.

"Rosa," I said, calling out to the bartender. "I'd like an order of flautas to go, and let's order another round for..."

"This round's on me."

Floyd Huckabee stepped between the stools that separated Sheriff Gilbert and me and placed a familiar roll of money on the counter.

"Rosa, bring these men whatever they like. The rest of their night is on me."

"That's not necessary," Chance said, standing up next to Huckabee.

Huckabee was shorter than Chance but challenged his girth and steadfastness.

"Nope," Huckabee said. "But since when is actin' neighborly ever...necessary. Keep the rest fer yerself, darlin'."

Rosa picked up the roll and smiled as if she had just won the lottery.

"*Gracias*, Mr. Huckabee."

"Floyd," he said, pointing at her. "Every pretty señorita I know calls me Floyd. You should, too."

The men with whom he had been sharing a table stood close by, each with looks of inappropriate intent. Rosa's smile fluttered. Huckabee reached out and embraced Chance's hand, giving it a good shake before turning to me.

"You fellas have a good night."

Huckabee offered his hand. He looked up at me, eyes seeming to churn like thunderclouds building on a darkened horizon. We shook longer than normal and the pressure with which he squeezed made me feel that this was not a gesture of kindheartedness, but a message that I had offended him and should not let it happen again.

Kill 'em with kindness, I thought.

When he released my hand, Huckabee smiled and turned for the door. His geriatric entourage stood waiting behind him, lingering like a malodorous fart. They nodded as they followed Huckabee out of El Hefe, each as clueless as the next, but not so inept that they failed to understand their place.

"That was..." Chance said, sounding perplexed.

"That's a sample of what I have had to endure since word spread about me inheriting the CR."

"You know if anyone is harassing you..."

"I know," I interrupted. "It's nothing I can't handle."

Rosa returned with fresh drinks and chips.

"You okay?" I asked.

"Yes. *Gracias*. It's part of the job to put up with men

like him. I may not have liked what he said, but who's going to the bank tomorrow?" she said, patting her front pocket where the remainder of the money rolled was tucked. "Enjoy your drinks. And your food to go will be ready shortly."

We resituated ourselves atop our stools, both of us leaning forward on our elbows. A sprinkling of salt dusted the counter between us, escaping from the endless baskets of chips served. Drops of water from our glasses plinked into the salt, forming small globs as we worked to finish our drinks. A beam of light slipped through the window shades on the opposite side of the restaurant, causing a glare to reflect on the mirror before us. I squinted at the sudden stab of light before turning to Chance.

"Before we were interrupted, I was going to tell you what happened in Houston, if you'd like to hear."

"I would," Chance replied, his interest noble, yet curious.

With my thumb and forefinger, I twisted my half-empty margarita on the counter.

"Too many bad guys get less than they deserve these days," I started. "You work hard to get them off the streets only to turn them over to a judicial system that is so politically drunk with an absolute disregard for what is right and wrong, fair or just, and well-ah, the same schmuck you hauled in one day is back on the corner the next, and right back to work. It's a frustrating cycle, and it finally came back to bite me in the ass."

Chance nodded, listening as I shared my frustrations and told him about a life-altering home invasion gone terribly, terribly wrong.

INTERLUDE 1
GORDO

Tuesdays always seemed to be the one day where the thrum of two-cycle engines and music from *KLTN Qué Buena* blended with harmony into good vibrations that accompanied the many trucks and trailers filled with eager workers along the streets of Walnut Bend. The buzz of the mowers and the roar of blowers filtered out the sounds of the surrounding city but never overpowered the music.

A bright summer sun pulsed overhead, but how most workers dressed for the job suggested that the temperature did not coincide with the day. Long sleeves, old jeans, boots, and hats of all varieties were the usual uniform, all to protect them from the burning rays on cloudless days like today. Their work was a welcomed sight for lazy or incapable homeowners, and most treated their workers with decency. Smiles could be seen all around on the faces of people who were feeling quite fortunate to have the work.

This Tuesday happened to be June 14, Flag Day. Thanks to Boy Scout troop 1000, most curbs held an eight-foot flagpole with Old Glory sailing in the summer breezes. The whap and fwap of fabric and the twisting of red, white, and blue made it look as if the streets themselves were on parade.

All the activity and shine on the streets made it easy for Guillermo Morales to blend in, watch, and wait for the perfect time to make his move. Known as Gordo to the "Tiny Flips" clique of the West Side Primera Flats gang, he had been arrested for assault and possession of a firearm. To Gordo, this was no big deal as he always claimed innocence for the crimes he was accused of committing. What made this time personal was the disrespect he felt from the arresting detectives. His dirty looks and big talk were of no consequence to the detectives. To them, he was just another *pinche cabron* waiting to be busted for one thing or another. He had seen them around and had run from them on more than one occasion, but this time his luck had run out, or so he thought.

Overcrowding and soft-on-crime pundits allowed Guillermo Morales, a.k.a. Gordo, to slip through the cracks of a judiciary system in need of an overhaul and a solid reminder that the bad guys really do need to be locked away. Gordo did not think so. He was more than happy to promise to change his ways, attend the outreach classes mandated by the judge, and fulfill the community service in exchange for his freedom, but he also made a promise to himself that he would send a reminder of his own not to disrespect anyone in Primera Flats.

The arresting detectives were beside themselves when Gordo was released, but the job had them already looking in another direction. In Houston, there was plenty of murder, rape, assault, invasion, gang violence, drug and human trafficking, and robbery to fill every police department's case log and then some.

Now, Gordo sat eating a brown bag lunch across the street from 1983 Chevy Chase, an address he obtained with the help of his Tiny Flips brothers. He was dressed as any other day laborer, and being that it was just after noon, no one paid any attention to him as most were off on a siesta of their own.

Beneath a shade tree, the shadows helped to conceal him, acting as cover to passing cars, but did nothing to obstruct his view of the sidewalk leading to the front door, the closed windows each of which perspired with condensation from an air conditioner running full blast inside, or the driveway gate recklessly left ajar so that even a man of Gordo's size might fit through with ease. And then there were the flags. The front curb held three in all. Two on either side of the driveway and one stationed by the industrial-sized mailbox near the front walkway.

It looks like America threw up over there, he thought.

He squinted his eyes, took a bite from his sandwich, and chewed, all the while waiting for Detective Callahan, *el pinche la chota*, to get home.

As time passed, so did Gordo's patience. What food he had was gone. The workers who had been two doors down now began cutting the yard he was sitting in, each looking at him and wondering who he was.

Leaving his trash for others to pick up, he stood and walked to the edge of the street. He stopped next to a utility trailer that held various tools and equipment for a local landscaping company called Lawn Concepts. Ignoring the questioning looks from the workers, he crossed the street toward the house. He walked along the sidewalk, passing over the driveway, and took a long look at the sheltered drive that ran the length of the left side of the house. No windows, just solid brick.

He continued until he reached the corner of Chevy Chase and Wilcrest, stopped as if he were contemplating crossing the street, then turned on a dime and walked back the way he had come. As he walked, he picked up his pace. His heart started to race. His eyes tracked the workers across the street. Each person was engrossed in their task, eager to finish and move on to the next job. Time was money, and to a day laborer, the more work completed meant a handsome bonus at the end of the day if they were lucky.

Gordo slipped his right hand into his rear jeans pocket and pulled out a golden-handled OTF knife. A decorative black scorpion twisted its body around the casing, and the letters PF had been scratched into the paint, memorializing his gang, Primavera Flats. His fingers flexed around the metal body as he advanced on the house, yet he waited to activate the spring that would release the blade. Tucked into the front of his pants was a Smith and Wesson Model 642 Airweight Centennial .38 Special he had stolen from a house in River Oaks. He felt the steel press against his gut as he walked.

You'll get your turn, he thought.

Without hesitating, he turned left up the driveway to 1983 Chevy Chase, turned sideways at the cocked gate, and slipped through without being noticed by anyone. He crept along the edge of the house. The driveway was empty, but the two-car garage door was lifted just enough to let the summer heat filter out through an eighteen-inch gap that revealed the tires of a mid level car parked inside. It was not an Explorer, but someone was home.

As he moved forward, everything around him blurred into obscurity except the path on which he walked. His breathing intensified, causing his nostrils to flare. His chest pounded with each rise and fall of his lungs. He could almost feel the snake and dagger tattoo that stretched down his sternum slither and jab, striking in rhythm with his racing heartbeat.

He reached the back corner of the house and peeked around. A large tree grew from the center of the yard, fanning out with giant limbs that drooped under their weight and age. A wooden deck encircled the base of the tree and acted as a pathway from the yard to the rear door of the house.

With his back sliding against the textured Acme brick, he advanced on the back door of the house. For Gordo, there was no going back. He would make his entrance quick and powerful, rushing into the house with only one thing in mind...payback.

Like a spider, he crept along until the doorknob was an arm's length from him. He frowned as if something had set him askew as if he was losing a part of himself to the deed he had yet to do, and yet he felt a rush of excitement at the same time that fueled his desire to finish what he had planned to do.

"We'll see how the *pinche* cop likes me now," he said to himself, then reached for the knob and turned.

Locked. As expected, but not an obstacle that would deter him. Not. One. Bit.

INTERLUDE 2
RAVEN

𝕽

It was Tuesday, and Raven was free. Summer had arrived for this schoolteacher. She soaked in her newfound schedule, or lack thereof, with a mid-day mimosa and a watch list full of new *Outer Banks* episodes, an old favorite in *Gilmore Girls*, and a whole series of *Glee* worth binging again.

She sat crossed-legged and barefoot on the couch. The remote for the television balanced over the crease between cushions, then slipped out of sight when she reached for her ringing telephone on the far armrest. She leaned forward to grab it, then looked at the caller-ID and pushed the send to VM button. Making a face at the phone, she tossed it onto the recliner adjacent to the couch.

"No, I don't need to talk to you about an extended car warranty, thank you very much!" she said with a hint of sarcasm to the half-empty glass of mimosa she held in her free hand.

She took a sip, closed her eyes, and swallowed. The coolness of her drink soothed her insides as did the extra helping of champagne she had decided to add to the mix. It was summer, so who was going to stop her from indulging in herself for once? It tingled, making her shudder, then switched gears, sending warm sensations throughout her body as the alcohol did its best.

Raven loved teaching. It made her feel good to know that she was making a difference in the lives of others. Each student was special to her, even those that other teachers were so glad to see leave for the next grade level. "Hope you don't get stuck with so-and-so," they would snicker. Raven did her best to ignore her coworker's snide comments, choosing to give each student a fresh look regardless of their history. More often than not, she reached those kids in ways no other teacher could. Raven was that one-of-a-kind teacher that felt as if her students were more like family than a number on a roll sheet. The results spoke for themselves, and that was the most important thing of all.

However, like any other teacher, Raven did enjoy her summers off. Over the years she would spend time carpooling Spencer from play date to activity to sporting event, but now that he earned his coveted driver's license, she remained at home waiting for his safe return. There is a definite sense of worry having a teen driver in the family when the streets they have to cruise are in crazy-lane Houston, Texas. Until they return home safe, that worry never goes away. Now that he was off at college, Raven spent her days doing the one thing she had no time for during the school year...relax.

The whir of blowers signaling the end of one job and the buzz of mowers starting on a new one was her only complaint. And then there was the background music that faded in and out as mowers pushed closer, then farther away. Raven did not mind the Spanish music, though on days like today she could have gone without it.

She stood up and walked to the front door, sliding open the partition that separated the entryway from the main living room. She first tried to peek through the peephole in the door, but all that did was make things look as if she were in the fun house at the fair where all the mirrors distorted whatever image they reflected. She leaned to one side, pulled aside the doorway curtain that covered the thin entryway window, rubbed her palm on the glass to wipe away the building condensation, and peered into her front yard.

American flags blew in the breeze, slapping on themselves, then straightening again to reveal Old Glory in her best form. Just this morning, Raven watched as the Boy Scouts placed the flags in front of the house. The street looked colorful. Patriotic. It reminded her of when Cass returned from his tour in Iraq and the overwhelming pride that filled everyone's hearts as they celebrated being American. It was a feeling she treasured, yet worried about because today, in 2023, where had that patriotism gone? It was a different country now. Too much fighting, positioning, and finger-pointing and not getting anything done but being the positive person she was, Raven held on to hope that people would come to their senses and realize that there is a better way. It made her cringe when Cass said, "we should make the bed, not shit the bed." There was at least a little something to that, though she could have gone without the visual.

Before drawing the curtains, she noticed two men standing near a trailer of landscaping equipment.

"Lawn Concepts," she whispered, then giggled. "I guess they see themselves as the artist and the lawn as their canvas."

Closing the blinds, she returned to the couch, this time opting to use headphones to listen to her shows until the workers were finished and the noise pollution of mowing day drifted away from her street.

"*Glee*, it is," she said, smiling.

She reached for the remote not noticing that it was missing.

"Where'd you go?" she called out.

Crawling on her hands and knees, she looked under

the couch, then ran her fingers in the crevasse between the cushions until she located it.

"Ha!" she said. "Nice try, but we're watching *Glee* whether you want to or not."

She plopped on the couch, activated the button on the remote that read Hulu, and turned her noise-canceling headphones to ON. Reaching forward, she picked up her mimosa and took a triumphant sip. All the world around her went silent as she slipped the headphones over her ears and waited for *Glee* to load. She bobbed her head to the beat of a song building in her head. Then, doing her best Steve Perry, she squeezed her eyes closed and sang, "Don't stop...believin'..."

INTERLUDE 3
INVASION

Gordo glanced down at the door and saw that while the handle was locked, the dead bolt was not set. He shook his head in disappointment as if he had hoped his intrusion would have been more challenging. He stepped back, lowered his shoulder, and rammed the door like a semi flattening a Subaru. Wood splintered as the latch bolt tore the strike plate from the doorframe.

Gordo rushed inside, finding himself in a small walk-through laundry room. Just beyond the washing machine was a doorway that led into a kitchen. He could see a pitcher half-full of ice and drink sitting on the counter, the left side of a refrigerator, and a doorway that led into a room on the far side of the kitchen.

He pressed a lever on the OTF knife handle, and the blade sprang forward into view. Five inches of hardened, polished steel extended from its metal sheath. The blade knew its task, for this was not the first time it had been pulled for action such as this.

With small, deliberate steps, he moved through the laundry room and into the kitchen. A small wall blocked his immediate view of the room to his left. He rounded the corner, rushing into the living room like a rogue wave.

DEAD LAND

The T.V. was on, but there was no sound. Standing next to the couch wearing headphones and a look of extreme terror, was Raven. She held an empty glass in her hand and stared at Gordo as he ran in. Music still blared through her headphones, but all she could hear was the scream born within her. It started low, then like lightning, shot through her throat and filled the room and the house and Gordo's ears.

Gordo felt pleasure from her fear. It was arousal spawned from evil and at a level he had never felt before. He liked it. No. He loved it. A smile sliced across his face as he charged.

Instinct took over, forcing Raven to act, to do anything but stand and be overrun by the beast in her house. She threw her glass at Gordo, hitting him in his chest, which did nothing but heighten his mindful invincibility. She ripped the headphones from her head and threw those as well, then turned and ran for the front door. Terrified, she let out a gurgled yelp as she tried desperately to turn the doorknob and escape. The door was locked.

Steam-rolling ahead, Gordo smashed the headphones in one stomp of his boot. Bohemian Rhapsody blared from the television now that the blu-tooth had disconnected.

"Mama, just killed a man, put a gun against his head, pulled the trigger now he's dead..."

In three lunging steps, Gordo was at the doorjamb leading to the entryway, watching Raven scramble to insert a key into the deadbolt on the front door. He paused for a split second and grunted.

His grunt caused Raven to jump. Fear, like icicles stabbing at every nerve ending from her heels to the nape of her neck, caused her to lose her breath so much so that she could not scream out. She turned, cornered against the door, the fortified oak and steel barrier bought and installed by Cass as a means to keep the house safe from unwelcome intruders. Now, it was the prison door meant to keep her in. Raven's only option was to dart into the dining room to the left of the front door.

She moved fast, but Gordo was faster. He reached out with his free hand and pushed Raven between her shoulder blades. The sudden increase in force caused her to surge uncontrollably ahead and stumble into the chair at the head of the dining table. She hit her forehead on the solid wood backing of the chair and rebounded onto the carpet, landing on her hands and knees.

"Yeah, *como una chucha*, little bitch," Gordo said.

Raven was dazed but not willing to give up. She crawled toward the table, grabbed the rear leg of the chair she had just rammed into, and pulled as hard as she could. The chair toppled over, landing on top of her, but it cleared a path under the table.

Gordo slowed his advance, deciding not to rush the fun he was having. Between the noise on the street and the music from the next room, no one would be the wiser as to the danger that Raven was facing. He stepped forward as she tried to hide.

"Ain't nowheres to go, bitch. Might as well give up."

Raven held enough breath to speak or scream or both. "What do you want!"

That made Gordo smile again. He switched which hand was holding the knife, reached down, and grabbed Raven's ankle before she disappeared under the table.

The touch of his fingers on her made her flesh wriggle. She screamed and kicked, but Gordo was stronger. An adrenaline-filled excitement roiled through him. He pulled hard, sliding Raven into view. The carpet burned her knees and caused her shirt to bunch up around her torso. Tears flooded her eyes. She prayed that by some miracle Cass would break through the front door and save her. He always promised to protect her, no matter what. Where was he now?

Between sobs and through the teary blur before her

eyes, she stared up at Gordo and the knife he now held before her. He squatted over her, teasing her as he poked the tip of the blade closer and closer to Raven's face.

"Please, please let me go. Take what you want, just...please."

Gordo felt in complete control. As he looked at her, his face softened as if he were now more comfortable and able to regulate the electrifying feeling that pulsed through him. He had wanted revenge. He had wanted payback. Now, in the midst of all this, he wanted more. It was not enough to scare the woman. He wanted to leave a lasting mark that Detective Callahan would never be able to rid himself of, nor forgive himself for.

"Oh," Gordo said almost with surprise. "I'll take what I want all right."

It was then Raven knew. The color of her attacker's eyes seemed to turn black, flooding even the bloodshot white that surrounded it. Another wash of fear, now knowing what she may be facing caused her to almost wet herself. She stared at him, frozen beneath this beast, then as if flipping a switch, flailed about as if she was having a seizure, punching and kicking and clawing.

Gordo swiped the knife in front of him catching Raven's forearm. The blade sliced through the skin, stopping when it met bone, then slipped away as he recoiled. Blood trailed across her arm, spattering on the carpet and across her shirt like a paint-a-whirl at the fair. She screamed, feeling the burn, but was also awakened from her aimless thrashing. As Gordo shifted to swing across her again, she lifted her foot as hard as she could, kicking him in the groin.

Gordo huffed, losing his breath, and felt the warm, terrible cramping pain of a direct ball shot. He sucked wind and wobbled back, giving enough time and separation for Raven to scoot further under the table.

She glanced to her left and saw that the french doors

leading into the kitchen were ajar. Beyond that, she saw the back door to the house was still open. That was her way out, but she had to act now. She rolled onto her hands and knees, arm throbbing and bleeding, and pulled herself toward the doorway into the kitchen.

Gordo rocked with a pulsing pain of his own, submitted to rage, and yelled aloud, "I'll kill you, bitch!"

He got his feet under him, leaned his free palm on the table for balance, and resumed his pursuit. The steel of his pistol against his sweating gut felt heavier now, but he wanted to do this with his hands.

"I'm coming. I'm coming."

Raven heard words but did not understand as everything drowned together in a mix of threats and '70s rock and the hum of two-cylinder engines just outside. Spit dribbled from the corner of her mouth as she crawled out from under the table. As she emerged, she pushed two chairs out of her way and into Gordo's path. She felt dizzy. A lump had formed where her forehead hit the chair, and the loss of blood from the knife wound was beginning to have an ill effect on her remaining strength, yet she knew that if she stopped, it would mean the worst for her.

Gordo stumbled into the chairs, kicking one with his right shin. Pain shot through his leg but only intensified his rage. He yelled like a bull, thrashing about as if attempting to dislodge a flank strap from his body. He kicked the chairs away to clear a path.

Leaving a trail of blood, Raven dragged herself into the kitchen and tried to stand. As she rose to her knees, she felt the world tilt. Everything around her spun. The color that filled the kitchen drew shadow, fading to blackness before revealing itself again. Her eyes rolled back into her head. Her stomach felt queasy, and for a moment she lost track of where she was. Her fingertips felt fuzzy as did her cheeks. She wobbled for a moment longer before being tackled from behind.

Gordo was on top of her now. She felt the full weight of his body press onto hers. She breathed in his stench and suffered through his hot breath as he lowered his face to hers and whispered something in Spanish. She slapped at him, but he was too heavy and too wide, and struggling only made the world spin faster.

As if terror had not seized her enough, a whole new world of fear awakened as she felt his knee dig in between her legs, then force them apart. Her eyes bulged. She screamed out again but was muffled by his large palm and the steel body of the knife he held.

In a swirl of blood and sweat, they wrestled on the kitchen floor. She pushed at him again but still had no leverage to gain an inch.

Their eyes met, inches apart. He squinted, and she cried. Terror met ecstasy, and she felt herself begin to submit. Gordo smiled, ready to have his way. He pressed his lips together.

"Shhhh, ain't a thing you can do."

Raven unwillingly relaxed, though her hands still dug at his body. Gordo raised his hips and reached for his belt. In a last attempt to save herself, Raven reached for his hand, but all she found was the brass belt buckle before he pressed the knife against her cheek. It did not break the skin, but his message was received. She released her grip on his belt buckle. He smiled and shook his head.

As she pulled her hand away, her fingers brushed by something else hard and cold, and damp from sweat. A short tube and curved features spoke to Raven.

My turn. I want to play too.

Gordo shifted to press his other knee into position and removed the knife from Raven's cheek. With a final surge of strength and sheer will to live beyond this disaster of a day, Raven grabbed the grip of the snub nose .38 tucked in Gordo's waist, slipped a bloody finger over the trigger, and pulled back. She fired and fired, each time feeling

Gordo's body convulse from the bullet that tore through him. Each time feeling the heat of the blast against her hands and waist. Each time feeling the weight of Gordo's body become heavier.

Their eyes met again, but his time disbelief spawned from her attacker's gaze. He wheezed. Warmth rushed over Raven's hands and waist while a trail of blood leaked from Gordo's mouth. Raven turned her head, catching the stream in her hair instead of her face. Her finger cramped, and she realized she had continued to pull the trigger even after the last round had been fired.

Gordo slumped forward over Raven, heavy and lifeless. Letting go of the gun, she slithered in the slick red mass dripping around her and shifted his body just enough to break free of his clutches. The tile floor acted as a bloody Slip-N-Slide as she moved away. Newborn deer standing for the first time had more grace and balance than Raven, but she muscled through, pulling herself to her feet.

She leaned against the counter, trembling. She saw her cell phone on the floor near the couch. Bracing herself against the counter, and then the wall, she moved toward the phone. Feeling sick, she dry-heaved once, then dropped to her knees. On all fours, she crawled to the phone, staining the carpet as she moved across the floor. Coming within arm's length, she reached out, grabbed the phone, and collapsed. Between shudders and sobs, she lifted the phone, activated the facial recognition security, and unlocked the home screen. She pushed the phone icon, opened her Favorites tab, and tapped Cass's name.

Bohemian Rhapsody was winding down on the television as Cass answered.

"Hey, babe."

Raven sniffled, then coughing a wetted sob, placed her palm on her forehead, and squeezed her eyes shut.

"Rave...What is it?"

Raven struggled to speak.

"Is everything all right?" Cass said with heightened concern.

"Nothing really matters, Nothing really matters...to me." The final lines of the infamous song played out, and the music faded into silence.

"I...I killed him!"

CHAPTER THIRTEEN

The neon above the bar fluttered and hummed, daring the glass tubes on an old Corona Light sign to burn out. Chance sat looking at our reflections, his lips pulled to one side.

"That's a hell of a thing to experience." He lifted the remaining slush of half-consumed margarita and polished it off in three long draws from the glass. "Y'all been through the wringer. And with the fire an' all. Cass, you did right by gettin' outta Dodge."

I lifted my glass, examined the contents before bringing the rim to my mouth, then decided against finishing it off. I placed it down again and reached for my wallet. "Rosa," I called out. "What do I owe ya?"

Rosa walked over to us, her black hair bouncing along her shoulders, and smiled more with her elongated fake eyelashes than with her lips.

"It's all covered. Your friend, Mr. Huckabee, remember?"

I smiled back at Rosa, then opened my wallet.

"That was nice of him, but I cover my own tabs," I said. "Fifty take care of the drinks and food to go? And don't forget Sheriff Gilbert's drinks, too."

Rosa held back a laugh, more as a result of the windfall she had found herself in with tips tonight than anything else.

"It is just fine, Mr. Cass," she said.

Rosa turned and walked toward the end of the bar, stepped out from behind it, and disappeared into the kitchen.

Chance stood up and stretched. I knew just how he felt. Overworked, worn out, and hard-pressed to obtain any extra help. He covered his mouth and turned his head to conceal a well-deserved yawn.

"Get some rest, my friend," I said.

Chance nodded, but we both understood that it was not in the cards. He would be back in the field for one reason or another before too long. It was like I said before, guys like us were never off duty.

Rosa returned with a plastic bag filled with Styrofoam containers that held more than a typical order of flautas for one.

"I put extra in. Also, some chips and queso."

"You didn't have to..."

Rosa raised two fingers at me showing teeth with her biggest smile of the night.

"*Es mi regalo*, my treat. It's been a good night."

She patted the bulge in her front pocket, then turned away before I could argue. I looked at Chance. He shrugged his shoulders, then slapped me on the shoulder.

"Come, *amigo*. I'm sure Raven is wondering where her dinner is."

Together, we walked away from the bar and the lights and the reflections of two friends with a lot on their minds. I grabbed a mint from a silver dish at the hostess station near the exit, squeezed it out of the wrapper with one hand, and popped it into my mouth. Chance opened the door and held it as I walked through.

The evening was warm. Music found its way out of the restaurant and into the night air, welcoming new customers while serenading those who left with full stomachs from an authentic, fulfilling meal. A breeze blew across the parking lot creating small dust devils in the crushed gravel and sending swirls of powder to race between vehicles like tiny tornadoes in search of tiny trailer parks to ravage.

El Hefe was located on RR170 on the north side of Brewster. I looked out toward Presidio. All I could see was the blacktop road and a few dull house lights in the distance before the horizon and the night sky blended into one black space where ambient light was swallowed and starlight shone over a million miles away. It was peaceful, yet a dark and dangerous drive this time of night.

"Take care, Chance. Thanks for joining me."

"You make sure to keep those windows up the next time you feel like singing along with the radio," he joked.

We laughed and shook hands.

"I'll see you around," he said.

"Will do," I answered. "Just remember one thing."

Chance looked back at me before entering his vehicle. "What's that?"

"You're off duty."

He tipped his hat and gave me his patented, contagious grin, then hopped in and fired up the engine of his Dodge Challenger patrol car. He blinked the lights once as I watched him drive off.

I opened the door to the Explorer and got in, placing the bag with Raven's dinner on the floor in front of the passenger seat. I pushed the ignition switch and rolled down the windows. The West Texas air was much cleaner than that of Houston. I took a deep breath and felt the fresh, warm feeling comforting my insides. The radio played a tune I was unfamiliar with, so I turned the volume to low, then put the Explorer in gear and drove to the driveway leading out of the parking lot. I pulled onto RR170 and headed south into the small town of Brewster. In the distance, I could hear a siren chime to life.

"So much for being off duty," I said to myself.

With the radio volume set to low, I drove home in relative quiet. The music was there, but my mind had drifted off into thought. The warm air and the desolate road hijacked my memories, drawing out visions that were so obscure it was like remembering scenes from an old movie without recalling the title.

A silent flash of distant lightning was the extra push my thoughts needed to transport me back to the months I spent in Iraq during the war.

The road was long, disappearing into the deep and dark as if swallowed by an unseen enemy. The night air was hot and thick. Dust on the wind made it uncomfortable to breathe, and the lingering smell of burning oil made this a memorable ride, but for reasons better off being lost in the mind. It was the hum of the tires as we bounced along the war-torn road and the spattering of stars above, though foreign to my eyes, that soothed me as my unit pushed forward on patrol. The Humvee's engine roared along as if singing cadence in the line of Mine Resistant Ambush Protected vehicles that led Dragon company.

"0200. What's our ETA again?" Sergeant Murphy asked.

"We're eleven clicks to the checkpoint, then another twenty-three before we head back." Specialist Daniker replied.

"These night jobs are the worst. Can't see a damn thing out here." Murphy complained from his raised position in the turret as he manned the Humvee's M2 .50-caliber machine gun.

"Shut it, Sergeant. Stay focused and do your job," Lieutenant Tucker said from the commander's seat.

I propped my PVS7-3 goggles on my forehead and looked out the front window without the assisted night vision tech. The glow of burning oil wells pulsed on the horizon. Trapped behind a filter of dust and distance, the fire's bright yellow and orange hues were masked, causing the blazes to look like puffs of auburn, as if the desert suffered from infectious sand, causing it to swell in agony.

"Hey, Private Callahan, you know why it's better to be in the Army than the Marines?" Sergeant Murphy asked from the elevated gunner's turret.

I ignored him, but he pressed the matter. We were all a captive audience, and this was not the first time we had been made to suffer through Murphy's jokes.

"Come on, why do you think?" he said, starting to laugh at himself.

"Jesus," Specialist Daniker said from the back seat. "Put us out of our misery already."

That made me smile.

"Okay. Okay. It's 'cause when them Navy boys take them places, they're up to their ears in seamen."

The groans from the Humvee momentarily drowned out the roar of the engine.

"Keep that shit to yourself, Murphy," Lieutenant Tucker said, leaning back to look up into the turret. "Eyes out, not down! I'm not willing to get shot while you're acting the comedian."

"Fucksake! That was funny!" he said, defending himself.

Lieutenant Tucker turned around and looked at Specialist Daniker.

"He opens his mouth again except to breathe, feel free to use that duct tape to wrap his mouth closed. Or shoot him."

Laughter erupted from Specialist Daniker.

"Now that's funny," he said.

Dejected, Sergeant Murphy glared down at him.

"It's not like I'm..."

The next few moments thrust us into a maelstrom of loud explosions, bright lights, and a flurry of radio calls as our convoy was hit by a surprise grenade attack.

The first explosion jolted the MRAP behind us, causing the vehicle to bounce violently. With little time to react, simultaneous explosions from two more grenades targeted the MRAP in front of us. One exploded beneath the lead MRAP's front axle while the other detonated on the driver's side between the front and rear wheels. The flashes were immense. The vehicle rocked as if it were an airplane and had just experienced a massive bout of turbulence. Sand flew and flames spouted, but the armored construction of the MRAP would not falter.

Chatter on the coms sounded more like an auctioneer's mash-up battle to the untrained ear, but to us, each order and report came through crystal clear.

Dragon 1, "Anyone have eyes on the enemy?"

Dragon 3, "Negative contact. All clear."

Dragon 2, "Contact, 90 degrees, fifty meters."

Base, "Dragon 2, lay down suppressing fire. Dragon 1 and 3, continue with the primary directive."

I slid my night vision goggles in place and accelerated the Humvee, veering off the pavement to position us in the direction of the insurgents while Sergeant Murphy manned the .50-caliber.

The MRAP convoy powered ahead as we stayed behind and Sergeant Murphy lit up the night with a barrage of gunfire. From our line, tracers cut through the thick air in a fiery trail. After a flurry of rounds were spent, Lieutenant Tucker ordered Murphy to cease fire.

The desert was still. An eerie calm settled in as if we had passed into the eye of a hurricane after riding out the first half of a tumultuous storm. Seconds clicked in my head, sounding like rounds being loaded into a magazine, as I waited for orders.

"All clear, Lieutenant Tucker," Sergeant Murphy called out.

Lieutenant Tucker twirled his left pointer finger in the air, then pointed ahead.

"Callahan, move out."

I stared through my night vision goggles, realizing I was clutching the steering wheel so tight that my fingers began to prickle and sting from lack of circulation. This was my first deployment, and while I had been in Iraq for almost two months, this was my first experience in which someone had tried to kill me.

I loosened my grip and followed Lieutenant Tucker's order. The Humvee's V-8 diesel engine roared as I pulled us back onto the road.

With a racing heart and cautious eyes, I drove ahead to catch up with our convoy. The blackout lights on the Humvee cast only a dim swatch of light, but as we proceeded ahead, they caught the terrified gaze of two faces standing in awe on the side of the road just ahead of our position. With hands raised, two young boys stood frozen, then, without warning, darted away into the night. It reminded me of how deer back home seemed to wait until the last moment to flee an oncoming car...deer!

With only a split second to react, I slammed the brakes, narrowly missing a white-tailed deer as it leaped across the road, its eyes gleaming in my headlights. I pulled over and stepped out of the car. The warm night wind engulfed my face, and I could have sworn I smelled the distinct stench of burning oil.

With a feeling of relief, a worrisome thought occurred to me. Where was I? Sometimes the memories are so vivid that it takes me a moment to realize it was all in the past. My heart pounded in my chest, both from reliving a memory and from realizing that I was not sure how far past the CR I had driven. The roads were twisty and acted like rolling waves in the ocean, except one wipeout here, the only sand that would cushion a fall would also have rocks, trees, bent and burning metal, and shards of sharp glass mixed in one horrific wreckage. I was lucky.

I slapped my cheek, then looked up at the enormous sky above. A river of stars flooded the heavens. I felt small beneath something so grand. So many pass through the night without a second thought to look up. Lives are busy, minds are full, and most have no idea what amazing sights they are missing. In Houston, I would never get the views I have tonight. I took a moment to gaze into the abyss that was space above. My heart settled, and my mind cleared. Satisfied, but not wanting to leave, I hopped back into the Explorer and made a U-turn for home.

Ten minutes later, I reached the turnoff that led to the entrance of the CR, turned left across the dark, barren road, and was driving the final stretch when my cell phone rang. I picked it up and glanced at the caller-ID. It was Raven.

"Hey, Rave. I'm two minutes away."

"I was wondering if you were lost. I was about to call the sheriff," she said with a hint of sarcasm.

"Chance? Ha! He was with me."

"Did you bring me what I asked for?"

"And some. I'm about to pull in."

"Oh, I see your lights. Love me?"

"Every day, Little Bird."

As we ended our chat, I drove over the final cattle guard and under the tall ranch gateway. Light glowed behind a covered window of Flint's tiny house, then, as if on cue, turned off as I passed by.

Raven opened the front door of the ranch house, polluting the immediate area with light from inside and noise from whatever show she had been watching. She waited at the front door as I retrieved the bag of take-out and locked the Explorer. It beeped and blinked its lights, then sank into the dark of night in wait of our next adventure.

"You bring enough?" Raven said, looking at the full bag of food.

I walked right up to her and kissed her forehead.

"It's a long story."

CHAPTER FOURTEEN

I woke before dawn and slid out of bed without disturbing Raven. She snored in small spurts that sounded more like chirping than the guttural rumble I had always been accused of making. I never understood the fuss. I don't snore.

The house was dark, but in the short time we lived here, I had become accustomed to maneuvering around with limited visibility. It took some getting used to, but I eventually mastered the art of ninjitsuing around the house with the lights out.

I made my way to the kitchen and gulped two glasses of water I filled straight from the faucet. That always made Raven cringe.

"That's just like drinking from a garden hose! Why don't you use the filter on the fridge?" she would say.

Most times, I shrugged off her comment with a dopey grin, but what I thought was... *Garden hose? That was the best way to get water as a kid. Didn't do anything to me.* Then I'd catch myself amid the goofy look I gave her and wondered if there was something there after all.

I was no stranger to early mornings, but today was different. It was nearing 4:30, and I felt wide awake. I walked to the front door, opened it, and stepped into the dry, warm morning air. A few clouds lingered overhead. The moon was nowhere to be seen. The CR was black as the fur on the belly of a bat. It was quiet too, except for a scraping sound like a mouse gnawing on a piece of old wood, and it seemed to originate in the barn.

I stepped off the porch for a better look. The gritty texture of sandy loam and sifted soil covered my calloused, bare feet. Dull light escaping through old nail holes in the barn siding that needed repair piqued my curiosity. I glanced at Flint's house. It was dark, as was the one next door. It remained empty for the time being, although Raven wanted to repurpose it as a "She-Shed." That chore was not very high on my to-do list, but it was not out of the question.

I felt no cause for alarm, as who would be up at this hour rummaging around in an old, empty barn way out here? Flint was the most likely answer. I wore an old Astros T-shirt but went commando in basketball shorts, my favorite pair that were oh-so-comfortable to sleep in, and headed to check out the noise.

The scuttling continued as I drew nearer the barn. The barn door was opened a crack, allowing me to peer inside before entering. I took a moment to look, and sure enough, Flint was on the far side of the open work area near the tack shelves and toolboxes. I opened the door wide enough to slip through, and stepped inside.

Flint's back was to me, and he did not hear me come in.

"Morning," I said.

"Jesus-H-Christ!" Flint yelled as he whirled around.

His eyes bulged wide as if he were a teenager and had been caught watching porn by his mother. His left hand pointed straight out to me, while his right hand sprang to his hip. Flint wore a hip holster and carried a replica Colt .45 when he worked in addition to the rifle sheathed on his horse.

When he realized it was me standing there, he

straightened his posture and relaxed both arms. As he moved his right hand away from the holster, I noticed he was carrying what looked like a semi-automatic instead of his usual .45.

"Scared the shit outta me," he said with a growing scowl.

Flint's rough edges were growing on me. It seemed to be his way. I guess after years alone, working in the middle of almost nowhere, calluses have a way of growing on a man's soul as well as his hands.

"Sorry about that," I said. "Saw the light in here and thought I'd check it out."

Flint looked me over.

"Dressed like that and unarmed at this time of night? There are dangers you just haven't caught onto yet, Mr. Callahan."

He walked toward me, dressed as if he had been up for hours. Sweat stained the armpits of his shirt and bubbled just over his upper lip.

"You think that because you're out of the big city there ain't nothin' ta worry about, but you're wrong. The kiyotes'll sneak up on ya. Wolves, too, if ya aren't careful. Hell, and that ain't the worst of it. You know that just on the other side of that river is Mexico. Ain't no wall 'cept them cliffs on the far side between us and a whole country of brownies just itchin' ta come over here without being caught. Most of 'em are poor as dirt hopin' for somethin' better, but a handful have other things in mind. You understand that, I'm sure of it."

I let him rant, but he made some good points. Instead of challenging his thoughts or touting my resume, I let him have his say. When he finished, he stood as if he expected me to turn tail and head back for the house. Instead, I doubled down.

"There's no question about it, Flint. We're new. *Green*, is that the word? But this is our home now, and Raven and I are not going anywhere. Hell, I'm glad you're here to run things. Actually, been trying to learn a thing or two from you, from a distance. I wonder if it isn't time to get my hands a little dirtier than they are used to."

Flint looked me up and down.

"Got lots ta do. You'd slow me down."

"It's Saturday."

"So?"

His irritation was on the rise again.

"Cows don't know what day it is. Neither do the fences that need repair or the predators that need killin'."

I stepped forward one step.

"I see your point. Tell you what. I'm going back inside and throwing on my city jeans as so many of you have pointed out since our arrival. I've got gloves and a hat and flask with just enough whiskey in it to last the morning, and I'm coming back out here. You say there's work to do. Let's fucking work."

I noticed Flint's eyes dilate. He glanced down to the left, then looked up and locked eyes with me, a challenging smile forming across his lips.

"All right, Mr. Callahan. We leave in ten minutes, and we'll both be on horseback. That crotch mule of yours'll scare anything that breathes out there. Can't help what we can't catch. Can't kill what we can't see, neither."

Flint turned his back and walked to the tack shelf, gathered a few things, and disappeared down the walkway between stalls.

That went better than expected, I thought.

I whirled around and jogged back to the house. I dressed in the oldest pair of jeans I could find, a Houston P.D. softball team T-shirt, a pair of knee-high socks, and a worn but comfortable pair of Adidas basketball shoes. I'd get scorned for them, but I had yet to settle on a pair of work boots. I grabbed a long-sleeve Dri-FIT fishing shirt Raven had bought me for Christmas last year, slung it over my shoulder, and put on my favorite yet weather-beaten and aged Astros ball cap.

I poured out the remnants of a day-old gallon of milk into the sink and filled the jug full of water from the faucet, then slipped a flask three-quarter filled with twelve-year-old Glenlivet into my pocket and wrote a brief note to Raven to leave on the counter.

Out with Flint. Be back later. Love you
Little Bird.

Before stepping out the door, I slipped my Sig Sauer between my jeans and the small of my back. Snug and in place, the steel hugged me, as if showing how much it missed me.

Eight minutes later, I was out the door and headed for the barn. I decided right then that I would endure without complaint any task Flint had in store. Had Raven been up to see me off, she might have suggested I bring a ruler along to measure in inches what I had set out to prove in worth. It was time I got my hands dirty on the CR, just as long as I did not get myself killed in the process.

Upon entering the barn, I saw Flint walking a second horse from the stalls. It was the same one I had ridden when he gave me the dime tour last week. It was saddled and ready to go. I could feel my ass already questioning *why*.

Flint tied the horse to a rail, then walked over to me. He did not hide that he was inspecting my preparedness. I felt as if I was going through review and that my staff sergeant was about to tear me a new one, though I would be hard-pressed to cave to the likes of Flint. I made a mistake or two at the start, but today would be the day that we would either come to blows or part ways with a touch more respect than before.

Good chance of both happening, I thought.

"You sure yer ready for this?" Flint asked.

"Don't let the high-tops fool you. I'm in for a hard day's work."

We locked eyes, neither willing to break the stare. It took a gruff whinny from my horse to remind us that even though there may be two alphas in the room, the work was not going to get done on its own.

"Well," Flint said in a low scratchy voice. "Got a rifle?"

"Wasn't expecting a hunt," I said.

Flint turned around and walked to his horse, pulled an old Winchester .308 from the pack on his horse's back, and returned to me.

"You handle this?"

Flint and I had not sat around to shoot the shit or to swap stories, but I know word had gotten around that I was not just a city simpleton. His question was more like a raise of the stakes in a friendly poker game where the pressure to win supersedes just tossing chips around the table and slugging back a few drinking beers.

I reached out and took the rifle in my hands, inspected the barrel, and noted the weight of the gun. I estimated it was loaded with six cartridges in the tube as one had yet to be chambered, then brought it to my shoulder and swept left and right along the far inner barn wall. I felt comfortable with the rifle and moved it into a collapsed low ready position.

"Yeah, I can."

Flint did not seem impressed, but I saw a flicker in his eyes that suggested I might have struck a chord for the positive.

"Let's go then," he said.

Without another word, we headed for our horses and mounted up. I was first out the door and walked my horse to the pasture side of the corral and gazed out into the dark that blanketed the CR. A coolness tickled my exposed skin, reminding me to slip on my long-sleeve shirt. Flint rode up next to me.

"We'll head to the far end first. There's brush to clear

and a few trees that need cuttin', then work our way back from there. Keep that hog handy in case we come across anything needs shootin'."

I glanced at the rifle now resting in a sheath fastened to the right front of my saddle. Flint continued.

"Ki-yotes, rattlesnakes, drug runners. They all pose a threat, so don't hesitate."

I listened and heard him, but I would judge whether shooting at a person was warranted. Law was law, even way out in this desolate part of Texas.

"Lead the way," I said.

Side by side, we rode into the black, soupy morning. The storm I saw from a distance last night had pushed a touch of moisture in our direction, causing a thin sheen of fog to form as the sun hinted at its awakening.

Daybreak was by far my favorite time of day on the CR. Every morning was unique. The call of wildlife, the slathering of color across the rims of the mountains to the south and west signaling the valleys to pull back the cover of shadow and reveal their rustic self, the subtle lift of the winds and the aromas it carried, each of these fit in place within the daily mosaic that was a West Texas sunrise.

This morning was no different save the strands of fog that stretched like ghostly fingers across the land. They made no attempt to grasp at us, though a coolness tempted my cheeks and lips as we passed through each thin layer. To the east, an onset glow pulsed higher and higher until the raging sun made its claim on the horizon as if boring itself out of the earth to burst into full view. And, like the waves that retreat from the shore then return in rhythmic, patterned harmony, blue sky poured in around the sun, filling the morning with a luster so clear, it was as if fresh water had been poured from the Big Dipper to wash away the night before the day.

We rode along at a slow, steady pace, reaching the farthest work area where I could see the attention it required. The sun was in full view, shrinking in size but not intensity as it ascended into the sky. Stopping at the far end of a tangled bramble of dead cottonwood limbs, we dismounted and secured the horses. Flint carried the necessary supplies. He tossed me a ten inch folding handsaw with steel teeth ready to do some real damage, and we set right to work.

The sawing and crackling of breaking limbs were the only sounds aside from the calls of a pair of foraging Green jays or the distant covey call of a bobwhite whistle. There was no conversational work chatter between me and Flint. Most of our communication was nods and grunts with a curse thrown in as needed to get our point across when the current branch or limb on which we were focused failed to cooperate. We were diligent in our tasks, each working on opposite sides from one another, cutting then dragging and stacking limbs in preparation for burning once the county burn ban was lifted. Although there was rain south of us, this summer had set a record-breaking dry spell.

By mid-morning, we were finished with our first task. My hands were hot and raw, but the gloves I wore prevented any blistering, for now. I walked to my horse and pulled the water jug from a pack on its back and took a swig. The coolness that ran down the inside of my throat was refreshing. I looked over at Flint. He took off his gloves, wiped his brow, and took a drink from an old green Army canteen, then gave me a satisfied nod. Was he offering a hint of approval? I figured at least it was a positive sign, and one I would gladly take. I walked over with my jug in hand and took another swig.

"We close to the river?" I asked.

"Fer the most part. She snakes along as she goes. I'd say 'bout half a mile give 'er take."

I looked in the direction of the Rio Grande and nodded.

"We'll head over toward the Huckabee lease. Check on

the cattle. Maybe have a chat with one of the hands, then get ta work on mending some fence."

I pulled my cell phone from my pocket and took pictures of the work we had completed with plans to send them to Raven. I texted, but it failed to deliver. I looked at my phone's signal strength to see there were no bars of service available.

The CR is a dead zone, I thought.

I turned and faced the direction of the river and took another picture, then ninety degrees to my left for another. As I lowered the phone, I noticed movement in the distance.

"You see that?"

"What?" Flint grunted.

"Thought I saw something running."

"Two legs or four?"

I turned to look at Flint. "Four. You have binoculars?"

"Nah. Left 'em in my go bag next to my camo pants and M-16."

I ignored his gut punch and turned back to see if I could locate the movement again. Sure enough, another blur scuttled in and out of view, appearing to be headed for the cottonwood grove.

Looking to the sky, I saw three vultures circling on updrafts as they surveyed something below.

"Something's going on over there," I said.

Flint dismissed my interest and mounted his horse before replying.

"Probably somethin' dead er dyin'. Breakfast time if ya ask me."

I untied my horse and mounted up. I was getting better each time, swinging my leg up and over like a seasoned regulator.

"Not worried it could be a stray cow or calf?"

Flint walked his horse over next to mine.

"Where, exactly, are you looking?"

I pointed in the direction of my first sighting, then the

second. Together, we watched for any further movement but saw none.

"Ain't been cattle near there for a few days. Been moved to the north pastures. Come on, let's move out."

"We're not going to check it out?" I asked.

Flint's shoulders dropped, and he turned to look at me square in the face. Exasperation seeped from his pores.

"Go on, if it's in yer ass that bad. I'm headin' north like I said."

I am sure Flint expected me to drop it, but he had said that coyotes posed a threat, so I was going to check it out. The only question I had was, why did he not want to? I admit there are things out here I still did not understand, and if this was another lesson learned the hard way, so be it.

"I'll catch up to you," I said.

With a pull of the reins, I headed off to investigate.

CHAPTER FIFTEEN

Alone on the range with the wind in my face, I felt free. I was determined to prove to myself that I was not in over my head and was just as motivated to show Flint I was not just a city slicker in search of a Western fantasy life. The leather reins began to feel natural in my grip, and the saddle was not as angry at my crotch, so I kicked my heels and picked up a little speed.

As I drew nearer to the cottonwood grove, I noticed two more vultures had joined the kettle, swooping and gliding as they circled in a wide observational pattern. I surveyed the immediate area, then turned my attention to the horizon before me. Other than the birds, nothing looked out of the ordinary. I glanced behind me, thinking maybe Flint was in tow, but I did not see him following.

Just as well, I thought. *If this turns out to be nothing, it will be better not hearing his crass way of saying I told you so.*

Still, I pushed ahead. Something in my gut told me to keep going.

I approached a hundred yards out and reined in, stopping my horse to have a clear look ahead before charging the rest of the way into the grove. Binoculars or a rifle scope would have been ideal for zeroing in on the underbrush of the trees. I squinted my eyes, focusing as best I could on a small target area before turning my attention to a different spot. When investigating a crime scene, I found that details were the keys to solving most every case. It was in the irregularities that clues came to light. Now, at a distance, these honed skills came into play.

"What are you so interested in?" I asked the vultures.

My horse's ears perked up at the sound of my voice, twisting around to listen for a command. When none was given, they settled again, twitching every so often while we stood and looked ahead. At first, I saw nothing to warrant any unreasonable concern. There were no cattle around, and I did not see any more movement coming or going from the trees. I was about to give up and head to meet Flint when I noticed my horse's ears perk up again.

Standing at attention, they aimed straight ahead. I watched and listened for anything that might be of interest. Still on heightened alert, the horse snorted, then pawed its front hoof in the dirt. The depth in which animals can sense danger is far beyond that of humans, but it takes human awareness to recognize such behaviors in animals. My curiosity rose. I pulled the rifle from its sheath and nudged my horse's ribs with my heels.

No sooner had we begun to walk on, that I heard faint yipping, followed by high-pitched barks.

"Yup, figured so," I said. "Whatcha doin' over there, Wile E.?"

With Flint's .308 in one hand and the reins in the other, I walked my horse cautiously ahead. What breeze remained blew toward us, which helped mask our position. At fifty yards, the yipping became easy to hear but sounded as if it came from beyond the grove instead of within. At twenty yards, the grove looked undisturbed.

I turned my focus to the sky again. The vultures seemed to have tightened their position. I thought their area of interest was in the grove, but they seemed to circle further away from the trees where the ground turned rocky on its way to the river.

I rode into the heart of the cottonwood trees, feeling an immediate temperature change beneath the shade. I looked among the branches and trunks. It was peaceful here. The way the limbs swayed as if rocking themselves to sleep, and the rustling of leaves in the canopy forced an unexpected yawn to stretch its way out of me. I was tempted to hang up my search and make for one of the wider trunks to study the backside of my eyelids.

With rifle in hand, I dismounted, then led my horse by the reins as I walked along. The yips continued, but I took a moment to enjoy the underbelly of what was to become my favorite and most memorable spot on the CR.

I inhaled a deep breath of air through my nose, then released it. I repeated this two more times, looking from tree to tree.

On the third exhale, I caught sight of something peculiar in the dirt. It looked similar to a coffee stain on a dress shirt. I tied the reins to a low-lying limb and walked over to the spot.

I kneeled and studied the dirt, the spot, and the area around it and noticed two additional stains a few feet away. The discolored areas were dry, having formed a crusty film. I stood up and looked around.

Blood?

With the presence of the coyotes, that was not out of the question, but if that were the case, where were the carcasses? I kneeled again, looking over each of the spots. This seemed out of the ordinary, but then again, was I overthinking things?

I made a sweep of the area, walking in a grid-like pattern, searching for anything that might explain what I had discovered. I found paw prints and hoof prints but had no way of telling when they were made. I decided to make another pass, walking ninety degrees from my original path. I started from the innermost section of the mental grid I had created and worked toward the perimeter of the grove when a change in the dirt caught my eye.

I looked from left to right along the ground, spotted the paw prints, then noticed a sloughing in the soil that smoothed an area behind the stains and continued beyond the edge of the grove. A few of the prints disturbed the smoothed sandy soil, looking like tracks in drying cement. Something had been dragged along the ground prior to the coyote's activity here.

I followed the trail on foot and saw that it led in the direction of the yips and barks. I returned to my horse, untied it, and mounted up. Circumventing my area of interest under the cottonwoods, I headed out of the grove following the drag marks until they disappeared where the ground hardened, turning to rocky, packed earth.

Fifty yards ahead, I saw three coyotes each wrestling over something on the ground in front of them. They competed for the best angle, positioning themselves for what I thought to be a bloody morning feast. But why would a coyote drag a carcass so far away from a kill? It did not add up. Maybe their prey was injured and ran, but that would not explain the drag marks.

I lifted my rifle and fired. When the blast sounded out, all but one scattered.

"Got one."

My horse was startled by the gunshot. A tug of the reins helped her regain her composure. I aimed at a second coyote and was about to fire but lost my target when it dashed behind a boulder. I looked for the third, but it was gone with the wind as well.

I sheathed the rifle, then patted my horse.

"Good girl."

She snorted and gave me a sideways glance as if to say *a little warning would have been nice*. I gave her a nudge, and we trotted ahead.

Halfway to my kill, I dismounted and tied the horse to a branch on a small patch of mesquite brush. Walking over, I confirmed that I had made a clean shot and killed one coyote. The bullet entered just behind its shoulder, penetrating whatever vital organs were in its path. It lay near a sharp crevasse where the rising boulders and shifting rock beds pressed together, then separated to make deep fissures in the ground. Flint had warned me about these tectonic abnormalities once before.

I was so focused on the coyote before glancing around that my heart jumped into my throat before settling again in a deep thump within my chest as I laid eyes on a grisly sight. On approach, in addition to the coyote, I expected to find the remains of a dead calf or maybe deer. Now, stretching out on the ground before me with the bottom half of its body concealed by the rocky overhang and narrow crevasse drop-off, were the ravaged arms and hands, head, and torso of a man.

PART THREE
DEAD LAND

CHAPTER SIXTEEN

"Holy shit!"

I had seen my fair share of dead bodies on the job, but none of them had been clawed and nibbled at quite like this one. The scene looked more like something out of *The Walking Dead*, but this biter had no chance of reanimating.

I leaned over and identified the victim as a man, late twenties, dark hair, caramel complexion, and no more than one-hundred forty pounds, but that was hard to estimate with only a partial view of the body. He lay face down, his nose tilting his head to one side. His eyes were fixed in an eternal stare, and his mouth lagged open just enough to make me think he had yelled out at least once before the end.

"What were you doing down there, *amigo*?"

He was covered in dirt, and by the buildup under his fingernails, it appeared he had tried to climb or crawl his way out of the thin chasm beneath the overhanging rocks.

His gut rested just over the shallow ledge. The lower portion of his body dangled out of sight.

I stepped back and looked around. The remaining two coyotes had disappeared, but the vultures remained interested, hoping for a turn to peck at the buffet below them. To the north, I saw a rider heading in my direction.

"Flint," I said to myself.

I walked away from the body to meet him, holding my hands up so he would stop well short of the scene. As he closed the gap, I could see an angry look on his face. He scowled. Flint must have heard the gunshot and figured I had gone and done something stupid. A time waster kind of thing.

He reined up but did not dismount. Instead, he let a cherry bomb of profanities rain down from his saddle before I could explain.

"What the fuck is going on? You know how far a bullet will goddamn fly out here if you miss your target?"

His rant continued until he paused long enough for me to respond.

"Shot a coyote. Didn't miss," I said. "Found something else, and I need you to listen very carefully."

Flint looked at me as if I had lost my mind. He hopped down from his horse and began to walk toward the coyote carcass and my crime scene.

"Stop right there, Flint," I said in a commanding voice I had not summoned since leaving the force in Houston.

My tone and directness surprised Flint, causing him to stop, which was what I wanted, and then to whirl around, take a step, and throw a right hook at my face. I did not want that.

I dodged his punch, feeling the wind from Flint's fist as it missed my nose. He followed up with his left, but I was faster. My hands blocked his second swing, deflecting them away. Then with a sudden shove on the backside of his left shoulder, I sent him stumbling to the side.

I did not want to fight Flint. I needed his help, but it seemed that he had some things to get off his chest. Like a bull stung by a bee, he charged at me, wrapped his arms around my midsection, and buried his forehead into my chest. We fell together, but I was able to use our momentum to continue the backward motion to my advantage. I grabbed his arms and dug my thumbs between his biceps and triceps and squeezed my fists. At the same time, I bent my right knee back to bring my foot against his hip. I kicked out as we rolled, sending Flint sailing over my head and onto his back just behind me. The steel body of my pistol dug into my back as I fought off Flint. His gun dislodged from its holster and landed out of reach under some ground cover. He landed hard enough to knock the wind out of him, but he was a bear of a man.

"You son of a bitch!" he yelled.

I whirled around before he had a chance to get up. I jumped on him, grinding my right shin into the meat of his forearm just above the elbow, quickly stapling his right side to the ground under my body weight. Knowing his left arm and head were his only options to continue the fight, I leaned in as he tried to surge up with a swing of the fist. It connected just above my kidneys but was a far less powerful attempt from his submissive position.

As he swung, he lifted his head and sat up just enough to allow me to slip my right arm under his throat. I brought my left arm down along the back of his neck, clasped my wrists together, and squeezed. His left arm flailed, chipping away at me, but the fight was over. He was pinned and unable to breathe.

"Chill out, Flint. I don't want to fight you. I need your help, damn it!" I said while increasing the pressure around his neck.

Sweat dripped from my nose as he made a last-ditch effort to wrestle out from under me, but it was no use. I felt his muscles relax. With the full weight of my body pinning him to the ground and my arms locked like a vise around his neck, he had no choice but to submit.

"Come on, Flint. Ease down."

Realizing defeat, I felt Flint surrender. His left arm flopped to the dirt, and his legs stopped wriggling. I eased the pressure around his neck, pushed up from his body, and stood. He crumpled onto his back, coughing and wheezing, sucking for fresh air while massaging his throat with one hand. His eyes watered, but his face quickly returned to its normal, weather-beaten color. He bent his left knee, placing his foot flat against the ground. Flint's breathing regulated, but he continued to cough.

I glanced around and noticed we had an audience. Both horses locked their gaze on us as if sharing the same thought, *bound to happen sooner or later*.

It was nearing noon. The sun blazed overhead, burning up any hopes of cloud cover. Flint turned his head, and we locked eyes. Though his glare remained gruff and divisive, something behind his eyes told me there was no more judgment aimed my way. I stepped forward and reached out a hand to help him up.

"Here," I said. "As you like to say, let's quit fuckin' around. We have a shit-ton ta do. Only thing is, what we were planning on doing will have to wait."

Flint coughed again, then squinted his eyes as if questioning what I had said. My hand remained outstretched and open. With a relaxed exhale, Flint reached for my palm. I lowered further and grabbed a hold of his wrist.

Flint was a hefty man, solid like the trunk of an oak, but even the strongest of trees are sometimes felled by forces beyond their control.

With a solid pull, I helped him to his feet. Both of us were covered in sweat and dirt, some of it mixing together and forming a thin crust of filth over our clothes and exposed skin. Though it seemed we were at peace, I remained on alert for a possible second attempt by Flint. He did not challenge me again. Instead, he looked at me and shook his head in disbelief.

"Son of a bitch. Where'd ya learn ta fight like that?"

"Call it a lifetime of always being prepared," I said. "Something I learned back in basics."

"You ex-military?"

"Among other things, yeah."

"Shit, wouldn't have believed it if I hadn't seen it myself."

We stood a moment, and I wondered if this was a turning point for us. It is uncommon for two alphas to coexist without one asserting dominance over the other. My guess was Flint felt as if he had just been dethroned, but that did not mean he would not challenge me again down the road.

"I need you to ride back to the house and call Sheriff Gilbert. Tell him we've got a 10-50 out on property at the CR. Do you have a radio or sat phone?"

"Sat phone, yeah. Got one stored out at the workshop in the barn."

"Good. Grab that and wait for him to arrive. When he does, bring the sat phone and lead him out here."

"What's this all about, Cass?"

First time you've called me by name, I thought.

"Found a dead body just over there. Coyotes led me right to him."

Flint leaned around me to look, then changed his gaze in the direction of the river, the border between us and desolate Mexico.

"What do ya think happened?" he asked.

"No idea, but I aim to find out."

"How ya figure?"

I turned to look at the crime scene. All the training I had set aside, all the thoughts and complexities of being a detective I had suppressed, and all the experience and drama from a life I thought I left behind washed over me like a flood.

"It's what I do."

I walked away from Flint and retrieved his gun. I saw where it had landed, and though I was a little wary about returning it to him, I felt it would be a sign of good faith. Leaning over, I saw its walnut stock and picked it up, then looked it over.

Smith and Wesson model 25, .45 caliber A.C.P., polished stainless-steel frame...*revolver*.

I turned to Flint. I had questions but now was not the time. I needed his help, and with the day half over, every minute counted.

"Flint," I said.

He had walked to his horse and was whispering something to himself. Flint looked over when I called out and saw I was holding his gun. He felt the empty holster on his waist and walked over to me.

"Damn, if that don't blow the head off a beer."

I gave it an admiring glance before handing it over.

"Nice piece."

"Yeah."

"Listen," I said, changing my tone for the serious. "We've got major problems out here. I have to secure the scene and filter through quite the mess without the proper tools. The sooner Sheriff Gilbert can get out here, the better. He will have everything we need and the connections to see this through."

I looked at the body, then at the vultures circling above.

"You have a rain poncho, blanket, anything I can cover him up with until you get back?"

Flint rummaged in the pack on his horse and pulled out a green rain poncho.

"Picked this up at Army Surplus a while back. Can't say I've ever used it."

"Perfect," I said. "When Sheriff Gilbert arrives, bring him straight out. If he's not in a 4x4, the keys to the Ranger are in the middle compartment. He can drive that out here."

"We've other horses," Flint said.

"Yeah, but we may need the towing and hauling capabilities of a UTV."

"Horses are more reliable. Won't break down 'er give up on ya."

"I see your point. Still, the Ranger's there if he needs it."

We talked a moment longer when I saw his eyes skip past mine and follow something just over my shoulder. I turned to see one of the vultures had decided to swoop down, landing too close to the corpse for my liking.

"Shit," I said, then ran with the poncho, waving my arms like a madman to scare the bird away.

"Gone on. Git!" I yelled.

The vulture bobbed its shoulders and hopped a few feet away but hung around until I was almost on top of it.

I drew my leg back like a kicker attempting a field goal. At the last moment, the bird gave in to my aggressive approach. It was like Lucy pulling the football away from Charlie Brown. My foot caught nothing but air as it flew away.

I turned to the body and draped the poncho over it. I used four small rocks as anchors to secure it in place. I stood and turned to look at Flint, who was already mounted on his horse.

"Soon as you can, get the sheriff on the horn and bring him out here."

Flint gave a wave, then reined his horse around and set off for the barn.

With the body covered, it would not be long before it started to turn ripe in this heat. The smell alone would attract a slew of curious diners looking for an easy meal.

Sweating and tired, I felt the beginnings of bruising come to life on my body as I walked to my horse for a drink. I reached for the water jug, then changed my mind, opting for the whiskey I had brought along instead.

The horse turned its head as I unscrewed the cap of the flask. Our eyes met, and I immediately felt judged.

"Yeah, well, it's turning out to be one of those days."

I took a swig, feeling the burn trail down my throat. I wiped my mouth with the sleeve of my dusty fishing shirt, then raised the flask toward the horse's snout.

"Care to join me?"

Her dark eyes seemed to look through me. Then as if making a long overdue connection, it nudged ahead, pushing my hand up and over its nose in search of an affectionate rub. I slipped the flask into my pocket and obliged vigorously.

"What's your name, horse?" I asked.

I waited as if I expected it to answer.

"I suppose I'll call you Tucker until I learn your real name. It's better than just Horse, anyway, and Tucker is an old friend of mine. Let's get you over to the grove and into some shade. I've got a lot to do."

As I walked Tucker toward the grove, a thought reentered my mind. Flint's gun. I was certain that the one I handed to him after our fight was not the same gun he carried when I walked in on him at the barn. Why swap guns? There was more to that story, and I would look into that later. For now, I tried to let it be, but it nagged at me like a sticker burr caught inside my shoe.

I tied Tucker to a low-lying limb near the center of the cottonwood grove. A gentle breeze blowing through and the shade from the trees made the temperature bearable. It would be at least an hour before help would arrive, and I had much to do between now and then.

"All right, Detective Callahan. Looks like you're back on the job."

CHAPTER SEVENTEEN

The sun was relentless, and as expected, a putrid aroma lingered in the air around the dead man. It made my nostrils tingle each time I came nearer to the heart of the crime scene, but that was unavoidable. Training taught me to ignore my senses. It also encouraged me to rely on them. The trick was to juggle both skills, allow them to complement each other, and focus on one aspect of the investigation at the time.

In the city, securing the crime scene was of utmost importance. Barriers would be erected, police tape would be strung creating a border around the area, victims would be taken to a secure location for treatment and questioning, while casualties would be assessed and preserved in wait of a medical examiner to arrive, and all the while, an inventory of evidence would be processed by a team of investigators led by one ranking detective. Out here, it was me, me, and me. Until help arrived, I was the whole nine yards.

I began by creating a perimeter. Using a dead tree limb, I traced a line in the dirt fifteen feet out on either side from where the victim lay to the cottonwood grove over seventy yards away. Then, every five yards in between, I placed medium-sized rocks to mark the lines and estimate the distance. When I was finished, it looked as if I had the beginnings of a makeshift runway.

Once the drag marks were isolated, I returned to the corpse and placed smaller stones around the body, allowing for three feet of workspace within the perimeter. No one was to step inside that zone unless cleared to do so. Using my phone, I took what seemed like a thousand pictures from every angle I could think of around the body, of the body, and the areas butting up to my secure zone of crime scene stones. I walked the runway again from corpse to grove, taking pictures in five-yard sections as I went, then repeated the process on the opposite side, walking from grove to corpse.

I stopped after the second pass to review the quality of the pictures and noticed my phone battery had fallen under twenty percent. I looked to the horizon in the direction of the ranch house, wondering when the cavalry would arrive.

Feeling the full power of the mid-afternoon sun beginning to take its toll, I walked back to the shade of the grove and sat down near the tree where Tucker was tied. My jug of water was only one-quarter full, optimist by choice as always. Leaning against the tree, I took a swig and stared at the stains in the dirt, realizing they, too, needed attention.

"On your feet!" I heard a voice command from inside my head.

I was tired and hot, but I got up and collected more stones. A five-year-old would have been the best partner for this job, but seeing as how none were around, rock collecting was all up to me. Where was a young Spencer when I needed him?

The time on my phone read 2:17. It was taking much longer than I expected for Flint to ride home, call for backup, and return with Chance. I closed my eyes to rest, and for a moment I felt calmness overtake me. The breeze, the shade, even the breath sounds from Tucker mixed in a hodgepodge of comfort as I sat alone in the middle of the cottonwood grove seventy-five yards away from another man who was much less fortunate than I.

As I sat there, I ran through scenarios of what might have happened, from the ridiculous to the gruesome. I had no idea how, or who, or why, but that is how an investigation begins. Think of a crime scene as a thousand-piece puzzle dumped on a table and the box top used to guide where the pieces go has disappeared. Then, consider that when the puzzle pieces landed on the tabletop, some may have fallen onto the floor and bounced in any number of directions. Any detective worth their salt will start at the beginning and work through the process, making sure each detail, no matter how small, is given its proper attention.

Investigations take time. A lot of time. To make things worse, you can do the very best job with the very best people and still sometimes come up short. It has been said numerous times, but was ever so pertinent in this case; failure was not an option. Finding a dead body so close to home opens a whole new can of worries I thought to have left back in Houston, and with Raven still emotionally fragile, I was determined to make sure that I could look her in the face and promise her that we were safe.

Lost in thought, I heard Tucker snort. I opened my eyes and noticed her ears were pricked.

"What is it?" I asked. "We have company?"

Fighting against my stiffening muscles, I got up to see what interested Tucker. I ran my palm along her neck to the top of her muscular front shoulder, whispering to ease her nerves. Her ears acted like sonar, zeroing in on the approximate location of whoever or whatever was approaching. I used the end of her muzzle as a sight and located two horses with riders coming our way. I watched as they drew nearer, then reached around and pulled my gun. It was not Flint with Sheriff Gilbert.

I continued to track them as they entered the far side

of the cottonwood grove. The riders slowed to a walk when one noticed me standing next to Tucker.

"Hey! Mr. Callahan," one of the riders called out.

He gave a wave and headed straight for me.

"Heard you might need some help?"

I squinted, then recognized the man who spoke. It was the first time I heard his voice, but we had crossed paths once before. The Black Hand tattoo clawing its fingers up his neck was a dead giveaway. I tucked my Sig into the front of my waist in plain view for anyone to see, then stepped away from Tucker to greet the riders.

The tattooed man and the other rider, a younger man who looked to be about the same age as my Spencer, reined up and dismounted beside a cluster of low-lying cottonwood limbs. They tied their horses and walked over.

"You Sinclair's men, right?"

"That's right. I'm Ramón López. This is Joe Sinclair," the tattooed man replied, rolling his *r*'s.

"Sinclair?"

"Roy Sinclair is my grandfather," Joe said with unexpected politeness.

That was the extent of the pleasantries exchanged. I remained on guard, as these men were far beyond the boundaries of the Sinclair lease. I noticed that Ramón wore a black-handled semi-automatic on his right hip, but Joe was unarmed as far as I could tell.

"Who told you I needed help?" I asked.

Though Joe was a Sinclair, it was clear that Ramón was in charge of the two. He spoke up, his voice accentuated with a mix of Texan English and Spanish tones.

"We were working the pasture when we received a radio call from Mr. Sinclair. Told us to ride over and see if you needed a hand."

Ramón looked around. He did not hide his curiosity, which made me wonder if his intentions were honest. I also considered that his purpose here was to gather information for Sinclair, but why? Joe stood next to him looking innocent, but I had dealt with my share of guiltless trash over the years, so I just was not ready to buy the well-mannered grandson bit, at least not yet.

I looked at both men, but before I could ask how Sinclair knew something was going on at the CR, I heard the rev of engines from beyond the border of the trees. I turned to look. Ramón and Joe heard it, too. From the corner of my eye, I caught Joe glancing at Ramón before looking out to the range.

Two Ford Bronco deputy vehicles bounced along the uneven ground on a direct path for the grove.

"That'd be my backup. Sheriff Gilbert and Flint. Guessing a deputy or two as well." I turned to face Ramón and Joe. "I appreciate Sinclair sending you out to help, but I've got everything under control."

Joe glanced at Ramón again, then summoned what I expected to be a genuine Sinclair-bred attitude and spoke up.

"Not bein' very neighborly. We come all the way out here ta help an' you turn us down?"

Any semblance of a polite young man was quickly deteriorating.

"Kinda shitty if ya ask me."

"Well," I said. "I didn't ask."

Joe pursed his lips. He began shifting his weight side to side as a child might when being told *no*. Ramón remained surreptitiously calm, yet it was his eyes that gave me the same scrutinizing look as he did the first time we met.

"Joe, I shouldn't have to tell you that while your grandfather and I have a lease agreement for a portion of northern CR land, you are now well beyond that border. One might call that trespassing, regardless of your intentions."

I turned my attention to Ramón.

"Pass my thanks along to Mr. Sinclair, but I have all the help I need."

Joe drew a breath to speak again, but Ramón stopped him with the touch of his hand to Joe's chest. Without a word, he turned into Joe, forcing him to move toward their horses. I watched them untie and mount up. Before they rode off, Ramón said something to Joe I could not hear, then walked his horse over to me.

"Mr. Callahan. You are new here. *El que juega con fuego, se quema.*"

With calm hands, Ramón reined his horse back toward Joe Sinclair.

What the hell did that mean? I thought, watching him ride away.

The rev of the approaching engines grew louder, causing me to put yet another concern on hold for the time being. I jogged to the tree line, motioned to the drivers to swing wide left of my position, and parked along the west edge of the grove. The lead Bronco's lights flashed, and then, one following the other, the vehicles rambled to the parking location. I walked over to meet them.

The Broncos parked next to one another at a forty-five-degree angle from the grove. Sheriff Gilbert opened the passenger door of the lead vehicle and stepped out. A man wearing a Brewster County Deputy uniform emerged from the driver's side. Two others got out of the second Bronco. A woman dressed in a similar deputy uniform and an older man wearing slacks, a dark blue polo shirt, and sunglasses walked over to Sheriff Gilbert forming a small crescent-shaped huddle in wait of me.

I walked over and was introduced by Sheriff Gilbert as Detective Cass Callahan.

"Cass, this is Deputy Javier Santos," he said, motioning to the man who had ridden out with him. "Deputy Marie Bostwick and Special Agent Dylan Sharp, FBI liaison on loan from El Paso."

Special Agent Sharp extended his hand.

"Was about to head back when your call came in."

We shook hands. I did so with Deputies Santos and Bostwick, shaking Sheriff Gilbert's hand last.

"Thanks for making the trip out, Chance. Where's Flint?"

"Said he'd swing by later. Had some things to see to. Said he'd show us the way, but I've been out here before with Stewart."

I nodded but thought it strange Flint did not see them out. This was, according to Flint, his backyard after all. I dismissed the thought and focused on the task at hand.

"I've secured the scene as best I could. Starts in the grove, then stretches out from there," I said, drawing an arc with my finger from one end of the crime scene to the other.

"Let's go have a look," Chance said.

I led the way to the blood-stained patches within the grove, then along the drag path seventy-five yards to the body.

"Whew," Special Agent Sharp said, fanning the air in front of his face. "It's getting pretty ripe out here."

"You can thank the vultures for that. I had to cover the body to prevent them from..."

"An early lunch," Sharp said, tastelessly finishing my sentence.

Chance and I shared the same glance of disapproval.

"I wouldn't have put it that way," I said. "It was important to preserve the crime scene as best I could with the limited resources I had at my disposal."

"Crime scene?" Sharp questioned. "Jumping the gun a little, Detective?"

Chance intervened. "Show us the body."

I stepped inside the stone perimeter I had created and bent over to remove the poncho.

"Ready?" I asked.

"Do it," Chance said.

I removed the small rocks that held the corners, then lifted the poncho off the dead man. It was just like opening the oven door on Thanksgiving Day when the turkey was done. The aromas of a freshly baked bird spread throughout the kitchen causing hungry stomachs to rumble as the delicious smells permeated the air, except now, the smell was putrid, causing Deputy Santos to gag at the warm, noxious fumes that had been festering beneath the poncho.

The scratches and chewed portions of the victim's back were bright red and seeping into the shredded cloth surrounding the wounds. I stood up so everyone could have a look.

"Coyotes did a number on him before I found him. Killed one. Gunshot scared the others away."

"How did he get down there?" Deputy Bostwick pondered.

"This has foul play written all over it if you ask me," I said.

"Run us through your thoughts, Cass," Chance said.

I explained my take on the situation, doing my best to paint a picture for them as I walked through what I thought happened.

"My best guess was he was attacked in the grove, then dragged by some means to the fissure and stuffed inside. The attacker must not have realized the man was not yet dead, which allowed the victim to try and climb out. Looks like he died shortly after wriggling over the top edge, leaving him to spend his last moments calling for help in a spot where no one would hear his pleas."

"Very entertaining story, Detective," Sharp said. "But who attacked him, and why? I'd put money on an illegal border crossing deal gone sour. Two men struggled. One killed the other and stuffed the body where he thought no one would look, then crossed over your wide-open property to freedom. Hell, he's probably enjoying a margarita somewhere nearby, and you wouldn't even know it. Most everyone looks the same around here."

Chance turned to Sharp, a disgusted look brimming over his face.

"Don't be an ass, Sharp. Illegal or not, he died in my county in the United States. That makes him my problem."

"Well, we agree on that at least. He's your problem. Sometimes these bodies lead to more exciting things to discover. Looks like a run-of-the-mill wetback got only a small taste of Texas before he bit the dust."

"Sharp," I said, later realizing my mouth was leading me to a place I preferred not to go when purported help was at hand, but sometimes it had a mind of its own. "If all you planned on doing out here was disparaging the death of an unknown victim, you can take your smug FBI comments and shove them in the fissure you seem to think with."

Special Agent Sharp could take his xenophobic remarks and shove them up his ass.

He removed his glasses, looked to the ground, and smiled as if he had heard this bit before but simply did not care what anyone else was thinking.

"Look at this however you want, Detective," he said, accentuating my former title. "You'll be wasting your time with this one."

He started to walk away from us, then stopped and turned around.

"But hey, stay out here long enough, maybe you can arrest the next round of wetbacks that come across. Just make sure you call the men in green and leave me out of it."

He looked at Chance.

"Sheriff Gilbert, I'll be in the car. When you see what I see, and believe me, it shouldn't take that long, I'll be more than ready to go."

He turned and walked toward the grove and the Broncos, but we could all hear him grumble as he went. "And I thought El Paso was a shit assignment."

Sheriff Gilbert, his deputies, and I stood dumbfounded at how unprofessional Special Agent Dylan Sharp had acted. There is something to be said about a man who earns his way up the ranks, doing his time while waiting for the right opportunity to seize advancement. Sharp was FBI, but not the kind I was used to, though I could see why a man like him was stationed out here.

For the true patriot, there was plenty to do in West Texas. Terrorism given open passage to the southern border of the country, drugs flowing in like a constant hundred-year flood, human trafficking running in both directions and a never-ending influx of illegals, most of which lose everything for the chance at what they hope will be a better life, while the hidden bad apples slip through and wreak havoc on the barrel that is the established communities of the United States of America; Agent Sharp forgot the most important thing of all, FBI does not only stand for Federal Bureau of Investigation but moreover, Fidelity, Bravery, Integrity.

Agent Sharp disappeared within the underbelly of the grove of cottonwoods. It was just as well. I was not jumping to any conclusions. If I knew Chance, we would be on the same page.

"Santos, Boss," Chance said. "This is not Detective Callahan's first day on the job. He may not be employed by the county, but as far as I'm concerned, if he chooses to assist, he will have the full cooperation of my team. He's one of us."

Santos and Bostwick nodded, looking at me with a reverence I had yet to earn, but it was clear that when Chance had your back, they all did.

"I appreciate that, Sheriff Gilbert."

He did not correct me and ask to be called Chance this time, but he did speak up, and the words that rolled off his tongue were directed at me.

"Seeing as how you're officially an unofficial detective for the South Brewster County Sheriff's Office, we'll let you have first go with the victim."

He pulled a pair of purple latex gloves from his rear pocket and tossed them to me.

"Put these on and pull him outta there," he said through his inimitable, contagious smile.

CHAPTER EIGHTEEN

The biggest ass-chewing I have ever received was from Dr. Monte McCord, a now-retired medical examiner from Harris County. It was my first week as a detective when my partner and I received a call to respond to Herman Park near the Houston Zoo. A jogger had seen what they described as "a frumple of clothing" and that "maybe it was a body" about fifteen feet away from the jogging path. It was just after sunup, and I was coming off the graveyard shift, but my sense of duty ran high, and I was out to impress anyone who would notice.

At the time I was partnered with Detective Larry Cline. He was twice my age and had the drive of a 1974 Volkswagen bus. Clock in, do your job, and clock out. He was running on fumes as it was and wanted more than anything to pass on this call.

———

"DON'T ANSWER THAT," he said. "Let a day roller handle it."

His face contorted from a yawn to a disgusted scowl when I picked up the mic.

"6-FOXTROT-98, Callahan, Cline en route," I said, revving the engine of our Ford Crown Vic.

We arrived on scene seven minutes after taking the call. A group of morning overachievers dressed in reflective shirts and hundred-dollar running shoes was huddled together in the middle of the path. A tall, slender man, shirtless and wearing aerodynamic sunglasses, saw us walking down the path toward them and frantically waved as if we should be running to the rescue. It must have been my slacks and Doc Martens that said, "We're not here for our health, but show us the body before it gets away." Nervous chatter erupted from more than one bystander as we approached.

"It's over there," the waving man said.

"I think it moved," said another.

The whole group began to chatter. Cline rolled his eyes at me and sucked a frustrated huff of air.

"You wanted this," he said. "It's your shit show."

I raised my hands as if I were standing behind a pulpit preparing a congregation for the most enlightening message they had ever heard.

"Settle down, everyone, please. Everyone, just take a breath," I said in a gentle yet authoritative voice. "Which one of you made the call?"

The crowd separated until a small woman was left standing in front of me. With a frightened look on her face, she raised her hand.

"Me," she whispered.

"What's your name, miss?"

"Terry. Terry Michaels."

Her lips quaked, and her body shivered. The adrenaline of discovering the body was wearing off, and the reality of the situation was beginning to take its toll on her.

"It's going to be all right, Miss Michaels."

I asked her a few questions while Cline milled about the rest of the bystanders doing the bare minimum to keep them occupied. To the chagrins of the joggers, two uniformed officers arrived and began securing a perimeter. They escorted the group away from the scene, then ran police tape across the jogging trail to close off the area. One officer remained with the ambulance chasers while the other walked back past Cline, Miss Michaels, and me to close off the path in the opposite direction.

After Miss Michaels answered my questions, Cline escorted her to the police barrier where she was received like a hero, worn out from battle. The group absorbed her, showered her with offers to whisk her away and drown out the morning with posh-sounding drinks from any number of uptown, hoity-toity coffee bars.

Cline returned as I was finishing up the notes from my chat with Miss Michaels.

"Let's go have a look," he said. "Hate to wake everyone up over an old bushel of discarded homeless crap."

I saw no reason to disagree and was excited to uncover what was to be my first recovery. We stepped off the jogging trail into the tall grass that wound its way into a tangle of tree limbs and dead ground cover, most of which was hard and prickly. My slacks would not survive.

I could hear the murmur from the crowd lessen as we slipped out of sight. With careful steps, we approached what looked like a makeshift campsite. Chip bags, cigarette butts, and beer cans littered the ground around a sky-blue sleeping bag. Lying face up and dressed in clothes more suited for a mountain climber than one who wished to survive the blistering Houston summer sun, was a deceased man.

He appeared peaceful at first glance. I observed no immediate indications of foul play, leading me to hastily conclude that he had passed away in his sleep. His skin had taken on a grayish hue, with a faint purplish glow emerging around his eyes. Tracing across his forehead and descending along his cheeks on both sides were dark veins resembling a map of winding rivers. Similar black streaks extended from his neck, vanishing beneath his worn flannel shirt. I kneeled beside him and was reaching out over him when a nasal voice screamed at me from behind.

"Keep your hands off and step away from the victim!"

I turned to see a round, stocky man wearing glasses and a

black necktie short tied over a plain white dress shirt. He pointed a firm finger at me and repeated himself with a heated shake of the wrist.

"Hands off and step away!"

Cline looked at me, his face cracking a smile.

"Now you've done it," he said.

"What," I replied, backing away. "You're the one who wanted to look. That's all we were doing."

I was beginning to get mad when my partner, the outdated Larry Cline, grabbed my arm and whispered into my ear.

"It won't matter to Doc McCord. He's very particular about his investigations. Kinda think he'd be a better Proctologist than medical examiner, seeing as how many asses he likes to chew."

"Great," I said.

Cline and I walked back toward the path, meeting Dr. McCord halfway. He didn't bother to stop. Instead, he barreled between us like an angry bowling ball out to splinter any pins in his way.

"Good morning to you, too," Cline said.

Dr. McCord stopped, then turned around and stepped close to the both of us. I could feel heat radiating off him. His nostrils flared, squeaking like a damaged bicycle tire with each breath. He spoke in a rumble.

"Either of you two see the victim expire? No? Either of you kill him? Shoot him? Hit him over the head? Jam a hypodermic needle into his neck? Feed him pills? Strangle him? Stab him repeatedly with an ice pick?"

He rained ridiculous accusations on us with no signs of letting up.

"I'm sure in all your vast experience, you've already uncovered the cause of death. Maybe we should all pack up and go home. Leave it to you two experts. Case closed. Stop by my office later and crap on my credentials if you like. But remember this, until then, don't think you know a goddamn thing about what I do. Stay the hell back and let the real expert decide how this poor son of a bitch died."

Feeling a bit raw on the backside, I stood next to Cline as Dr. McCord whirled around and headed for the body, grumbling as he went. My partner shook his head, smirking as if this had been a fun outing after all.

"Come on," he said. "Let Dr. Kevorkian work."

"I didn't even touch the guy," I said.

"No, but that was still fun to watch."

"What? Did you know he was on the way?"

"Yeah. Came across the radio when you were talking with the girl. Figured I'd set you up for a proper introduction with Dr. Dickhead."

"Thanks, Cline. Really had my back there."

"Hey, I told you to let a day roller have this one, but you wouldn't listen."

He slapped me on the shoulder as if to say better luck next time. "Payback's a bitch ain't it, Callahan?"

I LOOKED at Chance with an inquisitive smile of my own.

"Shouldn't we wait for the medical examiner?" I asked.

Deputy Santos chuckled.

"Does South Brewster County even have an M.E.?"

"We do. Dr. Frannie Lopez-Tasker," Chance said. "However, we share her with North Brewster County. I called in a request, passed along all the pertinent information, but unless you want to wait 'til dark...?"

I looked skyward. The sun seemed to race for the horizon. Even in retreat, the bright burning ball of yellow spared no one except those tucked away under a shade tree or impatiently waiting in the comfort of an air-conditioned Ford Bronco.

"Let's give her the benefit of the doubt. I'm game to wait if you are."

I stuffed the gloves into my pocket and gestured to the trees.

"I say we fan out from blood stains in the grove and see if we find anything else out of the ordinary. You bring any evidence identification markers?"

"I've got some in the Bronc," Deputy Bostwick said.

"Good. Grab them, and let's get started," I said.

"What about the body? Looks like the smell is already making the rounds."

Chance pointed to two coyotes pacing in the distance.

"Bet those are the two I missed," I said. "I'll cover him up again. Everyone just be cognizant of your position. Those coyotes or anything else moves any closer, I'll fire off a round to scare 'em away."

With only the surrounding wildlife as possible crime scene contaminators, I felt that the sooner we worked to uncover clues that may shed light on what happened, the better off we would be. When night falls, it falls hard. Searching for clues in the dark is not something I was looking forward to. Tending to the victim, on the other hand, was something we could do with flashlights or the headlights from one of the deputy Broncos, and he was not going anywhere.

We spread out under the canopy of the cottonwoods, each searching a predetermined grid I had outlined using landmarks and small markings in the dirt. It was as if we were kids again and I was drawing up plays to score the winning touchdown in a game of neighborhood street football. *Who wants to be the bottle cap?*

With our heads lowered, each of us meticulously canvassed our designated sections, scanning for any signs of unnatural presence within our search area. Beyond the bloodstains I had already marked, we were on the lookout for shell casings, discarded ammunition, abandoned weapons, torn clothing fragments, footprints, and possible tire tracks, all of which could be easy to spot and designate using the E.I.M.'s Deputy Bostwick shared among us. However, it was the trace evidence that I hoped we would not overlook, should any exist. Clothing fibers, strands of hair, bodily fluids other than blood, shards of glass, and fingerprints; all of these could be elusive to the untrained eye. It was crucial for us to remain attentive to every detail, familiarize ourselves with the surroundings, and approach each step with the understanding that even the tiniest uncovered evidence could hold the key to solving the entire investigation.

We each searched in a clockwise pattern, starting at opposite ends of the grove, then systematically worked our way toward the center. It was a painstaking task, but other than the occasional crack of the knuckles or flex of the back, no one complained. Agent Sharp remained in the Bronco, unwilling to lend a hand.

Shadows grew longer as we continued to comb the area. Our search came to a halt when we heard Deputy Bostwick give a sharp whistle.

"Over here," she said.

Before heading to see what Deputy Bostwick had uncovered, I marked my position within the grid so I could resume my search from the exact same spot. I stepped backward, making sure to place my feet within the footprints I had already made. Once I was at the edge of my grid, I walked around the perimeter to where Deputy Bostwick had called out.

Chance and I walked up at the same time, each noticing the E.I.M.s on the ground. Three small, yellow triangles with large black numbers on them had been placed on the ground near the base of a large cottonwood. It was one of the older trees in the grove, located near a cluster of fallen, dead branches. The rotting limbs lay in tangles. It was the perfect hiding spot for any number of poisonous snakes in the area and looked more like kindling set before a big fire was to be lit.

"Whatcha got, Deputy Bostwick?" I asked.

"Boss is enough," she replied before answering my question. "Shell casings. Look to be 9mm. Located three so far. I have a hunch there are more, but I'm not about to go traipsing into that bramble."

"Okay, Boss. Can you see any more from where you are standing?"

"No, but I'd bet there are more. A 9mm can hold up to eighteen rounds depending on the magazine. Hate to speculate, but I bet we find the bullets that match these casings in our vic over there."

Chance and I shared a glance, each knowing what the other was thinking.

"Time we checked the body?" he said.

"Yep. M.E. or no M.E.," I agreed.

Chance yelled over to Deputy Santos.

"Santos. Get on the radio and see if Dr. Frannie is heading our way, and tell Sharp we're gonna be a while."

While Santos went to make the call, Chance, Boss, and I headed for the fissure to finish exhuming the body. We had only just stepped out of the grove when Santos caught our attention with a whistle of his own. We turned to see him waving his arms over his head, then point in the direction of the ranch house. Pivoting, he waved again as if directing someone in from a point we could not see. A moment later, I heard the distinctive hum of my UTV as it drew nearer.

I walked over to see and felt a wave of discomfort wash over me as I saw who was driving. Flint was on horseback riding next to my offroad beast of a side-by-side, but it was Raven behind the wheel, and she had a passenger with her.

"Son of a..." I said to myself.

I had not noticed Chance walking up behind me.

"Look at that girl go," he said.

"She does not need to see any of this," I replied with eyes still on Raven.

"Well, you weren't gonna keep it a secret. Maybe this way she'll look at it differently. Like she's doing her part to help."

"Maybe," I said.

I was more worried that a glimpse of the dead body might trigger one of Raven's emotional episodes. She had made good progress since we moved to the CR but was far from a full recovery.

Raven did not park next to the Broncos. Instead, she circled wide of the grove and came to a sliding stop ten yards from us. She wore a concerned look but also spouted a genuine smile.

A woman sat in the passenger seat. She held a bag in her lap and had a stoic look about her as she scanned the area. Her face softened when she looked over at Raven. She spoke, then reached out and placed a hand on her shoulder, a simple moment of gratitude between the two women.

"That would be Dr. Frannie," Chance said out of the corner of his mouth. "She's a firecracker."

We watched Dr. Frannie Lopez-Tasker step out of my Ranger UTV as if she owned the land she walked upon. Her posture was elegant. Her figure was stunning. She had long, flowing black hair that delicately framed her face. Her skin was a swirl of dark mocha with a sheen of bronze that caused her to glow. She held a leather bag at her side which swayed in rhythm with her hips as she walked over to greet us. She wore a cream-colored blouse and navy pants, but instead of matching shoes to complement her professional appearance, she wore a pair of Lucchese pointed-toe snakeskin boots. Her slacks were tucked into the shaft of the boots displaying an ornate stitching design that ran jagged-like down and around the leather to her ankles. A tan-and-gray diamond-shaped scaled pattern covered the bottom portion of each boot from instep to toe. It was as if she walked among the rattlesnakes, and she was their queen.

Her smile broke our stare as we watched her glide over to us.

"Sheriff Gilbert," she said, extending her hand.

"One of these days, you'll call me Chance, Dr. Frannie."

"Maybe," she replied with a sly grin.

"This is Detective Cass Callahan. He's what I am calling a special addition to the investigative team I established to help investigate this investigation," Chance said, bumbling his words.

Dr. Frannie covered her mouth to hide her amusement, then cleared her throat and offered me a hand as well.

"I'm Dr. Fran Lopez-Tasker. Your lovely wife was kind enough to drive me out."

"I see that. She's always willing to pitch in when necessary," I said, secretly wishing she had stayed away from this one. "It's nice to meet you, Dr. Lopez-Tasker."

"Dr. Frannie is enough."

Her hand was firm as we shook.

"Who's up for giving me the tour?" she asked.

"Chance, let's show her the blood stains first, then lead her over to the body. I'm going to touch base with Raven."

I left them and headed over to greet Raven. Her face beamed in the late afternoon light. She seemed happy, but I knew her well enough to notice that she was feeling uncomfortable.

"You okay?" I asked.

"Yes. It was a little nerve-racking watching the sheriff's vehicles drive past the house and onto the property. I saw Flint watching from the corral and walked over to talk with him. He looked a little dirtier and was more open to conversation than usual. You two bury the hatchet out here or what?"

"You could say that."

"Well, he said I shouldn't worry. That you were all right, but that something was going on that the sheriff needed to see. Something about illegal brownies?" She looked confused. "I thought you found some drugs or something out here?"

"No. No drugs."

"Right, well, I figured that out when another car pulled up and parked outside the house. A little electric thing. I was curious to know who the beautiful woman was who stepped out of the car, so I walked out to meet her."

Raven gave me a tilt of her right eyebrow, the kind of look that insinuates guilt, but in a more playful and innocent manner.

"She's Chance's girlfriend, I think," I said with a smile.

"He wishes. Anyway, she asked if I knew the location of..." Raven leaned in and looked around as if sharing a secret. "...the body. Imagine my surprise. Can't say I've ever been asked that before."

Raven's words flowed faster as she talked. It was clear her nerves were pushing into overdrive.

"Everything's okay," I said in a soft voice. "Flint and I did discover a body, but it's just an unlucky illegal who ended up getting hurt and was not able to get help before he died."

Raven's cheeks began to sag. She looked over my shoulder, trying to catch a glimpse but not knowing what to look for.

"That's so sad," she said.

"Happens more than it should, but the important thing to know is we are safe."

Raven leaned into my chest. I felt her exhale a long, relieved sigh. I wrapped my arms around her and squeezed.

"How did you know where to find me?" I asked, resting my chin on her head.

She leaned back in the cradle of my arms to look at me.

"Flint. He led us out here, but now that I think of it, he disappeared once we got close. One minute he was by our side, the next minute, *poof*. Kinda weird, but I guess he had things to do."

"Speaking of things to do," I said. "You gonna be all right to drive back on your own?"

Her eyes deepened. I knew she wanted me to ask her to stay. Ordinarily, I would not give in to such an unspoken request, but this was our home, our land, our problem. At least if she stayed a while, I could keep an eye on her.

"Tell you what," I said, brushing her hair away from her face. "Drive the Ranger over and park it next to the deputy Broncos. Hang out in the grove where it's cooler. I have Tucker tied in the shade under one of the trees. She could use some company and a drink if you're willing."

"Tucker?"

"Yeah, the horse. I had to call it something."

"If Ray only knew," she said with a smile returning to her face. "I can do that. Just...just be careful. This isn't your job, but it is obvious Chance wants your help. I can see him glancing over here, wondering what's taking you so long. And I know I am a handful in my own way but talk to me about this. If it isn't a mystery, it won't cause me to wonder and turn it into something bigger in my mind than it already is, okay?"

I leaned forward and kissed Raven's forehead.

"I can do that. I love you, Little Bird."

"I love you too," she said.

CHAPTER NINETEEN

The grove buzzed with more activity than it was used to. Deputies Santos and Bostwick continued to comb the area for evidence, documenting and photographing each discovery while Dr. Frannie collected and categorized samples from the crusted, blood-stained patches of earth.

"We can identify specific genetic markers, including ABO blood type and DNA for starters that will unequivocally confirm or deny whether they all are from the same person. The most important step is to collect a viable sample from the victim as well as any other spatters we can locate. Once I get back to the lab, I can begin analysis."

Chance and I stood by and listened to Dr. Frannie talk as she worked through each of the sample areas. With surgical precision, she cut, scraped, and collected fragments of dried blood using a scalpel and micro tweezers, placing each sample in separate color-coded Vacutainers. She repeated the collection process using several small, moist cotton squares, blotting each until she was satisfied with the collected blood smear, then packaged them in similar medical-grade blood collection tubes for transport.

I glanced behind us and saw Raven spoiling Tucker with attention.

"That does it," Dr. Frannie said.

Before standing, she placed the last of the samples into a storage box, then tucked the container into her bag. She stood, removed her purple latex gloves, and brushed the dust from her knees. A strand of hair dangling in front of her face gave her a sexy, disheveled look. She brushed it away with her polished yet unpainted nails, then smiled at us. It was then we both realized we had been staring.

Chance let an approving grin slip from the corner of his mouth while I adjusted my ball cap and glanced at Raven once again. There was always something hypnotic about a beautiful woman who was not afraid to get her hands dirty, and we had both fallen into that awkward trap.

Dr. Frannie cocked her head to one side and gave us an inquisitive look. "Everything okay?"

"Yep," I said, my shame following me like a flat tire. "Ready to move on to the body?"

"I am," she answered. "If Sheriff Gilbert is."

Chance's smile widened. "But of course," he said. "Lead the way."

He held his arms out like a maître d' offering a grand welcome to his new guests.

"You're too much, Sheriff Chance," Dr. Frannie said with a giggle.

It was obvious she liked the attention but also that it did not make her uncomfortable. We walked side-by-side along the drag path with Chance following close behind. When we reached the transition from packed earth to rock, Dr. Frannie stopped and looked back at the grove. She stood for a moment without speaking, but her eyes spoke in volumes. I did not interrupt her train of thought, nor did Chance, but we both were wondering the same thing. As if deep in contemplation, she turned to me, her eyes still calculating.

"Why isn't there any blood along the path?" she said. "It seems to me that there would at least be traces marking the way from the trees to here."

I looked back and had to agree.

"And by the looks of it, the drag path seems swept."

"Swept?" Chance replied.

"Take a look. When a body is dragged, wouldn't the victim's heels or arms leave marks behind? Kinda like plow divots in the dirt?"

Chance *hmmm'd* to himself, nodding his head in agreement and thought. "Yeah. It's like he was dragged on top of something. A tarp, maybe?"

We each turned to look at the dead man still lying under the poncho.

"Come on," I said. "We're losing daylight. Let's pull our guy out and see what he can tell us."

The three of us walked toward the body, coming to a halt at the stones I had arranged around it. Dr. Frannie retrieved two sets of gloves from her bag. She put on one pair and extended the extra gloves to me.

"You're gonna need these."

I smiled, then reached around to my back pocket and pulled out the gloves Chance had given me earlier.

"One step ahead of you."

Without missing a beat, she balled the extra pair and tossed them to Chance.

"Here. Wouldn't want you to feel left out," she said, a playful glint in her eyes.

Chance looked at me and smiled, mouthing the word, *firecracker*.

With gloves in place, I stepped around the body and pulled the poncho off the man, letting the stones that held it down tumble aimlessly away.

"Well," Dr. Frannie said. "He's pretty ripe. Let's slide him into full view. Grab ahold of his right armpit. I'll get his left. On three?"

"Allow me, Dr. Frannie," Chance said, stepping around to stand next to her.

He crouched across from me. His forehead and the space between his mustache and upper lip were covered with sweat. I could feel wet trails sliding down my back, and I smelled the mingling odors in the air.

She counted down and watched as Chance and I pulled. At one point, the man's left foot snagged on the edge of the fissure, then jostled loose when his shoe slipped off. It bounced once along the rock wall, but I never heard it hit the ground.

With a final slide, we pulled the man into full view. He was dressed in tattered jeans and worn tube socks. His lone remaining shoe showed extensive wear, leaving me to wonder how long it had been his only pair.

"You ready to get a look at his face?" I asked.

"Yes," Dr. Frannie replied. "I'll help you roll him."

She positioned herself at his waist and reached across his body, grasping the opposite hip.

"Again, on three."

On her count, we rolled the man onto his back. Two bullet holes, three inches apart, off-center to the left of his sternum, were visible. His shirt was stiffened by dried blood and dirt. Despite any lingering hope for an accidental cause, the evidence we had already uncovered left no room for doubt. He had been murdered. This realization raised the question: why?

"Two entry points. Looks to have missed his heart," Dr. Frannie spoke in spurts. "Most likely did not die right away. My guess is that he used the last of his strength to try and climb out of there."

She pointed to the crevasse, and I thought back to my first visit out here and how Flint had warned me to stay back. I walked to the overhanging rocks and bent down to look underneath.

As I kneeled, a distinctive warning rattle erupted from somewhere within the shadows, causing me to jump back in alarm. My sudden movement startled both Chance and Dr. Frannie.

"Be careful," Chance said. "There may be poisonous snakes hiding in there."

"You don't say?" I said while watching out for the threatened snake to emerge.

Dr. Frannie shook her head. "We don't need to drag two stiffs outta here. But go ahead, take another look if it pleases you."

I glared at both of them, my heart pounding, and for a second, I wondered if I should be checking my shorts. When the rattle died down and the snake did not show itself, Chance patted down the dead man's pockets.

"No ID, no money. Who are you, *amigo*?"

"Let's get him bagged up," Dr. Frannie said. "Maybe I can help answer that question after running some tests. Can you transport him to the lab, Sheriff Gilbert, or should I call for a van to meet us?"

"Nope, Deputies Santos and Bostwick will take him wherever you ask."

Chance stepped away and radioed for Deputy Bostwick and Santos to drive one of the deputy Broncos over. Looking back at the grove, we had a small audience in Raven, but also Agent Sharp. He stood near Raven at the tree line, arms folded. It looked as if he were speaking to her, though Raven did not appear to be interested in what he was saying.

A few moments later, I helped place the dead man into a long, black HRP—human remains pouch. The sound the metal teeth made as Dr. Frannie pulled the zipper was stark, adding a real finality to the lost life packaged inside the thick, plastic bag. Deputy Bostwick opened the hatch while Deputy Santos helped me load the body bag into the rear of the Bronco.

"Gonna have to roll with the windows down for a week to get rid of that smell," he said to me.

I ignored his comment but thanked him for the help. "Appreciate the assistance, Deputy Santos."

"Javier," he said, offering his first name. "You coming to work full time with us after this?"

I shook my head, but deep down, I knew I could not walk away from this case. My mind raced with questions. With a murder on the CR, just how safe were we? What was the motive? Was this an isolated incident or the beginning of something more complicated?

Deputy Santos handed Chance the keys to his vehicle, then joined Deputy Bostwick for the ride to Dr. Frannie's office to deliver the body. The rest of us walked back to the grove, agreeing to meet up at the house before parting ways for the day. Special Agent Sharp returned to the remaining deputy Bronco and loaded up without so much as a final word. Dr. Frannie declined an offer from Chance to ride back with him, saying that Raven was so nice to bring her out that she hoped a return trip was in order. Raven smiled, happy to have a female companion, and the two walked side-by-side to the Ranger. The engine fired up, and they were off.

Chance stood with me as I took a final look around before mounting Tucker for the ride back to the house. He could tell something was bothering me.

"¿Que pasa?"

As I stood there, another question entered my mind. "We found at least three casings, all 9mm."

Chance nodded, listening.

"Don't you think it odd that the body only had two entry wounds?"

"Maybe the shooter missed?"

I walked a few steps away, thinking and speaking as I moved. "Those shots were placed in a tight pattern. The distance from the expelled casings to the bloodstains would have been far enough apart for a bullet to enter a body, but not exit. Any closer, and those rounds would have torn right through him. We would have seen blood on the dead man's back when we first found him."

I turned to face Chance.

"What are you saying, Cass?"

"From that distance, the shooter couldn't have missed. What else or who else was he shooting at, and where are those bodies?"

"Maybe they got away?" Chance paused to look around, ending with a glance at the sky. "It's getting late, Cass. You know by now how fast things go dark around here. Let's head back. Come down to the station in the morning, and we can talk about this more. Maybe Dr. Frannie will have some answers by then."

I had simple questions before, but now every possible outcome raced through my mind, including that while Chance was doing everything he could right now, was he ready to sweep this under the rug? Was I overreacting, or was my gut leading me to another possibility? I needed to regroup and work this from the beginning. Chance was my friend, a lifelong Texan, and was experienced with the problems everyone living on the border faced. It was a lot to take in, but I had experience, too.

"Come, my friend. Let's decompress and pick this up tomorrow," Chance said.

As if on cue, the horn from Chance's Bronco sounded out in three long, impatient bursts. I could see Agent Sharp raise both arms and mouth *WTF?* He opened the passenger door and stood looking over the top of the door.

"Jesus! Let's go already!"

Chance waved at him as if to say, "*We're coming*," then turned back to me and rolled his eyes.

"You wanna ride back with that prick, and I'll take the horse?"

"Not on your life," I said.

"Figures," he said. "See you back at the house."

He walked back to the Bronco, taking his time as if

only to irritate Agent Sharp further. I untied Tucker and mounted up. It had been a long day, but I still had a few questions I wanted answered before I hung it up for the night, the most curious of all being where Flint had been all day and where the gun was I had seen on him first thing this morning. I reined Tucker around and headed for the edge of the grove.

"What do you think, Tucker? Do we have more problems than I realize, or what?"

Tucker's ears perked up at the sound of my voice, but she did not offer further insight into the case.

The sky, which had been so blue this morning, now transformed into shades of black and purple, as if the colors bled into the glazed horizon. A mixture of red and orange fought back the night, but as was the routine, fell victim to an overpowering force from which there was no escape.

I looked around, felt the warm evening air on my face, and thought about the dead man. In a desolate place like this, what were his last thoughts before death claimed him, and what drove him to try to make an escape even after being left for dead?

CHAPTER TWENTY

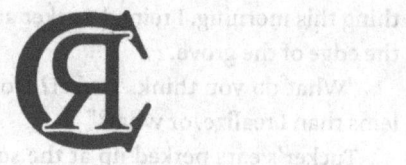

As was natural for night to flood darkness across the vast reaches of West Texas, light too came with it, burning and pulsing throughout the heavens. Stillness also accompanied the fold, birthing new sounds yet swallowing them up again as if caught in a never-ending tug-of-war between mystery and solace.

By the time the house lights appeared in the distance, I could see two sets of headlights trail off along the dirt road as they aimed for RR170. I figured it was Chance's deputies, followed by Dr. Frannie, heading for the lab. A few moments later, another pair of headlights bobbled off as well.

"Guess I'll see you tomorrow, Chance," I said.

Tucker remained disinterested in what I had to say but did a good job of giving me a smooth ride. I patted her neck and scratched between her ears. When I stopped, she snorted and tilted her head back in hopes of more.

"You're as needy as a dog," I said, laughing. "But since we're becoming pals, I'll bite."

When I arrived home, except for my Explorer, the drive was empty. I led Tucker to the barn, removed the saddle from her back, and stowed the gear, including securing Flint's Winchester .308 in a cabinet near the barn workbench. I returned with fresh water and offered her a drink, then hosed her down and brushed her as I had seen Flint do, also as recommended by *horseandrider.com*. My recent late-night internet perusals found me reading about horse care and western gear, and now my Facebook feed was filled with ads of the same. One might think I had become a true Texan rancher, but they would be mistaken. I was learning a thing or two which had paid off, especially when Flint was nowhere to be found.

After seeing Tucker to her stall for the night, I walked on stiff legs for the house and was met at the door by my beautiful bride. She held a green-bottled, longneck beer in each hand and wore a look of relief on her face.

"Thought you'd never get back. You doing okay?"

She handed me one of the beers, then stepped outside and sat on a bench at the end of the porch. I followed and sat next to her.

"Dos Equis?" I said, looking at the bottle.

Raven nodded, but I could sense the coming questions masked by her thin-lipped smile. Her eyes gave her away. It was how I knew she loved me after our second date and how I knew I was on her shit list when I had done something stupid. It was also her way of communicating that she needed me more than ever without having to say a word.

I took a long drink, taking in the smell of corn and sweet malt, feeling the bubbles swish across my tongue and down my throat, coating my insides with a cool, refreshing feeling. Raven laid her head against my shoulder.

"Do you...I mean, are we..."

"Safe?" I said, finishing her sentence. "Yes, Raven. We are."

She nuzzled in closer. I could feel her warmth beyond that of the night air. I reached my arm around her and pulled her in. Her heart pounded against my chest.

"Who would have shot that man?"

I took another drink then rested the bottle on my thigh. "Honestly, I don't know." I stopped short of giving examples of who I thought it could have been, but that would do nothing to comfort Raven. "But when I find out, I will tell you right away."

"Are you going back to work?"

I looked out past the corral into the deep, dark of the CR and wondered what things went on beyond where I could see. I had as many questions as Raven, but before I could look for my answers, I would first have to answer her.

"Only for a short time. Nothing official."

Raven sat up and looked at me. Her face drained of color. "I thought we were starting over," she said.

"We are, Raven. But this is not something we can ignore. You asked me to keep you in the loop. I will. I promise."

I reached my hand out and traced the soft skin of her cheek with my thumb. Raven leaned back against me.

We stayed on the porch long after the beers were gone. As evening aged, my body relaxed, allowing the reminders of a long day's work to return in the form of achy muscles and fresh bruises. Raven's chest rose and fell in a rhythmic flow of shallow breaths. She was asleep, peaceful in every way, safely tucked within my grasp from which I would never want to part.

I kissed the top of her head. She murmured something I could not understand, then shifted positions and wrapped an arm around my waist as if I were a body pillow and the bench was our bed.

An unseasonal coolness wafted in as the breeze picked up. Fresh aromas drifted with the air, filling my nose with new scents, one of which had a particular taste about it. I took a deep breath, then glanced around and discovered a faint orange glow appeared, then disappeared like a lightning bug playing hide-and-seek, except this was no bug.

Squinting my eyes, I caught the glow rise and fall

again. Though the smell was faint, I realized that it was from a cigar originating on the side of Flint's tiny house.

How long have you been standing in the shadows, Flint?

Each pulse of orange toyed with my curiosity, but now was not the time to approach him. He might have been out for a smoke, but my gut told me otherwise.

When the glow failed to return, I continued to observe until a time when I had to consider that Flint was no longer there. The evening had grown late, and my rumbling stomach reminded me its last meal was well before noon, and that had been a snack at best. I shifted my weight on the bench, causing Raven to stir. Before she settled, I eased out from under her and stood.

"Come on," I said, bending down to pick her up. "Put your arms around my neck. I'll carry you in."

Like a child being brought to bed after a long car ride, she hooked her hands around my neck. I cradled her in my arms and lifted her, then walked to the front door of the house. Using my foot for leverage, I opened the door and passed through. I used my heel to close the door behind me and carried Raven to the bedroom, gently placing her on the mattress. She rolled to one side as I covered her with a blanket and fell back into a deep sleep.

I stood for a moment and considered the promise I had made her. *If it isn't a mystery, it won't cause me to wonder*, her voice said over and over in my mind.

"I'll do what I can, Little Bird," I whispered as I watched her sink into the safest place she would ever know.

CHAPTER TWENTY-ONE

Raven drifted into a deep sleep while I lay next to her grappling with thoughts, schemes, scenarios, and past cases, all presenting themselves before me in scattered disarray. Even as I lay with my eyes closed a colorful display of images and memories, both real and fabricated, engulfed my vision. I drifted in and out of thought and dream not knowing which was me contemplating being awake or a shallow slumber of sifting through tunnels in my mind searching for answers. At one point, I caught myself staring at the red numbers of my alarm clock and realized that this was not a terrible dream, but a sleepless reality.

For the second day in a row, I found myself awake and wandering through the house well before dawn. The difference was that this morning, I carried a mental burden that weighed heavier than the dead man pulled from the rock yesterday.

I walked to the kitchen and opened the refrigerator, grabbed the gallon of milk, and slugged two large gulps straight from the jug. I replaced the milk and wiped my mouth on my sleeve. Glancing at the microwave, I read the time.

4:35

I stretched, feeling the pull of yesterday's war bruises I earned fighting off Flint, and let a satisfying yawn act as the final marker that I was up for the duration.

"Fine," I said to the blue digital numbers staring me in the face.

4:36

It was far too early to head into Brewster. Anxious for answers, I dismissed the dark and decided to return to the crime scene, retrace my steps, and see if I could uncover anything new.

I threw some clothes on, being careful not to wake Raven. I opted for my Safariland ALS belt holster, locked my SIg in place, and packed a bag with three fifteen-round magazines, two sets of handcuffs, a canteen of water, Streamlight ProTac flashlight, and my Bushnell tactical monocular. I slung the pack over my shoulder, left Raven a note on the coffee table, and crept out the front door.

I stepped off the porch and surveyed my surroundings as I headed out. The Ranger was parked in a garage attached to the backside of the barn. As I walked through the barn, I pulled the flashlight from my bag and shone it around. A large circle of light illuminated the walls like a spotlight at a burlesque show. I swept right, then left, stopping on the workbench. The satellite phone I had asked Flint to bring out yesterday stood wired to a charger with a small, solid green light signifying a complete charge. I unplugged the phone and placed it in my bag.

Next, I opened the cabinet where I had placed Flint's Winchester .308 rifle last night. It was still where I had left it, and took the liberty of borrowing it again for the day. I had only fired it once, which meant I had at least five cartridges remaining in the tube.

Feeling satisfied and fully equipped, I headed for the Ranger and loaded my gear. I swung the garage door open. Its old hinges creaked, boasting of age but determined to continue the job for which they were meant. I fired up the Ranger and pulled out just beyond the door.

Rule number one Uncle Stewart made sure I would never forget was always to close and secure the gate. In this case, it was the garage door, but the meaning still held. I left the Ranger to idle, followed Uncle Stewart's rule to the letter, then returned to the rhythmic hum of the UTV.

Slipping into the driver's seat, I checked the gauges for fuel level, switched on the headlights, and pushed a button that set the wheels in 4x4-H mode. With nothing but CR land in front of me, and Mexico beyond that, I pressed the accelerator and was off.

The bright beams of the Ranger's headlights cut a clear path as I drove into the predawn darkness. Drying cow pies, desert shrubs, and patches of grama grass were no match for the UTV's offroad tires. They ate through each encounter, but it was mesquite, large stones, and other obstacles of which I had to be more aware. A head-on encounter with one of those, and I would be walking home or waiting for someone or something to come along and find me. I suppose the vultures would be a dead giveaway. Even though this was my land, I did not yet have home-field advantage and was not about to enter a man versus nature duel in the middle of the night, so I kept my speed low.

It was times like these that brought about flashbacks from Iraq or the job back in Houston, but now as I drove alone, my mind flashed images from the crime scene like floating pieces to a three-dimensional puzzle. Answers to my many questions were the links I needed, but so far, I had no leads, no motive, and no way to solve this case.

After a mind-racing thirty minutes and one brief stop to relieve myself, I found myself approaching the grove. It swallowed the landscape and skyline behind it, growing like a wave swelling before the shore.

I circled the north side of the trees and continued until I reached the rocky crags and outcroppings that pierced the ground, resembling a geological maze reminiscent of the child's board game, *Mousetrap*. The area was filled with potential hiding spots for wild and venomous creatures, and the treacherous rock formations posed a constant risk of twisted ankles. The cracks and fissures between the weathered slabs and ancient granite uplifts held unknown depths, demanding extreme caution if I were to avoid being caught and losing the game.

I brought the Ranger to a stop ten yards from where we had found the dead man, leaving it running to power the headlights. It would not be long before sunrise, so I felt I could afford the extra juice running from the battery so I could see what I was doing.

Stepping out of the UTV, I had a momentary thought that tried to persuade me to stop, turn around, and head back to the house. A kind of *What are you doing out here so early, and all alone...are you crazy?* moment. It was a rational thought that I dismissed, opting to follow my borderline obsessive need for answers instead.

The LED beams from my headlights illuminated the ground leading to the crevasse in front of the Ranger, but they cast dark shadows to either side of the scene. The fissure beneath the rocky overhang looked like a pool of black ink. It reminded me of the 1980s movie *The Gate*, in which a group of teens unwittingly unleashed Hell's wrath from a mysterious hole in their backyard.

"This is the part of the movie where you are supposed to run, Cass," I said to myself.

Instead, I leaned into the Ranger and rummaged in my bag for the flashlight. The cool, steel cylinder felt good in my palm.

"Time to unleash the demons," I said, clicking it on, then off again.

I stepped toward the rocks, remembering the warning rattle from yesterday. Watching where I stepped, I moved closer to the overhang. I noticed that we had left the poncho behind yesterday and made a mental note to retrieve it before leaving. I also saw the small stones used to secure it. I reached down and picked up three of the larger stones, then tossed them along the ground toward the opening of the dark crevasse as if I were attempting to skim them across a lake. Each clanged along, crashing into different points under the rocky overhang, all of which disappeared into the fissure in a crackling bounce as they cascaded out of sight. I listened to see if there were any venomous guardians lurking about.

Lacking confidence that my most scientific method of discovering and locating any creatures that might be waiting for me to have a hold-my-beer moment, I repeated the process using three more stones. Still nothing. I stepped forward and swiped my foot along the ground just shy of the overhang, then jumped back as if I was under attack. I must have looked ridiculous, but it was all I could think to do at the time. Satisfied that there was nothing around to slither over and attack me, I clicked on the flashlight, dropped to my knees, twisted my ball cap around backward, and aimed the beam into the inky chasm.

"All right, what secrets do you have for me this morning?"

With caution, I crawled closer, shifting my eyes to either side as I swept the flashlight in front of me. With my head and shoulders beneath the rocky ledge, the drop-off was only an arm's length before me. I was drawn to look inside as if all my questions would be answered with one curious glance. As I moved the light from right to left, I noticed a small twinkle like a reflection from a disco ball. I figured it was a piece of quartz or pyrite, but it was intriguing enough that I had to see what it was.

My hand blocked the beam as I reached ahead. My fingers inched forward and latched on to the reflective object. It was not a rock. Its plastic feel and slender, geometric shape told me without seeing that whatever it was, it was man-made. I pulled my hand back and shined the light where I could have a look.

"USB drive?"

I slipped it into my rear pocket and scooched ahead another six inches.

I extended myself to the point where my hands dangled over an edge. With a determined effort, I pulled myself forward, sliding headfirst into the crypt in which the man I had discovered had been left for dead. The stench of decay permeated the air, intensifying as my face drew nearer further in. I cast a glance back at the opening, inhaling a deep breath of fresh air, before turning my gaze forward and directing the flashlight into the gaping crevice in the earth. Into the *gate*.

Had I more in my stomach than a few chugs of milk, I might have lost it all at once. My gut lurched and my eyes bulged when the beam from my flashlight illuminated a new, glassy surface. Eyes. Not the reptilian predator or multi-eyed arachnid variety, but the glazed-over stare of a dead man. A dried trail of blood extended from a single wound above his left eyebrow, meandering across his hairline to his left ear, forming a crusty mat in his hair and sideburns. A shudder coursed through me at the sight, causing me to squeeze my eyes shut for a brief moment before opening them again.

I swept the light from the face of the corpse to his chest, then toward his waist, where I found another body entangled with him. This one lay face down, but in the beam of my flashlight, I could see that a sizable chunk of the back of the victim's head was missing. My light caught the white shards of fractured skull, the mix of blood and dirt and brain matter, mixed in what looked like a nightmarish helping of human oatmeal. Lying on its side, as old and tattered as I remembered the other being, was the first dead man's shoe that had come loose when Chance and I pulled him out yesterday.

"Ho...lee shit!"

I started to back my way out, doing my best reverse army crawl. My heart descended from my throat, and my stomach began to settle, but my mind raced with one gruesome fact. I had found a mass grave, hidden smack dab in the middle of the CR.

Covered in dirt, I slid the rest of the way out of the crevasse, stood, and brushed myself off. Sliding the flashlight into my pocket, I turned to walk to the Ranger, thinking I had to get Chance on the line immediately when I froze in my tracks and reached for my gun. I pulled it and aimed at two figures standing in front of me within the beams of the UTV's headlights.

CHAPTER TWENTY-TWO

"Don't move!" I commanded.

In front of me, their faces were veiled in shadows cast by the high-powered LED headlights shining from behind, outlining their bodies. One figure appeared to lean in, grasping the other.

"*Por favor*," a trembling voice cracked. "*Por favor, no nos dispares.*"

I stepped one step closer and to the side, changing my view of the two until my vision became less impeded by the headlights. Except for a slow turn of the head, the two did not move. A whimper escaped the one clutching the other.

"Please...no...shoot," a terrified female's voice spoke in choppy English.

Without lowering my gun, I motioned with my free hand for them to step away from the Ranger. Using my limited Spanish, I told them to sit on the ground.

"*Siéntate. Siéntate.*"

Shuffling their feet, they moved together, then sat down. As I moved around them, I saw that the one clutching the woman was a little girl no more than eight years old. She held tight, staring over her shoulder at me. Tears covered her cheeks beneath eyes that looked like disturbed brown pools that on any other day would shimmer with life and innocence, absent of worry while soaking in wonder.

"It's okay. You're okay," I said, altering my tone.

The sun had yet to tease the horizon. The early morning breeze carried an anomalous chill about it. It could have been my adrenaline erupting after discovering the dead men, then finding myself with unexpected company, or it may have drifted in as a warning of weather yet to form overhead. Either way, I felt it. By the looks of them, they felt it, too.

Their clothes were soaked. The woman wore blue jeans, a long, dark patterned flannel shirt buttoned to the top, and red imitation Converse shoes. The girl wore jeans as well, brown canvas sneakers and a purple hoodie with a picture of a large kitten licking a lollipop on the front. Below the picture were the words, "Best Day Ever!"

The woman carried a cloth bag overflowing with what looked like everything they owned. One strap was frayed to the point of breaking.

"What are you doing out here?" I asked.

It was a dumb question. I knew the answer, but it was out of my mouth before I had a chance to hold it back. It did not matter, anyway. The woman looked scared and confused as she struggled to understand what I had said.

"*El Rescatista?*"

I looked back with the same want of understanding. She pointed at me, then repeated herself.

"*El Rescatista?*"

What did that mean? *El Rescatista*. *El Rescatista*. I thought hard, but the translation was not coming to me. Señora Lemos would be crossing her arms about now for my not understanding the phrase. Or was it a name? I shrugged my shoulders and presented a calm demeanor as I approached them.

I crouched down and smiled, trying to alleviate their fear. The woman looked down at the girl. The girl caught my gaze. I made a silly face at her to which she cracked a small grin of her own.

Good, I thought. *Now what?*

"*El Rescatista*," the woman said again.

"I don't understand," I replied.

Her eyes traced from side to side, searching for a way to bridge the language gap between us. A fourth time, she spoke the word.

"*El Rescatista*," she said, pointing to me.

"Me?"

I motioned to myself. She nodded, her face brimming with a smile as if we had just broken an unsolvable code.

They are looking for me, I thought. *Why me?*

I stood up and looked around. Sunrise was just around the corner. It was still dark but there was a feeling that the CR was waking up.

The girls remained where they were, shivering in their wet clothes. I had no idea how they made it this far or why they claimed to be looking for me, and I was incapable of understanding why they would risk so much to cross at night. The terrain across the river in Mexico was as wide open and barren as the CR, but here they were.

I had seen the mass illegal border crossings on the news. It was all too common these days but without the proper management and support of those tasked with securing the border, Texas and all the other southern neighboring states were left to bail out what was becoming a sinking ship with bare hands.

"Come," I said, motioning them to stand.

Against my better judgment, I decided to take them back to the house, ensure they had something to eat, and give them a chance to change into some dry clothes. While I struggled to consider myself an abettor, seeing a woman and child to safety was the right thing to do. I already had at least two new reasons to call Chance this morning. What were two more?

"*Por favor*," I said, motioning once again.

I opened the passenger door to the Ranger, lifted my supply bag, and placed it behind the seats. The woman hesitated, then, glancing at the girl, stood up. The girl rose with the woman. They watched me with deep concern, although I felt a small amount of trust was beginning to work its way into the fold. Hand in hand, they walked toward the Ranger.

"It's okay," I said. "Come."

"Okay," the woman repeated.

She sat in the passenger seat, placed her bag at her feet, then reached both arms out for the girl, pulling her onto her lap. I closed the door behind them, then walked to the driver's side, pausing to look back at the dark entrance where my latest discovery of dead bodies lay. From the Ranger, I heard the girl ask the woman something. I did not understand her words, but from the care with which the woman replied and the manner with which she consoled the girl, I was certain she was reassuring her that everything was going to be all right. As far as I was concerned, it would. I loaded up and started the engine. The mild roar startled the girl, but a subsequent rev of the motor and a playful smile from me was enough to settle her down.

I eased the Ranger away and headed toward the south side of the grove. The fresh air felt comforting. The horizon began to show signs of life, turning from black to dark purple. With so many bad things happening on the CR, I felt that if I could help these two, it might just be enough to balance the building frustration I was facing with a bit of joy. They were safe, and for now, that was all that mattered.

I saw the muzzle flash at the same time I heard the shot ring out. I yanked on the wheel, making a sharp right turn with the Ranger Metal clanged as the bullet zinged by, puncturing the rear panel of the driver's side door. I felt the impact radiate just under my seat.

At once, a mass of flood lights shone from all sides of a

large vehicle parked at the edge of the grove. Like a fearsome dragon, its engine roared to life as it set off in pursuit of us. The bouncing beams of intense light overwhelmed my vision, forcing me to squint as I glanced into the rearview mirror.

"Hold on!" I yelled.

The girl was crying again. The woman held tight to her with one arm while clenching the passenger side grab handle with her free hand. I pulled my gun, ready to return fire while focusing on the dark terrain before me. My headlights only reached so far, and with my accelerated speed, my reaction time for dodging large objects was one second at best.

I could hear the savage thrum of what was a large diesel engine behind us, and it was growing louder. We were sitting ducks out here with no way to outrun the danger gaining behind us. With only one thought at a chance of escape, I elevated the risk of certain disaster for us and turned off our headlights.

I pulled hard to the left and pressed the accelerator until it touched the floor. The instrument panel glowed in the cab, and the speedometer systematically calculated our increasing speed. At the rate with which we were going, one wrong move, one over-correction, one jarring bounce or oversized obstacle in our path would end the chase in an instant.

The dragon veered away from us before correcting its path, then raged forward, closing the gap behind us once again.

Where are we? Where are we!!!

There was a mere thread of light powdering the horizon now but still was not enough for me to see what was ahead. I was turned around, driving blind in the hopes of finding a place to hide or a chance to break further away.

We raced ahead at what felt like break-neck speed when we hit a sunken patch of earth. The Ranger jolted forward, then bobbed back like a cork fighting the weight of a large fish. The girl slipped from the woman and bounced into the dash. She let out a scream of pain and terror matched by the woman's fearful shrieks. My knees buckled forward, ramming into the console, and my left thumb bent backward with force enough to break bone.

I slammed my foot on the brakes, ending the trauma of a near-disastrous crash as we slid to a complete stop. I swallowed the pain in my legs and thumb and hopped out of the Ranger. With my gun still in hand, I turned to face the oncoming horde of lights and the roar of an engine.

"Eat this, you son of a bitch!" I yelled, then emptied my magazine into the night.

Sparks flew, metal groaned, and glass cracked as each round penetrated through the barrier of lights. I had no idea who or how many were in what I could now make out as an oversized truck or if I had hit anyone, but my barrage of bullets caused the driver to swerve to the left and high-tail it away without further incident.

I stood and watched as the truck sped off, then lost sight of it when its lights were shut off. My blood boiled. My body hurt. My mind was made up. There would be few who could stop me from finding out who had attacked us.

I turned around and walked back to the Ranger. The little girl whimpered as the woman cradled her. Both cried from pain and fright. I opened the door and gingerly slipped into the driver's seat. The pain in my legs felt like wet fire draining from my knees. My thumb throbbed. I leaned around and reached for my go bag, pulled out the sat phone, and grabbed one of the extra loaded magazines, then sat back in my seat and let out a long, relieving breath.

I laid the sat phone in my lap while I replaced the empty magazine with the fresh one, chambered one round, and slid my gun back into its holster. The woman watched every move but did not indicate that she wanted to get away. She knew they were safer with me than on their own. Before starting the engine, I turned and looked at the woman.

"Do you know who that was? Were they waiting for you?"

She looked at me, her pale face muddled with a blank expression. I could tell that she felt the intensity in my voice but did not have a clue about what I had said. She shook her head, then offered a single word, spoken as a question but making her point all the same.

"Okay?"

I nodded.

"Okay," I said. "Let's get outta here."

As the sun bore light on a new day, fiery streaks of orange and yellow reached out like fingers calling us home. The stars faded, giving way to blue sky overhead, and the CR awakened with life teaming all around. Yellow beams filled the cab of the Ranger, uncovering the injuries and damage sustained in our flight but also revealing the resolve of three strangers will to survive the things that go bump in the night.

I grabbed the satellite phone and pressed the power button until it surged to life. A chime sounded out followed by a pulsing image of a small, digital satellite on the screen signifying it was connected and ready for transmission. Next to that was the time.

6:21

I keyed the numbers for Chance's cell phone. It was early, but guys like us were never off duty. I pressed send, then placed the receiver against my ear.

Ring...Ring...Ring...

My call was answered just shy of the fourth ring.

"This is Chance."

His voice was muffled as if his mouth was filled with cotton.

"This is Cass. Sorry to wake you."

"What is wrong, *amigo*, that you must call so early?"

"We've got problems."

"I know. Dr. Frannie is supposed to—"

"Chance," I interrupted. "Bigger problems."

"What could be bigger than the dead guy? He's not going anywhere."

"Try three dead guys, two illegal migrants, and a bullet hole in the side of my Ranger."

A faint clicking noise invaded our call as I waited for Chance to say something. I glanced at the sat phone's screen and saw my reception had diminished by half.

"Chance," I said, breaking the silence. "I need you to meet me at the house as soon as you can. I have a woman and a young child with me."

"*Espera, espera, espera.* Where are you now?"

"I went out to the scene to retrace my steps and..."

"In the middle of the night?" Chance said, his voice rising with surprise. "Are you crazy?"

"Apparently, I am. I've been up most of the night thinking things through. We can talk about it more when you get here."

"Okay, okay. I'm on my way."

I could hear Chance moving, and then the line went dead. I pressed *END* on the sat phone to disconnect it and placed it back on my lap. Out of the corner of my eye, I could see the woman looking at me, listening. Was she able to understand? I twisted my head and gave her a reassuring nod.

"Help is on the way," I told her.

"Okay."

I made for the house at a comfortable speed, checking my mirrors as well as my right and left flanks for anything out of the ordinary. I thought we might come across Flint, but if he was already out on the CR, I did not see him.

As the house came into view, I glanced at my passengers, my refugees, and wondered what obstacles they overcame to get here and what they had yet to face. There was no judgment, no procedure, and no rush to turn them over to the system, though I could not simply look the other way once they were back on their feet. I would look to Chance to handle their situation going forward. He had the necessary contacts and would see they were processed and cared for once they left the CR. They had come a long way and were lucky to be alive. We all were.

In the morning shine, streaked by old tears and sweat, the little girl's sleepy face showed signs of peace. The woman closed her eyes, cradling the child in her arms as the UTV rocked back and forth over the uneven terrain. I could not help but think that as crazy as it sounds, maybe, for them, the words on the little girl's hoodie were right.

CHAPTER TWENTY-THREE

As I pulled into the yard with a full cab, I noticed a few lights were on in the house. I gave a beep of the horn, hoping she had seen the note I had left, and prayed that what had happened this morning would not cause her emotional recovery to regress.

Since our arrival at the CR, Raven had made considerable progress in overcoming the trauma of the home invasion, rediscovering herself bit by bit. The new surroundings, weekly therapy visits in town followed by a stop at La Mariposa Mística, helped her begin to find normalcy again. She was sleeping better, smiled more often, felt further in control of herself and her routines, and grew stronger with each passing day.

I parked the Ranger in front of the porch and turned off the engine. The girl lifted her head to look around, wincing in pain as she shifted her weight on the woman's lap. She placed her left hand on her right arm and gritted her teeth. The rattle of the front door captured my attention. The woman noticed as well, then looked at me with nervous eyes.

"Home," I said. "This is my home."

She shook her head and shrugged. The door opened,

and Raven stepped onto the porch, her gait slowing to a stop as she saw I was not alone.

"Cass?" she said, looking at me. "Who are they?"

I opened the side door of the Ranger and saw Raven's stare widen and her mouth open with surprise as she looked past me at the bullet hole in the UTV. Nothing got past her.

"I'll explain everything, but right now, they need our help. The girl is hurt. I'm not sure about the woman."

Right before me, a change came over Raven. I saw it flash across her face, then blend in with the tones of her skin. She looked at the woman and the girl and stepped off the porch, bypassing me altogether to walk straight over to them. She flowed with compassion, and for a moment, the Raven I knew, the teacher, the giver, the fighter, was back. I watched as she approached the Ranger.

"Do they speak English?" she asked, stopping at the passenger side door.

"No."

Without missing a beat, Raven took over. "*Mi nombre es Raven.* Can I help you? *¿Puedo ayudarle?*"

The woman sighed with relief, then burst into tears. "*Gracias a Dios. Gracias a Dios,*" she repeated over and over.

The girl tried to sit up, then groaned with pain, still clutching her arm. Raven looked across at me.

"We had a bumpy ride," I said. "At one point, she slammed into the dash."

Raven gave me a stern look, then pulled the latch on the passenger door and opened it. She squatted and spoke to the girl in a gentle voice.

"*Te ayudare. Es esta tu madre?*"

The woman answered for the girl.

"*Si. Soy su madre.*"

"*Cómo te llamas?*"

"*María. Esta es Isabella,*" she said, looking down at the girl.

Isabella tried to smile as she fought through her pain.

"Come," Raven said, motioning to Maria and Isabella. "*Ven a limpiarse.*"

Watching Raven interact with the two was amazing. It was the first Spanish I had heard her speak since she left teaching, her fluency as natural as ever.

She first helped Isabella off her mother's lap, being careful not to further irritate her injured arm, then offered a hand to Maria as she stepped out on wobbly legs. They had both been through quite an ordeal this morning, not to mention the dangerous miles they had to travel just to get here. But why here, I wondered, filing away that thought as answers would come soon enough?

"Cass, get the door," Raven said.

My knees burned under my jeans as I walked to open the door. Raven led Isabella by the hand with Maria following close behind.

"We'll be in the kitchen. Bring me some clean towels from the bathroom closet. Then get changed yourself," she said as they passed by. "You smell funky."

The girls headed for the kitchen, and I went to gather some towels as requested. When I entered the kitchen, Isabella was sitting on the counter while Raven wiped her face with a moist dish rag. Maria stood next to them and was washing her hands in the sink. I placed the towels on the breakfast table and stood by and watched.

Raven whispered things to Isabella as she helped get her cleaned up. Maria took a towel from the table, thanking me with a look of gratitude and comfort that made me realize how many things in life I took for granted.

While in the Army, I had been deployed overseas and met people from all over the world who lived in the most debilitating of conditions, yet every day, I returned to my barracks to rest and regroup before the next set of orders came through. It was no different stateside. In Houston, the number of homeless men, women, and children was staggering and continues to grow at an alarming rate. There is hardly an underpass that is void of pieced-together structures, some of which stand abandoned, others that remain occupied, yet every day when the job was done and the cases solved, I got to go home. Brick walls, a shingled roof over my head, a stocked refrigerator, cable television, and hot showers with clean towels always awaited my return. Always.

Looking at the girls, the way Maria held the towel to her face and inhaled the fresh smells of clean cloth, and seeing their dirty, fraying bag lying on the tile floor in my house was like a kick in the teeth. I had things others only dreamed of having, which made me wonder to what lengths I would go to make sure my family, my child, had an opportunity for a better life.

"Go get cleaned up, Cass. I'll be okay," Raven said, catching me in a transient stare.

It seemed she was *okay*.

I headed back for the bathroom, took off my shirt, then sat down on the toilet and removed my socks. I tossed them both in a hamper behind the door and looked at my legs. The knees of both jeans were stained and soiled with dirt from my spelunking and blood from ramming them into the steering column and instrument panel during our near-disastrous crash on the CR.

My thumb pulsed and had swollen to look more like an eggplant growing out of my hand. While it had not dislocated, it was considerably sprained. I flexed my hand, trying to work out the growing stiffness, but it was my legs with which I was most concerned.

I stood, undid the button of my jeans with my good hand, and unzipped my fly. Slowly, I slid the jeans down below my thighs before sitting once again. I could already feel the pull of skin where crusted blood adhered to flesh and denim. Leaning forward, I pulled from the bottom of one pant leg, then the other, each time activating a mix of burn and sting from my kneecaps to my shins.

Come on, Callahan! Suck it up, I heard my old partner Ray Tucker yell from some back room in my head.

Damn it, Ray!

He was always quick to criticize, but when it came to injury, he whined with the best of them.

I held my breath and with one long tug, pulled both legs out of the jeans, feeling the fire as the damaged skin ripped itself free. Both knees began bleeding. I removed my briefs, added the rest of my dirty clothes to the hamper, and stepped into the shower. I turned the knob and felt the chill of well water run down my thighs and over my knees, cleaning away the dirt and grime with each stinging dribble. I used a washcloth to blot each knee.

Probably should have used a junk towel instead of one of Raven's floral favorites, I thought after the fact.

I applied a small amount of liquid soap to each leg, wincing in pain as I cleaned each wound. Stitches were not necessary, but my legs looked as if they had skidded across a cheese grater.

My left shin was worse than my right. A flap of skin almost an inch long sagged to one side. I dabbed soap from my flower towel on the raw skin and bit my lip to keep from telling it what I really thought. The cuts bled but were only superficial. I turned off the water, figured I would go for broke, and used a matching floral patterned bath sheet to dry myself. She would get a brand-new set after I ruined these anyway.

I stepped out of the shower, patted myself dry, lubed my cuts with triple-antibiotic, and wrapped them with gauze I found under the sink, then opened the medicine cabinet and grabbed a small bottle of ibuprofen. Cursing my thumb for its lack of cooperation when opening the bottle, I swallowed four pills. With the towel draped around my waist, I walked to the bedroom, where I dressed in fresh clothes.

When I returned to the kitchen, Isabella was sitting at the breakfast table, sipping a glass of milk. She was wrapped in a throw blanket and was swallowed up by one of Raven's T-shirts. Her arm rested in a makeshift sling comprised of two bandanas tied together and looped around her neck. Having lived a life with two boys, Raven was accustomed to patching us up with whatever was lying around.

I heard Maria and Raven talking through the open door that led to the laundry room just off the kitchen. Isabella set her drink on the table and stared up at me. With her white, dribbly mustache and half-empty glass, she could have been the poster child for a "Got Milk" campaign. I took a seat across from her at the table. She glanced at the empty doorway, then back at me, wearing the look of a rescued animal not yet sure if she should trust her rescuer.

"You know, it tastes much better with chocolate," I said.

She looked at me without blinking.

"Cho...co...late?" I said slowly.

Isabella scrunched her face a bit, turning her stare into a curious gaze as if wanting to say something. Then, taking a chance, she softly broke her silence.

"*Chocolate?*" she said, sounding more like *cho-co-la-tay*.

"Yeah."

I got up from the table, opened the refrigerator, and found the brown pear-shaped bottle of Hershey's syrup. I pulled a teaspoon from the silverware drawer and returned to the table, sitting back down to show Isabella.

"Chocolate. It's the only way my Spencer would drink milk when he was a little boy."

I opened the bottle, leaned forward, and added a short stream into her glass. She watched as I mixed it with the teaspoon, her eyes growing wide with interest as the milk turned from white to brown.

"Go on," I said. "Try it."

Isabella raised the glass to her nose and sniffed as a sommelier might when scoring wine, then placed the glass to her lips and sipped.

"Good, isn't it?"

Isabella's face transformed from little lost puppy to happy child ready to watch Saturday morning cartoons. I smiled at her and watched as she continued to sip away.

"It's good to see you haven't lost your touch."

I looked up and saw Raven in the doorway.

"How long have you been standing there?" I asked.

"Long enough," she said, smiling. She walked over and sat next to Isabella. "Cass..." Raven paused. "...Maria told me a story I think you should hear. It's so sad. I really want to help them."

My heart understood, but the reality was that Maria and Isabella illegally crossed the border into the United States.

"There is not much we can do at this point, Raven. I've already called Chance. He is on his way out right now."

"You want them deported? If you heard their story. If you knew what they've been through." Raven's voice wavered.

"Hold on. Chance is their best shot at getting the kind of help they need."

Raven turned to look at Isabella. She reached out and gently stroked her hair. Isabelle looked at her and whispered.

"¿Puedo tener un poco más de leche, por favor?"

"Of course, you can. Cass, pour her some more milk."

To Raven, it was more than a glass of milk. It was a lifeline. I could tell she had already made up her mind to do whatever it took to help Maria and Isabella. It was noble, and I loved her for it, but my concern was how she would handle things should they not go the way she had hoped.

Trying to mask my thoughts, I made a silly face at Isabella, then stood to get the milk.

"One glass of milk, coming right up."

As I was pulling the jug from the refrigerator, I heard a small voice make a simple request. "Chocolate?"

CHAPTER TWENTY-FOUR

I found myself standing on the front porch twenty minutes later watching Chance pull up to the house, but he was not driving either of his usual county vehicles. He parked a red-and-white two-toned 1985 Ford F-150 pickup next to my Explorer. It was a two-door extended cab with a matching box shell placed over the bed of the truck and large offroad tires worn down from miles of wear and tear. Chance cut off the engine and opened the door.

He wore aviator sunglasses and a vented straw hat with a large pheasant feather decoration that fanned out from the band to the crease. His shirt, jeans, and boots were nondescript. He nodded as he walked to the porch.

"*Buenos dias.*"

"Morning."

"Cass, you got a screw loose or something? I know it's your land, but it's not always safe to be riding around in the dark, especially alone, *amigo.*"

"Thanks for the tip, but you're a little late. Getting shot at and almost run down kinda had me thinking the same thing."

I pointed to the bullet hole in the side panel door of the Ranger.

"You're lucky that wasn't any higher," Chance said. "At least now you have an excuse to get rid of the doors. It's rangeland, not freeways across the CR, Cass."

"Tell that to the truck that just about ran us down," I said. "Felt like I was back in Houston after an Astros game, everyone racing to get home and damned be anyone in their way. I'll tell you this, whoever it was took considerable damage to their truck. Should be easy to spot the fifteen rounds I emptied into it."

Chance looked across to the barn, then to the entrance of the ranch.

"Get a good look at the truck?" he said.

"Lots of lights. Some on the roof, two mounted on the front between the factory lights, and bright. Couldn't see if it had a grille guard, but I wouldn't doubt it. Loud son of a bitch too. Diesel probably."

"Color?"

"Too dark to tell."

Chance turned back to face me and removed his glasses.

"A lot happens in the dark out there. More than you'll ever want to know, Cass," he said in a tone more serious and darker than I was used to when we spoke. "Your uncle knew that and was wise to be careful. You should be, too."

Another warning? I filed that away with all the other cautionary bullshit that had flung my way and told him about the additional bodies I found.

"Two victims, both shot through the head, both looked to be transients. I suspect they were all traveling together until they ran into some trouble."

"Or maybe trouble was waiting for them," Chance offered.

"That one of those things I should be the wiser for, Chance?"

"Look, *amigo*," Chance shifted his weight and softened his tone. "I just don't want to see you get wrapped up in something beyond your understanding."

"What I do understand is that we've found three dead bodies on the CR, I've been warned by multiple people, one of which I consider a friend, to mind my own business or await some unspoken consequence, and now I have two illegal migrants in my house who Raven is determined to see are properly cared for, and oh, by the way, I've been shot at on my property. The way I see it, I am consumed by the very fucking fabric of the whole thing." I paused briefly, lowering my voice. "Everyone has been wondering if I was going to step in and join the county to serve and protect. It worries the shit out of Raven. Your deputies have even asked, and I know more about your intentions than you think I do, Chance. Hell, even that FBI douchebag had that look like I was pissing in his pool. The fact is, you want me? You got me but on my terms."

Chance cocked his head to one side and slid his thumbs into the belt loops of his jeans. A crafty smile emerged from his lips.

"I knew you'd come around," Chance said.

"Oh, yeah? Fuck you then."

"Look. *Amigo*. I will gladly take you, but remember that this is not the city. It can be like the Wild West out here except the *pendejos* we have to face can be as harmless as a frightened pup or as savage as a *sicario* with a death wish."

I heard what he was saying, but at the moment I was only concerned about one thing, and one thing only: keep Raven safe. If that meant I was back on the job, so be it. I may not be from the sticks, but I am from a jungle every bit as rough and dangerous. Whether it's the open range or spread out over blacktop streets, blood spills the same, no matter the location.

I nodded my head, then offered Chance a hand. We shook and did not release my grasp.

"This is no game to me. I'm not signing up to be Wyatt Earp, but I want to find out what is going on and why it seems to be located on the CR. Murder is murder regardless of where it happens. In this case, it's happening way too close to my family. If I am to keep the promises I made to Raven, you must trust me to do my job just as much as I trust you. I'm not just some city slicker in a baseball hat. You may know that, but from what I've seen, you're the only one."

We shook one last time, solidifying my intentions to him and my commitment to my family. His face softened, giving way to his Cheshire smile. While it may seem out of place to some, it was Chance's calling card, saying without words that he had my six.

"Let's head inside. Raven will want to say hello, and you will want to meet our guests."

I pulled the door open and followed Chance into the house. As I turned to close the door, I saw Flint standing in the doorway of the barn, eyes locked on me, arms folded across his chest. I paused a moment, returning his stare with a steely one of my own. We had battled and bonded, and I thought I had made some headway with him. Maybe I was wrong. With nothing more to see, Flint lowered his arms and disappeared into the barn.

I walked to the kitchen and saw Chance had already earned the attention and interest of Maria. He sat across from her speaking Spanish in a calm, soothing tone. It was clear he wanted to make her feel comfortable, but what he was saying, I did not understand. She nodded her head as he spoke to her.

Raven stepped through the opposite doorway from the laundry room with Isabella in tow no longer wrapped in a throw blanket. She wore a different pair of jeans, these showing through at the knees. It was not the fashion statement most over-privileged American girls pay for; instead, it was pre-torn and stone-washed for that ragged, aged look. These had been worn to the point of almost no return, but they were clean and dry, and they were hers. A thudding sound reverberated from behind them as the girls' shoes bounced around inside our dryer.

Chance noticed Isabella and smiled, then waved her over to the table to join them. Maria opened her arms to receive her. Isabella looked concerned, unsure if she should trust Chance. She glanced at me, looking for what I considered to be reassurance. I smiled, then made a face and gave her a thumbs up. She leaned into Maria's chest, then turned and sheepishly greeted Chance for the first time.

Their conversation lasted longer than I expected. Chance talked while Maria listened, then the other way round. Raven moved over to stand near me. She wrapped an arm around my waist and leaned on my shoulder, whispering translations of some of what they were saying. Raven's Spanish was conversational, and while it had proved valuable already, she was not nearly fluent enough to keep up with the speed with which they talked.

When they finished talking, a washed look of relief overcame Maria. She smiled, then kissed Isabella on the head. She looked at us and said one word I did understand.

"*Gracias, gracias, gracias.*"

I could feel the pull of Raven's arm around me as Maria's words, simple as they were, meant a great deal.

"You're welcome," I said.

Raven let go of me and walked around the table to Maria, paused, then leaned over and hugged her. Maria returned the embrace and whispered something to her in Spanish. When Raven let go, her eyes showed signs of welling up, but she found the strength to withhold the flow for now.

"Okay," Chance said, turning to look at me. "We're all set. I'll bring them with me and see that they are taken care of properly."

Raven's jaw dropped to speak but Chance beat her to it. "Everything will be all right, Raven. Trust me."

Raven nodded. She did trust Chance, but to her, it was like dropping Spencer off at kindergarten for the first time. She had no control over what would happen to him once he entered the classroom, and she worried all day until it was time to pick him up. The difference was, Raven would not be going to pick up Maria or Isabella at the end of the day. This was more like a giant leap of faith in what Chance had planned because she might never see them again.

"Maria looks okay," I whispered. "Look at her."

Indeed, Maria had a hopeful look about her. Whatever Chance had said seemed to brighten her day. I grabbed Maria's tattered bag and followed them outside. Chance walked to the truck. He opened the passenger door and helped Isabella into the cab. I stood and waited while Maria climbed in and buckled up. Raven walked over to Chance as he rounded the front of the truck.

"Will you tell me what's going to happen to them?"

Chance opened the driver's side door, then turned to face Raven.

"I will when the time is right an' they are safe," he said.

Raven leaned in and kissed Chance on the cheek. "Thank you," she said.

I handed Maria her bag and closed the passenger door. Before walking away, I knocked once on the window to get Isabella's attention. When she looked at me, she found my tongue sticking out of my mouth and my fingers wiggling behind my ears. Her Saturday morning cartoons demeanor revived itself once more, smiling wide enough to show her young, crooked teeth. A genuine smile from the luckiest girl I knew.

I joined Raven on the porch and watched as Chance backed away in a semi-circle before driving off the CR. It was anticlimactic, seeing them drive away, but I felt good about how this part of the day had gone.

I tugged at Raven's waist, encouraging her to walk inside. At first, she resisted, then dipped her head and grabbed my hand.

"Come," I said. "They're in good hands."

"I know," she sighed.

"It's still early. Let's grab some coffee. There are a few things I want to discuss with you."

"I know what you are going to say."

I stepped close to her and rested my chin on top of her head. "I keep my promises. You know that."

"I know," she said. "It's how you intend to keep them this time that worries me."

PART FOUR
GATEWAY TO PARADISE

INTERLUDE 4

1911 was a dark year for the Callahan family with the loss of their eleven-year-old daughter Rose to scarlet fever. It was a nightmare no parent should ever be forced to endure. Though surrounded by close friends, in the end, the death of their only daughter proved to be too much for Jack and Molly Callahan. Grief-stricken, they left their longtime home in New Mexico with their son, Timothy, heading south into Texas in search of a place where they could bury the trauma of their loss within a new landscape.

After weeks of travel, the wear on their bodies and minds led them to begin questioning whether they had made the right decision to move on. Yet, on August 17, 1911, what would have been Rose's twelfth birthday, a gift was laid in their path. As if God had placed his own blank canvas before them, pure white and waiting for a painter's touch to bless the finely stretched hemp, they came to a land rich with beauty which they felt was solely comparable to that of their sweet, lost girl.

It was the wash of colors that painted the sky every morning, the distant mountains that caught the rays of the sun, reflecting its brilliance like tiny dew drops clinging to a rose, the winding river teaming with life, and the long, open reaches of rangeland that seemed to transform with the rise and fall of every day that captivated their souls and eased their minds. There was no question that the Callahan family had found a place to start anew. On October 3, 1911, Jack and Molly purchased a large stretch of that very land and established the CR, the Callahan Ranch.

Stories tend to become lost over time, shifting points of view or challenged for meaning, but what was not lost upon the Callahan family were the very words shared between Jack and Molly when they finally found what they felt was a bit of heaven on earth.

"If we were ever to reunite with those who went on before us, it would be through this very stretch of land. This *Gateway to Paradise*. Should all else crumble around us, let this path be saved."

It was in these words that hope was born, not only for the preservation of the land but for the opportunities that lay within that solemn pathway.

Through the years, the CR thrived as one of the largest ranches in West Texas and was passed down from one generation of Callahans to the next. When extreme drought conditions plagued the region and an outbreak of brucellosis ran rampant through the livestock, resulting in considerable financial losses, Pat Callahan, third generation Callahan rancher, was forced to sell a large portion of the CR. In 1958, longtime family friend Len G "Tuffy" McCormick bought what amounted to ninety-five thousand acres of CR land, adding to his already plentiful stake in the area, Big Bend Ranch. The remaining five thousand acres still stand as the most brilliant section of the CR, and one that will remain in the family for generations to come, thanks to the financial stability and profitable investments made by Pat after the sale was completed. It was this stretch of land that was Jack and Molly's Gateway to Paradise and would remain a family heirloom for many generations to come.

CHAPTER TWENTY-FIVE

"What do you mean, *they took the body*?" I asked.

After changing into clothes more appropriate for a professional work environment, I kissed Raven, told her not to worry, and hopped into the Explorer for the drive into Brewster. The South Brewster County Sheriff's Office was fifteen minutes from the CR. With Chance having left less than an hour ago, I had expected to beat him to his office. I had not, which surprised me, considering the morning's events.

Immigration and Customs Enforcement (ICE) and Enforcement and Removal Operations (ERO) had been working full throttle since the change in administration back in 2020, resulting in long delays for processing undocumented persons and implementation of directives for detention and deportation or asylum acquisition. Chance may have had some clout to expedite the process through local contacts or his position as County Sheriff, but even then, it would have taken time to drive to the nearest detention facility unless the South Brewster County Jail held a subcontract from ICE for holding detainees.

Everything has an explanation.

I tumbled this thought around in my head with a bevy of others as I walked through the front doors of the Brewster County Sheriff's Office. To my surprise, Chance met me at the reception desk with a look that spoke of annoyance.

"You heard right, amigo. They took the body."

I gave Chance a confused look.

"Not here," he said, motioning for me to follow.

The front office clerk buzzed us through a secure door that led away from the waiting area to a walkway through a cluster of desks, ending at the open door of Chance's private office. He ushered me in, closed the door behind us, and twisted the rod on the blinds so that we could speak with total privacy.

I sat in a chair in front of a grand walnut desk. The wood grain created a captivating pattern, dancing gracefully across its surface. I reached forward and ran my hand along the lines in the wood. I glanced at a clock on the wall, hung central to the room. It reminded me of an old, black-and-white elementary school hallway clock with its red second hand smoothly advancing around the dial, passing large, black numbers as time marched ahead. The time read, nine-thirty-five.

Chance sat down, leaned forward, and folded his hands on the desktop. A tiny American flag and Mexican flag stood side by side in a small desktop display at one end. A shiny brass nameplate was placed at the other.

Behind Chance, a large, framed map of Texas and Mexico hung on the wall below the clock with the date 1912 inscribed in the bottom right corner. The paper had faded, showing stains from years of incandescent light damage, and yet, the map held an antiquated history that captured my attention. The illustrated topography was brilliant, and the old-style script was written with a flair that spoke to the artist's creative nature. Though the words were in Spanish, it did not take a linguist to appreciate the artistry.

"The map is speaking to you, Cass?"

My eyes shot from the map to Chance.

"I suppose." I leaned forward as if studying an invisible chessboard between us. "Chance, tell me who *they* are."

"FBI."

"FBI? Special Agent Dylan Sharp playing some sort of cross-jurisdictional mind game or something?"

"I doubt it. Dr. Frannie called this morning as I was leaving the CR sounding pretty upset. She told me she went right to work when she reached her lab with the body last night and that to her surprise, was able to identify him through fingerprints."

"What? The guy must have a record. Another catch-and-release failure?"

"That's what I thought, too, but Frannie had more to say. When she ran the prints through IAFIS, Integrated Automated Fingerprint Identification System..."

"I know it."

"Yeah, well, what she found was more than any of us could have bargained for."

Chance leaned back in his chair and placed his folded hands across the shelf of his gut and continued.

"The match was registered as classified and held FBI flags. Less than two hours later, an unmarked SUV and a black van pulled up outside her office with a team of agents holding a seizure warrant for the body and a gag order for her. They were in and out, loaded the body in the van, and were off again, and all Frannie could do was watch."

"What the hell? FBI doesn't swoop in for just anybody."

"Nope, my guess is the guy must have been a plant in some cartel or organization and was maintaining his cover until he got back into the United States."

"So, he just randomly decided to cross in the middle of nowhere and ended up on the CR? He must have been followed. Who else would target him?"

Chance bore a look on his face as if he knew the answer but was unsure if he should share it with me. He shifted in his seat, reached both palms forward, laying them flat on the desktop, and looked at me without blinking for what seemed like minutes. The red second-hand on the wall clock surged ahead. I sat back, crossed my legs, and waited for an answer I was not sure I wanted to hear.

Chance exhaled and pulled the figurative trigger.

"There are things about the CR that you do not yet know. Things that Stewart kept from you." He paused dead eye on me. "But you must understand it was for your own good."

Not the best way to start a story, but there was no going back now.

"Lay it on me," I said, crossing my arms over my chest.

"Your family has a history of helping others. It's in your blood. It's what you *do*. Look at you now...soldier, detective, and for what purpose? To serve for the benefit of others. Cass, this links back over a hundred years and has been kept secret for most of that time. It was not until recently that the wrong sorts have been infiltrating what was truly a humanitarian effort."

"What are you talking about?"

Chance stood up and walked behind his chair, placing both hands on the headrest for support.

"Your family has been helping select Mexican nationals cross the border through the CR since your great-great-grandfather purchased the land."

"Illegally? So, you're saying my family, the ones who you proclaim to help people, are doing so by breaking the law?"

I glared at Chance with mixed emotions. My mind

raced with questions. The detective in me wanted answers. Truthful answers. Why would Uncle Stewart, and all the rest for that matter, go to such lengths? Why was it kept from me? Why didn't Chance do anything to stop what he knew was going on? I looked away from Chance for a moment, glancing at a freestanding coat rack in the far corner. It was bare except for the hat with the large pheasant feather decoration Chance had worn earlier. I looked back at him and realized he was still dressed in the same plain clothes. No badge visible, no gun, but he wore a look that suggested I already knew the answer to my next question.

"You're helping them, aren't you?"

I stood up and squared off in front of him. In front of my friend.

"How could you be a part of the problem this country is facing? You of all people know the consequences of allowing undocumented illegals into the United States. The problems they bring with them, the trouble they cause, and the stress they add to a system of governance that has already been stretched to its breaking point. It's treasonous, Chance."

Chance walked from behind his desk and stopped nose to nose in front of me. The look in his eye and the twitch in his upper lip revealed a side of him I had never seen before. His determined stare replaced his usual welcoming brown eyes, and his trademark smile was buried beneath a defensive scowl growing across his face. His breath was warm.

"Because we are friends, I will pretend I did not hear the last few words you so easily vomited in my office. *You*, of all people, know that judgment should never be cast until the whole story has been explained. Show some deeper respect for your family, sit down, and I will finish what I was saying."

Anger and confusion urged me to respond with an

objection, but a voice from deep inside broke through the turmoil and stopped what would have been regretful actions. Three words were all I heard, but the power of truth within those words was enough. *Chance is right*, it said.

I backed away from our standoff. I walked to the blinds and slid a finger through one of the slats, glancing out into the heart of the station. Work continued as normal. Phones rang, keyboards clicked, coffee steamed from small Styrofoam cups, and no one was the wiser about the bombshell that reverberated within Chance's office.

Chance returned to his side of the desk and took a seat, waiting until I was ready to move forward.

I dropped my finger from the blinds and turned to face him.

"Tell me everything," I said.

Chance motioned to the chair before him. I sat and listened as the story unfolded, finding more pride from what I heard than malice for the actions which I knew nothing about.

"For years, the Callahans have had friends on both sides of the border," he said. "As the years passed, there were times when it was necessary to aid one or more of these friends or acquaintances of friends. Most times it was to escape a dangerous situation. Other times it was to seek medical attention that was either unavailable to them in Mexico or beyond the means of the person or persons in need. It was decided early on to avoid the red tape and bypass a traditional border crossing to expedite the process. Each time, the ones that were helped were given asylum and then properly documented and processed, once their safety was ensured. I have a lawyer friend in Presidio and two others within ICE who have been a part of this for many years.

"More recently it has been a safety concern for the traveling party. With the rise of the cartels, there was no way to know who to trust. It is no secret that they have their hands in everything from the lowliest peasant to the highest offices within the Mexican government. With the cartels becoming too powerful and too integrated, more often than not, their presence goes overlooked as their influence runs rampant like a sickness.

"You see, Cass, your family is not smuggling people to the United States for any other reason than showing concern and love for humanity. And yes, I know. I have known for many years. It was your great-uncle Patrick Callahan that arranged safe passage for my father and mother to pass through the *Gateway to Paradise* only days before I was born.

"My parents were teachers in Sinaloa. I know you are familiar with the goings on in that region of Mexico. When my father stood in the pathway of cartel soldiers who were recruiting children, he was marked for execution. He was lucky to escape at all after facing them. Word passed through the right channels very quickly and Pat Callahan acted. With help from some brave friends in Sinaloa, they were able to flee from the region. They changed their last name from Gutiérrez to Gilbert, hoping that would help protect them during their escape, and ended up adopting it once they reached the United States. In this instance, as I am unaware of any other, your great-uncle Pat met them on the Mexican side of the border to personally escort my parents through the barren stretches of eastern Mexico and cross into the United States right at the CR.

"Now, fast forward forty or so years. The crossings were infrequent but made possible when there was no other way to solve whatever situation through appropriate measures. Keep in mind, Cass, this is not a daily occurrence where tens or hundreds of people are being funneled in by your family. It is a select few. There are others, such as Maria and Isabella, who have fallen into the trap of promises made for duties carried out which have caused more trouble than either you or I know, but it happens. When I learn of such things, I handle each on a case-by-case basis. Not everyone gets the free ride they hoped for. Those who were selected and offered assistance by your family are the lucky ones.

"The problem now is that somewhere along the chain, someone has found a way to use the same route as a means to smuggle things other than refugees. I fear there is a snag on both sides of the border, but I have yet to learn who is responsible or on which side of the river the issue originated. To further complicate things, we now have three dead bodies, one of which is of great importance to the FBI, and someone has taken a shot at you.

"The good news is now that you are here, maybe we can make some headway, as I am already understaffed and overdrawn. I had my hopes set on you the moment I learned you were taking control of the CR, though at the time I had no idea how messy things would get. I am sorry it has come this, but I am glad you decided to come on board, even if it is under your conditions, which, by the way, we should discuss."

The room went still at that moment. I had never heard Chance speak for so long or with such emotion about anything before. It was easy to understand, and while everything was still sinking in, I did not take any further issue with him, or my family, for that matter.

Everything has an explanation.

Hearing Chance out was difficult, but in the end, it made my decision to join forces with him much easier.

"My conditions, Chance, are very simple. I am here for one reason and one reason only...ensure the safety of the CR for my family. I'll help you uncover who is responsible for the murders and will back you up as I would any partner. You are my friend, Chance, and as I am learning, a pillar within the Callahan family, and I wouldn't have it any other way. Should the tradition of the *Gateway to*

Paradise need to continue, who better than a Callahan with the law on his side to see things through?"

Chance sat across from me, nodding as I spoke. When I finished, he did not say a word, but his infectious smile had reappeared, and it was beaming.

CHAPTER TWENTY-SIX

I stood outside the front doors of the South Brewster County Sheriff's Office and looked at the badge Chance had handed me after swearing me in as a Special Deputy Investigator for South Brewster County. The badge, a silver star attached within a silver circle at each of its five points, represented my official position within the county. The seal of Texas was displayed in the center of the star with the number 16 engraved in an antiqued finish, hovering just below. The words *South Brewster County* on the bottom arc of the circle and *Special Investigator* along the top were similarly engraved with the same antique finish, allowing the contrast to highlight the bearer's title while enhancing the shine of the badge. It glimmered in the sunlight as I held it in the palm of my hand.

"Here we go, sixteen," I said to myself.

I had never intended to inject myself into the local law enforcement scene, but here I was, nonetheless. I was given little choice in the matter, but still, it felt right. Now that I was the official lead in the CR murders investigation, I felt a surge of normalcy fill gaps I had kept empty since leaving Houston. It was as if I had put on a pair of old basketball shoes before a pickup game but felt that same excitement of tightening my laces prior to the year's championship back in the day. They still fit and felt just the same.

I slipped the badge on my belt, tugging the leather against the pancake holster that held my Sig over the small of my back and walked through the parking lot.

"Back in service," I said to my jet-black Explorer as I patted the hood before getting in.

I rolled out of the parking lot intending to first get in touch with Dr. Frannie, then stop at Javi's Autoparts on my way back into town.

I had done a good amount of damage to the truck that tried to run me down on the CR with Maria and Isabella. Bullets do that kind of thing to a target. Lightbars and spotlights are not an inexpensive fix and would need someone to special order parts for repair or replacement. Javi's was like an O'Reilly or Autozone without the corporate overhead to support the same multitude of automotive repair options, but it was the only parts store in town and would be as good a place as any to start asking questions.

Chance had written Dr. Frannie's number on a Post-it for me before leaving his office. I retrieved it from my front pocket and uncrumpled the paper to read the numbers. I pushed the numbers on the keypad and clicked the phone to Bluetooth so I could speak to her through the car. When she answered my call, I could sense a lingering bout of frustration in her voice.

"Hello, This is Dr. Frannie Lopez-Tasker."

"Hey, Dr. Frannie. It's Cass Callahan."

"They took the damn body already so..."

"I know," I said. "But I need your help again. Two more bodies were discovered this morning on the ranch."

"How did..."

I interrupted.

"It's a long story, but I could use your expertise. How soon can you get down here?"

"Not until one-thirty at the earliest. I'm finishing up my report on the first victim now. Soon as I'm done, I'll head your way with a small team and a van. Tell Chance he won't need to delegate his deputies this go-round."

"Sounds good. Will see you at the house."

The line fell silent for a moment before Dr. Frannie spoke again, her voice tinged with concern.

"Cass, it was very strange the way the FBI swooped in here. What do you think is going on?"

"I'm not sure. Let's see if there is a connection between these new bodies and the one they already hauled off. Either way, that ought to tell us something."

"It doesn't make any sense to me," she said.

"Yeah, no kidding."

I came to a red light at the corner of Main and Trinidad Street. Javi's was two blocks away just past the VFW and Mary's Feed Supply.

"I'll text you when we're twenty minutes out. Tell Chance he owes me one," she said.

"Sounds like I'll owe you one as well. See you in a few," I replied, then ended the call.

I sat at the light and thought through my next lines of questions for the clerk at Javi's. With any luck, Javi will be there himself, but these days, no local truly kept blue-collar hours.

Glancing at the parking lot of the VFW, I noticed two trucks parked parallel to Main Street so that the driver's side doors opened up to each other. Two men stood between the trucks and seemed to be arguing about something. I watched with the interest of a nosy bystander until the blare of a horn told me the light had turned green. I gave an apologetic wave out my open window and proceeded through the intersection and past the arguing pair of men.

As I rolled by, I saw that one of the men was Flint. The other man's back was to me, and I did not recognize either truck. Come to think of it, I had not yet seen Flint anywhere except the CR.

I drove past until I came to the driveway of Mary's Feed Supply and pulled into a parking spot between an old Ford F-150 and a vintage Monte Carlo and rolled up my window. The truck was covered with surface rust, and its rear bumper was tied and wound in place by an old, fraying rope. A worn MAGA sticker was displayed on the driver's side rear window directly below a newly placed NRA decal. The Monte Carlo needed new tires and a fresh coat of paint, but other than that looked well-maintained.

I sat and observed Flint and the man become more heated as time wore on. At one point, I could hear shouting through the closed windows, but their words never came to blows. The confrontation escalated when the unidentified man pointed an angry finger at Flint, tapping it on his chest like a woodpecker going after a worm.

"That was a mistake," I said to myself.

Flint reacted as I would have expected. He grabbed the man's finger and in one violent move, twisted and yanked down. I could not hear the snap of bone, but the stiffening of the man's body and the reaction he made when Flint let go suggested that he would not be jabbing that finger into anyone else in the future. Recoiling in pain, he cradled his injured hand with the other before forcefully passing by Flint and climbing into his truck. After slamming the door, he unleashed a flurry of obscenities at him, then revved the engine and roared away, leaving Flint engulfed in a cloud of black smoke.

With hands on his hips, Flint watched the man speed off. Before turning to get into his truck, he paused, looking in my direction. He lowered his arms to his side, then turned and loaded up. He sat for a moment before pulling out of the VFW parking lot onto Main Street and drove away.

Who the hell are you, really, Levi Flint? I thought.

Before backing out of my parking spot, I jotted down a few notes: make and model of the trucks, color, what license plate information I could remember, and the descriptions of Flint's adversary with asterisks next to the words *broken finger*.

It took no time to drive the hundred or so yards to Javi's Autoparts, park, and walk inside. The shop smelled of fresh oil and cardboard. A glass display counter near the entrance held trophies from pro/am stock car races dated nearly thirty years ago and two plaques with the inscription *Off-Road Derby*, one from 2005, the other 2008. A picture of three men standing before a large-wheeled truck lifted at least ten inches, painted in clash-color racing stripes of red and green and orange, and spattered with mud along the side, was centered between the trophies in the display case. An old cash register sat on the counter. In front of that was a chrome service bell with a notecard taped to its base that read, "Don't ring, I'm probably busy."

I found the crass note amusing and was tempted to ring it anyway. Instead, I slid my hands into my pockets and looked at the stacks of stock shelves that ran from the counter to the far side of the building. Nothing. I looked out across the store to the bins that made up each endcap. One filled with new cloth rags bundled together and on sale, BOGO. Another bin held canisters of oil. The rest held similar items on sale and ready to move at discounted prices.

"This place is a ghost town," I mumbled.

From somewhere behind the stacks, a loud thud and the clanging of metal sounded out followed by a mix of English and Spanish of which I only recognized the bad words.

"Carlos! Where ju at, boy?"

It was a man's voice, laden with Tex-Mex drawl, frosted with irritation.

"Come clean up theese mess."

When Carlos did not reply, I heard another thud and saw a cardboard box fly across the backside of the aisle behind the register. The man in the back grumbled to himself, then came into view as he went to retrieve the box. He glanced down the aisle toward the front of the store and saw me. As if he had better things to do, he huffed his way along the stacks of shelves to the front counter.

"Why you no ring the bell?" he said, gesturing to the chrome ringer on the counter.

"The sign says..."

"Yeah, eet does. That wuz a tes'," he said with a laugh. "Ju pass."

The man's demeanor changed now that he had had fun with me. He was plain clothed in jeans, boots, and a long-sleeved tan cloth shirt buttoned only halfway to his neck. His dark brown eyes set back in sunken sockets over a rough-looking face. A scar trailed along his chin looking like a third lip, and his cheeks were pitted as if a cheese grater had dragged along the skin leaving a discolored redness behind. He grew a thick, black mustache that gave Tom Selleck a run for his money. The hairs at the ends of his mustache curled up as the man mustered a smile, despite the trouble he was having in the back of the store.

"What can I do for ju?"

"I'm looking for Javi."

"Ju foun' heem, señor. Javi ees right here stan'ing in fron' of ju."

I smiled with squinted eyes and pursed lips.

"My name is Cass Callahan. I..."

Javi cut me off.

"Ju are related to Stewart Callahan?"

"I am his nephew."

"I wuz sorry to hear of hees passing, amigo. I have known heem for many years. He wuz a good man."

"Yes, he was," I said. "Javi, I am new to town and am wondering if this is the place someone might come to for replacement parts for lightbars, rooftop spotlights, you know, things like that. You know what I'm talking about?"

Javi nodded.

"What are you looking for?" he asked.

I pulled my new badge from my belt and laid it on the counter for him to see. He glanced down, eyes widening slightly, then shifted his weight back away from the counter. It was subtle, but I noticed.

"I want to know if you have replacement parts in stock or if it is something you would have to order, that's all."

Javi relaxed, then placed his hands on the counter and leaned in.

"I can geet anytheeng for ju, Mr. Cass, but eet weell take a day or two for a sheepment to arrive."

"Fair enough," I said, slipping my badge back onto my belt. "Here's what you can do for me, Javi. Give me a call if someone comes in and orders anything that might be used to repair or replace a lightbar for a truck or jeep, UTV. Will you do that?"

Javi gave me an inquisitive look but nodded.

"I can do that, Mr. Cass. Has somesing happened? You are workeeng for Sheriff Gilbert, no?"

I smiled at Javi.

"Yes, I am working for the county. Just started. Thanks for your help, but I can't tell you anything more right now."

I wrote my name and number on the back of a business card I found on the counter, then slid it over to Javi. He picked it up and read the name and number aloud.

"Cass Callahan, Special Investigator, 346-222-0192."

He slipped the card into his back pocket. "If someone ees asking for the light, I weel call you after."

"Good," I said, offering Javi a handshake.

Just then, a teenage boy walked through the front door slurping a Big Gulp, head bouncing in rhythm to whatever music blared through his earbuds. He was lost in himself as many kids are, oblivious to anything or anyone around them. Javi watched the boy walk past and his disposition changed to resemble that of an angered junkyard dog. I looked at the boy, then back at Javi.

"Carlos?"

"Yeah," he said, with a grumble in his voice.

Javi stepped sideways to the end of the counter, then slipped past a floor-standing display rack of key chains, sunglasses, and air fresheners, falling in line to stalk Carlos from behind.

"Poor kid," I said to myself walking out of the store.

As I opened the door to the Explorer, I heard the familiar roll of Spanish vulgarity with the name Carlos sprinkled in every so often and wondered how the kid would make it through the day after the tongue-lashing.

I put the Explorer in reverse and backed away from the building. It was nearing lunchtime, and Raven would be wondering about Maria and Isabella. I had little to tell her except to reiterate that Chance was making sure they would be all right. The question I had to answer for myself was, would I tell her about what Uncle Stewart and the rest of the Callahan family had used the CR for, and that I had decided to continue the tradition of the *Gateway to Paradise* for the same purpose should the need arise?

CHAPTER TWENTY-SEVEN

Things felt different as I drove under the gateway arch at the entrance of the CR. Things were *different*. I pulled up to the house and sat with the motor running, my mind a twist of questions, some of which had no solution, others so simple that all they did was cloud my thinking with nonsense and improbability. The past thirty-six hours had changed my life, changed my plan of why Raven and I came out west in the first place, and thrust me back into the daily gamble of tempting fate against my very life. What concerned me most was I had not realized how much I missed it.

As the new steward of the Gateway to Paradise and Special Investigator for South Brewster County, I found that my role on the CR had changed dramatically. I was now both law and outlaw, and it would take some serious soul-searching to separate the two. Out here, there was more at stake than what was right vs. wrong.

I glanced at the digital screen on the center console, noting the time.

12:34

As a child, Spencer called this "magic time," and would have told me to make a wish, I thought. *If wishes were horses...*

My thought was interrupted by the rumbling sound of a vehicle pulling into the drive. I looked in my rearview mirror and saw Floyd Huckabee behind the wheel of his massive truck. He drove toward Flint's mini-house, then circled back and headed over to where I was parked. The truck's monstrous tires spit stones and kicked up dust as he drove over and parked next to me. The gravel seemed to groan as it crunched under its weight. Huckabee shot me a glare before he hopped out. He left the diesel engine to idle, rumbling like a fearsome dragon.

As he rounded the front of the truck, all I could see was the top of his hat moving across the hood like a shark's fin atop the water. He didn't stop until he reached my driver's side door. Floyd Huckabee was not intimidating. His wide, shapely stature made him look more like a Weeble Wobble character, non-threatening and insignificant, but I knew better than to underestimate him. He stood at my door, fuming.

Calm and measured, I turned off the Explorer and opened the door, bumping his gut when he failed to move out of the way. Stepping out of the air-conditioned cab and into the natural West Texas sauna, I felt the heat of both the sun and Floyd Huckabee's breath bearing down on me.

"Flint! Where is he?"

His eyes bulged up at me. His usual nonchalant flauntings were nowhere to be seen. His lips curved downward like a disgruntled church secretary, and his jowls wavered under a clenched jaw. I looked down at him with fortified patience.

"Well? Where is that son of a bitch?"

"What do you need with Flint, Floyd?"

I had not called him by his first name before and make it a habit to maintain a respectful disposition with guests, but he had shown up uninvited and was being demanding with no explanation as to why he was here or what he wanted with Flint, so I opted for a direct assault of my own.

"I'll tell you what, eye for eye comes to mind."

I stroked my chin as if giving his threat considerable thought, then looked over at Flint's tiny house.

"Tell you what. Why don't you head on home and settle down, and I'll see if I can locate Flint? Wouldn't want you to have a stroke. And as it were, regardless of how you feel the need to retrieve a pound of flesh, I'll have you know that the law doesn't permit acts of revenge."

"The law?" Huckabee spouted. "There's city-folk law, then there's the law of the West. Somethin' a man like you ain't never gonna understand."

The more he talked, the more agitated he became, causing his words to drift into an underlying drawl I had not heard from him before. He wanted control. Hell, he demanded it but here on the CR, he was about as powerful as a gnat in a thunderstorm.

"Let me tell you what I do understand. I know that some men feel that the way things were in the past is the way they'll always be. I'm sorry to be the one to inform you, but those days are over." I slipped my badge from my belt and cupped it in the palm of my hand for him to see. "Why don't you head on out, Mr. Huckabee."

My tact had returned, but this was my last effort to act polite. His face drooped in disgust.

"You the new sheriff in town, Callahan? Gonna see things handled how you see 'em now?"

He placed his hands on his hips as if I owed him an explanation. I met his stare with a stone-faced glare of my own.

"Ol' Stewart woulda steered clear of all this. He knew a man should handle his own affairs and would never have gotten in the way. If he was here now..."

"Well, he's not, Mr. Huckabee," I said, the floodgates bending to a river of building frustration inside of me.

"Have a nice day. I'll tell Flint you stopped by when I see him."

I brushed past, forcing Huckabee to twist out of my way with a bump of my hip against his bulging belly. He huffed his displeasure, then stomped around the grille of his truck, pausing once to glare at me as I stood on my porch waiting for him to leave.

The truck's continued rumble seemed to emulate the foul thoughts Huckabee displayed through a nasty scowl. The massive grille was hard to forget, and the roof lights... wait, where were the roof lights?

"What happened to your lights, Mr. Huckabee?" I asked.

He turned his back on me and threw his left hand in the air to brush off my question.

"Wouldn't you like to know," he said as he loaded up.

Like a wronged teenager, he stomped the accelerator, spewing gravel into the air as he reversed away. Sliding to a halt, he thrust the truck into drive and sped off sending a mix of gravel dust and thick exhaust to swirl away in his wake.

The last thing I noticed was how the dust clung to the panels of his truck. It was almost as if it had been washed and was not yet completely dry.

"What was that all about?"

Raven stood in the doorway behind me with a curious look about her.

"Floyd Huckabee," I said. "Something's got him all riled up."

"What'd you say to him?" she asked, walking over next to me.

"Nothing. He was looking for Flint."

"Oh. I saw him drive in just before you. Must have parked over by the barn. Did you know he had such a nice truck?"

I shook my head and glanced at my phone for the time.

12:42

It would not be long before Dr. Frannie showed up with her team.

"I'm going to go chat with Flint for a minute. You eat lunch yet?"

"Not yet. Want me to fix something?"

"No, I'll handle it today. For both of us. Go dive back into whatever you were doing."

"Okay," she said, pushing up on her tiptoes for a peck on the cheek.

I stepped off the porch and headed for the barn, hoping Flint was still inside. I had questions for him, some of which he might take exception to, but it was my job to ask even the tough ones. Rounding the corner of the barn, I headed through the side door that led to the stalls and the work area. The room was empty, but I heard noises from the stalls.

"Flint?" I called out. "That you back there?"

"Do ya have ta ask that, Callahan? Who else would it goddamn be?"

I laughed to myself, thinking what a lucky guy I was to have a man like Flint running the ranch. I mean, who would not want to put up with his foul disposition on a daily basis.

I paused, shifting my thoughts from how he annoyed me to what it was that made him so important to Uncle Stewart. If he trusted Flint enough to keep him around even after he died, there might be something more to him of which I am not yet aware.

Did he know what the family had been doing on the CR? Did he have a hand in the Gateway to Paradise? How could he not?

I headed down a musty walkway past a series of stalls, one of which was my new pal Tucker's, though she was out to pasture. A stocked tack shelf ran along the opposite wall, ending outside a ten-by-ten-foot washroom designed to bathe the horses. A steel ring dangled around a rope that draped across the entrance, allowing a horse to be tethered inside the wash area but still allowing for some movement while being attended. There was a gradual slope in the floor toward the rear to a drain that led out of the barn.

Flint appeared from the last stall. His shirt was stained and wet, and his hands seemed to be dripping blood.

CHAPTER TWENTY-EIGHT

"Holy shit! Are you hurt?"

"Hell no, I ain't hurt. Mare just delivered her foal. Been keepin' an eye on her since last night. Ain't a picture more worth seein' than a newborn and its proud mama. She did good, too, but I'll be around here for a while watchin' over the both of 'em."

His hands dripped with funk the likes of which I had never seen in person before.

"Why are you so..."

I gestured to his hands. He looked down, shook both hands, flicking small tendrils of thick fluid from them, then wiped what was left onto his pant legs. I clenched my teeth, swallowing a lump of dry air down my throat.

"I didn't know we had a pregnant mare."

"How could you?" Flint said. "You *live* on the ranch. You damn well don't work it." He paused as if making an honest attempt to speak without disparaging me further. "Until yesterday," he continued. "Yer city through and through, but maybe there's some hope for you yet, Callahan."

I smiled at the thought.

"Wanna see 'em?"

"Yeah," I said.

Flint led me into the stall, motioning for me to stay at the edge near the door.

"Don't want to stress mama out too much," he said with a hint of care in his voice that suggested he may have a gentle side after all. "It's important for me ta be here, to watch over 'em both. The foal needs to see me around, feel the touch of my palm, and make a connection with something that from its eyes, looks nothing like his mama. The more I can interact with it, the better the imprint."

"Imprint?"

"The sooner the foal imprints on a human, the more trusting it will become of us."

It was fascinating to watch Flint work to soothe both the mare and the foal. He whispered reassurances as he moved closer and spoke with the grace and skill of an experienced rancher. The mare allowed Flint to approach and remained calm when he reached out to stroke the newborn foal. Its long, lanky legs shook as if cold or nervous, but I imagined it was more from the shock of its new environment. How safe and secure and warm it had been for so long inside its mother, and now the foal faced a wide-open space covered in fresh straw and two funny-looking beings staring at it.

Flint turned his attention to the mare. He looked her over, then offered a gentle hand to rub her muzzle. She was more accepting of his attention than I would have expected, but I suppose her familiarity with him and the exhaustion she must have felt were enough to allow it.

I watched from the side, amazed at the miracle before me, but my need to speak with Flint was still fresh.

"Flint," I said in a low voice. "I'd like to—"

"Help?" he said, interrupting.

That was not what I was going to say, rather more like, *I'd like to talk to you, speak with you, chat a minute, tell you this is beautiful, but I have shit to do and need your cooperation*...something along those lines, but I bit my tongue.

"We need to maintain a clean environment. Grab some gloves off the tack shelf and give me a hand."

I hesitated, then exited the stall and found a pair of gloves that fit. When I returned to the stall, he was waiting for me with something in his hands. Without a chance to ask, he dumped what looked like a tangled helping of wet, skinned roadkill into my arms. The weight of the glob caught me off guard, straining my injured thumb, and the stench was enough to make my stomach lurch.

"Take this out back to the burn pile. I'll light it up before dark," he said.

"What the hell, Flint?"

"Never hold a horse placenta in yer arms before? You want ta ranch around here, it won't be the last, Callahan."

His face was serious, but his eyes laughed wildly as if he was enjoying the library scene in the movie *Ghostbusters* when Dr. Venkman was told to take a sample of dripping ectoplasm for Egon.

"Yeah," I said.

He turned around and left me to my disgusting job of disposing of the horse's afterbirth. It felt more like hazing, but if it would get him to open up to me, so be it.

I handled the task quickly, placing it on the burn pile as requested, then went straight back inside. Flint was washing his hands in the utility sink attached to the wall just outside the washroom stall.

"Ever seen anything like that before, Callahan?" he said, drying his hands on a shop towel.

"Only when my son was born, but I wouldn't call that a true comparison."

"I s'pose not," Flint said.

He stepped away from the sink and tossed the spent rag into a garbage barrel.

"What's on yer mind?" he said, turning to face me. "Seems like ya didn't just wander out here for shits and grins. Fact is, feels like you've been keepin' yer eye on me."

"Kind of feels like that's going both ways, Flint. You know anything about what went on this morning?"

"Nah. Been here since midnight watchin' the mare. Heard you come through, though. Early too. Where'd you head out to?"

I ignored his question to ask another of my own.

"You hear anything strange before sunup?"

Flint walked over to the stall and glanced inside, then leaned his back against the wood slats and crossed his arms over his chest.

"Someone shootin' at something. Ain't strange ta hear that. You got ranches on both sides of the CR an' hands doin' whatever work they've meant ta do. Back in the day when yer uncle had cattle, we'd always have two or three men ride out overnight a couple of times a week huntin' fer scavengers or scarin' away little packs of wet brownies that try and cross over in the dark. We'd mix it up, too, keep the wildlife guessin'. Didn't lose as many head that way, and tell ya the truth, them overnights was more fun than you'd think."

"So you heard some shots but dismissed them?"

"You know how far sound travels out here. Hell, them pops coulda been miles off. Even over in Mexico."

"I'll tell you firsthand that they were not miles away. I was out at the crime scene this morning and discovered two more dead bodies that had been stuffed into the crevasse beneath the guy we pulled out yesterday."

"That why Sheriff Gilbert come out this mornin'?"

I nodded.

"Among other things. Someone was hiding out near the grove and took a shot at me, then tried running me down with what sounded like a large diesel truck. Rooftop lights, grille lights, looked like a damned UFO chasing us across the CR. They fled when I returned fire. Guess they weren't used to being on the receiving end of a bullet."

"Us?" Flint asked, dropping his arms to slip his thumbs behind his belt.

"Came across a couple of transients. A girl and her mother. The woman said she was looking for *The Rescuer*. That mean anything to you?"

Flint did not reply.

"Look," I said, taking a step closer to him. "There has been a lot of shit happening around here, and I'm trying to figure out who is behind it. I'd like us to be on the same page."

I took a deep breath and dove into the hard questions. Questions that could make or break trust. This would be the turning point for Levi Flint and me.

"How long have you been working for the CR?"

He stepped away from the stall to stand directly in front of me. His eyes were intense, yet starting to come alive with emotion.

"We having one of them, what do you city boys call it, an exit interview?"

"Just answer the question, Flint."

"I been workin' here nearly thirty years. Stewart Callahan's always been good to me. I owe him a lot though he'd never seen it that way. When he died, I figured my time was done out here 'til some lawyer told me otherwise. Said I'd have job security for life if I wanted it and that I had your uncle to thank. I ain't never had a family of my own, but I'll tell you this, there ain't nothin' I wouldn't have done for him. Nothin' at all."

"You ever heard him mention the words, 'Gateway to Paradise'?"

Flint squinted his eyes, searching for a read on me like a poker player deciding whether to call my 'all-in' bet. His breathing deepened, and his nostrils flared as if he had detected a foul odor as he contemplated his next statement. I returned his gaze patiently waiting, watching him just as intently. Finally, Flint spoke.

"Be careful with them words, Callahan. Yer uncle Stewart was a good man. He helped people whenever he could. Can't say I agreed with all of it, but it weren't fer me to say. I did my job, didn't ask questions, and kept the CR and yer uncle safe."

"You shoot that man that we found, Flint? Try hiding him in the crevasses you warned me about on our first ride?"

Flint's eyes widened. He did not seem all that surprised by my accusation but did not answer the question either.

"The morning I went to work with you, the same morning I discovered the first body, you carried a revolver, but before we left the barn, you had a semi-auto holstered on your hip. Why switch weapons? Where is that gun now?"

"Yer askin' a lot of questions, Callahan."

I pulled the badge from my belt and held it up for him to see. Flint smiled, not deterred by my display.

"You were loyal to my uncle. I'd like to think you'd remain so to the CR and to me, but I have a job to do and a family to protect."

I slipped the badge back in place.

"Follow me," Flint said.

We walked through the rear door of the barn to a large shed beyond the burn pile. Flies had already begun to swarm above the sticks that covered the discarded membrane. On the backside of the shed was a garage. Flint wasted no time, leaning over to pull open the wide garage door. Its old hinges creaked as it rose.

I followed Flint into the shadowy interior. Cobwebs dangled in the far corners of the ceiling. A dead wasp nest clung to a rafter in front of a cracked, frosted window on the right side of the garage. Parked in the center was a blue 2016 Chevrolet Silverado 2500HD LTZ 4x4. It was as elegant as it was rugged. Large Toyo MT tires on wheels lifted just enough for style while maintaining the versatility of a work truck, a well-used Tractor Supply toolbox set beneath the rear window, and a ranch hand full replacement front bumper with grille guard made this truck hard to forget. It was odd I had only just seen it, but it was the truck Flint drove away after the confrontation I witnessed in town.

He opened the driver's side door and leaned in. I moved behind him, watching his movements while remaining on guard. I did not want to draw on him, but I was prepared. He reached an arm into the cab, then paused. My hand had instinctively reached for my gun, my thumb and palm resting on the grip.

"I'ma turn around now. Don't fuckin' shoot me." Flint turned, holding the barrel of a black, semi-automatic pistol in his hands. "Safety's on. Take it and look fer yerself."

I reached out and took it from him, depressed the magazine release, slid the loaded magazine from the gun, then did a press check of the barrel. Loaded as I expected. I pulled the slide back far enough to eject the bullet, then inspected the weapon.

"Colt 1911," Flint said. "Stewart gave it to me some years back. Carry it for protection when I'm not workin'."

".45 caliber," I said. "It's a beaut."

The shells we found in the grove were 9mm, I thought.

"Protection, huh," I said.

"Don't forget where we live, Callahan. We call the river a border but it ain't doin' a damn thing ta keep people out. There's a buffet of foreign turdwads tryin' ta get into our country every day. Most of 'em Mexican, but not all."

"Yeah, I see the news."

"Well, now you live it."

I handed Flint the pistol and the magazine, then bent over and picked up the ejected round.

"Keep it," he said. "I didn't kill those men. Coulda been any number of people, but it wasn't me."

"Any idea who might have been out on the CR this morning?" I asked.

He turned away to lean back into the cab. I heard the

click of the magazine as it slid into a locked position. After stowing the Colt, Flint shut the door of the truck and turned back to face me.

"This is wide open land, Callahan. Ain't hard ta get somewhere if ya have a mind to."

I considered his answer but felt there was more to it than he was letting on.

"Anything else, officer?" he said with a sarcastic tone.

"Two things."

His irritation was growing. I was on borrowed time but felt that the heavy lifting was over.

"Who were you arguing with in town earlier?"

That got Flint smiling, looking more amused now than agitated.

"Curly Yates. Son of a bitch works for the *Flyin' H*."

"Floyd Huckabee's ranch?"

"The very one. They've had Doc Blackstone tied up with piddly crap these past few days. I need him out here checkin' up on the mare and her foal. Needed ta grab a few things ta help her out, so I ran inta town," he said, then paused as if he had a bad taste in his mouth. "Hate goin' inta town. Anyway, met up with Curly by chance this mornin' an' gave him a piece of my mind."

"And a broken finger by the looks of it."

"Saw that too, did ya?" Flint said, looking pleased with himself. "Ain't no man put their hands on me."

I raised an eyebrow at him, remembering and still feeling the lingering effects of our altercation yesterday morning. He laughed aloud.

"You took yer lumps, Callahan. Gave some too. Consider that a frog-strangler."

"A what?"

"Gully washer? Water under the bridge? Hell, Callahan, ya survived, didn't ya?"

"If I recollect, I came out on top," I said, sporting a satisfied grin of my own.

"Been so long ago, don't remember that part of it. What else you got on yer mind? I got shit ta do."

Building bridges and patching potholes could go a long way between us if we were to coexist on the CR. Stewart's estate paid Flint, so unless I forced him out by legal means, he was here as long as he wanted. Thirty years is a long time to be in any one place, which made the CR more Flint's home than mine. Maybe it was time I took a page out of Stewart's book. If he trusted Flint, maybe it was time I did, too.

"Well, Raven and I were thinking of bringing you in for supper one of these nights."

"Her idea?"

"Don't matter. It's a good one, anyhow," I said.

I stepped closer to Flint, doing my best to change my tone.

"I need you to know I've got your back if you need it. I'd like to think that you might do the same should the need arise. I'm not asking to be buddy-buddy, but if you stopped thinking of me as a useless prong on the CR, I might surprise you with what I can do."

I offered Flint a hand. He looked me dead in the eye, then smirked and took hold.

"You may have some of Stewart in you yet, Callahan."

We shook hard and released. I had a better feeling about Flint, now that I knew the weapon he showed me did not match the ballistics we had collected at the crime scene, although I would see if I could pull a print off the .45 round he told me to keep. If we had any viable prints from the casings we collected, I could rule him out with certainty, as long as he did not turn out to be a match.

Keep me filled in on the mare's progress if you don't mind.

"Robin," he said.

I gave Flint a confused look.

"The mare, her name's Robin."

"Gotcha," I said. "Also, there will be a few vehicles

arriving shortly to retrieve the bodies. I'll lead them out on the CR. I'll take the sat phone to reach you, but right now I don't see the need."

"You'll know where to find me."

I nodded and headed for the house.

"Hey, Callahan," Flint called out after closing the garage door behind us. "You might want to talk with Ramón over at the Double S. Sinclair may not like it, but you've got that all-access pass on yer belt. See what he thinks about that."

"Thanks," I said.

Walking back to the house, I mulled over what Flint had told me and regarded what he had not said as curious. *Talk to Ramón*, he had said, *but Sinclair won't like it*.

A rising dust trail from the road parallel to the CR caught my attention. Dr. Frannie and her team were early. I walked into the yard to greet them as they crossed under the archway at the entrance to the ranch.

"Sorry, Little Bird, lunch will have to wait."

CHAPTER TWENTY-NINE

"How 'bout making these the last bodies we pull from the CR this week?" Dr. Frannie said, stepping out of the lead van as I walked over.

"Fine by me," I said. "It's been a helluva day already."

"Tell me about it. Nothing like spending the majority of the night examining the first one only to have your lab overrun with agents and a medic of their own with a federal seizure warrant and a gag order. I'd barely sown him up again when they burst in."

"You learn anything before?"

"Not much. The cause of death was primarily attributed to exsanguination resulting from the chest wounds."

"Exsang...what?"

"Blood loss, Detective. Keep up," she said, smiling.

"Upon examination, I retrieved two 9mm projectiles from his body, one lodged adjacent to the posterior rib cage behind the lung, and the other located in the upper left region of the chest, slightly superior to the heart. The latter shot proved fatal, inflicting critical damage. Even with prompt medical intervention, the likelihood of him surviving would have been grim at best."

I shook my head, disappointed.

"Well, at least we can confirm the ballistics results against the evidence we collected."

"There is a little more. When I ran the fingerprints through IAFIS, his file was flagged and secured."

"Right," I said. "But..."

"Hold on, cowboy," Dr. Frannie said. "Before they hauled him away I ran a search in CODIS, Combined DNA Index System, and was able to pull a name from a case file from 2017."

"I'm starting to really like you, Dr Frannie."

"If you like that, you'll love this. His name is Balde Ramos. He is connected to a homicide scene in New Mexico that had ties to the Aristas Asesinos. Cass, the Sinaloa Cartel has a history of using gangs like them as drug traffickers and enforcers. You know, the kind you read about in all those Don Winslow books about the cartels. They're some really dangerous men. If he was already dead, why did the FBI act so quickly, and why was his file flagged?"

"Dunno," I said. "Maybe they've been looking for him, or maybe..." I paused. *Even the most ridiculous of theories may hold merit*, something my old partner Ray Tucker would say when we came to a dead end on a case. "Maybe he cut a deal and was undercover?"

"I suppose," Dr. Frannie said. "But that's pretty thin, Cass."

"Yeah," I said. "Maybe these other two will tell us something we don't know. Let's load up and get this over with. I'll grab my keys and you can follow me out."

Dr. Frannie turned back to the van, and I ran inside to fetch my keys, calling out to Raven as I came into the house.

"Hey Rave, gotta take a rain check on lunch."

Raven appeared from the kitchen with a paper sack in one hand and a water bottle in the other.

"Figured you could eat on the way out," she said.

I walked over to her and wrapped my arms around her waist.

"You're more than I deserve," I said.

"I know," she said with a hint of jealous pride. "Just remember that as you're bouncing around the countryside with the beautiful Dr. Frannie."

"Hey," I said, pondering, then losing control of my next thought. "You asked me to keep you in the loop. Ride out there with me. It won't be pretty, and it may take a while before we are done, but I'll tell you everything I can along the way."

Raven's eyes sparkled, catching fire with excitement as well as a deep-seated boil of emotion that caused them to grow teary.

"You'd bring me along?"

"You're the only partner I ever wanted. Plus," I said with distinction as I pulled the badge from my belt. "I'm Special Investigator of South Brewster County, Cass Callahan, and what I say goes."

Raven leaned in, kissing me with a passion that had been missing for far too long. It made me want to forget about Dr. Frannie, the waiting vans, the dead bodies, and all the troubles I had faced since this morning, but what caused my knees to buckle was what she said as our lips parted.

"Go ahead. I'll be waiting for you...in there when you come home."

Her eyes danced toward the hallway that led to the bedroom. A sly, seductive smile crept across her face, and the palm of her hand slowly slid down my chest. Pulse be damned, she had my full attention.

"I love you, Cass," she said, handing me the lunch she had prepared.

Without another word, she walked past me and down the hall, looking back over her shoulder once before disappearing into the bedroom. She left the door open.

"Damn," I whispered to myself.

I took a deep breath, forced thoughts of gutting fish, lifting weights, and Mattress Mac's Gallery Furniture commercials where I could *save, save, save, money today* all to soothe the necessary parts of me that needed relaxing before stepping out of the privacy of my home.

A look out the living room window showed the vans lined up and waiting. Satisfied with my readiness, I started for the door. My feet worked as they should but felt heavier as I stepped off the porch and walked to the Explorer. With a push of the ignition button, the engine roared to life.

I shifted the Explorer into drive, spinning the wheels over the loose gravel as my lead foot pressed a little too hard on the gas, and drove around to lead Dr. Frannie's team out on the CR to recover what I hoped was the last of the dead bodies.

"One helluva morning's turning into a bitch of a day," I said to myself.

Distant clouds lingered over Mexico, teasing us with hopes of drifting shade or a brief shower to cool things off, but they stayed south of the border for the duration of the afternoon. It did, however, offer a southerly breeze, but by the time it reached us, it was more like the blast of heat that fills a kitchen when a working oven door is opened.

Over the next two-and-a-half hours, Dr. Frannie's team staged a work area and extracted the two bodies, lifting each from the crevasse using a series of pulleys, harnesses, and rope. The team worked methodically, taking careful measures to keep themselves safe while preserving the integrity of the crime scene as much as possible. They had one brief run-in with a testy rattlesnake, but once it had been relocated, they powered through their work.

My job was easy: stay the hell out of the way. This was not one of the glorious perks of the job. Handling dead bodies never is, but it was necessary for many reasons, most important of which was to see if there was a connection between these two men and the one that had the FBI scrambling to collect.

Dr. Frannie went right to work assessing the bodies as they were pulled from their rocky tomb. She took photographs, measured and noted wound size, drew blood, collected skin and hair samples, then swabbed both of the victim's mouths to be used for additional DNA testing. She used a digital fingerprint scanner to catalog the victim's prints, then removed her cell phone and snapped a pic of the scanner's screen after each print had been digitized.

"Whatcha doing there, Doc?" I asked.

She looked at me without a shred of guilt on her face.

"Just in case anyone wants to leave us out of the loop again."

She flashed a crafty smile as she slipped her phone into her back pocket. I can not say that what she did was by the book or even right by ethical standards, but I understood the frustration of someone taking over her work without so much as an explanation. FBI, ICE, DEA; three-letter agencies usually only play nice when forced to do so. Otherwise, it's pull out the ruler and let's measure. That old "there is no 'I' in team" speech never made it out of fifth-grade gym class.

Once the extraction and initial inspections of the bodies were completed, Dr. Frannie and her team loaded up the vans, and we were off. I checked the time on the Explorer's heads-up display.

4:14

If I played my cards right, I could still get out to the Double S to talk with Ramón before dark, but I wanted to look in on Raven first. She had left me with a lot to think about before coming out here, and I hoped that once I returned, those feelings were still open for exploration.

The vans pulled next to me when we reached the house, stopping only long enough for Dr. Frannie to roll down her window and lean out. I pushed the control to open the Explorer's window.

"I'll call you as soon as I get to the lab and run the prints. If they're flagged, too, we may have stepped into an even bigger pile of shit than we initially realized."

"Thanks, Dr. Frannie."

She nodded, then gave me a thumbs up before telling her driver to move out. I parked in my usual spot in front of the house, feeling a tingle of anticipation creep over me. Raven had made so much progress in her recovery since arriving at the CR. I had expected a long, harrowing road, but the change of scenery and quiet isolation on the ranch turned out to be just what the doctor ordered.

I opened the door and headed inside to see if Raven was still in a romantically inclined mood.

"Home, Little Bird," I called out in an overtly childish hide-and-seek voice.

No reply. I walked down the hall and into the bedroom.

"You in here?"

The room was empty.

Okay, I thought. *Where are you?*

I walked through the entire house, unable to find Raven anywhere. It was strange, but not out of the ordinary for her to leave for a run or to head into town, but I had the car, and I had seen her running shoes in the basket next to the front door. I stepped out onto the porch and looked around.

"Raven?" I called out.

I walked outside wondering if Flint, however unlikely, had seen her. I stepped through the barn so as not to disturb the new foal or its mother and found my answer. Raven's face beamed with newfound love as she knelt next to the foal watching it fight to balance on wobbly legs. Flint occupied the mother with soft clicks and soothing words while Raven gently stroked the newborn's back.

I watched over the railing. Flint noticed me first. He caught Raven's attention with a subtle whisper and nodded toward me. She turned, eyes catching mine, mouth stretched wide in a smile to rival all smiles, and mouthed the words, *Oh. My. God!*

CHAPTER THIRTY

Forty-five minutes later, I walked hand in hand with Raven to keep her from floating away with the high she was feeling after spending time with the new foal. It was as if she had been at a Taylor Swift concert where each note released another batch of endorphins that nearly had her flying. And, like a diehard fan, when it was all over and the encores had been played out, the last thing she wanted to do was leave. Flint had shown Raven a gentleman's kindness. He waited with her as she stroked and whispered and ogled over the CR's newest baby.

"That was the sweetest thing ever," she said, her eyes looking starstruck. "And Flint said that I could name it, but I couldn't think of anything good on the spot. Oh, Cass. Wasn't she beautiful?"

"So, it's a girl?"

"Yes! Weren't you paying attention?"

"To be honest, I was more interested in watching you."

Raven squeezed my hand three times, our secret way of saying *I love you*.

"Let's celebrate," she said.

I smiled. Though, through all the darkness that had descended over the CR the past two days, Raven found the silver lining of which we were all in need. I could put off talking with Ramón until tomorrow if it meant spending the evening with my beautiful wife.

"Sure," I said. "What do you have in mind?"

Raven came to an abrupt halt, tugging hard on my hand, causing a sharp strain on my injured thumb. I clenched my teeth, but a grunt of agony escaped. She pulled herself in front of me and wrapped her free hand around my back.

"Three things," she said, laughing, unaware of the pain she had caused.

"Dinner in town, a drive along RR170, and finally..."

She leaned in and pressed her soft lips to mine, nibbling on my bottom lip.

"...some steamy star gazing. What do you say?"

Without hesitation, I grabbed her around the waist and lifted her over my shoulder as if I was carrying a green Army duffel bag and double-timed it to the house. She giggled as I carried her along. Truth be told, my bruised and cut body screamed at me for doing so, but I had been through extensive training to cope with such things in the Army and while on the police force, but it was my innate male understanding of what I had to look forward to that took over and dulled any pain I might have had.

"Let's gooooo!" I said, my voice bouncing with each lunging step.

Dinner at Rancho Arroyo Steakhouse was the perfect way to start the evening. The smells from the kitchen made me want to order one of everything on the menu, and the list of drinks seemed endless. When a waiter took our order and explained that beers on tap were served in a frosted mug, I looked at Raven and, in a playful voice, announced that we had found heaven. There is no better way to enjoy a frothy lager than from an ice-cold mug pulled fresh from the freezer.

The waiter was quick to return with our drinks, then delivered a tray of utter goodness to the table next to us. I watched the steam rise and could almost hear the sizzle of meat from platter-sized plates, surrounded by veggies and warm pieces of bread as each was set before its lucky dinner guest. I took a deep breath, stealing a whiff from their order, then leaned across the table, careful not to topple the small, decorative candle holders that glimmered red in the center of our corner table.

"Can you believe this place?" I said.

"It's great, Cass. Reminds me of Taste of Texas back in Houston," she said, tapping the menu with her fingers.

"I'll drink to that."

We each lifted our mug, clinked them together, and enjoyed a long swallow. I could not have thought of a better way to end the day than this.

When our plates arrived, they were every bit as delicious as our taste buds had come to expect. The meat from my T-bone melted in my mouth. I added a baked potato that burst with sour cream and chives, was heavy on the bacon, and dripped with melted butter. Fresh rolls steamed in my hands, smelling homemade fresh and tasted even better when sopped with escaping juices from my devoured steak. Raven's filet was generous, was as tender as Turkish delight, and the mixed veggies on her plate looked to be hand-picked for size and quality. In a hundred years, I could not have hoped for a better meal than what we had been served. Though feeling rather full, I was disappointed when I took my last bite.

"Are you as stuffed as I am?" I asked Raven.

"And then some," she said, patting her stomach.

"You still up for part two of your evening plan?" I wondered.

Raven grabbed the handle of her beer and lifted the mug to her lips, eyes dancing at me over the rim as she sipped the final drops. She set the mug down again and let her lips slowly part to allow her tongue to clean up what fermented moisture remained behind. My heart skipped a beat, and I felt myself sigh. Whether Raven heard it was debatable, but her gaze on me did not change one bit. She reached across the table and grasped my hands with a tender touch.

"You settle the bill while I go freshen up in the bathroom. Meet you out front when I'm done."

She brought my hands to her mouth and delicately kissed my outlying fingers, trailing her crafty tongue along my knuckles before pulling away with a smile that said, *take me now*.

I watched as Raven stood up and walked to the ladies' room.

Damn, I thought. *I may not make it for the drive.*

I was much less graceful leaving the table. I hurried to the cashier, fumbling with my wallet along the way. I paid the bill, added a sizable tip, and stepped outside to wait as she had asked.

The evening air was kind tonight, easing itself into a mellow warmth that felt like a downy pillow wafting against my exposed skin. The sky was pale blue, hinting at twilight to come. I paced away from the doorway, looking along the roadway that ran northwest and southeast in each direction from the restaurant, wondering how far we would have to drive before finding the perfect spot to pull off and dive into each other's arms. I sucked in a long breath of fresh air, the tantalizing aromas of Rancho Arroyo riding bareback on the breeze and felt my heart thump when I heard footsteps approaching from behind. I turned, spreading my arms for a quick embrace.

"I missed..."

"We have to talk."

I dropped my arms, my face contorting with surprise as Ramón walked over to me. Veins pulsed in his neck, causing his hand tattoo to twitch as if it were preparing to strike.

Muscle memory is caused by repetitive movements of

specific body parts or a combination of multiple parts over an elongated period where practice does not necessarily make perfect. Instead, it encodes a routine reaction within a person's reflexes. These reflexes know to act before the brain can make the connection, then assign the movements that are required resulting in an increased response time. When seconds matter, these engrained actions could mean the difference between life and death. As it were, I had already moved my feet into a defensive position, my arms bent at the elbows ready to block or strike, and my eyes homed in on Ramón's, and all before he had finished saying the word *talk*.

"Yes," I said. "We do."

Ramón's brown eyes locked on me, his eyelids closing to a concentrated squint. He was dressed as if he had just been out on the range. His jeans were soiled and dusty, his shirt soaked at the armpits and around his collar. He was hatless, but how his hair was pasted to his forehead suggested it had not been removed for long. Such a gesture was rare for a man like Ramón to remove his hat until he turned in for the night or in the presence of a lady if he played by those rules.

"Where were you..."

"Not here," Ramón said, interrupting me with a hushed, firm voice. "Come with me."

"Ain't gonna happen, Ramón."

I glanced at the entrance to the restaurant. *Stay inside, Little Bird*, I thought.

"You must. There is no time."

He was insistent almost to the point of being scared, which raised questions about what could be making him feel so on edge. When I did not move, his eyes dropped from mine. They twitched from side to side as if he was expecting something to happen but was unsure of how or where or when. Sweat beaded above his lip and across his brow.

"Fine," he said. "Meet me at El Lobo Vista. Ten o'clock.

Take Camino de la Leche south of town. Drive until you come to a dead end. There is a path for you to follow from there. It will be dark, but you will be able to see. Come alone."

His words accelerated as he laid out my instructions.

"Ramón," I said, interested yet agitated. "Follow me to the sheriff's office. If you're worried about..."

"No," he said, eyes bulging. "You want to know who is doing these killings on the CR, you come tonight."

I looked past Ramón, expecting to see Raven walk outside at any moment. He followed my gaze, then looked back at me.

"Your woman, she is inside?"

The mere mention of her caused me to take one aggressive step closer to him.

"Be very careful, Ramón."

The tension in my body was palpable; fists clenched, legs ready to spring, even my swollen thumb poised for action. Ramón glanced down at my prepared stance and nodded.

"Do not be late."

As he passed by me, Raven walked through the door. Her hair had been fluffed, and she had a sway about her as she looked around for me. I stepped back toward the entrance, signaling her over with a wave.

"Hey, Rave. Over here."

Curiosity laced her laughter as she approached, questioning my behavior. "What are you doing?"

"Just waiting for you."

She smiled, then rocked up and down on her tiptoes. I admired her excitement, though I could not share in it fully. There was another reason for my unease that I did not want to reveal to her.

"Ready to go?" I asked, reaching my hand out to her.

She wrapped her pinky finger around mine and pulled. Without realizing it, I resisted. That caused her intuitive radar to activate. She released my finger and stepped closer to me. There were no hiding secrets from Raven, and now was not the time to start trying.

"What's wrong?" she said.

CHAPTER THIRTY-ONE

The ride home was direct. No searching for a secluded place to park. No stopping to watch the sunset. And though the late summer sun still cast its warmth all around us, the cab of the Explorer felt cold and distant.

"I don't understand why you don't call Chance," Raven said with genuine worry. "He's the sheriff. He's your boss, right?"

"He is both, but I have nothing to say that he hasn't already heard one way or another. Meeting the guy I'm meeting is just that...a meeting."

"If it's only a meeting, why not have it in town at a bar or behind a gas station, for Christ's sake? Why meet on some cliff in the middle of nowhere?"

She made an excellent point, but my hands were tied. The cost of information was high, and trust was a valued commodity, especially when it was offered as take it or leave it.

"What if I go with you? I'll stay in the car. I can keep a lookout or get Chance on the phone if..."

"Raven," I interrupted. "This is not as dangerous as you are making it out to be."

"Then let me come along. You were going to take me

out this afternoon, and that was to dig up dead bodies. If it's not dangerous, give me one reason why I shouldn't come."

I could think of a myriad of reasons why this meeting would be dangerous. Ramón's tattoo, a clear testament to his dark past, hinted at the perilous nature of our encounter. Whether he had turned himself around, escaped from a life where crime and villainy were worn like a badge of honor, or was still working for some faction of the Mexican mafia, he had something important to share and was unwilling to risk being seen with me. The limb he stepped out on to get my attention at the restaurant was what piqued my curiosity. If he had viable intel on who was behind the killings, there might be those who would not want that information to come to light. I suspected he knew that which already suggested what he had to say had weight.

"I won't be long," I said.

"No," she replied with a wavery voice. "Take all the time in the world."

Raven leaned her head against the window and watched the landscape hurl by. A partial reflection of her face in the glass showed tears running down her cheeks, making the drive home an emotional blur of frustration and hurt feelings.

The sun hovered just above the horizon as we pulled onto the CR. Raven's door was open before the Explorer came to a full stop, and she was in the house before I had even a chance to close the driver's side door. Nothing I could say would make things better right now. I understood the disappointment she was feeling, and I know she was worried for my safety. I had concerns of my own.

Instead of going inside, I made my way toward the barn, hoping to find Flint. It was he who had suggested I speak with Ramón, and now, almost miraculously, I found myself face-to-face with the man. I needed more from Flint.

All was quiet as I entered the barn. The smell of fresh hay filled my nose, overpowering the lingering musty smell to which I had become accustomed. I made my way past the workbench and cabinets to the stalls. Tucker was back and approached the railing as I drew near.

"What's the word Tucker? Flint still around?"

Tucker ignored my question. What did she care, anyway? She was a horse. What she did want was a good scratch behind the ears and a treat. I gave her some of the desired attention, scratching the soft hairs and skin at the base of her ears, then gently rubbed her snout. The moment felt therapeutic. Her large eyes were calming, and the shallow grunts of satisfaction from the attention helped me recenter my focus on the job I had to do.

"Gotta go, girl," I said, giving her a final stroke of her muzzle.

As if understanding, Tucker retreated from the rail and stood in the growing shadows as evening fell.

I peeked over the rail of the final stall and saw the mare with her new foal lying on a bed of fresh straw. The mare rested her head along the side of her baby, blinking when she noticed me but stayed still so as not to disturb her tiny sleeping miracle. Flint was not in the barn.

I returned to the house and sat on the porch for a while before going inside. I had a few hours to kill before heading off to meet Ramón, and I figured it better to leave Raven to herself for the time being.

As the sun disappeared over the vistas across the Rio Grande, the CR fell into the shadow of night. The swirl of color at twilight looked watered down, less brilliant than usual. Maybe it was an anomaly, or maybe it was my distracted perception, but darkness surged forward like the tide rolling over the shores and the land with all its color disappeared.

CHAPTER THIRTY-TWO

A glance at my phone told me the time.
9:03
I stood from where I had been sitting for what felt like hours as I racked my brain to fit the pieces of this case together. Amid the sea of uncertainties and unanswered questions, I hoped that after talking with Ramón, things would fall into place.

I opened the front door and went inside. The house lights were on, and I could hear the television from the bedroom. I walked through the kitchen and laundry to a room in the front corner of the house. This had been Uncle Stewart's office, a room I seldom entered. I did, however, use it to store certain things that I had collected and carried with me over the years which I never considered bringing back to use while living on the CR: gear from my Army days, gear from my life as a Police Officer, and later, Detective.

I stepped into the room and flipped the wall switch. The overhead light flickered, then came to full bloom, illuminating the office and all its contents. I walked around a large walnut desk stained to display its gorgeous grain and patterning anchored in the center of the room. An oversized leather wingback chair stitched in a crossing pattern that made for bulbous cushions across the seat and back rolled with ease from its commanding spot. I reached into the knee hole and removed a chrome-cast, reinforced aluminum tactical case and placed it on the desktop.

I dialed the code on its combination lock and depressed the mechanism that released the clasps. A simultaneous *click* sounded out, and it was unlocked. Opening the case was like rediscovering a long-lost group of friends.

Resting in the center of the custom-cut foam inlay was my battlefield green Glock 17. The overhead lighting glinted away from the steel barrel as if fleeing from want of reflection. This harbinger of controlled chaos demanded precision, firing with deadly accuracy in a symphony of rounds dancing in rhythm with each pull of the trigger. Nestled in a cutout to the beast's right were two polymer-coated magazines fully loaded with 9mm NATO, 124-grain FMJ bullets. On the opposite side of the case were two rectangular cutouts. One held a Nitecore P20 tactical flashlight. The other cradled a Holosun HS507C red dot sight. Two larger custom cutouts below the Glock 17 held the upper and lower receivers of my Colt AR-15.

I pulled the Glock from the case. The gun fit perfectly in my hand, its form molding to my grip, and its weight feeling like a seamless extension of my body. I depressed the magazine release button and slid it out to inspect its load. It was full but hungry. After sliding the magazine back into place, I performed a quick hand press check. A single bullet was revealed, chambered and ready. I placed the two additional magazines in the rear pocket of my jeans, then tucked the firearm into my belt. I slid the flashlight into my front pocket. Leaving the sight and the AR-15 for another day, I closed and locked the case and exited my uncle's office.

As I passed through the laundry room, I grabbed a

fresh long-sleeved button shirt that had been hanging in wait for mending. I slipped it on to conceal my weapon, buttoned the bottommost button, and rolled the sleeves up three times. My navy Astros trucker cap hung on a hook on the back of the laundry door.

"You brought me a championship last year, maybe you'll bring me some luck on this case," I said, putting it on.

The digital numbers on the microwave glowed blue.
9:30

If you're on time, you're late! a voice from the distant past rang out in my head.

Nothing had changed in the house since I went inside to prepare for the meeting. The lights remained untouched, and the television continued its rambling in the bedroom. I started to walk in to speak with Raven, but what could I say that would do any good? The best thing I could do was come home. It was all she ever asked of me when I was on the job, and it was I promise I kept each and every time.

I slipped out the door and got into the Explorer. As I backed away from the house, I saw Raven appear in the window of the living room. She pressed her hand against the glass and watched as I drove away.

CHAPTER THIRTY-THREE

If not for the blanket of stars and a sliver of moon, I would not have been able to see two feet in front of me. *El Lobo Vista* was a secluded overlook that once catered to picnickers and day hikers. It had been a well-known spot just outside of town but had become rundown and forgotten over the years. Now, with the scattered beer cans and litter, it was more suited for vagrants or used as a teenage late-night rendezvous.

I got out and waited next to the Explorer until my eyes adjusted to the surroundings. Looking around, I saw it was the only car in the gravel lot. Closing my eyes, I remained quiet and listened, tuning in, then filtering through every sound my ears could hear. Aside from the scurrying noises among the brush and the distant high-pitched warble of a screech owl, I heard nothing that would cause alarm until I took my first step away from the Explorer.

I pursed my lips at the crunch my shoes made on the gravel.

If anyone was watching, driving in would have already given away my position, I thought.

My senses were on overload as I walked the short path from the parking area to the overlook. I could see three concrete tables and benches, each with a rusted-out grill freestanding on a single steel pole. One had corroded to the point of toppling over leaving a jagged stump where the pit had once perched. Beyond the tables was a chain-link fence, bent from misuse and age, that acted as a boundary between the picnic area and the edge of *El Lobo Vista*. It sagged in spots where people had climbed over to tempt their fate near the dangerous ledge.

I walked to the fence and looked out into a pit of darkness. The old, galvanized steel wires groaned as their webbing stretched under my weight when I leaned my palms on the rickety railing. Absent of light, there was no telling how deep the cliff fell. In the distance, headlights traced the curves of RR170. A warm breeze climbed the drop-off carrying dry smells of dead grass and old dust.

I turned around and focused on the path leading to and from the gravel lot. It seemed to grow longer, stretching out like the cursed hallways of the Overlook Hotel. As if materializing from the darkness, a shadow grew, slowly filling the center of the walkway, then taking the shape of a man.

"Here's Johnny," I whispered to myself.

I watched with interest as the man drew near. My fingers tingled, yearning to slip into position around the grip of my concealed Glock, but I remained steadfast. The man made no sudden movements as he ambled his way into the heart of the picnic area. He spoke up when the ambient light began to uncover his face.

"You are very trusting."

"You left me no choice, Ramón," I said as I stepped away from the fence. My senses were on high alert, my legs and chest filling with adrenaline.

He lifted his chin and turned his head to one side. The hand tattoo looked like a black hole on his neck. "When you have lived a life like I have lived, you learn not to take chances."

"You took a huge chance turning your back on whatever cartel you were working for, or are you still under orders?"

Ramón fixed his eyes on mine. Black on black, details swallowed within the dark. He studied me.

"I thought loyalty was taken to the grave."

Undeterred, he spoke. "When I was ten years old, I was forced to work for *Diablos Muerte*, a gang in Sinaloa with direct ties to the cartel. The jobs were small at first. Follow a man and return with his location, deliver a package, steal a wallet or passport. They told me if I did not do what I was told, not to worry, they would not kill me. Instead, they would cut the fingers from my mother's hands, then take her feet, but they would make sure that she did not die. Not right away. If I continued to disobey, they would cut her more until they took her head."

Ramón's face was stone, but his words wavered when he spoke of his mother. I had heard of the horrifying methods used by the mafia and the cartels to punish their enemies and to place fear among the people.

"You speak of loyalty, but you have no idea. I did what I was told to protect myself and my family. I killed a man when I was thirteen. From there, it was no looking back. I became someone else. A dangerous man."

"And now you expect me to believe whatever you say you know about the killings on the CR?" I paused, eyes locked on his. "Was it you?"

"No, it was not me. The last man I killed was the man who killed my mother."

"So, you turned?"

"No!" Ramón said, his voice becoming heated.

Watch his eyes, Cass, I told myself. *Look and learn, learn and look.*

"When a Halcón..."

"¿*Halcón*?" I interrupted.

"Falcon. A man who watches like a spy."

I nodded, and he continued.

"Most we know, some we do not, but they are always

watching. This *Halcón*, Miguel, one day he come out of nowhere. I was with my mother walking from the plaza in town. He says I am not doing what was asked of me. I call him a liar. Without warning, he pulled his gun and hit me with the barrel here."

Ramón pointed to a scar on the side of his head.

"*¡Pinche cabrón!* I fell to the ground, bleeding everywhere. My mother..." Ramón paused, nostrils flaring as the memory replayed itself in vivid detail. "She yelled and cursed him for being a coward. She was very proud and would not back down. At first, Miguel found it funny. He laughed, then returned his attention to me, telling me things he would do to me if I was not *loyal*."

As he talked, we moved together toward the railing. He leaned forward and grabbed the crossbar with both hands and squeezed, continuing his story.

"I spit at him and tried to get up. He kicked me in the stomach and stood over me with the gun pointed at my head. 'All dogs should know their place,' he said. My mother's yells turned to pleas. She begged him not to shoot, not to kill her son. Miguel grew tired of her whining and turned to face her. 'All dogs,' he said again. 'Especially this bitch.' He laughed, then raised his gun and shot her in the head. My mother fell face first on the ground, eyes wide, staring right at me. Miguel kicked me over and over until everything went black. When I woke up, he was gone. My mother was on her back. Three fingers had been cut from her right hand and stuffed into her mouth. It was Miguel warning me not to say anything. It took more than a week to find him and get him alone with me. When I did find him, it was Miguel who begged for his life. When I finally had my revenge, he did not die for many days, much like I had been warned when I was ten. After that, there was no going back."

"So, you came to the United States."

"Yes."

"And now you work for Sinclair."

"Yes, but not always."

"Who else did you work for?"

Ramón turned to face me resting his waist on the sagging fence. His chest puffed out like a rooster. He breathed in slow, determined puffs in and out of his nose.

"Callahan."

"Stewart Callahan? My uncle?"

"Yes. He was the first to take me in."

I stepped away from the fence, trying to decide if I could believe anything Ramón was saying.

"Mr. Callahan, he give me a chance. If not for him, I would be in jail or probably dead."

"Why did you leave the CR for the Double S?" I said, turning back to face Ramón.

"Because of Flint. He did not like me. We had too many problems. Mr. Callahan talked to Mr. Sinclair about taking me on."

"Just like that?"

"When you live out here, men respect the word of another. Sinclair took me on, but it was hard for a long time. Still, I was alive, and no one in Mexico knew where I was. That all changed when..."

As if jolted by a volt of electricity, Ramón thrust forward. His head snapped back, and his arms flailed to the side. In a split second of whiplash, the distinct, thunderous report of a rifle shot followed. Ramón toppled to his knees, doubled over in a bout of violent, hoarse coughs. Blood sprayed from his mouth with each forced breath.

A second shot rang out from the dark beyond the failing fence. The bullet zinged off one of the galvanized steel line posts, ricocheting so close to the side of my head that I felt the wind from its path. I caught a hint of flash that looked like a distant firefly as I dove to the ground. I quickly rolled to my knees and pulled my Glock, filling the air with a barrage of bullets flying at the shooter's defiladed position. I ejected the spent magazine and replaced it with a full one, then paused.

The depth and distance and the blackness that engulfed the area between us made it impossible to know if any of my shots hit their mark. As the echoes of gunfire drifted away, a void of silence hovered over *El Lobo Vista*.

I turned and crawled to Ramón. He lay flat on his stomach. I could see blood oozing from a bullet hole in the middle of his back. His gasps for air sounded more like someone trying to inflate a wet balloon.

"Shit!"

I tore off my outer shirt and wadded it into a ball, then pressed firmly against his wound. Ramón wailed under my hand.

"Easy, Ramón," I said.

With my free hand, I fished my cell phone from my pocket and called Chance. 911 would take too long, and Chance would have the capabilities to mobilize the help we needed.

RING...RING...RIN...

"*Hey, Amigo. How 'bout that first day on the job, eh?*"

"Code 2, 10-71. Chance, I need an ambulance as fast as you can get one to *El Lobo Vista*. I've got a man down. GSW to his back. The shooter was downrange somewhere between the highway and the overlook just north of the construction cutoff. Get Boss and Santos, whoever is on duty out on RR170, and sweep in both directions."

"*What the...?*"

"We need to move quickly on this, Chance. I can't lose this guy."

"*Hold on*," Chance said.

I looked at Ramón, his head lay cheek-down on the ground. His mouth dripped with spit and blood. I could hear Chance through the line talking with someone over a radio. Ramón groaned, then began coughing violently again. If I did not do something, he was going to die right here.

"Chance!" I yelled into the phone. "Where are we on the ambulance?"

"They're coming, but it's going to be at least fifteen minutes."

"He doesn't have that long. Stay online with me so we can coordinate a transfer to the ambulance en route. I'm getting him outta here."

"10-4 Cass."

I clicked the phone to speaker and slid it between my belt and stomach. I stuffed my gun on the opposite side of my belt. The barrel was still hot, but I had no time to lose.

"Come on, Ramón. Time to see how tough you really are. Stay with me."

I carefully rolled him onto his back, then bent both of his legs at the knee. Pressing down on the top of his feet with my right foot, I leaned over and grabbed both of his arms at the wrist. With a firm pull, I brought Ramón to his feet. Then, I squatted and ducked my head under his right armpit so that the weight of his body rested on my right shoulder. I wrapped my arms around the back of his knees and lifted straight up.

Ramón moaned at the force my shoulder made against his weakened, injured body, but he was secure and ready to move. As fast as my legs could go with the added weight, I carried him down the pathway and across the gravel parking lot to the car. The muscles in my thighs burned, and my back ached from the exertion. Sweat dripped from my forehead. As we approached the Explorer, I dug into my left front pocket and found the key fob to unlock the doors. A quick press of the correct button, and we were in business.

I opened the passenger side door and eased him into the cockpit. The interior light illuminated Ramón's ghostly face. He had lost a significant amount of blood, and his breathing was so shallow that only the bubbles forming on his lips gave me hope that he still had time. Once he was secured inside, I closed the door, ran around to the driver's side, and hopped in. I pushed the ignition switch, and the Explorer roared to life.

I dropped the car into reverse and punched the gas. With enough room to turn around, I slammed on the brakes. We slid backward as I shifted into drive, kicking up stones and dirt and spinning the wheels. Finally gaining traction, the Explorer lurched ahead, thrusting us back into our seats behind the powerful engine.

I flipped on my brights and activated my hazard lights as we sped along the windy road toward the cutoff at the construction site. As we descended, I could see flashing blue and red strobes in the distance racing toward us on RR170.

"Hang on Ramón. Damn it, hang on!"

CHAPTER THIRTY-FOUR

"What the hell is going on?" I asked Chance as we talked in the ambulance bay at Brewster Regional Hospital. "I mean, damn! Have things always been this bad around here?"

Chance's radio squawked. Deputy Santos was on the other end of the call.

"Completed a sweep of the immediate area around El Lobo Vista picnic overlook. I'll head north to El Povo road, then circle back."

The radio squawked again followed by a female voice.

"The cutoff is clear. Proceeding southeast on RR170," Deputy Boss announced.

Two additional patrol units were scouring the low ground in the vicinity of where I had estimated the shooter to be hiding, but they had yet to report anything substantial.

"Cass," Chance said. "South Brewster has its problems just like everywhere else, but my friend, you have stumbled onto something."

I looked through the sliding doors to the emergency room, wondering if Ramón would pull through. We had met the ambulance on the road and were successful in transferring him into the EMT's care, but his prognosis was grave.

"What were you doing with him up there?"

"Ramón approached me in town earlier this evening and said he had information about the killings on the CR. Said he wanted to speak with me in private and that I should meet him at *El Lobo Vista* at ten o'clock. Oddly enough, I had planned to seek him out tomorrow morning."

"Why Ramón?"

"Flint's idea. We had a come-to-Jesus moment earlier today. Among others, I had him pegged as a possible suspect. Turns out my suspicions about him were unfounded. He suggested I speak with Ramón but didn't offer an explanation as to why."

"And now Ramón is fighting for his life. Cass, you may have just led the lamb to slaughter."

I paced away from Chance, then spun around and pulled my hat off, slapping my side in frustration.

"The only person that knows I went to meet Ramón was Raven." I walked back to Chance and lowered my voice. "How well do you know Sinclair? Ramón's been a part of the Double S for a while now. Maybe he's involved. Maybe Ramón saw or heard something and figured if he didn't come forward, they'd pin the blame on him. The guy has a seriously checkered past."

"I know all about Ramón, Cass. As for Sinclair, he may be an old, crotchety S.O.B., but that's about the end of it. He's been around these parts as long as Stewart. Aside from dealing with his crass personality, I've never had an issue with him."

"What about his grandson?"

"Joe?" Chance chuckled. "That boy is greener than you ever were. Plays the role well though. Talks fancy. Acts tough, but always had 'ol Roy to hide behind."

"Or Ramón," I added.

Chance tilted his head and gave me an inquisitive look.

"The morning I found the first dead body, they happened along, offering to help square things away. Ramón did most of the talking. Joe was polite, at first, but when I declined their help, he turned into more of what I would have expected from a Sinclair. Ramón pulled him out of there before Joe had a chance to say or do something regrettable."

I paused, replaying the scene in my head for details I might have missed before, then remembered Ramón said one final thing.

"Ramón said something to me in Spanish before they rode off. *El...que...fuego*, something about fire maybe?"

"Your Spanish is terrible, *amigo*, but you are close. I think what he probably said was *El que juega con fuego, se quema*."

"That's it. Was he threatening me?"

"It means, he who plays with fire gets burned. It is an old Mexican proverb, not a threat, although maybe he was trying to tell you something."

The two of us stood without an answer. We had no motive for the killings on the CR. No witnesses. The evidence we did have was insufficient until we found the gun that had been used in the murders. Now with Ramón fighting for his life, there was no telling what information he wanted to share.

"Is there anyone else who might know something?"

"Cass, your guess is as good as mine. Let's just hope Ramón pulls through."

I put my crumpled cap back on my head and glanced inside once more.

"There is nothing more you can do tonight. Go home to Raven and start fresh in the morning." Chance said, slapping me on the shoulder. "If one of the patrol units turns up anything, I will call you."

I did not want to admit it, but he was right. I nodded, then started to walk away.

"Hey, Cass," he called out.

I turned to look at him over my shoulder.

"Go home means, *go home*."

When I reached the Explorer, the interior of the passenger seat looked like a scene out of a Stephen King novel. There were blood spatters on the dash and a circular smudge on the window where Ramón had propped his head. The carpet floor had drying patches of red mixed with gravel dust. The seat was in ruin. The backrest was still moist. Trickles of blood had created trailing stains that made the leather look as if it were crying. The base of the seat held sticky puddles of coagulating blood accumulating around the stitching and in the concave corners of the cushion.

I rolled all the windows down to help clear out the stale air. Still, as I drove away from the hospital, a distinct metallic tang lingered in the Explorer. The time on the center console scolded me for being out so late.

12:34

"Twice in one day," I said. "I gotta clean this shit up."

I turned onto Main Street and headed for a Texaco gas station that I knew had a self-serve car wash. I pulled into the closest bay and rummaged around for a few quarters but came up empty. I looked in my wallet and found a five and three one-dollar bills. I rolled up the windows, then turned off the Explorer and went to look for the change machine. It was easy to locate, but the bright orange light near the bill feeder was illuminated, signaling it was out of change.

"Figures," I said to myself.

I turned and considered my options. The gas station was closed, and Tío Andrés, a local dive bar across the street, looked like it was shutting down. I could drive home and use the hose from the house, but I was going to need a high-power spray and someone else's vacuum to tackle the mess in question.

"Whelp, Tío Andrés it is."

I left the Explorer in the washing bay and jogged across the street. The wooden exterior of the building showed years of wear with minimal upkeep. It was in need of fresh paint, and portions of the outer wall looked like a carpenter's worst nightmare. Scrap boards and wood had been nailed over wood rot, then heavily caulked, giving it a zombie-like appearance.

The building that never dies, I thought, slowing to a walk.

The perimeter was well lit except it looked as if Tío Andrés, whoever he was, had missed the memo that Christmas was over. The back corner of the building looked as if a vehicle had missed its parking spot and rammed into it. If I was able to get change and make it out before this shack of a bar collapsed, I would call that a win.

As I walked toward the entrance, I saw two barflies loitering on the deck. They both wore biker jackets that looked familiar, and each gave me a wary look. I was taller than both men, but what I had in height, they doubled in girth. One wore a durag and sported a bird's nest mess of a beard below his chin. The other had long black hair pulled into a ponytail behind his head. A thick, black mustache covered his upper lip. He wore black, fingerless gloves and a tangle of chains around his neck that clanked when he moved in my way.

"Bar's closed," he slurred.

I walked around him and reached for the door's pull handle. The glass front door, although frosted to keep onlookers from gawking at what went on inside, had a crack that ran from the top of the frame to the bottom.

"You deaf?" Durag said. "The bar ain't open."

"Thanks for the tip," I said. "But I'm not looking for a drink."

"Well, what the...what the hell are ya doin' here, then?"

I ignored Neck Chain Guy's attempt to trap me in a debate and headed inside. The smell was overwhelming. A haze of lingering smoke hung just below the ceiling like a cloud of toxic fog. I could feel the stickiness of the floor as I stepped over to the bar. I glanced around, looking for the barkeep, but all I saw was dirty glasses and unattended spills on the counter. I turned to see two men sitting at a booth near an ancient-looking jukebox. Neon lights hung all over, providing most of the lighting save one fluorescent light that hung above a raggedy pool table.

"What'chu want? De bar ees closed."

I spun around and had to look down to see who had spoken to me. Behind the bar stood a man no more than five feet tall. When our eyes met, he stepped onto a pedestal on the floor and glared at me.

"Ju 'ave a pro'lem?"

Feeling more amused than attacked, I calmly answered the little man's question.

"No. No problem," I said. "Just looking for some change."

I pulled my wallet from my pocket and pulled out the five and three ones, placing them on the counter.

"Ju theenk we are a bank?"

His mix of temper and alcohol did nothing but excite his little-man syndrome.

"No, but I could use some quarters if you have any."

The man reached out and grabbed my money, then stepped down from his pedestal and reached under the bar. As his hands disappeared from view, I immediately shifted into alert mode, ready for any sudden move. In a flash, he remounted the pedestal, producing a handful of coins that he splashed onto the counter with surprising speed, as if a skilled bank teller had counted the exact change due in a mere instant.

"That shoul' do eet," he said.

I looked at the pile of change, noting the quarters, but also the mix of dimes, nickels, and pennies strewn about. I smiled, realizing what was going on.

"Looks to be a little light," I said.

"No," he said. "The res' ees a teep for dee har' work I do for ju."

I thought so.

I cupped one hand below the counter's edge and slid the change into it, then dropped the load into my front pocket. I gave the man a pursed smile.

"Thank you, friend," I said. "I'll probably see you again."

The man looked at me as if I had just slept with his sister.

"Ju ain't no frien' of mine. Ju een dee wrong place. Get to walkeeng eef you know what ees good for ju."

As I turned to leave, his attitude seeped in, giving me a moment of hesitation. I stepped back and whirled around to face him.

"Look. I have no problem with you or anyone else in this town," I lied. "Hell, I'm pretty new around here."

With a slip of my hand, I pulled my badge into view and slammed it on the counter, then reached across and grabbed the little man by the collar. It was not my style, but I had had a long, exasperating day, and this speed bump of a barkeep just jostled loose the last string of my remaining patience. I pulled him close to me, lifting him off the pedestal and sliding his chest across the bar.

"But...since I've been here, I've been shot at, nearly run down, lied to, threatened, shot at again, and now because some asshole decided to try and kill a friend of mine, I'm stuck cleaning out the blood from my favorite car while I hang around to see if he'll pull through. So, if I call you a friend, believe me, I mean it because if we are not friends..."

I paused and picked up my badge with my free hand and tapped the barkeep on the nose.

"...we may have a problem after all."

The men at the corner booth stood and were watching our altercation at the bar.

"Now," I said with a calm voice. "What is your name?"

"Andrés. It's Andrés."

"This your place, Andrés?"

"*Sí*. Eet ees mine."

I let Andrés go and stepped away from the counter. He wiggled his way onto his pedestal and stood glaring at me in what looked like a mix of disrespect and fear.

"Here's a tip, Andrés. The next time someone is made to leave a little extra cash for you on their bill, use it to clean this place up. I may want to bring a few more of *my* friends around one of these days."

Without another word, I turned and headed out the door. Durag and Neck Chain Guy were still grumbling on the front porch as I walked past.

"Night, fellas," I said.

Inebriation responded with a friendly farewell of its own before they realized it was I who had been the target of their bullying mentality when we had first met. Durag stuttered as his words fumbled from his lips, causing Neck Chain Guy to lose interest in me and laugh at him. I heard them squabble as I jogged across the street. I still had a disgusting job to do, and then there was Raven to consider once I returned home.

CHAPTER THIRTY-FIVE

The CR was quiet. A single light remained on in the house, illuminating the windows with a dull yellow hue as the beams fought to reach out from its source. I left the Explorer running, leaned my head back on the seat, and closed my eyes. Scene after scene from the past few days played themselves out in my head, causing my thoughts to blur and a pulsing ache to form beneath my temples. A multitude of possibilities tugged my suspicions in alternating directions, and yet I had no justifiable leads in the case.

The damp smell of leather and pine scent fragrance filtered into my nose, interrupting my thoughts. I opened my eyes and glanced at the passenger seat where Ramón had nearly bled out. A combination of the soapy foam brush and high-powered sprayer at the car wash removed most of the blood and grime, and the industrial-strength vacuum sucked up its share of the water and funk. I added a spritz of what had been described as auto-enhancing deodorant to the carpet and seat, but it ended up smelling more along the lines of watered-down Pine-Sol all-purpose cleaner.

Before turning off the ignition, I lowered the windows of the Explorer. It was well after one in the morning. A warm breeze kept a steady current, blowing from the southwest, straight past the house and barn. Without the possibility of rain, I was optimistic that all would be dry by daybreak.

My shoes squeaked on the porch boards as I walked to the house, leaving wet footprints with each step. I had a brief notion to walk to the burn pile, strip down, and torch everything I had been wearing. Blood and sweat and grime inundated my shirt and pants, and there was no forgiving at the carwash for my basketball shoes. Maybe it was time I bought a pair of boots.

I thought better of it and kicked off my shoes, leaving them outside the front door, another mistake at which Flint would have scoffed. *Just gave a snake er a scorpion a nice little hidey-hole there, slick.* He would not have been wrong, but right now, I did not care.

Turning the knob, I found the door was unlocked and slipped quietly inside. I walked into the living room and placed my badge and gun on the coffee table, then continued to the kitchen. The stovetop light was on, lighting my way to the laundry room. I removed my clothes and tossed them directly into the washer, added a Tide pod, and turned the dial to heavy duty. Leaning forward, I balanced myself on the rumbling washer, relieved to finally be home yet anxious to find answers to questions still racing around in my head.

I walked to the refrigerator and opened the door. The pressurized blast of air felt refreshing on my bare skin. I stood motionless for a moment, enjoying the escaping cool. The soft white light of the refrigerator shone over my naked body. Looking down, I saw the gauze on my knees sagged and needed changing. My thumb was less swollen but had turned shades of purple and green along my palm. The rest of me looked as if I had spent the afternoon in the pool, clammy and shriveled. I removed the jug of milk from the bottom shelf, took three long gulps, then replaced it and closed the door.

The light over the stove was all I needed to see. I returned to the laundry room and was lucky enough to find a pile of fresh clothes on the folding table. I pulled on a pair of boxers and an Aggie Parent T-shirt Spencer had sent home from school and was turning away from the folding table when I noticed something out of place.

Sitting by itself near the edge of the table was a small, black USB drive. I dismissed it as one of Raven's and walked back into the kitchen to the breakfast table and had a seat. It had been an exasperating day, yet I was wide awake.

I grabbed a banana from a fruit bowl in the middle of the table and began peeling away the skin. Biting through the fruit, I chewed on more than just its tenderness. I reversed my line of thinking, playing through the most recent events first, then moving backward through each in turn. This method forced me to focus on the specific timeline and details from a whole new perspective and would sometimes trigger even the most minute bit of information that may have been overlooked.

Ramón is shot...the shooter...Ramón coming up to me after dinner...Raven and the foal...removing the last two dead bodies...my chat with Flint...Javi's Autoparts...swearing in with Chance...the Gateway to Paradise...helping María and Isabella...being shot at and chased on the CR...discovering María and Isabella...discovering the bodies in the fissure...the jump drive...crawling into the...

I dropped the banana on the table and stood up.

"Holy shit!"

With four lunging steps, I stood in the laundry room staring down at the small, black USB drive. I picked it up and examined it as if it were a rare diamond, discovered by chance in the most unlikely of places.

"What secrets are you hiding, my friend?" I asked.

Clenching it in my fist, I retrieved my laptop and sat back at the breakfast table. The bright flash of the screen and the hum of the hard drive spinning to life gave me a moment of hope as I searched for a light, any light at the end of the dark tunnel in which I had felt trapped.

The chimes of the computer sounded out, and the home screen appeared displaying a picture I had taken of Raven and Spencer during a road trip through the mountains some years ago. I inserted the drive into the USB port and waited for the computer to discover it. Another chime sounded out, and a text box opened asking how I wanted to proceed.

"Open sesame," I said to the computer while clicking the option to *explore device*.

A new window opened on the desktop with multiple saved folders and documents. It was a load of information to sift through, but there was a problem...they were all listed as numbers or in Spanish.

"Fucksake!" I grumbled.

"What are you complaining about at this hour?"

I flinched, startled by a voice I did not expect to hear until morning if she was even talking to me by then.

"Shit, you scared me, Raven."

"Good. It's the least I could do."

She reached for a glass from the cupboard and filled it from the filtered refrigerator spout, then walked over and stood across the table from me.

"What are you working on now?" she asked. "And what's that smell?"

"It's been a crazy couple of hours," I said.

She sipped her water and gave me a look that suggested I owed her an explanation. I skipped over the part about Ramón having been shot and began with the USB drive and the information within.

"How well can you read Spanish?"

"Depends."

"On what? Dialect, slang, regionalism?"

She shook her head and took another sip. I did not have time for guessing games or to figure out what exactly she was expecting of me.

"Rave, I could use some help."

"And I could use an apology."

Raven lowered her glass to the table and glared at me. A moment before, I enjoyed the cool of the refrigerator, but now the whole kitchen felt as cold as ice. To add to the mounting headache I had from swirling around speculative scenarios in my mind, I felt terrible. I did owe her an apology, and I would give her an explanation.

"Look," I said standing up. "I am sorry about earlier tonight. This whole mess has become one big clusterfuck. I want to make it up to you, but I have to see this case through."

She watched me as I inched around the table toward her. Expecting the remainder of her water to be splashed across my face, I extended my arms and offered her an easy target. Instead, I felt the warmth of her embrace and the press of her cheek against my chest.

"You're a mess, Cass Callahan. What the hell am I going to do with you?"

"Anything you want, Little Bird."

She pivoted her head to look up into my eyes. The anger was gone though I could tell the hurt still lingered.

"I love you," I said.

I leaned down and kissed her forehead. I could feel the rise and fall of her chest and the tightening grasp of her arms around me. She squeezed three times, returning the sentiment without the need for words.

We stood in the kitchen in each other's arms, comfortable and at peace.

"Rave," I whispered. "Would you help me?"

With her head pressed against me, she nodded, then released her hold of me.

"What are you working on?" she asked.

"It's on the drive."

"Hey, I found a black one in your jeans. It's on the..."

"I found it."

"Hope it still works. I didn't know it was in your pocket until after the wash was done."

"Looks to be running properly. The problem is all the folders and titles for documents are in Spanish. Think you could help me translate?"

Raven walked over and took my seat behind the laptop. She glanced over the open window, mouthing words to herself.

"Have you tried opening any of these folders yet?"

"Was about to when you came in," I said walking around behind her to look over her shoulder. "Let's start at the top and work our way across."

We started with the first folder titled *Agua Prieta, Sonora 31.3278_109.5490*. Raven double-clicked on the folder, opening it to reveal two documents. The first file was named *Industrias Azteca*. The second file read *Muertos o Feria*.

"Industrias Azteca?" I said, sounding very American.

"Aztec Industries," Raven said, translating the words. "Wonder what that is?"

I pulled out my phone and typed the name in the search engine and had a list of immediate answers.

"Google says it is a textile factory located in Agua Prieta, Sonora, Mexico," I said, scrolling through the results. "It's also a disco club in Argentina and a roofing company out of Phoenix. What about the second file, *muertos o feria*?"

"*Muertos* means death," Raven said. "*Feria* is another way to say money without calling it money. It's slang that refers to a medium of exchange, like silver."

"Death money?" I said, confused.

"Sort of," she replied. "But put together, it reads, death *or* money."

"Click on it. Let's check it out."

Raven double-clicked the icon over the file name, opening *Muertos o Feria*.

"It's a spreadsheet," she said. "Look at the heading.

Industria Azteca Entregas. Below that, there are subheadings over the columns. *Contabilidad*...accounting, *Entregas*...deliveries, *Obreros*...laborers, *Miembros de la Junta*...board members..."

Raven paused.

"What is it?"

"The last two. I don't understand. Why would they be on a company spreadsheet."

"What do they say?"

"*Familia de los Miembros de la Junta*...family of board members, and, oh God! *Orden de Matar*..." Raven's voice wavered. "Kill Order. Cass, there are names listed below."

"Let's not overreact. Close this folder, and let's go to the next one."

She clicked on folder *Bacalar, Quintana Roo 18.68031_88.39190*. Two files appeared, one titled *Autopartes Chilero*, and the other *Muertos o Feria*.

"This is unreal," Raven said, astonished.

We spent the next hour opening and combing through each folder in turn.

Ciudad Mante, Tamaulipas 22.74290_98.972

Dolores Hidalgo, Guanajuato 21.15640_100.93320

El Fuerte, Sinaloa 26.41941_108.62087

Ruidoso, Chihuahua 33.49203_105.38387

Izamal, Yucatán 20.93486_89.01753

The list went on and on, each naming a different factory or business, each with a spreadsheet that included a *Kill Order* column. The amount of information we had at our fingertips was mind-blowing.

As we worked our way through the USB drive, we found rows of saved documents below the folders. Most were correspondence, all in Spanish, and were quite lengthy. We opted to focus on the files that were easier to decipher and to flag ones that were more difficult for later review. There were documents with travel routes and directions, lists of military checkpoints, lists of churches and priests for each, addresses of government offices, and the names and ranks of police officers in all the major towns from Monterrey to Mexico City.

One file named *Cruce de Mulas* caught my attention.

"Know what that means?" I asked Raven as I leaned over her shoulder and pointed.

Raven paused. She had already been a tremendous help, but I could tell she was losing steam quickly. We both were.

"It says 'Mule Crossing'."

"Let's take a look at that one," I said.

Raven double-clicked the file, opening another spreadsheet with lists of coordinates, dates, times, weight, and cargo. We delved into this document, noting the specified dates and cargo, and did our best to cross-reference the coordinates to see if there were any commonalities or connections related to the stretch of Mexico just south of the CR. Raven read the first set of numbers.

"26.10781° N 98.27112° W"

I punched the coordinates into my phone.

"Reynosa, Tamaulipas. That's near McAllen, Texas. Keep 'em coming," I said.

One by one, we discovered the location of each set of coordinates, all of which were in or near a border town or crossing from Texas to California. They were not organized geographically, which kept us bouncing around on the map to locate the next spot. As we neared the bottom of the list, Raven called out the next set of numbers.

"29.45824° N 104.21875° W"

When the location revealed itself, my fingers tingled as if they had fallen asleep and my chest burned as if desperate for oxygen. Raven sensed my concern.

"What is it? Where is this location?"

I showed her the map on my phone.

"It's right here. Just across the river from the CR."

It was then I began to understand. Balde Ramos had stolen highly sensitive information from either the

Mexican mafia or one of the cartels. We could confirm that one of their smuggling routes cut straight into the CR from Mexico. As disconcerting as that was, we still had no idea with which organization we could be dealing because the drive lacked the name of the cartel responsible.

The last icon we discovered at the very bottom of the list of folders and documents was a .mp4 file.

"It's a video file," Raven said. "Should I play it?"

I needed to see what was on the file, but I was concerned that it could be a video of something that might upset Raven. The mafia and cartels were brutal. From their perspective, the acts they carried out as punishment or the lengths they went to to send a message were effective techniques that instilled fear and maintained order but were some of the most inhumane atrocities ever to come out of Mexico.

"Maybe I should watch it alone," I suggested.

Raven looked at me. Her eyes were bloodshot from the late night and bright computer lights. Her cheeks sagged with exhaustion.

"I can handle anything that is on that video, Cass."

She paused to look at the computer screen again. The cursor blinked in place like a warning light hung above the crossroads of a one-stop town.

"If it looks like something I don't want to see, I'll stop the recording and let you finish on your own. Deal?"

"Okay," I said reluctantly.

We both focused on the laptop as Raven moved the cursor into position and double-clicked the .mp4 icon. The screen flashed, and a video window appeared. The picture was black. Raven dragged the cursor to the bottom of the window and hovered over the play button.

"Ready?" she asked.

I nodded and Raven double-clicked the mouse.

The black screen wobbled at first, then using a flashlight to illuminate his face, Balde Ramos sat in front of the camera. His face was covered in sweat, and his eyes looked as if he had not slept in days.

"This message is for FBI Special Agent, Thomas Zuñiga. My name is Balde Ramos," he began. *"If you are seeing this and I am not standing with you, something must have gone terribly wrong, and I am dead."*

INTERLUDE 5
BALDE RAMOS

It's three-thirty in the morning, and the shit is getting too thick to stay put. I was able to locate and copy files from the Camargo Cartel accounting firm's mainframe detailing everything about their illegal dealings on both sides of the border from Texas to California. This is big. Bigger than we expected, and now I've got to get the hell out of Mexico. This drive is the key to bringing them down. I don't know how the cartel knows, but they discovered that data had been accessed at the firm and have already executed two of the accountants in charge of that information. I don't think they suspect me, but I'm not waiting around to find out. I had to kill my way into a smuggling job that will get me to the border somewhere south of Presidio, Texas. I overheard the other two mules saying the place was like paradise, but the terrain was extreme. Not sure what that means. We are scheduled to cross around two a.m. and are to wait for our contact to meet us near a place called the Double S. Someone named Sinclair will take the drop. Once he does, we are instructed to return to Mexico immediately. Fuck that. My only hope lies with Agent Zuñiga; he's the only one who knows I'm undercover and promised to protect my family should something happen to me. This drive must reach him—his word is all I have left. Keep your promise,

Agent Zuñiga! I've held up my end of the bargain. Get my family out! Now!

CHAPTER THIRTY-SIX

𝒞𝓡

My mouth nearly dropped to the table when I heard Balde Ramos say that his contact was...*Sinclair*!

"Skip back," I said abruptly.

Raven dismissed my urgency and did as I asked. We listened again, and there it was, plain as day, plain as the twisted scowl on the old man's face.

"Sinclair," I said aloud. "Now we have motive."

"You think Sinclair killed those men and then tried to hide them on the CR?"

"Think about it. If he were running a smuggling ring, what better place to discard the bodies than on land that is standing unused, except for his cattle? And he had access whenever he wanted."

"What about Floyd Huckabee?"

"Yeah, he's got access to the CR as well, but to the south. Until his name is mentioned or I have reason to believe he is working with Sinclair, I do not need to pursue him at this time."

"Wasn't he just out at the house this afternoon?"

"Yeah. And he was pissed. One of his men crossed hairs with Flint this morning. We both know how that ended up."

"Bad for the other guy?"

"Right. I think Huckabee would be more likely to seek revenge on Flint than be involved with smuggling. He's West Texas all the way, God, country, land, history. He's not likely wired to think like a criminal."

"And Sinclair is? Seems to me they aren't that different. Most of these ranchers run in the same circles. Your uncle Stewart, too."

Raven had a point, but I had an iron-clad accusation from beyond the grave staring me right in the face. *Sinclair*. Balde had just named him as the contact, and now he was dead.

I glanced at the clock on the microwave.

4:17

It was early but there was no way I was going to sleep on this.

"Phone," I said, patting myself down. "Where's my phone?"

I looked first in the laundry room, then cringed as I considered it may be tumbling around the washer with the rest of my dirty clothes. I opened the lid and rummaged through the soaked load, but came up empty.

"You leave it in the Explorer?" Raven called out before I started tossing her neatly folded clothing aside to look.

I skidded barefoot out to the Explorer and found my phone still resting in the wireless charging pad in the middle of the cockpit.

"Fully charged," I said to myself. "Perfect."

I returned to the porch and pulled up Chance's number. Raven stood in the doorway watching as I dialed. I raised the phone to my ear.

"Don't you think he is asleep?" she asked.

"Probably."

"He may not be too happy about you waking him up in the middle of the night."

"Probably not, but this can't wait."

I waited impatiently for Chance to answer. After the

fourth ring, a voicemail message responded. I promptly hung up and called him back."

RING...RING...RING...

The line activated as Chance answered the phone.

"This better be a beautiful woman wanting to show me her new bass boat, or I'm hanging up," he said, still sounding half asleep.

"Chance," I said. "This case may have just been blown wide open."

Over the line, I heard a fumbling, then a thud as if Chance had dropped the phone or fallen out of bed, or perhaps both.

"What? What have you found so early in the morning, Cass?"

"Meet me at the station, and I'll fill you in."

"You gotta give me more than that, or I'm going back to bed."

"The body, the one the FBI snatched from Dr. Frannie. His name was Balde Ramos."

"I know that, Cass. I talked with Dr. Frannie. FBI won't let us touch him. He's nothing but a dead end unless you can bring the man back to life."

I paused, then turned to face Raven still hanging out in the doorway.

"I think we just did."

"Say that again, amigo. You did what?"

"Look, there is a lot to explain. Throw some clothes on and meet me in town. When you're done looking at what I have..."

Raven cleared her throat and bulged her eyes at me; message sent and received.

"...at what *we* have uncovered, you'll be running to the holding cells to make sure there is a free bed available."

"All right, Cass. You have my attention, but if this turns out we're *buscarle cinco patas al gato...ay, dios*. I should be so lucky to find a five-legged cat at this hour."

The line went dead. I lowered the phone and turned around to walk off the porch.

The night sky towered above me, yet I felt as if I could reach out and pluck any star from the firmament I wished. Glancing to the open range beyond the barn where the CR ran wild all the way to the Rio Grande, I felt for the first time that I truly belonged. Each stop in my life had been but a stepping stone as I worked through where I had been until, at last, I discovered where I was meant to be.

Excitement and anticipation grew inside of me. The more I considered the events leading up to this moment, the more confident I was that what Balde Ramos had served us was more likely true. I was sure I would find a connection between Sinclair and Ramón's attempted murder as well. I just needed to pay him a visit and watch his eyes turn gray as I read him his rights.

"You just gonna stand there, or are you gonna go?" Raven called from the porch.

I whirled around and lunged to the porch and through the door as Raven pulled it open. As I passed her, I slid to a stop, nearly crashing into the sofa before catching my balance.

"You coming along?"

Raven's face blossomed with a smile that read into the offer as a *thank you*, and *I'm sorry*, and *I'll love you forever*. She stepped over to me and laid her palm against my cheek.

"You go to work. I'll be here when you return."

She pushed up on her tiptoes and kissed me on the lips, then headed into the kitchen.

"I'll make some coffee for you and Chance. God knows you're going to need it."

"Thanks, Rave."

I took a quick shower and dressed in the most functional clothing I had still hanging among my everyday clothes. Navy blue tactical pants with enough exterior pockets to make a mob of kangaroos jealous, a black, form-fitting Dri-FIT shirt, boot-length socks, and a pair of solid black 5.11 A/T Mid Boot trainer shoes had me not only looking the part but feeling the part of determined badass.

I retrieved my badge and gun, slipping each into place, then walked through the kitchen on my way to Uncle Stewart's office. I could smell fresh coffee beans and savored the aroma as it wafted into my nose. Raven winked at me as I passed by.

Once in the office I collected a pair of handcuffs, two sets of handcuff keys—one of which I slipped into a hidden pocket in the waistline of my pants—a small canister of pepper spray, a box of fifty 9mm NATO, 124-grain FMJ bullets, a small tactical Benchmade D2 Griptilian folding knife I won off a Navy SEAL friend of mine some years back, and a Case folding knife my grandfather, Pat Stewart, gave me when I turned eighteen. I placed all the gear in a small canvas bag, zipped the zipper, and slung it over my shoulder. The last two things I grabbed were a black mesh baseball cap made from quick-drying fiber and a pair of Ray-Ban aviators. I walked back into the kitchen to the cat calls from my wife. She whistled in jest, but it lightened the mood and told me regardless of how she was feeling about my returning to law enforcement, she had my six.

I removed the USB drive from my laptop and securely zipped it inside my right front pocket, then took the thermos of coffee Raven held out to me. Together, we walked to the front door.

"Be careful, Cass."

"I always am."

"Come home to me."

"I promise, Little Bird."

She took hold of my hand and squeezed, then in a single motion, gently pushed me away. We never embraced when I left for my deployments, nor did we when I was working on the force in Houston. We agreed before the first time I left her behind to answer duty's call that we would save those embraces for when I returned.

I got in the Explorer, placed my bag in the back seat, and looked at my beautiful wife standing in wait of me. The engine fired up at the push of a button, and the lights cut through the early morning darkness, illuminating the porch and reflecting off the windows. As I pulled away, I flashed my brights, then made a wide U-turn and waved out my open window.

The car smelled damp, but my mind was fresh, and my thoughts focused. I did not hear the gravel crackle under the tires or the clang of the cattle guard as I crossed under the archway at the entrance to the Callahan Ranch, nor did I notice the dull flicker of light that turned on behind Flint's front window as I left for town. I was in the zone and ready to face the day, whatever may come. This city boy, as so many had come to think of me, was about to show South Brewster County that there was more to Cass Callahan than a baseball cap and faded blue jeans.

PART FIVE
DOUBLE CROSS

CHAPTER THIRTY-SEVEN

Hot coffee billowed in wisps of steam from two Styrofoam cups, their warmth permeating the air. As I sat back in my chair opposite Chance, I waited while he devoted the next 1:17.49 to watching the video from the USB drive featuring Balde Ramos. His eyes remained fixated on the screen, and his mouth and mustache were pulled up to one side of his face, a testament to his unwavering focus on every word that Balde said. When the video concluded, he replayed it, pausing once to scribble a note on a scrap of paper before slipping it into his pocket.

"Sinclair, huh?" Chance said, breaking the silence.

"Straight from the lips of a dead man," I responded.

"In all my years of living and working out here, I can't believe I let this one slip past me."

"According to the data in the *Cruce de Mulas* folder, the route through the CR only became active recently."

I stood and walked next to Chance. Leaning over beside him, I opened the file to display the information. My finger scrolled through the spreadsheet, guiding his gaze to the "Dates" column.

"If you compare the dates in this column to the corresponding coordinates, you'll see that it's been an active route for just over a year. Unlike the other crossings, which boast extensive records and a long history of traffic, this one, Ojinaga, Chihuahua, just up the road from here, is the newest entry on record."

Sheriff Gilbert studied the data, his meticulousness a perfect complement to his usually cheerful demeanor. It was this combination that made him not only a thorough investigator but also the ideal Sheriff for South Brewster County. If there were any inconsistencies with my report, he would uncover them, although I doubted there were any to be found.

"Okay, *amigo*. Not only am I wide awake before the sun has even scratched its ass, but this has my undivided attention."

I walked back to my seat and sat down facing him. He reached for his coffee, took a measured sip, and reclined in his chair, his face stretching into his trademark smile.

"Diego Leo and Javier Santos come on at seven. You know Santos, and you'll like Leo. He's as laid-back as you and I, but when it comes to the job, he's all business. Tough as nails, he is. *Él es duro como un cactus*. Are you ready to pay a visit to the Double S?"

With images of Roy Sinclair in custody lingering in my mind, I met Sheriff Gilbert's gaze with squinted, determined eyes and nodded.

"Hooah."

CHAPTER THIRTY-EIGHT

I stood in the parking lot of the South Brewster County Sheriff's Office, watching the sunrise paint the town. The buildings came alive, their surfaces bathed in a kaleidoscope of colors as the golden beams of sunlight danced with the earthy tones of adobe, painted cement, and aluminum-sided structures. Windows crackled with brightness reminiscent of sparklers twirling in a child's gleeful grasp. Shadows formed behind the buildings, road signs, and cars parked and left to ride out the night alone on the streets, then gradually retreated as the sun climbed higher. There was nothing dull about this morning. With each passing moment, the day grew brighter, banishing the remnants of night to reveal a cloudless, cerulean expanse. It was our sendoff, a celebration of the day's events to come as if they had already been written. But it was up to us to determine the ending, as the story held no spoilers.

A gentle vibration in my front pocket interrupted the captivating sight. I reached for my phone and answered the call.

"Callahan."

"This is Dr. Frannie Lopez-Tasker."

"It's pretty early wouldn't you say, Dr. Frannie?"

"Yeah, well the dead never sleep in my world," she said with a sarcastic laugh. *"The two bodies we recovered yesterday ended up being just that, a dead end. Two Juan Does. No records or fingerprints on file. No clues to their identities. However, I did extract the same 9mm rounds from each that we found on our initial victim."*

"Balde Ramos," I said. "We discovered why he was so important to your FBI buddies."

I turned to a high-pitched whistle calling out behind me to see Chance wave me over. I acknowledged his call with a nod and began walking back to the station.

"Do tell, Cass," Dr. Frannie said with interest.

"There's a lot to it but I've got to run. Sorry. Will fill you in as soon as I can."

"Fine," she said, a tinge of disappointment creeping into her voice. *"You know where to find me. On my head with the dead."*

I ended the call as I walked through the front door. I flashed the receptionist my badge and was buzzed through the security door. Chance stood with Deputy Santos and another man who was introduced as Deputy Deigo Leo.

"Let's step into the briefing room and get these guys up to speed, Cass."

Chance led the way, swinging open the frosted glass door and ensuring it closed behind us. The deputies took a seat while we delved into the details of our findings, outlining our strategy to apprehend and arrest Roy Sinclair.

CHAPTER THIRTY-NINE

Three official South Brewster County Sheriff vehicles and one jet-black Explorer drove in a tight, code 2 formation along RR170 en route to the Double S ranch. No lights. No sirens. A simple yet structured and non-threatening approach. Sheriff Chance Gilbert's Bronco led the way. I followed closely behind with Deputies Santos and Leo bringing up the rear.

It was closing in on seven thirty, which meant we would most likely find Sinclair and his hands already up and moving. Ranchers kept God's hours, as Uncle Stewart had once called it, which meant they were up with the sun and worked until the heavens returned. As a kid, I never considered putting that much effort into a job, yet as most adults know, it comes with the territory.

My focus on the mission at hand was interrupted when my phone rang. It was Chance.

"Callahan."

"Just got an update on Ramón. He's listed in critical but stable condition. Looks like he's going to pull through."

"That's good news. Hope he has some insight as to who may have shot him."

"You and me, both. After wrapping things up this morning, we'll pay him a visit if the doctors will allow it."

"10-4."

The line went dead, and silence returned to the cockpit.

We rolled along at posted speeds, rising and falling with the undulating landscape. The road stretched ahead, empty of cars as far as the eye could reach. Each bend revealed familiar landmarks etched deep into my memory; the forlorn International pickup standing sentinel near the edge of Copperhead Canyon, the ramshackle remnants of Pepito's roadside fruit stand, a lone cottonwood tree defying nature's logic standing proudly on the edge of the Fresno ranch as if it thrived without a drop of water. These landmarks served as poignant reminders, guiding me closer to home or town, depending on the direction of my journey.

The Double S was located north of the CR with the main house and ranch complex erected at the end of Camino Alborotado. Departing from RR170, we rolled past a stretch of barbed-wire fencing, each juniper post thrust deep into the unyielding earth. At one-hundred-foot intervals, iron displays of the *Double S* ranch insignia hung from sturdy posts.

As we approached the entrance, the knock of displaced stones in the wheel wells and the plume of dust cascading into the air behind our caravan announced our arrival to anyone who may be watching. The cattle guard rumbled as our caravan pulled onto the ranch.

The yard was empty. The adjacent corral had two loose horses left to mill about, but there were no hands, nor Sinclair himself anywhere to be seen.

I followed Chance's lead as he pulled up to the house, parking next to him in a cover-and-conceal tactical position. Deputy Santos angled his Bronco behind us to cover our rear flank. Deputy Leo strategically parked his vehicle in a diagonal stance across the entrance to the ranch. His car formed an imposing barrier, sealing off any escape routes through the main gate.

Chance and I exchanged a cautious glance before stepping out of our vehicles. He tilted his head to the side, speaking into his shoulder-mounted microphone. A brief pause and then a nod from him indicated that he was ready to approach the house. In a place like Houston, the police would have rolled in with a tactical team, flexed their muscles, swiftly made the arrest, and left the property with the suspect in custody. Their bulldozer mentality was effective in gaining control and securing scenes and was seldom met with resistance.

However, South Brewster County demanded a different approach. Here, where everyone knew everybody else, tact was key when dealing with local accusations. Despite our objective to apprehend Roy Sinclair on murder charges, we acknowledged that achieving a peaceful resolution would better serve the community.

Before we reached the porch, the front door opened and one of Sinclair's ranch hands stepped out. Chance and I stopped our advance, making subtle movements in our stance that prepared us to take evasive action if necessary.

"Mornin', Sheriff Gilbert."

"Earl Crawford. Haven't seen you around in a while. Keepin' yer hands clean these days, I reckon."

Chance spoke as if they were old friends, but his body language hinted at a lingering memory of past altercations with Earl.

"What'chu you bringin' this greener around fer?" Earl said, looking at me with a snarky idle in his voice. "Needin' some ridin' lessons? Maybe a take a roll in the sack with one of our jackasses?"

Earl made an obscene gesture with his hands then rocked his hips back and forth like he was dry humping the air. Upon our first encounter on the CR, I got the impression that he was an undereducated, crude person. It appears my initial assessment was correct.

"Need to speak with Roy. He inside the house?"

Chance asked, still maintaining a patient, friendly demeanor.

"Ain't no time ta talk ta the likes of you." Earl took a step toward me and pointed with an angry finger. "Especially not him."

"Come on, Earl," I said. "That's not very neighborly. I thought we were friends."

Earl took two more steps toward me but was halted in his place by a commanding voice from the doorway.

"Hold up there, Earl!"

Roy Sinclair stepped into view followed by two men I had never seen before. His weathered face wrinkled with objection. The two men followed behind Sinclair as he marched toward us. Their stocky build and blocked jaws reminded me of bouncers at any number of Houston nightclubs. It was as if Tweedledee and Tweedledum turned cowboys. One donned a black felt hat, the other a dusted beige Stetson. Earl fell in line behind Sinclair's henchmen, wearing a fighter's scowl as his looks dared me to say something else.

"Not sure I like you comin' onto the Double S the way ya are this mornin', Sheriff. If I didn't know any better, I'd say you were huntin' fer someone."

Sinclair stood tall and stout. He slid his knobby knuckled fingers into his front pockets, tilting his head back, waiting for Chance's reply.

"Much as I hate to say it, Roy, but yer right." Chance took a step closer to Sinclair and spoke in a softer, calming tone. "Why don't you and I take a walk, Roy? I need to speak with you."

"You ain't goin' nowhere's with him alone," Earl spouted as he pushed his way between his boss and Chance.

Earl's forward momentum caused him to bounce into Chance's chest, knocking him off balance. That was my cue to intervene. Sinclair had warned Earl once before that I may not understand how things work out here because, at the time, they were on the CR. Right now, I was on the Double S, so my actions, or reactions in this case, warranted no intervention by Sinclair, which was fine by me.

I stepped forward with my right leg, grabbed Earl by the scruff of hair that dangled beneath his worn hat, placed my right palm on the back of his shoulder, and drove him three steps away from the group before anyone knew what had happened. Earl yelled, then violently pulled away, leaving me with a handful of torn hair in my fist.

In a rage, he turned and charged. With a quick sidestep, I evaded his assault. As he pivoted, I seized his left wrist with my right hand and twisted up. In a sweeping motion, I rotated his arm around behind him, applying vise-like pressure, adding excruciating distress to his shoulder. Capitalizing on Earl's vulnerability, I swiftly positioned my opposite hand on the left side of his neck, slipped my foot around his ankles, and made a calculated push forward. Earl's world suddenly turned upside down as he crashed face first into the unforgiving earth. Wasting no time, I released my grip on Earl's neck and placed my knee on his back, pinning him to the ground. With a deftness that rivaled the most seasoned cowboys roping and tying calves, I had cuffed Earl's hands behind his back, silencing his foul mouth as he ate the dirt.

I stood and faced Sinclair. Black Hat and Dusty Beige, as I identified them, both looked intent on joining the fight but had been restrained by the steady hand and authoritative eye of Sheriff Chance Gilbert. Sinclair, on the other hand, exuded an air of invincibility, his face etched with amusement as he watched the situation unfold.

"Guess ya didn't see that comin', did ya, Earl?" Sinclair said.

Chance lowered his arm. With a nod, he gave me the green light to announce our reason for being here. I stepped forward.

"Roy Sinclair, you are under arrest for the murder of Balde Ramos."

"What kind of horse shit is this?" he snapped. "Who the hell is Balde Ramos?"

"Roy," Chance interrupted. "I know you are aware that there has been some trouble over on the CR. I am also sure you are aware that your man, Ramón López, is fighting for his life at Brewster Regional as we speak. We have reason to believe that you are directly involved in the murders on the CR and are a suspect in the shooting of Ramón. Let's not make this any harder than it has to be."

"Have you lost your mind? What the hell are you talking about?" Sinclair spun around and shouted at the men behind him. "Either of you seen that lazy Mexican this mornin'?"

"No, Sir, Mr. Sinclair" was the answer of the day.

"Roy," Chance said, his words falling on deaf ears. "Roy!"

Sinclair turned back to face Chance, looking less commanding and more like an aged, confused senior citizen lost in the mall parking lot.

"Ya come with me voluntarily, I'll keep the cuffs off ya." Chance said, his voice returning to its calm, convincing manner.

"I ain't goin' nowhere. You wanna talk, we kin talk right here."

Chance lowered his head, his disappointment evident as Sinclair remained uncooperative. He had extended him the benefit of the doubt, but now, that phase was unequivocally behind us all.

The door to the house flew open, slamming against the exterior wall with a loud slap of cracking wood.

"What's all this?"

Joe Sinclair marched outside like a cock ready for a fight, his chest bowled out like ruffled feathers. He pointed at us with his left hand, but it was the right with which I was concerned. He held his arm down to his side, his wrist curled behind him. I stepped away from Earl, closing the short distance, and placed my hand on my gun.

"Slow down there, Joe," I said. "Show me both of your hands."

Joe stopped in his tracks. He glared at me, then lowered his left hand and pulled an empty right hand into full view.

"They're wantin' ta take me in for questioning," Roy said.

"About what?" Joe replied.

"These boys seem ta think I got somethin' ta do with the trouble over at the CR."

Joe's lips twitched.

"Oh," he said, sounding surprised. "You find three dead Mexicans so close to the border, and the first thing you're gonna do is look to blame one of us. We're Americans, if you haven't forgotten."

Chance and I shared a glance. Roy looked at both of us, seeming just as perplexed. I turned my attention to Joe.

"How do you know there were three bodies?"

Joe stood looking back and forth between us and Roy, his lip twitching turning into a continuous tremor.

"We know most folks around town heard about the first one. Shoot, you and Ramón rode over to see if I needed any help, but I turned you down. You remember that, don't you?" I said. "Only thing is, we only just discovered the other two bodies yesterday morning, and no one except Chance, myself, and the medical examiner were in the know."

Joe's eyes fluttered, and I could see the color of his face begin to sour.

"And we now have evidence that names the killer," Chance said.

The offer of this information, though a stretch of the truth, was the final piece of bait we needed to catch the big fish and put a killer behind bars. It was good detective work. Sometimes all that is needed to get an admission of guilt is to lead the suspect in the right direction, get him rattled, and let him fill in the blanks.

"That name..." Chance said as he turned his glance to Roy. "is Sinclair."

Roy shot Chance a look that teetered between anger and inconceivability. Joe, on the other hand, seemed nervous, flexing his fingers as he shifted his weight to his heels.

There was a noticeable change in demeanor in both Roy and Joe.

"Something tells me..." Chance said.

We shared a sideways glance and then spoke together. "We're looking at the wrong Sinclair."

Roy Sinclair turned his head away from us to look at Joe. A realization brewed as disbelief began to bubble in the splits on his wrinkled cheeks. Joe stepped back one step.

"Why are you looking at me?" he stammered, taking yet another step back. "That's fucking insane!"

"Joe!"

Roy Sinclair's voice bellowed, causing Joe to flinch. "What the hell did you do?"

Joe looked at Roy, tears forming in his eyes. "What they told me."

"Come on, Joe," I said. "Let's take a ride."

Joe truly looked frightened, but the source of his fear seemed to come from miles away and not because of his impending arrest.

"Ain't gonna happen," he said. "I'm dead if I do."

"Why would you say that?" Chance asked, stepping forward, his demeanor calm, his attention completely focused on Joe alone.

"Stay away from me, Sheriff. You don't know these people."

"Camargo Cartel?" I asked.

Joe shot me a glance, wonderment filling his eyes. "How the hell do you know that?"

Roy Sinclair turned, and with a heated voice, broke what little semblance of calm we had left between Joe and the rest of us. "You dumb son of a bitch," he growled. "You goddamn son of a bitch!"

"I...I..."

Chance had eyes on Joe, his right hand raised waist high, palm out. If there were to be a peaceful resolution, it would have to come now.

"Enough, Roy," Chance said, eyes still locked on Joe. "Settle down, son. I see that you're scared. We can figure this out, just..."

Roy, consumed with growing rage, lost control. He charged Joe, knuckles tightly bound over clenched fists. His two ranch hands looked on, looking unsure if they should intervene or stay the hell out of it.

"You kill those men?" Roy yelled at Joe, landing a solid punch on his chest. "Speak up! No Sinclair I know has ever been capable of backing down from a fight, so answer the goddamn question!"

Roy struck Joe again, causing him to stagger backward.

"Stop," Joe cried out, but Roy's fury overwhelmed him, driving him to deliver a third blow.

Chance lunged ahead and thrust himself between Joe and Roy, positioned to protect the very man we had come to arrest. It was at that tense moment it happened.

The blast severed time, creating a vacuum where every movement became slow-motion, and words and noise were deadened with unintelligible chatter. The gun sounded its cry, smoke curled away from the barrel, and the bullet shot through the air, searing and tearing through cloth and flesh, finding more than one target before lodging itself behind aged bone.

CHAPTER FORTY

I was five feet away. Five damn feet, yet I was unable to catch Chance when he fell. He toppled forward into Roy Sinclair as both men tumbled to the ground in a mess of blood and tangled limbs. With mouth agape, eyes stretched wide in disbelief, Joe retreated to the porch, a smoking semi-automatic pistol shaking in his grasp.

I pulled my piece and aimed at Joe, but Roy's two ranch hands had jumped into my line of fire as they rushed to his aid.

"Stop, Joe!"

My voice could have been amplified through stadium speakers, and Joe still would not have heard my command. He raced along the porch, disappearing behind the back of the house. Santos and Leo rushed in, guns drawn. Chance rolled off Sinclair's chest and tried to sit up.

"Leo," I yelled, waving him over to me as I kneeled next to Chance. "Call it in and get medical out here ASAP."

Leo tilted his head and spoke to dispatch through a shoulder-mounted microphone while I assessed Chance's injuries. Santos continued along the porch in pursuit of Joe.

"Easy, Chance. I need to lay you down."

His face was flushed, and he was in shock. I slid my pistol into my belt and used both hands to support his weight. His shoulder bled from both sides of his body.

"Bullet went clean through, Chance."

"Motherfucker shot me," he said in disbelief.

"Yeah, he..."

"Mr. Sinclair. Mr. Sinclair!" Dusty Beige called out.

I looked at Roy Sinclair lying on the ground, blood seeping from the corner of his mouth. A glance at his chest showed a growing saturation of blood on his denim shirt as it oozed from a hole in his chest. Garbled words, wet with blood and spit and growing fear made no sense as each attempt was met with spats of coughing and groans of pain. He wheezed and tried to speak again but had not the strength to spare.

"Apply pressure to the wound," I ordered.

I gently laid Chance on the ground while Dusty placed his hand over the hole in Roy's chest and pressed down. Roy flinched with pain under the added weight, causing Dusty to recoil. I shot a look at him like a wolf bearing down on a sheep.

"Do not let up until the EMTs arrive!"

Dusty reapplied pressure while Black Hat sat idly by, being of little help.

Adding to the tension, gunfire erupted behind the house. A quick burst of four shots rang out, followed by two shots and the loud rumble of a diesel engine as it fired up. A Super Duty F250 pickup with crusted dirt stuck along the wheel wells and lower frame of the door skidded into view near the Double S corral. The driver's side window had been blown out, giving me a clear view of Joe behind the wheel. The knobby tires spun ferociously and the engine's growl intensified as the truck surged toward us.

As the front of the vehicle came into full view, I noted the roof-mounted light bars, most of which were broken in their casings or dangling by the electrical wiring. The cattle guard held a shattered light bar, and the front window displayed cracks along a line of three bullet holes that moved across the glass from the passenger seat to the driver's. There was no doubt in my mind that this was the truck that tried to run me down.

Joe cranked the wheel to the right, fishtailing the rear of the truck around to point away from us. Santos sprinted from the house, gun in hand and ready to fire. Leo began to stand, but I reached out and held his arm before he could get to his feet.

"Watch after Chance and Roy until help arrives," I said.

I leaped to my feet and pulled my Glock, its weight and feel, the perfect balance in my grip as I aimed at Joe.

"Nooo."

Roy's raspy voice did not deter me from zeroing in on Joe, but his plea hit me like a hornet's sting.

"Don't...don't kill my grandson."

With fading strength and struggling breath, Roy's call for mercy struck a chord. Joe was no older than my Spencer. Should we ever be in the same position, would I beg the same of the man who had Spencer in his sights? Irrelevant to the thought that it was, the answer was still a resounding *yes*.

With a roar of the engine and a plume of black smoke rising from the exhaust, Joe sped away from us, crashing through the posts and beams of the corral, and headed for the open ranges of the Double S.

I lowered my gun, then turned and ran for the Explorer. Jumping in, I pushed the ignition switch and threw it into reverse. Slamming the brakes, I took a quick glance at Chance lying on the ground next to Sinclair before shifting into drive. Santos sprinted to his vehicle to join the pursuit as I punched the gas and raced to catch up to Joe.

I followed the F-250's tracks through the destroyed corral and out to the rangeland where the ground formed a hard, packed earth with scattered clumps of blackbrush, Texas grama, skunkbush, and other natural obstacles all waiting to get in the way of my pursuit. Joe's beast of a truck cut down anything short of a small tree or mesquite bush, carving a path for me to follow. I could hear Santos's siren rise and fall behind me as I increased my speed over terrain more suited for horseback or offroad tires.

"Where you headed, Joe?" I said to myself.

As the pursuit continued, I began to recognize landmarks that told me we were approaching CR land. The large brush pile Flint and I had started the morning we discovered Balde Ramos, the cottonwood grove in the distance, and the fence line that created a border between the CR and the Double S from the main road to the Rio Grande stood before me.

Joe barreled through the fence, snapping the barbed-wire and ripping the juniper posts from the ground. I watched, hoping the wire would get tangled in his axle or driveshaft and disable the truck, but its sheer power and the speed at which it drove sent the wires and posts flying into the air like deadly nunchucks in a Kung Fu movie.

He raced unimpeded onto the CR and looked to be heading for the grove. We sped over a long patch of flattened earth void of brush but growing rockier by the second. Joe's driving was erratic, swerving to one side and then the other as I closed the gap.

Santos pulled even with me on my right flank. I eased the Explorer left and accelerated so that the front wheels pulled even with the rear wheels of Joe's truck.

Seeing me pull closer must have spooked Joe. He wrenched the steering wheel to the right, veering the truck into Santos's path. Santos had to slam the brakes to avoid being hit by Joe's erratic driving. We approached the grove at speeds unfit for the terrain, but Joe continued by aiming the truck toward the rocky outcroppings and dangerous fissures that preceded the Rio Grande. It was then I knew, as stupid a plan as it was, what Joe was trying to do.

"Getting to Mexico isn't the answer, Joe," I said.

The path was a tight fit, but the manner with which Joe traversed the larger rock formations, cutting in and out and around them at just the right times, displayed a sense of experience with this area. He knew where he was going, but it would take only one mistake on his part to quickly end this chase. As scared as Joe was, he drove the gauntlet like a pro, shooting through and onto a flat expanse that led to the banks of the Rio Grande.

Now, in the open, Joe accelerated the truck. I had one opportunity to perform a precision immobilization technique, the PIT maneuver, now that we were in an open space, but at the rate at which we were traveling, one wrong move on my part might mean the difference between Joe losing control and stopping, or both of us losing control and violently crashing.

I decided against the technique, opting to continue my pursuit as Joe was approaching the river and quickly running out of road. I pulled up and fell in line behind him. At fifty yards from the water, I expected Joe to begin slowing down, but that did not happen. We passed by what I estimated to be thirty yards to go and still no wavering by Joe.

I pulled back and eased the Explorer to the left hind flank of the F-250 and watched the Rio Grande race at us. With fifteen yards to go, I had no choice but to slam on my brakes. Joe ran with a winner-take-all mentality, but this was not a game, nor was this about winning or losing. In truth, we had all already lost. Chance was injured. Roy's fate was uncertain; he was in critical condition, fighting for his life. Balde Ramos and the two mules with which he traveled had already met their fate at the hands of Joe, and I was in pursuit of him; a young, misguided man whose future looked grim at best.

Skidding the Explorer to a stop, I watched Joe and the

F-250 barrel ahead the final few feet before attempting a daring, and very dangerous escape maneuver. At the last moment, he accelerated, plunging the truck into the river. It skimmed the first few feet when the front tires left dry land, but its weight and power were no match for the Rio Grande.

As soft and inviting as water appears, its jaws opened, bared its teeth, and swallowed the truck whole. It pitched forward upon impact, causing the bed and rear wheels to lift out of the water as it met the full force of the river. The current was minimal, but the riverbed was soft and unsupportive of the heavy truck. As the truck recoiled, its front swiveled, creating an uneven distribution of energy, which caused it to shift and ultimately roll onto its side.

I exited the Explorer and watched as water rushed into the cab of the pickup. Racing to the water's edge, I looked for Joe to emerge. He did not surface. With only moments to act before the truck rolled upside down becoming submerged, I entered the water, running with giant leaps. Soon, I was forced to wade through depths that quickly rose to my waist. I could feel the tug of the river against my body as I fought my way toward the truck, still watching for signs of Joe.

The sound of Santos's approaching siren reassured me that I had backup on the way. When I reached the rear of the inverted truck and still saw no signs of Joe, I dove headfirst into the murky water. I ran my hands along the doors, feeling my way to the driver's side window. I found the door handle and pulled, but it would not budge.

Resurfacing for a fresh breath, I saw Santos's Bronco next to the Explorer and caught a glimpse of him racing for the water before I went back under in search of Joe. I found the door handle again and used it to pull myself down further beneath the water. Even the slightest movements were a struggle against the flow, the weight of the truck, and the murky mass of water that fought to claim Joe. I felt an opening in the window and grabbed a hold.

With more than just Joe's life on the line, I disregarded the gnashing glass cutting my hands and sunk to a point where I could lean into the cab of the truck.

Reaching in, I felt Joe's arms floating freely underwater. I ran my hands along his body to his waist, feeling for the seat belt. He was not buckled in, which meant I should be able to move him without restraint. Regardless of whether he suffered only a minor head bump or more critical injuries, I had to remove him from the truck, or he would drown.

I slid my hands to his armpits and pulled. I could feel Joe's head bob against my arms as I tugged at his body. My lungs screamed for air. My eyes burned as I fought to clamp them closed, but none of it mattered if I could not get Joe out. His clothing snagged once on the glass as I slid him through the window causing me a moment of near panic, but a determined grip and a forceful yank freed him from the jagged window.

As I surfaced, I felt a hand grab me from behind. Santos had made it to the edge of the truck and helped me pull Joe to shore. We quickened our movements as the water became shallower, racing to get out of the water.

"He's not breathing," Santos said.

"I know. I know."

We laid Joe flat on his back. His skin was turning blue. I positioned myself at his side and administered five chest compressions in hopes of expelling any water from his lungs. When that did not work, I began CPR.

Stayin' alive, stayin' alive, ah...ah...ah...ah...stayin' alive...

That song, as ridiculous as I always found it to be, invaded my mind but helped me keep a necessary rhythm through thirty chest compressions. I gave Joe two breaths of air and repeated the technique.

"Come on, Joe. Wake the fuck up!"

After two more rounds of compressions, I was beginning to lose hope until my second breath sparked whatever it was he needed to vomit what was an immense amount of brown water, some of which I am sorry to say, found its way into my rescuing mouth before I could pull away.

We both coughed. He gasped for air while I did what I could to get Joe's expelled river water out of my mouth.

Santos reported our position to dispatch as I wiped my tongue and spit. He confirmed our location and that medical assistance was on the way.

We were all drenched both inside and out, but Joe was alive. I rolled him over and cuffed his wrists behind his back, ending our pursuit while saving his life in the process.

"You have the right to remain silent," I said, patting Joe on the back.

Exhausted, he remained face down and did not say a word.

"You got 'im, Callahan. Good work."

"Well, Santos, I guess his dreams of joining the Dukes of Hazzard are over."

Santos gave me a perplexed look.

"What's that?"

I felt my age creep up on me as I realized Santos had no idea what I was talking about.

"Son of a bitch," I said.

CHAPTER FORTY-ONE

News of the shootings at the Double S spread throughout South Brewster County and beyond, reaching as far as KTSM 9 and KFOX 14 in El Paso and KSAT 12 in San Antonio.

Joe Sinclair, son of the deceased Henry Sinclair and Grandson of Double S magnate, Roy Sinclair, was arrested for triple murder, two counts of aggravated assault with a deadly weapon, evading arrest, destruction of property, and possession of an unlicensed firearm along with a slew of other charges. He suffered minor injuries during his botched escape attempt and was treated at Brewster Regional Hospital before being released into the custody of Sheriff Deputies Marie Bostwick and Javier Santos for transfer to the South Brewster County Jail, where he would remain until his arraignment. Investigations seeking to uncover the truth behind his alleged involvement in drug and potential human trafficking operations along the Texas/Mexico border have continued since his arrest.

Roy Sinclair was a tough old bird and put up one hell of a fight after being shot by Joe, though he claims it was accidental. Against the odds and tremendous loss of blood, he survived the ordeal and was well on his way to a full recovery.

Joe Sinclair's arraignment date coincided with Roy's release from the hospital. As word got out that Joe pleaded guilty to avoid what prosecutors were saying was a slam-dunk case and that they would be seeking the death penalty, the reality that his grandson would spend the rest of his life in jail was too much for his Roy, or his heart, to bear. Upon hearing the news, he dropped dead on the spot from what doctors say was a massive heart attack brought upon by stress and old age. Some locals joked that could not have been the cause of death because everyone knew Roy Sinclair was a heartless SOB.

Chance spent a few days recovering at Brewster Regional from a through-and-through wound to his right shoulder. He was being called a hero, though Chance would never see it that way. He did, however, allow the nurses to dote on him as they wished. Raven and Frannie, who until recently we called Dr. Frannie, visited him daily, only adding to the spoils of his recovery.

I remained busy with paperwork, answering or deflecting questions as they arose as to the details surrounding the events, and I helped hold down the fort until Chance was back on his feet. To my surprise, two days after the story broke, the parking lot outside the Sheriff's Office played host to an unexpected visit from none other than Special Agent Dylan Sharp. A man I did not know stood with him. Wearing dark sunglasses and tailored suits, the two FBI agents stood out like tourists at a rodeo. Before meeting with them, I donned a pair of sunglasses and adjusted my lucky Astros baseball cap, bringing my own enigmatic twist to the table.

"Special Agent Sharp," I said, walking up to the men.

"Cass Callahan, this is Special Agent Thomas Zuñiga," Sharp said, introducing us.

"You've made quite an impression only having been out here a short while, Mr. Callahan," Zuñiga said, shaking my hand. "An impression that is sure to be noticed by more than just the FBI."

"Agent Zuñiga, all this fell into my lap. I just had to pick up the pieces."

"You did more than that, Mr. Callahan. Are you familiar with the Hydra?"

"You're talking Greek mythology, right? Isn't that the creature that grows back its head once it's been cut off?"

"That's right, but in its case, it grows back two heads instead of one. The Camargo Cartel has been under our surveillance for more than a year now. It was a small but very ambitious group at the start that is now growing exponentially by the day. They are on pace to take a seat with the likes of the Sinaloa, Juárez, and Los Zetas cartels. When you uncovered their smuggling route, you lopped off one of their heads. Our concern is that they will work to reopen that route and double their presence in the area."

"So you got the information we sent you about Balde Ramos," I asked.

"We did."

"What about his family?"

Agent Sharp and Agent Zuñiga shared a look. I removed my sunglasses, dropped the charade, and squinted my eyes at them. They needed to see my eyes, *read* my eyes for the rest of this conversation.

"Your man said you had a deal. Did you get his family out?"

"We are working on a diplomatic..." Agent Sharp began.

"Bullshit," I interrupted. "You got what you wanted, and now you're going to break your deal and cut them out? Easy to do now that Balde is dead and no one else is the wiser to your agreement, Special Agent Zuñiga."

I paced away from the men, fuming. They took no risk but benefited from the rewards. I turned around to face them.

"Why did you drive out here, Agent Zuñiga?"

Zuñiga smiled and removed his glasses.

"We came because I like what I've heard about you these past few days. Your resume is impressive. Your experience in law enforcement combined with your military background make you a perfect fit for my team."

"Your team?"

"*Kill Hydra*. It's going to take more than one man to kill the beast."

I let his words sink in, but it took only a moment to give him my answer.

"Agent Zuñiga, hell no," I said. "I moved my family out here for a fresh start with no intentions of returning to law enforcement. I took my role with South Brewster County as a temporary assignment to protect my family. Seeing as how I am the only one here who thinks family is important, I'm going to emphatically decline."

"Just gonna sit back and do nothing while there is a war going in your backyard?" Agent Sharp said.

"Fuck you, Sharp. You didn't lift a damn finger to help us, so don't preach to me about sitting idly by."

Agent Sharp pompously smirked. "You are an ass..."

I rarely resort to violence when the high ground is within reach and the use of words is just...words. Sticks and stones, shit like that. This time, though, I took a pass.

My fist stopped Agent Sharp from completing the phrase. His nose cracked as his head popped backward, sunglasses flying from his face. Blood flowed from his nostrils, and his eyes watered from the impact. Agent Sharp staggered back. He palmed his nose with both hands and leaned forward as spatters of red stained his shirt and jacket. Agent Zuñiga pursed his lips and put on his sunglasses, his thoughts hidden, his intentions masked. He reached into his pocket and produced a business card, handing it to me.

"If you change your mind."

Special Agent Thomas Zuñiga turned and seized Agent

Sharp by the shoulder and pulled him along to their car. Sharp's face would heal, but he would not forget the day or the name Cass Callahan. He shot me a sour glare and a bloody middle finger before getting into the vehicle. I turned to head back inside and saw Deputies Santos and Leo standing in the doorway. Both wore smiles as wide as the Texas border.

I received pats on the back as I passed between them.

"Been wanting to do that for years," Santos said.

"Yeah," Leo added. "*Mi amigo*, Cass Callahan, Special Investigator *un campeón de lucha!*"

"Back to work, fellas," I said.

The receptionist buzzed us through the security door, and I walked to Chance's office, my mouth curling into a smile as I closed the door behind me.

CHAPTER FORTY-TWO

A warm breeze swept through the CR carrying the smell of rain. The sky overhead was void of clouds, but the cliffs to the west across the Rio Grande wore a building blackness like an angry shroud. Flickers of lightning added to the intensity of the distant storm.

Chance, Raven, and I sat together on the front porch talking and laughing as old friends do, even when work and worry linger nearby. Bottles of ice-cold beer sweated in our hands and made rings on the glass table between us. Chance wore his arm in a sling, never once complaining about the pain in his shoulder. We swapped stories and told lies, but most of all, we smiled. We chose to let the things with which we had no control slip haplessly away while we focused on more important facets in front of us. Family, friends, and the CR.

I watched Flint with our new foal and its mother in the corral. He was an effective, experienced ranch hand and could be a royal pain in the ass, but he was growing on me. Raven had invited him to join us, but he politely declined, saying he was going to take Robin and Luna, the name Raven had decided to give the foal, out for a bit of exercise. She did, however, slip a beer into his hands before he walked away. He twisted the top and polished off the last gulps before disappearing into the barn.

"You think Uncle Stewart ever sat out here drinking beers at the end of the day?" Raven asked.

I didn't answer, but I nodded and imagined him sitting just as we were: cold beer in hand, warm breeze across the CR, sitting back and enjoying life as the day shuts down.

"Oh," Raven said. "I heard Ramón is well enough to leave the hospital."

Chance leaned forward and placed his empty bottle on the table. He waved me off when I offered him another. "Yeah, he's gonna stay with my cousin until he gets his strength back."

"Any idea what he will do now, what with all that's happened with the Double S?" I asked.

"My advice," Chance said, leaning back in his chair. "Take one day at a time."

"I'll drink to that," Raven said.

Raven missed her mouth taking a drink, startled when her cell phone rang. "It's Spencer," she said, her eyes lighting up with excitement. She hopped up and walked off the porch to talk to him.

I sipped the last of my beer and added it to the line of dead soldiers on the table, then looked at Chance.

"What is it, *amigo*?"

"We ever get any closer to identifying Ramón's shooter?"

Chance leaned forward, dangling his sling, and placed his good elbow on his knee. "We found one .308 casing in the brush along the ridgeline across and away from *El Lobo Vista*. That's nearly five hundred yards, Cass."

"Think Joe Sinclair could have made that shot?"

"No way. He couldn't hit the broadside of a barn at fifty feet. No, the shooter had skills. Only a few people around here that I know could have made that shot, but I wouldn't put a collar on any of 'em."

"Anyone I know?"

Chance raised a hand and pointed at the corral.

"Flint?" I said. "You think he's capable of making a shot like that."

"He's good enough, but the question we have to ask ourselves is why? I have someone running tests on the casing, but don't hold your breath, amigo."

I watched Flint with the horses. As if he had some sixth sense about him, he turned his head and looked at the house. I raised my hand and gave a friendly, "damn, you caught me looking" wave. He looked away without returning the gesture. I sat back and mulled over what Chance had just said.

"You think..."

"He's coming out to see us!" Raven skipped over to the porch and plopped down on my lap, breaking my train of thought and gaining my interest in her excitement.

"Who?" Chance asked.

"Spencer. He has some winter break thing, and it's a bye weekend for football, whatever that means. Anyway, he'll be here this weekend!"

Raven squeezed my neck with excitement. I felt it, too. It would be good to see him. Lord knows I could use some guy time with my son. A chime from Chance's phone interrupted our mini-celebration.

"Don't answer that," I said.

Chance gave me an agreeable look but reached for the phone anyway. "It's Chance...uh-huh...uh-huh...I'm on the way." Chance ended the call and slipped the phone into his pocket as he stood up.

"Oh, Chance," Raven said. "Aren't you supposed to be resting your arm?"

Chance smiled, showing his sparkling teeth between dimpled cheeks. "It's like Cass always says..." He paused and shrugged his good shoulder. "Guys like us are never off duty."

"You want me to..."

"Nope, you've got your hands full already," he interrupted.

Raven stood up and kissed Chance on the cheek. "Be careful, Chance. Come back real soon," she said, walking to the front door.

"I will," he said.

I stood to shake his hand. "Call me," I said.

"*Amigo*." Chance glanced at Raven. "Something tells me you're going to be a little busy."

Raven gave him a deviously embarrassed but sensually accurate grin.

"*Adios, amigo*."

"Adios, Chance," I said.

As he pulled away, I glanced across the CR to the storm clouds building in the distance. A thought invaded my mind as I looked across the wide-open spaces.

Were there more bodies to be found hidden within the Gateway to Paradise?

A faint rumble of thunder found its way across the expanse but lost itself in Raven's gentle call. I turned to see her standing in the doorway of the house, barefoot, with a look I had missed for far too long. She pushed the door open wider with her toes.

"You coming?"

EPILOGUE

CAMARGO, MEXICO—27.70799° N, 105.18971° W

Beyond the electrified security fence and fortified cement walls of the Camargo Cartel compound, Luis Rojas nervously stood by as Señor de la Droga contemplated the news he had just delivered. It was no secret that vital information had been copied from a secure drive at Servicios Financieros Cortez y Asociados. Men had already been executed for allowing it to happen. *Someone must be punished*, Señor de la Droga had commanded, and it had been done.

Now, Luis worried he may also have to pay in punishment, but what he had to say could not be overlooked.

"So," Señor de la Droga said, stroking the black hairs on his chin. "This thing you are telling me, it is good but how can you be certain?"

Luis' mouth was dry. He felt a sudden urge to let his bladder flow.

"Six months ago, we implemented a comprehensive security upgrade across all accounting software in our firm. This upgrade introduced advanced features to enhance data protection and user monitoring. The software now tracks user activity, timestamps file access, and maintains a log of file durations. However, the most remarkable capability is our ability to trace data movements, even to external devices, anywhere in the world. Through secure internet portals, most devices have a seamless connection, but in rare cases where security is compromised, our cutting-edge technology employs a specialized nano-file beacon. This beacon acts as a powerful tracking mechanism, enabling precise localization of the device to specific coordinates on a map, with a margin of error of fewer than five hundred feet."

Señor de la Droga looked at Luis with eyes more suited for snake than man, then reached out and put a palm around the back of his neck. A menacing smile split his face, parting the hairs around his lips. Luis trembled as Señor de la Droga leaned his face mere inches from his own.

"This is very, very... good, Luis. You have nothing to fear. Go to Servicios Financieros Cortez y Asociados and report back to me personally when you learn the file's location."

Señor de la Droga let go and turned to walk away, but Luis remained where he was. The drug lord turned to face Luis, his face perplexed.

"Why are you still standing there? GO!"

"But...the files...they have already been accessed."

Señor de la Droga moved close to Luis and spoke delicately into his ear.

"Bring me the coordinates now or lose a finger. *Entiendes?*"

Luis shook his head, understanding the consequences should he fail to deliver. He balled his fingers into fists, then turned and hurried out the door.

Señor de la Droga walked behind his desk and picked up the phone.

"Get me *La Sombra Negra* and *El Despiadado*."

Silence filled the office as he waited for confirmation.

"Si, si... de inmediato."

He placed the phone on the receiver and sat down in his plush leather chair. Crossing his legs, he leaned back and imagined what his Sicarios would do to anyone who got in their way of retrieving what was his.

A LOOK AT BOOK TWO:
KILL ORDER

In the gripping sequel to *Dead Land*, life in West Texas takes a sinister turn.

Cass Callahan and his family yearn for a return to normalcy after the unsettling mystery and murders that shook their beloved ranch, the CR. However, their hopes for peace are shattered when the ruthless Camargo cartel sets in motion a disruptive plot that threatens the very fabric of their hometown.

When Cass's son, Spencer, returns for a visit and becomes embroiled in a life-altering confrontation where one wrong move could prove deadly, the cartel dispatches two sicarios to recover stolen technology, eliminate those who may have accessed the data, and leave no witnesses behind. With danger mounting, body counts rising, and Spencer now missing, Cass finds himself torn between his wife's desperate pleas to find their son and his unwavering commitment to stopping the cartel's murderous rampage.

Accompany Cass Callahan on a deadly journey, where danger looms, tensions escalate, and the town of Brewster is thrown into chaos.

"Chris Mullen's writing is sharp and action packed. His talent and enthusiasm are enviable." **—Chris Enss**, *New York Times* **bestselling author**

AVAILABLE MARCH 2024

ACKNOWLEDGMENTS

Beginning the journey with Cass Callahan and the cast of Dead Land was exciting. Some huge thank yous are in order, followed by a round on me at Clancy's. I want to start by extending my heartfelt gratitude to my longtime friend and Sergeant (Ret), Fort Bend County Sheriff's Office, Carlos Castillo. He provided a wide range of information about law enforcement, weaponry, personal and gun safety, and situational job procedures that helped create an aspect of authenticity for many of the characters, especially Cass. Brigadier General Edwin A. "Buddy" Grantham, TXSG and LTC (Ret) Chris Whittaker were instrumental in my understanding and correctly portraying military personnel serving in Iraq and the Middle East during the war. They were both open about sharing their personal experiences while stationed abroad and provided insight and perspective about some of the more dangerous moments of their tour. Also, SSG (Ret) Stephen Saunders for explaining sniper terminology and technique. A respectful thank you to Master Daniel Elkowitz and Master Chris Martinez of Fort Bend Martial Arts Academy, both of whom assisted with action sequences, solidifying Cass as a humble, yet formidable fighter. Represent!

I'd also like to thank Jeff, Libby, and Malcolm for their early reading efforts; Wolfpack Publishing for the opportunity to bring Cass to life; Author John Nesbitt for his chats, insights, and feedback about my writing; and my sons—Ryan for his encouragement, and Jackson for his automotive expertise.

A final and most enduring thank you to Jack and Margie Mullen and Julie Grantham for their eyes, ears, daily support, and expertise that helped me keep my wits, stay focused, and for telling me to "YARN ON." And to my wife Joellan, a lifetime of thanks for her unwavering support of my writing journey.

ABOUT THE AUTHOR

Chris Mullen is an accomplished and award-winning author, recognized for his captivating storytelling and literary talent. Hailing from Richmond, Texas, he is a proud graduate of Texas A&M University.

With a career spanning twenty-three years in education, Chris has been a dedicated teacher in both Kindergarten and PreK, cultivating his passion for storytelling and nurturing young minds. In 2019, he received the prestigious Connie Wootton Excellence in Teaching Award—a testament to his commitment to education and his profound impact on students' lives, bestowed upon him by the Southwest Association of Episcopal Schools (SAES). It was during this time that the idea for his young adult western adventure series, Rowdy, was born.

The first installment, *Rowdy: Wild and Mean, Sharp and Keen*, was met with critical acclaim and earned the esteemed title of 2023 Independent Press Distinguished Favorite. Notably, the third book, *Rowdy: Dead or Alive*, stands as a 2023 Will Rogers Medallion Finalist. Garnering numerous awards, Chris's Rowdy series continues to captivate readers of all ages, cementing his place as an author in the young adult western genre.

When he's not weaving stories, you can find Chris honing his craft in local coffee shops, pizza places, or even the neighborhood grocery store. Currently, he is hard at work on an adult, contemporary western mystery series for Wolfpack Publishing.

To connect with Chris, visit his website www.chrismullenwrites.com, where you can access updates, behind-the-scenes glimpses, and much more. Additionally, be sure to follow his Amazon Author Page and catch him on various social media platforms—Facebook, Instagram, Threads, and TikTok @chrismullenwrites, as well as on Twitter @cmullenwrites. For any inquiries or heartfelt messages, feel free to reach out directly at chrismullenwrites@gmail.com.

Printed in the USA
CPSIA information can be obtained
at www.ICGtesting.com
CBHW010756301223
3027CB00004B/8

9 781639 773817